TO ME YOU SEEM GIANT

TO ME YOU SEEM GIANT

GREG RHYNO

NeWest Press

EDMONTON, AB
2017

Library and Archives Canada Cataloguing in Publication

Rhyno, Greg, 1976-, author
To me you seem giant / Greg Rhyno.

(Nunatak first fiction series ; 47)
Issued in print and electronic formats.
ISBN 978-1-988732-00-8 (softcover).--ISBN
978-1-988732-01-5 (EPUB).--
ISBN 978-1-988732-02-2 (Kindle)

I. Title. II. Series: Nunatak first fiction ; no. 47

PS8635.H97T6 2017 C813'.6 C2017-901281-9 C2017-901282-7

Editor for the Press: Leslie Vermeer
Cover and interior design: Kate Hargreaves
Cover photograph: Markus Spiske; Interior graphics: junkohanhero
Author photo: Sarah Wyche

The words "To me you seem giant" are taken with permission from the song 'Penpals,' written by Sloan. The author and the publisher both thank the band.

NeWest Press acknowledges the support of the Canada Council for the Arts, the Alberta Foundation for the Arts, and the Edmonton Arts Council for support of our publishing program. We acknowledge the financial support of the Government of Canada through the Canada Book Fund for our publishing activities.

Canada Council for the Arts Conseil des Arts du Canada
Funded by the Government of Canada
Financé par le gouvernement du Canada
Canada

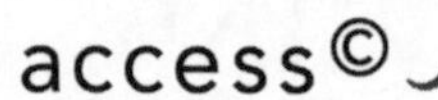

Alberta Government
THE CITY OF Edmonton

NEWEST PRESS
NeWest Press
#201, 8540-109 Street
Edmonton, Alberta T6G 1E6
www.newestpress.com

No bison were harmed in the making of this book.
PRINTED AND BOUND IN CANADA

1 2 3 4 5 19 18 17

For Sarah, Walter, and Ezra

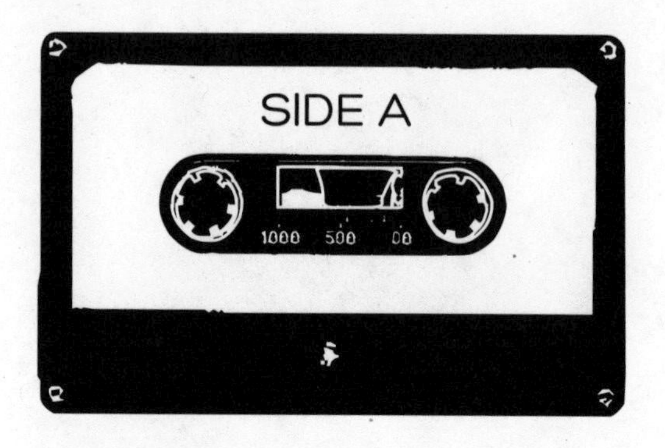
SIDE A
1000 500 00

SIDE B
1000 500 00

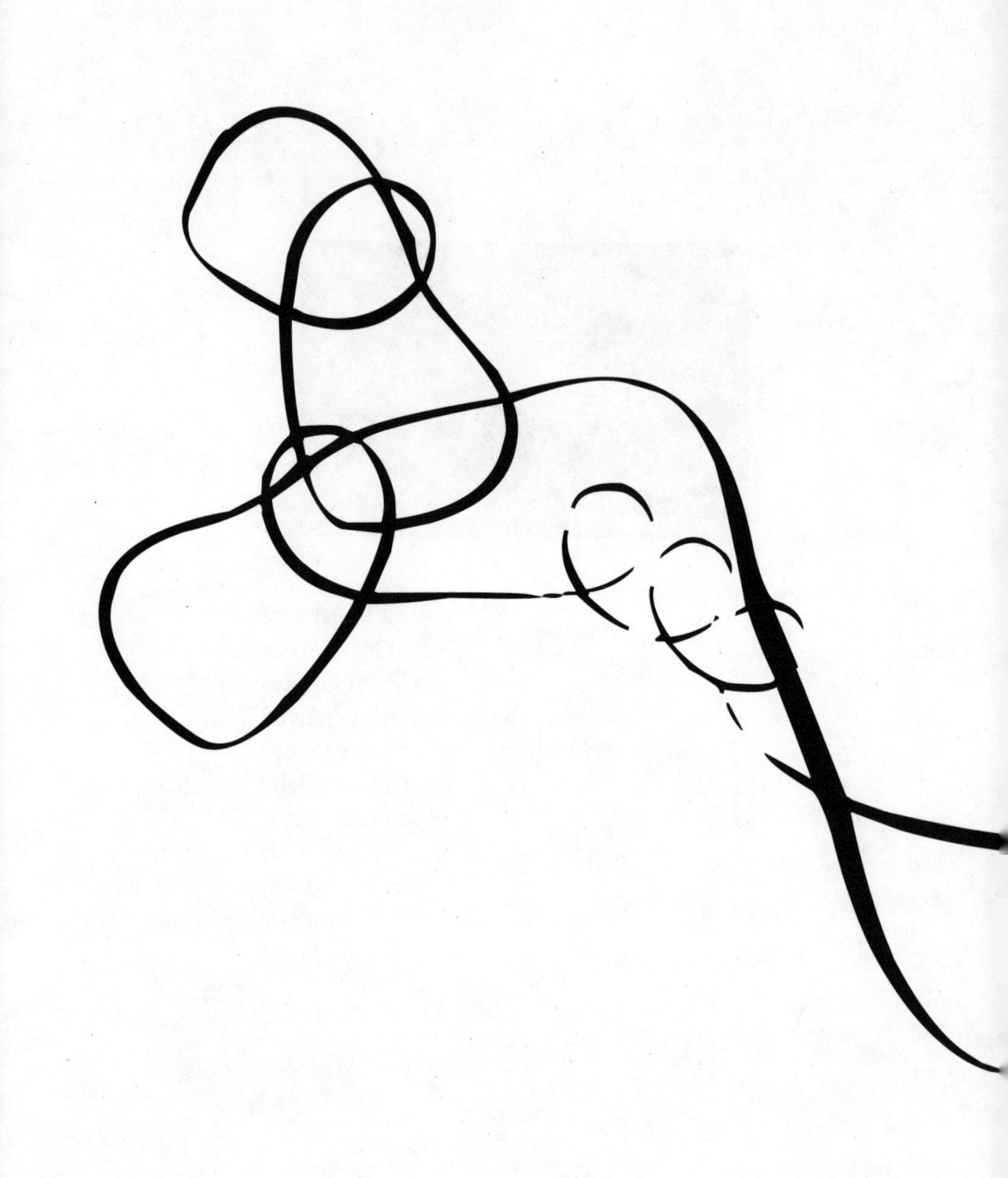

SIDE A

Looking for a Place to Happen

I don't pick up the phone, even though at this time of night it's probably for me. This'll make my parents crazy, but I figure it's their name in the phone book. Until they get me my own line, they can answer it.

A few seconds later, there's a knock on the door. My mom swings it open before I can say anything. Part of me wishes I was doing something really messed up, like performing Satanic rituals, or jerking off to *The Golden Girls*—something that would really burn her retinas.

"Peter?"

I turn down the chipmunky sound of high-speed dubbing.

"Jesse's on the phone for you."

"Okay. Thanks."

After she shuts the door, I pick up the receiver from the nightstand.

"Got it," I say into the mouthpiece. A moment passes and I can still hear the ambient laughter of a live studio audience from the living room. "I've got it!" I shout. There's a rattle and click as someone finally hangs up.

"Hello?"

"You coming out tonight?"

Soda's not the most talkative guy to begin with, but when he calls, you'd think he was getting charged for long distance or something.

"Uh, sure. Where do you want to meet?"

"Up top. Twenty minutes."

I get a cold flash of adrenalin.

"Sounds good," I lie. "See you there."

"Oh, hey," Soda says, "one more thing."

"What's that?"

Click.

Fucker. I hate it when he does that. I grin in spite of myself, but then I hear the mechanical *kachunk* of my stereo amputating a song halfway through, and I realize I've got a situation on my hands.

When faced with this kind of mixed tape timing crisis, most people opt for one of two strategies. The first is to let the song die when the tape runs out. It's the simplest solution, but I get kind of anxious waiting for that shitty, abrupt ending to come down like an axe. Alternatively, some people go back and record over the half-finished song with a blanket of magnetic silence. I'm not really into that either. As far as I'm concerned, two minutes of tape hiss can feel like an eternity in limbo.

Thankfully, there's a third option: you bring in a closer. *Love Tara*, the first full length from Eric's Trip, has no fewer than four songs that clock in under two minutes, not including 'Allergic to Love,' which is pretty much two minutes on the dot. So, to finish out the side, I pick 'June,' this weird, menacing little number that basically sounds like your stereo is going to come to life and murder you. It's perfect.

I rewind the tape a bit, then cue up my closer with a screechy fast-forward. I listen as the previous song dies out, wait a second or two for that crucial dead air, then start pushing buttons. PAUSE. PLAY. PLAY and RECORD. A minute and a half later, the song ends just before the reels groan and stop. In tiny black letters, I make a few final notes on the sleeve, then slide the paper back into the plastic case. I pop the tape out of the stereo and snug it into the sleeve. I can always finish the flip side later.

I grab my jacket and then walk through the house toward the cackling of *Roseanne*. My dad is stretched out on the couch, and my mom has her feet up in the recliner. There's a bowl of Bugles on a TV table between them.

"I'm going to stay at Soda's tonight," I tell them.

They look up at me then at each other, their faces changing shape in the television light.

"I don't remember you asking us," Dad says.

"Okay," I sigh. Sometimes you've got to play ball. "*Can* I stay at Soda's tonight?"

My dad looks at my mom, eyebrows raised. My mom nods in the affirmative. "Just call us if you go somewhere else."

"I wi-ill," I sing as I walk away. But I won't.

My parents aren't bad people as far as parents go, but I wish they'd had another kid after me. At least that way they would've spread their parenting a little thinner. People think I've got it made because I'm an only child, but the truth is, it sucks being constantly outnumbered by adults. I don't have older siblings to pave the way, or any younger ones to take the blame. Plus, I'm always outvoted. If I want to go Harvey's, we inevitably go to Swiss Chalet. If I want to watch *The X-Files*, I have to settle for *Dr. Quinn, Medicine Woman*. As a result, I've been suspicious of democracy since I was six and lying my ass off since I was seven.

By the time I get up on the roof, Soda's already polished off two bottles of Crystal and he's working on his third. I don't actually need to see him to know this. While I worked my way from the dumpster lid to the first floor addition to the terrifying second-floor lintel, I could hear the empties completing their journey to the teachers' parking lot. Mortality Reminders, Soda calls them.

He doesn't turn around when I find him. Instead, he slides another bottle out of the case, twists off the cap, and sets it beside him. It stands at attention while Soda dangles his feet over the edge and tries to light a smoke behind the shield of his jeans jacket. I get a wave of vertigo just watching. I keep a safe distance and reach down for the beer.

"Sodapop," I say.

"Ponyboy," he mumbles, cigarette bouncing up and down.

Up this high, there's a sting in the air and it doesn't feel like summer anymore. I guess in about a week it won't be. I tuck my hair behind my ears but a few mutinous strands escape and flap in my face. For a minute or so, we drink in silence and survey the view. Down and to the east I can make out the aging chain-link fence that circles the student parking lot across the street. It's empty except for Trevor Shewchuck's Fiesta, which rotted there all summer because he's too cheap to have it towed, and because there's no one left at school to care. Beyond that, the city becomes a dotting of streetlights, the red-brown roofs of bungalows and wartime houses, and the unfathomable blackness of the lake.

You know that song Neil Young sings about a town in North Ontario and how all his changes happened there? I always wanted that song to be about Thunder Bay, but it's not. Thunder Bay isn't the kind of place you write a song about.

"I can't wait to get out of here," I say.

I know it sounds a little rehearsed, like the kind of thing people say standing on rooftops in movies, but it's the truth. Soda nods. He doesn't say anything.

Sometimes, when he gets all stoic like this, I think he's trying to remind everyone that he's an Indian. His mom was part Ojibwe, and she was only nineteen or twenty when she hooked up with Mauri. He was this older guy, straight out of Finland. They had Soda about a year later, and sometime after that, she died of ovarian cancer.

"So that makes me a Findian," he said when we met in grade four. It was my second week at Balsam Street Elementary, and in some spirit of new-kid hazing, Brad McLaren had just spontaneously announced to the class that I'd tried to "bum him" in the cloakroom. I had trouble finding friends for a while after that.

Soda and I worked together for a group science project. We made one of those papier-mâché volcanoes that you fill with red dye, vinegar, and baking soda. He was just Jesse back then. He had failed a grade and the other kids were leery of him, partly because he was older and partly because of the whole Indian thing. In the beginning, we were just kind of friends by default.

That first day, when we walked home from school, I realized we didn't even live that far apart—just on either side of Hillcrest Park. His eyes got all saucered when my mom invited him in for some ants on a log. He told me my house was "really nice." Later, I'd learn that Soda's house wasn't really nice. On the other side of the park there were broken fences, uncut lawns, and dogs chained up in backyards.

"How's Mauri doing tonight?" I ask.

He raises his elbow in the air and flicks a beer cap into outer space. "He's fine."

Soda's dad is kind of an asshole when he drinks, which is pretty much always. On the upside, Mauri has been buying our beer since I was thirteen. Not that he knows or anything. He just assumes he drank any beer that disappears. I scratch at the gummy Crystal label with my fingernail, then brace myself for the bitter bottom. How does Soda scramble up here with a six pack in one hand, anyhow? I read that Mohawk Indians aren't afraid of heights. It's genetic, or something. Maybe it's true for the Ojibwe too.

I'm not so great with heights, so I get on my stomach and crawl toward the edge, the way you'd crawl over thin ice to pull someone out of the water. I learned how to do that in First Aid, along with performing CPR and treating minor burns. I did *not* learn how to treat falling two storeys down onto concrete steps. Still, I poke my head over so that my chin rests on the cold metal trim of the roof. I can feel the wind on my face, and my arms seem heavy. I reach back for the beer bottle and hold it in front of my face before I let it go. For about a second, it looks like it's just hanging in the air between the roof and the ground. Then the neck breaks on the concrete below and whatever's left inside spills out white and foamy. Watching it gives me this electric feeling between my shoulder blades, like I'm somehow going to follow the bottle down. I shimmy backward and push myself up into a sitting position.

"Catching up?" Soda offers me another beer.

I put the bottle to my lips and start to make a pretty impressive show of chugging it back, when I hear the voice from behind us.

"Hey!"

It's more like a dog bark than a word.

"What are you kids doing up here?"

I start coughing and sputtering and spilling down my front. Suds ejaculate from the neck, so I stand up and hold the bottle away from me at an arm's length. I wipe my hand on my jeans and listen to half my beer splatter on the ground. Soda shakes his head at me.

"Fucking *amateur.*" Deacon laughs and slaps me on the back. He collapses in a heap on the other side of Soda and grabs a beer.

The first time we really noticed Deacon, Soda and I were forced to sit through this excruciating school concert assembly, featuring such teen favourites as 'The Girl from Ipanema' and 'In The Mood.' As we watched the grade nine band wobble though a fairly soulless rendition of 'I Want To Hold Your Hand,' it became immediately clear that—regardless of the music teacher's enthusiastic baton waving—it was really the short kid on bass that was keeping it all from falling apart.

"Nice haircut," I say, still coughing a little.

"Thanks. Just set the ol' razor on Number Two."

"Your mom's Number Two," I mutter. He ignores me and twists the cap off his beer. The front of my jacket is damp.

"So," Deacon says after he winces down a mouthful, "I finally figured out how to do Johnny Cage's finishing move. He rips people right in half. It's pretty crazy."

Soda gives me a look.

"Sub-Zero still has the best Fatalities, though. Like in the first one? Where he pulls the guy's head off and you can see the *spine*? So awesome."

"Hey, did your mom let you have the Sabre tonight?" Soda asks, changing the subject.

"Yep."

"Are people still going to Wild Goose?"

"Think so."

"Well then?"

I finish what's left of my second beer. This time, I throw a hook shot over the road. It falls short of Shewchuck's hatchback and bounces off the chain-link fence.

"Shit. That sucked," I say.

"Your mom sucks," Deacon says.

"Jesus Christ, let's go!" Soda shouts. Somehow he's already waiting for us down in the parking lot. Indian blood. Has to be.

The Sabre is Deacon's mom's 1989 Buick LeSabre station wagon, a wood-paneled beast that is both hideous and frequently available. By the time I get down off the roof, Soda's already called shotgun, so I'm stuck in the back. I don't mind so much. There's something comforting about the back seat of that car. It's all beige and plushy and I can put my legs up across the bench. It's only after we've eased onto Van Norman Street and we're driving away that I look back to see all the dark windows of Mackenzie King staring at me like empty eye sockets. One more year of high school, I tell myself. One more year of the Pussies, of Fat Fuck, and one more year of Thunder Bay. Then I'm out for good.

"Anybody bring anything to listen to?" Deacon polls the car.

I can see Soda's arm reach into the front of his jacket, and at first I think he's fishing for smokes but instead he pulls out a tape. He pushes it into the player and hits rewind. The dashboard hums.

I'm barely buzzed and feel unprepared for what is supposed to be the last bush party of the season. Maybe I'll be able to swipe a few beers once I get there.

"I put something in the back for us," Soda says, his head half-turned toward me.

On the floor behind the passenger seat there's something covered with an old grey-and-red blanket. When I lift up a corner, twelve beer cans gleam like a miracle in the passing streetlight.

"Road pops!"

I dig one out of the carton and pass it to Soda over his shoulder. I hand the next one to Deacon, then get one for myself. Hollow cracks and wet slurps echo in the car. In the satisfied quiet that follows, the tape deck whines and the cassette crashes into the beginning. As Deacon turns onto Lakeshore Drive, Soda presses play and the first hopeful notes fill up the night.

SIDE B

The Rest of My Life

The sudden music feels like a cop's flashlight. Slowly, my hand creeps out from under the covers to slap at the snooze button on the clock radio. I haven't set it all summer, so why it's going off at seven in the morning—the *last* morning I can actually sleep in—is a cruel mystery.

Even crueler are the unmistakable symptoms I'm just starting to experience. I can remember a time when hangovers were brief explosions of vomiting and regret, but now they hang around all day and won't take a hint. It's like when Deacon crashes on my couch, sleeps until noon, and then starts watching my *Apocalypse Now Redux* DVD when he finally wakes up.

Despite my efforts, the clock radio continues to sing its evil electronica, until I realize it's not my alarm at all, but my cell phone. Driven by Pavlovian urgency, my legs kick themselves untangled, then find the cold floor of my basement apartment. I hunt through coat pockets and couch cushions until I finally find the thing underneath a pile of unopened mail. I stab the green button with my thumb and mumble an answer. It's Gail.

"Hi, Peter," she says. "How was your summer?"

My tongue is still cemented to the roof of my mouth. I peel it loose. "Good," I manage to say. "Yours?"

Gail describes the additional qualification courses she took online, how much money they cost, and how slow the internet connection was. Of all the people I'd like to hear from this early, Gail ranks pretty low on the list. Getting a call from your new department head on the last day of summer vacation is like an early visit from the Grim Reaper.

"So Peter, I hate to do this to you on short notice," she says, "but unfortunately there've been some issues with timetabling."

"Oh yeah? What's up?" I try my best to emulate the perky enthusiasm of a Dedicated Teacher.

"Well, *unfortunately,* there wasn't enough student enrolment for the Anthropology course, so it looks like you'll be teaching the Civics course this semester instead."

This semester. As in, tomorrow.

"Uh, okay. Sure." I can hear the perkiness in my voice fading fast. "There wouldn't happen to be any resources for that course kicking around, would there?" My eye travels to the Grade Eleven Anthropology binder on my kitchen table, the one full of step-by-step lesson plans, assignments, handouts, and quizzes.

"*Unfortunately,*" she says (I'm really starting to hate that word), "Jan Maki used to chair that course, and she retired in June. You could try calling her, but I think she's still in South Carolina. School's open all day, though, if you want to come in. There might be something in the storage room."

Unfortunately, it doesn't seem like I have any other options. I try to say *Thanks* in a way that doesn't sound completely insincere, but fail, and then hang up the phone.

When I walk out into the little kitchen, I realize the full extent to which my apartment is a mess. Partially empty glasses and beer bottles containing both questionable liquids and concerning solids crowd the counter. On the coffee table in the living room, there're a few greasy cartons from Eddy Lee's and a black soup of spilled beer and cigarette ash in the ashtray. A single pale noodle clings to the wall. From the sad little window near the ceiling, I can see a sunless smear of sky hovering above. It feels like the whole world has become an outward expression of my hangover.

After a little searching, I find my jacket in a wounded heap by the door and fish out a pack of smokes. I remember how there used to be a show on TV where this girl—I think she was half-alien or something—could put her fingers together and freeze time. If she forgot to do her homework, or felt like sleeping in, or I don't know, wanted to rob the 7-Eleven, it was no problem: *time freeze.* It was like having a pause button for the universe. As far as superpowers go, it always struck me as pretty practical. It would definitely come in handy right about now. Instead, I'm resigned to do the next best thing. I sit down, smoke a cigarette, and pretend for about six and half minutes that I'm not completely fucked.

North West High School was rechristened William Lyon Mackenzie King High School in 1950, just after our tenth prime minister died of pneumonia. The name change happened when C.D. Howe, our local member of parliament and one of King's closest cronies, leaned on the school board. The taxpayers weren't so fond of the name—King didn't have all that much to do with northern Ontario, and it was a little long-winded—but in the end they tolerated it. Fifty-four years of decreasing attention spans gave birth to a bunch of popular short forms including WLMK and Billy Mack (like the detective down in Texas), but for the most part people just call it Mackenzie King.

Personally, I think it's kind of awesome that the school was named after the only state leader who held séances with his dead mom and took advice from a dog. Stoner legend has it that if you burn a fifty-dollar bill—the one with King's picture on it—over the school crest then douse the flames with a bottle of Labatt's 50, you can commune with the ghost of King. I can't say I've ever had the money to burn or the beer to waste.

When I get to the school, it's relatively quiet. Office staff, admin, and guidance counsellors are milling about, but thankfully, there are very few Dedicated Teachers to exacerbate my headache. Dedicated Teachers aren't around today because they've already spent the week photocopying lessons, putting up freshly laminated posters, and organizing their desks into more effective learning configurations. Today, Dedicated Teachers are going for runs to reduce stress or looking forward to quiet evenings of watching *Two and a Half Men*. They are not, unlike some other people, spending the remainder of their Labour Day Weekend desperately hunting up course material.

I make my way upstairs to the history storage room and let myself in. The place is the size of a walk-in closet and smells like old coffee and paper. At one point, a few reclusive teachers must have used it as an office, but all that's left now is a couple desks, a phone, and an unplugged computer collecting dust. The shelves are lined with scintillating reads like *Confederation and Beyond*, *Imagine Canada*, and the 1981 classic *Canada Today: A Modern Perspective*, but there's nothing really specific to Civics. Some light archaeological digging in the file cabinet unearths hundreds of beige folders stuffed with mimeographs and photocopies of dot-matrix printouts. Another screeching metal drawer produces an array of peeling Trapper Keepers and a few VHS tapes labelled *Fur Trade Documentary, North and South,* and *Star Trek—Nazi Episode.* The place is a graveyard. I'm still completely fucked.

Don't get me wrong. It's not like I don't know my stuff; I know plenty. If they want me to talk about Roman aqueducts, the Reign of Terror, or the Beer Hall Putsch, I'm the man for the job. What I don't know is what I'm going to say to thirty stone-faced grade tens when the bell rings at 9:05 tomorrow morning. My best bet at this point is to pull some ice-breakers off the internet, figure out who else is teaching the course, and then get down to some serious mooching.

I leave the storage room and start heading toward the nearest exit. The web connection is faster at home and there's the added bonus of being able to smoke while I work. It's kind of tricky to do that around here. But then, as I walk through the English wing, I hear the sound of someone singing along to Joni Mitchell's 'Both Sides, Now.' It's coming from Room 207. When I look inside, I see Ruth Kipling standing on a chair and stapling a poster of Zefferelli's *Romeo and Juliet* to the back wall.

"Well, *ho-lee* shit," I say, walking into the room. "They'll let just about anyone work here, won't they?"

"Seems like it," she replies. "They hired you."

She steps down off the ladder and puts the stapler on her desk.

"You plan on spending all day in here?" I ask.

"Actually, I was just about to head over to Court Street Café for a reuben," she says looking at her watch. "Want to come with?"

The offer is tempting. Court Street does make a good reuben.

"I should probably head home," I decide. "I'm teaching Civics tomorrow and I have no idea what I'm doing."

"They gave you Civics? *Bastards.* That's half the reason I got out of History. Have fun with that."

I've known Ruth since high school. She's been teaching for a few years, but she was just transferred to Mackenzie King last semester, which works out pretty well for me. Ruth is funny and smart and has impeccable taste in music, but I'd like to think that the real reason we're friends is that she makes me dinner once a week. Plus, she married Deacon last spring, so we're kind of stuck with each other now.

I leave the building through one of the side exits, but about a minute later, as I'm walking through the teachers' parking lot, I hear the clomp of approaching sneakers behind me. I turn around just as Ruth catches up, a little out of breath.

"Hey!" she says. "I've still got some Civics binders I brought over from Churchill if you need them. They're from a couple years ago, but they should be okay."

"Seriously?"

"Seriously."

"*Thank you*. For a minute there I actually thought I was going to have to work on Labour Day."

"God forbid."

Crisis averted, I offer to buy lunch. She agrees, so we walk toward her car.

"You're really going to have to get your licence one of these days," she tells me.

"Meh. You'd be surprised how far you can get on learned helplessness."

She unlocks my door. "We can pick up the binders en route," she says as we pull out of the parking lot. "I want to check in on Pepperoni anyway. He's been barfing a lot lately. You should come in and see Michael. Maybe we can catch him *in flagrante*."

"Uh oh. Has Deacon been getting into the online porn?"

"I wish," she sighs. "*Grand Theft Auto*."

Deacon landed on his feet okay. Not that anyone was particularly worried. After everything went down with Soda, he took off to Laurier, and now he runs a website that manages other websites. I think. To be honest, I'm not one hundred percent sure what he does. I kind of stopped paying attention when he started talking about Boolean operators. All I know is, he gets to work from home, flies to Toronto once a month, and makes about twice as much money as I do. Fucking smart people.

The windows rattle a little as we fly down River Street. All things considered, the Sabre's held up surprisingly well. It's probably seen more than one transmission, but besides a little rust around the wheel well and a long crack across the back windshield, it's in pretty decent shape.

"I can't believe you guys still drive this thing."

"Hey, there's a lot of memories in this car." She surveys the interior for a second. "Lost my virginity in here."

"I did not need to know that."

"Yep. Right there where you're sitting."

"*Jesus!*"

I try to change the subject by way of turning on the radio. Thunder Bay has only a handful of stations, and they're all bad. I've never fully understood how there can be so many good songs in the world, but every time I turn on 94FM, they're playing 'One Week' by the Barenaked Ladies.

I open the glove compartment and rummage through a mess of battered cassettes to find something better. I take out one ancient mixed tape and through the scratched-up haze of the plastic case read the tracks. *Penpals—Sloan; Looking for a Place to Happen—The Tragically Hip;*

Helpless—Neil Young. They're listed in a faded but familiar handwriting. I hum a little note of recognition and smile to myself.

"What's that?" Ruth asks.

"Ah, nothing," I say. "Just an old tape Soda made."

She keeps one hand on the steering wheel and uses the other to crank down the driver's-side window.

"Oh, come on," I say. "It might be worth something."

Ruth takes the cassette out of my hand, then lobs it outside over the roof of the travelling car. I look out the window and catch a fleeting glimpse of magnetic tape unspooling on the sidewalk.

"Not to me."

She accelerates and keeps her eyes on the road.

SIDE A

In September

To me, it just doesn't seem worth it. Right now the floors are all waxed and shiny, but soon they'll be dull with foot traffic and sandwich guts. The lockers are graffiti free and the bathrooms smell like a chemical fruit, but by next week, someone will scratch a veiny cock into the paint, and someone else will take a dump on the floor. It must drive the custodians crazy to see a summer's worth of work destroyed in a matter of days.

My first two classes of the fall semester pass by uneventfully. It's all kind of old hat by now. Course outlines. Student profiles. Some bullshit get-to-know-you icebreakers that every teacher inevitably trots out to kill off the first day. Rotten was in my OAC History class, so I had to sit next to him. After a couple of weeks, I probably won't even notice the smell, like how I got used to the pulp and paper mill after we moved to Thunder Bay.

I don't see Soda or Deacon all morning. At lunch, I weave through student-clogged hallways and past manic banners that scream *Pep Rally this Thursday! Go Lyons!* When I finally make it out the front doors, I find myself in the middle of an afternoon that callously resembles summer. Immediately, I spot Evie sitting on the steps with a girl I don't recognize.

"Hey, Pete!" Evie smiles. "Good summer?"

We compare adventures. By now, we've both had lots of practice explaining How I Spent My Summer Vacation. She helped her parents build a sauna at their camp. (*Mosquitoes were insane!*) I worked at the Husky on Arthur Street for a week but quit because my boss was crazy. (*Wouldn't let me take lunch breaks!*)

"How come I didn't see you at Wild Goose last week?" she asks.

"Cops busted it up by the time we got there."

"Yeah, that was too bad. It was pretty fun while it lasted. We wound up going Cosmic Bowling after, but the shoe guy kicked us out for using our lane as a Slip 'n' Slide. *Never* go bowling when you're that wasted."

Evie's pretty great. We made out once at a party in grade ten when we were both really drunk. We'd been getting along famously all night, so when we found ourselves alone in an empty bedroom, it seemed like the thing to do. But just before we made the crucial transition from vertical kissing to horizontal groping, she stopped and threw up on my shoes. Romantically speaking, it was hard to come back from.

"So," she says, "when are we going to play a show together?"

"Uh, soon? I guess?" I hate commitment. "Lovely Rita's the brains of the operation."

"Well, tell Lovely Rita that you want to play with Martha Dumptruck as soon as fucking possible. Or else." She smashes her fist adorably into her palm. "Hey—do you know Ruth? Our new bass player?"

Evie nudges the girl sitting beside her who, until now, has had her nose buried in a battered copy of *The Bell Jar*. The girl looks up.

"Oh," she says, distractedly. "Hey." Then she returns to Sylvia Plath.

"She's actually very friendly," Evie assures me. "But not *too* friendly. You tell Sodapop she's off limits. Although, she does seem to have a thing for—" she whispers this part "*—other bass players.*"

From under *The Bell Jar*, Ruth blushes furiously.

Eventually, I make my excuses and head across the sloping front lawn. From the crest of the hill, it's easy to survey the familiar topography. The Dominion of Goth Chicks. Drama Kingdom. The People's Republic of Grunge. Metal Nation. Skaterland. Middle Earth. By now, I figure the Pussies have planted their flag in the cafeteria. In a way, it's kind of reassuring that all the old tribes have found themselves and reinstated their borders, no-fly zones, and passport policies. Though, to be honest, not a lot of people visit Middle Earth.

Even frightened-looking grade nines form their own weird Island of Misfit Toys. As they make their conspicuous attempts to look inconspicuous, someone shouts, "Gummer!" and I see something hurtle through the air. Barely pubescent children scatter, and the remains of two raw eggs cling to the brick of the school wall.

Without Soda and Deacon, I'm feeling like a man without a country, and I'm seriously considering running home to watch *The Monkees* and microwave a Pizza Pop. That's when I see Matty Wheeler making a beeline toward me with a fistful of handbills.

"Hey, brother," he says.

I try to keep things to a handshake, but Matty counters with a bear hug that blocks out the sun. For a moment, there is nothing but bristly dreadlocks and the smell of patchouli. Matty, or *Wheels*, as his disciples call him, is the Dalai Lama of Stoner Mountain.

"Great show back in August," he tells me. "Fucking *great*. That Soda, man." He pauses to let out a low whistle. "Terrific energy. You too. Nice drumming. *Amazing*."

I want to like Matty. He's a charmer and a true force of nature at Mackenzie King, but he's almost always working some kind of angle. And here it comes.

"So check this out," he says, putting a fluorescent orange flyer in my hand. "You'll like this. It's totally your bag."

I look down at the paper, wondering exactly what Matty thinks my "bag" is. I expect to see something about an Environmental Awareness Conference or a drum circle—which, bagwise, are decidedly not for me—but instead read *HAYDEN w/ Bunsen Honeydew, Saturday September 10th @ Whiskey Jack's. $5 at the door.*

From a fairly recent issue of *Pulse*, I know that Hayden is this screamy, folk-singer guy out of Toronto, but who is Bunsen Honeydew? I ask Matty.

"Bunsen Honeydew ..." he repeats, his voice full of stoned reverence. "Andy Thaler 'n' me started a *band* this summer."

Shit.

"We're into the Dead, Chili Peppers, Jamiroquai ... y'know, jazzy, funky improv stuff and super-extended grooves. I'm singing lead."

Shitshitshit.

"So, hopefully we'll see you Saturday. Awesome, dude." He walks away toward a semi-circle of grade elevens sitting on the grass. They smile at him expectantly. For a second, he looks back at me, then holds up a fist with devil horns. "Support the scene!" I hear him shout.

I've had enough. I start to make my way home when I spot Soda sprawled out underneath the big elm on the other side of the football field. As I get closer, I recognize the incredibly hot Emily Gardner sitting cross-legged beside him, wearing enormous sunglasses and cradling a bag of Hickory Sticks in her lap. Every once in a while he reaches in and steals a few. I drop my backpack beside them and immediately become a third wheel.

"Sodapop."

"Ponyboy. How's your first day back in the shit?"

"Not bad. Just ran into Matty Wheeler. You hear he started a band this summer?" I try to play it cool, but he can tell it's bothering me.

"Dude. It's not a competition. And besides, they're, like, a hippie jam band." He crunches a few Sticks between his teeth.

"I heard they're more like funk rock," Emily offers. She takes a swig from a can of pop.

It's hard to explain with Emily there, so I don't. The truth is, though, if I hadn't started a band with Soda and Deacon in grade nine, I'd probably be rolling twelve-sided dice with the Middle Earthers right now. I was a hundred and fifteen pounds of skinny, awkward thirteen-year-old. I wasn't good at sports, or talking to girls, and I had little doubt that my high school experience would be chock full of wedgies and swirlies. Instead, I got lucky. My Uncle Ted died.

Uncle Ted was my dad's younger brother who never really got the hang of being an adult. His massive coronary was likely due to his daily regime of cigarettes, fast food, and exercise avoidance. The only physical activity I ever saw him do was playing the drums. Why he willed them to me, I was never entirely sure. Maybe I said Ringo Starr was my favourite Beatle. *Maybe* I complimented the framed poster of John Bonham his girlfriend let him hang in their spare bedroom. All I know is, a week after the funeral, we drove home from Aunt Missy's house with a set of bright-orange 1978 Ludwig Jelly Bean Vistalites crammed in the back of my dad's Toyota. I spent the entire summer before high school learning to play them in the basement. It drove my dad crazy. What drove him even crazier is when Soda pushed his Peavey amp over on an old skateboard.

"Uh-uh. No way," my dad said. "You're not bringing that thing into my house."

In our defence, my mom asked if he'd prefer us out drinking and taking drugs. "At least this way we'll know where they are," she told him.

"Of course we'll know where they are. The whole goddamn neighbourhood will know where they are."

Eventually, after a few ground rules were set (no noise after ten o'clock and no noise during *Home Improvement*), the Peavey Bandit was allowed inside, where we proceeded to repeatedly butcher 'Enter Sandman,' 'Paranoid,' and 'Black Dog.' Of course, that was all before the fateful day Soda brought over a copy of this new album he'd taped off his older cousin.

"The cover's kind of weird," he described as he dropped the tape into the stereo. "It's got a baby swimming in a pool with its dong hanging out."

"Why would you put that on the front of your album?"

"I don't know. But listen ..."

So I listened, and everything started to make sense. Suddenly, my loud drums and Soda's power chords didn't sound accidental; they sounded ... I don't know ... relevant. We invited Deacon to play bass with us a few weeks later—much to my father's extended chagrin. Soon after, we started to play at punk shows in basements and community centres. People started paying attention, and all that underwear and toilet-related torture I anticipated never really happened. I successfully fooled people into thinking I was maybe even kind of cool.

But now, the naturally cool people—funny, confident, socially gifted people like Matty Wheeler—were starting to encroach on my territory. And I didn't like it.

"Well," Emily says, standing up, "I'm going to let you boys talk. Want the rest of these?" Before Soda can answer, she drops the Hickory Sticks on his stomach. "Bye, Soda," she says musically. "See you, Pete."

As she walks away, I try not to notice how good her ass looks in her low-riders. Soda's always been a bit of a chick magnet, but ever since the Battle of the Bands last January, girls were acting like he was Evan Dando.

"Sorry, dude. Didn't mean to cramp your style."

"No worries," he says, squinting his eyes as Emily waves at him from across the football field. "She's not going far. And look," he says, lighting a smoke, "don't sweat this whole thing with Wheels. That guy's just a tourist."

"I don't know. They've got Andy Thaler on board."

"Thaler the Wailer?" Soda holds the smoke in his lungs, momentarily impressed, then exhales. "Whatever. So what are your classes like?"

"I've got Mitchell and Hildebrandt, period three spare, and Maki in the afternoon."

"That's not so bad. Mitchell's okay, and Hildebrandt's a nutjob but harmless. Maki's a flake, but she never takes attendance, so there's that. Did you see Deacon in any of your classes?"

I shake my head and start to unpack my lunch. Ham sandwich and a box of fruit punch that, by now, will taste like warm poison.

"Haven't seen him at all today," I say. "He's taking a bunch of programming classes this semester."

"If he spends all his lunches in the computer lab again this year, he's going to finish out his high school career a virgin."

"I don't know. Gordana Novak seemed pretty into him last year."

"Is she the one with the wonky eye or the thing on her neck?"

"Thing on her neck."

Soda shrugs. "Guess you've got to start somewhere." He pushes himself to his feet. "Well, dude, unlike you, I have a class next period. Calculus. With *Gallo*."

"Ouch."

"Practice after supper?"

I give him the thumbs up as he heads off in the general direction of Mackenzie King and Emily Gardner. I finish my sandwich and then spear the little straw on my juice box out of its cellophane and into the silver dot on top. I take a sip and squint up at the blue sky. In the distance, a flock of birds changes course with the telepathic single-mindedness of iron filings following a magnet. If it wasn't for school, I'd be at Soldier's Hole right now, swimming, drinking stolen beer, and listening to *Twice Removed* or that new Guided By Voices album. And then I realize that it's still a beautiful day, and I've got precisely nothing to do for the next hour. I set my Timex so I won't be late for period four, wedge my jacket under my head, and take the first of what I hope will be many afternoon naps.

When I wake up, the first thing I think is I've pissed myself. I feel a cool wetness spreading in my lap and understand even before I'm fully conscious that peeing my pants at school would be an irrecoverable horror. Then I hear the giggling. I blink my eyes open to see an arc of red fluid that somehow begins at my juice box and ends between my legs.

"Wake up, Curtsey ..." a voice croons.

"Check it out," a second voice insists. "Curtsey's on the rag."

The first voice is Dave Greatorex, King of the Cafeteria. The second is Brad McLaren, Clown Prince. Greatorex is the real threat. He's been a Junior B Hockey enforcer since he was sixteen. He's always wearing those expensive jeans with writing on the butt, a gold chain, and too much hair gel. If there was a category in the yearbook for Most Likely to Commit Date Rape, he'd be a shoo-in. The other guy, McLaren, is a little hockey-haired third-stringer, but just like Greatorex, he walks around wearing a lame-ass varsity jacket as if he didn't look like the villain in every John Hughes movie. He's the one liberally squeezing Del Monte all over my button fly.

I'm wide awake now, scuttling back on the grass, trying to get away from the juice fountain.

"What the fuck are you *doing*?" I get to my feet.

"What are *we* doing?" McLaren asks innocently. "You're the one menstruating in public, Curtis."

"You forget your maxi-pad, Princess?" Greatorex adds.

As reasonable as my current standing in the Mackenzie King social hierarchy may be, the Pussies have always aggressively guarded their position at the top of the food chain. Don't get me wrong—I'm no jockist. I ran track in grade nine and ten, and Soda was a pretty decent forward until he sold all his hockey equipment to buy a Telecaster (Mauri was *not* pleased). We just don't have the necessary skill set to be Pussies. We don't enjoy yelling in public places or humiliating people with half our body mass.

If Soda was still here, they wouldn't mess with me. They've got a healthy respect for all six foot three of him. But he's not here. He's in Calculus, or having sex with Emily Gardner in her parents' Dodge Caravan. Either way, there's not much he can do now.

"Uh-oh, Dave. Princess looks right pissed."

"Don't worry, Brad. I'll have a chat with her." Greatorex leans down into my airspace and puts a paw on my shoulder. For a moment, everything smells like Drakkar Noir. "Cheer up, Buttercup. It's completely natural. This is a special time in a young girl's life." More sniggering. "You're just becoming a woman, that's all."

The worst part about this particular brand of abuse is that you're forced to acknowledge your own weaknesses. I'd love nothing more than to punch this guy so hard that cartoon birdies circle his head, but even if I landed that first hit, I know it'd be my last. Greatorex has knuckles like steel rivets and muscles I can't even name ballooning under his Mondetta sweatshirt. Another option is to say something—something that would put these two idiots in their place—but even if my brain wasn't a rage-and-adrenalin factory right now, even if I could think clearly enough to find the right words, I still wouldn't risk losing my front teeth. I don't even bother to shake his hand off my shoulder, and I know that later I'll hate myself for it. Guys like Greatorex rarely beat you up. They let you do it to yourself.

Eventually, the two of them get bored of discussing my dicklessness, and Greatorex adjourns our meeting by giving me a shove in the chest, hard. I trip backward over the elm root, and I can hear Brad making the sound in the back of his throat before I hit the ground. A second later, I feel a loogie pulling itself down my hair.

"Go home and clean yourself up," Greatorex tells me.

"Yeah," McLaren adds. "Get your mom to show you how to use a fuckin' tampon."

They walk away, congratulating each other with punches to the shoulder. I scrub my head with my sleeve, but it just pushes the disgusting wet further into my scalp. As I wait for shame to replace the fear, I hear a familiar voice.

"Hey, *Pussy* ..." Greatorex and McLaren, a good thirty feet away from me now, slow down and stop. All three of us look in the same direction at once and see Soda walking toward us, shedding his jeans jacket as he does.

Here's the thing. Originally, our sports teams were called the Kings and our mascot was this dubious, bearded character who playfully bashed the visiting teams with a foam sceptre. At some point during a basketball game in the early seventies, an overzealous King decided to use his sceptre to vigorously air-rape the visiting Sir Winston Churchill Bulldogs. It led to a bench-clearing rumble that landed half the home team in the hospital. As a result of the fiasco, the principal revoked the name *Kings* in favour of the more gender-neutral *Lyons*. Or *Pussies*, as they've been called by every visiting team since.

"The fuck you call me?"

Soda walks past McLaren and dismisses him with a roll of his eyes. He squares up in front of Greatorex. "I think you should apologize to my friend," he tells him.

Greatorex steps up to Soda and leans in close, like he's going to kiss him. "You want to start something, Chief?" he asks softly.

The two stare at each other for a little while. Greatorex's nose flares an inch away from Soda's, but Soda's cool is unshakeable.

"No, *Dave*," Soda finally says. "I don't want to 'start something'. I'm just asking you to apologize to my friend."

I wonder how far this is going to go. Soda's a big enough guy, sure, but Greatorex is a fucking kodiak, and all this testosterone has got to be testing the tensile strength of the school's zero-tolerance rule.

And yet, surprisingly, it's Greatorex who steps back. He cricks his neck. For a moment there's an unsettling silence. There's a look in Greatorex's eyes I can't place.

"Whatever," he says. "Wouldn't want to get my hands dirty anyway."

"Yeah, fuck this," McLaren sniffs. "I'm going home to wash the welfare stink out of my clothes."

I can tell Soda wants to say more, but he keeps his mouth shut. As we watch the hockey players fade away across the field, I feel the beginnings of relief. Soda picks up his jacket off the grass and pushes his arms through the sleeves. He walks past me to the elm.

"Where'd you come from?" I ask, remembering to be amazed.

"Forgot my smokes," he says, pulling a pack out from underneath an exposed root.

"Are you going back to class?" I ask.

"Think I'll stick here for a bit." He slides down the tree to where I was sitting before. "You should head home. Skip fourth."

"Yeah. See you at practice?"

Soda keeps his eyes closed and nods.

I start walking, trying not to run, trying not to look as cowardly as I feel. My head hurts, my pants are wet, and there's still loogie in my hair. I scan the football field and make accidental eye contact with a feather-haired headbanger—last of a dying breed—smoking a cigarette on the bottom seat of the bleachers. He looks away before I do. On the other side of the field, I can make out two girls sitting against the west wall of the school. I hope they didn't see what happened. I hope they aren't pretty.

It's my last year of high school. I thought I was past all this. You take a little shit in grade nine, no question, but I figured that by the time you were in OAC, you'd be old enough to forget about pecking order. Apparently, this is not the case. Apparently, the shit is never-ending.

SIDE B
Come on, Teacher

"*Jesus.* When is this going to end?"

I check my watch again. Class starts in four minutes and the photocopier is dribbling out assignments like a nervous twelve-year-old at a public urinal.

"We should've got new machines last year," Vicky Greene says, "but Trimble's too cheap to pay for them."

She leans against the counter beside me, and we both try to think of something to say. "So, where've you been hiding?" she finally asks. "I haven't seen you in the staff room for a couple weeks."

Against my better judgement, I tell her where I've been spending my prep time.

"That storage room? The one upstairs? Is there even a phone in there?"

Making small talk at the photocopier is the worst. It's like a water cooler you can't walk away from. I wonder if I should've just lied. I feel like I've divulged a critical element of Ruth's escape plan.

"You should come back to the staff room," she decides. "That's where the action's at. Besides, I need you around to keep Jim Lodge from looking down my shirt."

As if to demonstrate, her eyes flit down her low-cut blouse, and against every natural instinct, I keep my own trained squarely on her forehead.

Finally, she picks up a file folder and turns to leave. I realize she hasn't even made any copies. "Maybe I'll stop by later and you can give me a tour of your secret hideout."

"It wouldn't take long," I tell her. "It's pretty cozy in there."

"How cozy?" she asks. "Is there a lock on the door?" She laughs nervously and beats a hasty retreat.

The photocopier spits out the rest of my paper, and I find myself with exactly two minutes left to unleash half a pot of coffee from my bladder and get to class. After I hit the bathroom, I stop by History Storage to grab my bag. Ruth is in there flipping leisurely through a binder labelled *To Kill a Mockingbird.*

"I saw *Madame* Greene follow you into the copy room," she tells me.

"Yeah. She does that sometimes."

"You know she's married to a superintendent, right?"

"Hey," I say, "aren't you a member of the English department? You know this is a designated *History* room, right?"

"Hey," she replies as the bell rings, "aren't you teaching class this period? You know you might be kind of late."

"You're late, Curtis." The kid's shaved head looks small and pasty compared to the enormous, airbrushed head of Tupac Shakur on his t-shirt.

"Guess I'll have to give myself a detention." I don't exactly have the moral high ground to remind him it's *Mister* Curtis.

Already there's a cluster of bored-looking tenth-graders outside my classroom door. They watch skeptically as I try to balance my books and coffee in one hand and fish keys out my pocket with the other. I give up and drop my teacher's copy of *Civics Now!* and the course binder on the polished concrete below. The jaws of the binder spring open and barf out three units' worth of meticulously organized loose-leaf paper.

"Nice one," says Tupac.

I open the door and watch knees and ankles surge past as I gather my notes. By the time I get to my desk, things have already gone a little *Lord of the Flies*. Kids are at each other's seats, girls are sitting on each other's laps, and in the back row, three boys crowd around a laptop and hoot from under their hoodies. Amidst it all is the mosquito chorus of a dozen or so blaring earbuds, the repetitive bleepery of handheld video games, and the intermittent buzz of phones set to vibrate.

The classroom itself is also a disaster. Hildebrandt taught me history out of this room when I was in OAC, and I always thought it was mess because *he* was a mess, but with the exception of a computer on the teacher's desk and its tangled mullet of wire and ethernet cable, not much has changed. Dirty coffee mugs and a crumbling diorama of the Egyptian pyramids decorate the built-in bookshelves. An old beige file cabinet stands at the back of the room and commemorates in jagged white scratches that *Rotten Rules!* and *Mazz wuz here.* Motivational posters continue to encourage DIVERSITY, TEAMWORK, and DETERMINATION, and in a series of circles, another poster reminds me of all the other things I could've done with a history degree—journalist, librarian, museum curator, etc. They all sound infinitely more rewarding than what I'm doing right now.

"Okay, folks!" I shout. "Grab your seats, please. Tracey Adams?"

"Here."

"Colin Atkinson?"

"Present!"

"Thomas Bertrand?" Silence. "Thomas Bertrand?" More silence. "Okay. No Thomas Bertrand."

I've been teaching these kids for just over two weeks and a lot of them still blur together. The girls with the shoulder-length brown hair. The guys with the ball caps. The bus kids with their bed-head and wild-life sweatshirts. The well-dressed kids from Cherry Ridge. I can really only put a handful of names to a handful of faces.

"All right, so," I say, finally sorted, "today we're going to spend some time talking about democracy. We're going to talk about what a democracy is and what it means to live in one."

A hand goes up. I recognize Marshall Heyen-Miller at the back. Smart kid. Reads a lot. His parents are both profs at the university. I nod to him and he asks, "If we live in a democracy, why do we have to go to school? Shouldn't we have some kind of vote about it?"

In teacher's college they called this a teachable moment. I can use Marshall's question to segue right into the idea of free will and sacrificing personal rights to participate in a society. I might even get to talk about Rousseau's Social Contract.

"Actually, Marshall, it's interesting you should ask that—"

"I vote we watch a movie," Tupac says suddenly. "Does that TV work? I've got *American History X* in my bag. It's about history. Says so in the title." A chorus of agreement bubbles from the silence.

"Well ..." *Steve? Brandon?* I scan the seating plan. "*Dylan*, that's not quite—"

"All in favour we watch the movie?" Dylan polls the room. A number of enthusiastic hands bolt skyward. A few others follow along shyly to make up the majority. Marshall looks at me, shrugs, and also puts up his hand.

"All right," I say, "we're not—" but before I can kibosh the impending mutiny, Dylan is at the front of the room, squatting in front of the television cart.

"Where's the ... ?" He pokes experimentally at a button and white noise explodes into the room.

"Dylan!" I shout over the static. He points to his ear and mimes deafness. I reach down and yank the plug out of the wall. In the sudden silence, my voice sounds too loud. "We're not watching that right now."

Dylan lets out a heavy sigh and takes the DVD back to his desk, rolling his eyes like a dissatisfied customer. "This class *buh-lows*," he says. I ignore him and try to salvage my introduction.

"Okay. So, yeah, when you live in a democracy, you get to make decisions based on majority rule—like whether or not you listen to me or watch a movie—*but*, one of the things we decided as a society is—"

Before I can finish my thought, a short electronic melody sounds out from the vicinity of Dylan's desk. I look in his direction, and his entire attention seems to be suddenly focused on his own lap.

"Dylan, please turn your phone off in class." I'm still relatively new at this, but I imagine teaching was a lot easier before the invention of wireless devices.

"I'll put it on vibrate."

He slips it into his pocket.

"*Off*, please. And away."

More eye rolling. He pulls it out and puts it in his empty desk with a hollow clatter. Good enough.

"So," I return to the class, "because you're all under the age of eighteen—"

"I'm not," says a large and impressively bearded student in the back row.

"Okay, because *most* of you are under the age of eighteen—"

I'm interrupted again, this time by the sound of Dylan's phone buzzing against the metal of his desk. Dylan grabs it, but instead of sheepishly turning it off, he holds it to his ear and says, "Hello?"

I make a beeline to his desk and hold out my hand.

"Give me that."

He eyes me narrowly, raises a silencing index finger, and continues to talk. I feel something like a blood vessel burst in my head.

"Dylan, give me that phone *right now*," I say. I hear my voice getting shaky with anger.

By now, even the students who were only vaguely tuned in are watching hungrily, eager for a showdown. This is better than a movie. Definitely better than a Civics lesson.

Dylan holds his hand over the mouthpiece. "It's my *mom*!" he whispers viciously, and then, to his alleged parent, "Yeah. *I know.* I'll have to call you back. I know. Okay. Bye."

He puts the phone down on his desk. I snatch it away with an animal dexterity I didn't know I had.

"What the *hell*?" By some impossible teenage logic, Dylan is the victim. "That's mine!"

"I know it's yours," I say, walking back to my desk where I lock the phone in a drawer. "You can have it back after school."

He slides down in his seat and stares past me. "Fuckin' fascist," he mutters. The girl sitting next to him stares, wide-eyed and happily scandalized.

"I'm sorry, *what* did you just call me?"

Dylan sits up in his seat. "Did I stutter? I called you a *fucking fascist*."

"Get your things," I tell him, trying to keep my voice steady, "and go to the office."

"Whatever."

He reaches into his pocket, puts a cigarette behind his ear, and as he walks past me, casually pushes my coffee cup off my desk and into the garbage can. Sixty eyes watch for my next move, but I just let him go. At least I have everyone's attention now.

When I first started teaching, I wanted to be cool. I mean, I wasn't expecting kids to get up on their desks and recite "O Captain! My Captain," but I wanted to have interesting discussions about why the world is the way it is and how we can make it better. So far, it doesn't seem to be working out that way. I guess it's hard to stick it to the Man once you've become the Man.

At lunch, I find Ruth in the staff cafeteria and sit down across from her with my plate of chicken nuggets, fries, and gravy.

"God," Ruth says, looking at my food in disgust. "How can you eat that?"

"It's comfort food," I say. "I need comfort." I crack the tab on a can of root beer and dare her to challenge my choice of beverage.

"Any classes this afternoon?"

Through a mouthful of inferior chicken, I answer, "Physics. Third period."

"Did you even *take* physics in high school?"

I got hired this semester to fill in for a woman on maternity leave.

I teach a sleepy Canadian History class first thing in the morning, and then the nightmare that is Civics just before lunch. The office is usually pretty good at throwing me enough supply work in the afternoon to keep me busy, but that includes anything from girl's phys. ed. to woodworking. Of course, none of this is permanent, which means that unless someone retires, dies, or gets fired, I'll be out of a job by February.

"Well, why don't you come over for dinner tonight?" Ruth asks. "I'll cook you something that isn't slurry based, and you can distract Michael from whatever stupid video game he's currently obsessed with."

"Okay, but what if he seduces me with superior graphics and elaborate weaponry?"

"Then I'm feeding your dinner to Pepperoni."

"I can't imagine that's healthy for an octogenarian cat."

"He's *eleven*."

"That's pretty old for a cat."

In the background, I can hear a phone ringing. Just as I lift another bite of chicken to my mouth, Jim Lodge vies for my attention.

"Kovalski on the phone for you, Curtis."

I put down the fork and make my way to the staff cafeteria telephone. Chances are that someone went home sick and they need me to cover a class fourth period. I could use the extra money.

"Hi, it's Pete," I say into the receiver.

"Hi, Peter. Listen, I've got a parent in the office, and she's a little concerned about what happened in your period two class today."

In the background I can hear a woman's voice: "*completely unacceptable ...*"

"Did you confiscate a student's phone?"

Ah. Dylan's mom. "I sure did. And then I sent him down to see you."

"Okay. He never showed up. Did you fill out an incident report?"

A what? "Uh, no, I was trying to corral my class after he left. He was pretty disruptive."

"*That was private property ...*" Dylan's mom protests in the background.

"Right. Well ... you can't send a student down without filling out an incident report, and *legally*, we're not really supposed to take their phones away. I'm going to need you to come down and have a chat with us, okay? And bring the phone."

"*... and he has no right to ...*"

I sigh and look sadly at the gravy congealing on my plate. "I'll be right there."

I walk past Ruth and shove one last forkful of food into my mouth.

It's going to be a long day without a lunch.

"Problem?" she asks.

I take a final swallow of root beer. "Yeah. The crazy apple doesn't fall far from the crazy tree."

"Truer words, my friend," she says. "Hey, can I have the rest of your fries?"

SIDE A

French Inhale

"Hands off."

Soda swats Deacon away from the faders on our brand-new Tascam Portastudio.

"Hey, I paid for it. I can touch it all I want."

"We *all* paid for it, dumbass," I say. "It's *the band's* four-track."

"Yeah, and as a member of *the band*, I'd like to fix my levels. The bass sounds like a farted-out tuba."

"I thought that was your signature sound." Soda grins. He makes a few adjustments and then hits Record. "Okay. Let's try this again."

Our rehearsal space is a wood-panelled room in my parents' basement that's now plastered with photocopied show posters. Some of the shows were ours; others I wish had been ours: hHead and Mystery Machine in June; King Cobb Steelie in August; Hayden in September. My dad had some ambitions about turning this place into a rec room, with a big-screen TV and surround sound, but I think by now it's safe to say we've got squatters' rights. Of course, we're still subject to the will of the landlords. We get halfway through 'Glass Knuckles,' without making a *single* mistake, when the overhead lights flash.

Deacon stops playing first. Soda finishes the chorus and then drops out, but I can tell he's irritated. I unleash an indignant drum solo in protest. Soda hits Stop on the Tascam.

"Mom, we're trying to record down here."

"Well, I have a load of whites to do," my mom fires back, navigating the stairs from behind an avocado-coloured laundry basket. Before she's even halfway down, Deacon unstraps his bass and takes the basket out of her arms.

"Can I throw this in the wash for you, Mrs. Curtis? Permanent press?"

"Thank you, Michael."

Deacon smiles smugly in my direction, and I roll my eyes.

"Peter," my mom says, "Rita called. She wants you to call her after practice."

She pauses for a moment, like she's just now realized we're all waiting for her to leave. "You guys are sounding ... better."

"Thanks."

"Thanks, Mrs. Curtis."

Once she's gone I turn back to the other guys. With his thumbs and forefingers, Deacon is dangling one of my mom's bras in front of his chest. He winks at me.

"I can't even begin to tell you how gross that is," I tell him.

"What does Rita want?" Soda asks.

"I don't know. She probably needs us to confirm the Super Friendz show."

"Super Friendz ..." Deacon says, dropping the offending underwear back in the basket. "Who names their band after a cartoon?"

"Mystery Machine is from *Scooby Doo*," I say.

"Yeah, well, Mystery Machine sounds cool. Super Friendz sounds kind of gay."

"*You* named our band after a fairy tale," Soda reminds him.

"Well, I had another name, which would've been *infinitely* cooler, but you guys just didn't *get* it."

Soda groans. Deacon had wanted to name the band Kid Charlemagne, but Soda and I vetoed it: "We're *not* naming our band after a fucking Steely Dan song."

We eventually decided on Giant Killer. Despite its questionable origins, it did sound pretty badass. Plus, it was kind of a fuck-you to Thunder Bay's foremost geological wonder, the Sleeping Giant, this peninsula that everyone's so proud of because they think it looks like a man lying down on his back. Personally, I think it looks like a giant green turd floating in Lake Superior.

We agree to do the show and practise for another hour or so. After Soda and Deacon take off, I call Lovely Rita and confirm. Rita laughs and tells us she already booked it.

"As if you guys would ever turn down a chance to be on stage."

We met Rita Bachinsky one night last year at End of the Century. She was originally from Windsor and doing her first year at Lakehead. She came out to watch a couple guys from her hacky-sack club play covers of Soul Asylum and Sublime songs that were somehow worse than their source material. She stuck around to watch Giant Killer play, and right after our set she came up to us and announced that she wanted to be our manager for life. At first—I'll admit it—I was a little put off. I imagine the other guys were too. Basking in the sweaty afterglow of our best and most crowded show to date (almost twenty people!), I thought she might damage our newly established cred. I mean, she didn't exactly scream rock 'n' roll.

The thing is, Rita is fat. If I wanted to be politically correct, I might say she's big-boned, or husky, but that's not quite the truth. The truth is, she's just fat. Enormously fat. Like Rita MacNeil fat. In fact, the unfortunate coincidence that she shares her name with Canada's premier heavyweight songbird has led her to slap at least two people who were stupid enough to make the comparison.

It's possible that Rita sensed we were a little leery of her that first night. Maybe she was just used to having to prove herself. In any case, the next thing we knew, she had sneaked us a free pitcher of beer and talked the bar manager into paying us an extra fifty bucks. That's when I realized Lovely Rita got shit done. From then on she booked our shows, helped design our t-shirts, sold our merch, and drove the Sabre if everyone else wanted to get drunk. She couldn't play a note of music, but Rita was in the band.

The next day, Deacon picks me up around one o'clock so we can put up posters around town. Even before he pulls into my driveway, I can hear 'Rikki Don't Lose That Number' blaring through his windows.

"Where's Soda?" I ask, easing into the passenger seat.

Deacon plays drums on the steering wheel.

"He said he's not feeling well."

With Soda, "not feeling well" could mean a lot of things.

"Hey, check out the Super Friendz poster Rita made," Deacon says, reaching in the back and then handing me a piece of paper stiff with glue. "Think it's too obvious?"

“Nah. I like how she replaced Aquaman’s head with a Telecaster.”

Luckily, Deacon’s sister Deandra is working that day, which means we can get the photocopies for free and pocket the money from the club manager. But not before Deandra gives the poster a once over.

“Super Friendz?” The Bubblicious snaps between her teeth. “Like the kids’ show? Sounds kind of gay.”

“See?” Deacon says, elbowing me.

How Deandra “Double D” Deacon shares any DNA with her brother is something of a mystery. In her glory days, she was the Metal Queen of Mackenzie King, all hairspray, fishnets, feather earrings, and black leather. In grade nine, I was only lucky enough to spot her a couple times before she dropped out and moved to Calgary, but those rare sightings had a profound impact on my young libido.

She came home about a year ago and got a job at Business Depot. The rumour, as yet unconfirmed by Deacon, was that she had a kid, then gave it up for adoption. She seems kind of faded now—her hair’s a little out of date, and she’s put on a few pounds—but I love that she still wears those studded leather bracelets under the red uniform and plastic name tag.

“Hey, Mikey, tell your friend there to quit looking at my tits.”

Deacon glares in my direction, and I hold up my hands like someone’s got a gun on me.

“You wish, Deandra,” Deacon says.

Deandra shrugs, snaps her gum again, and winks at me. I experience a minor heart attack as she goes back to check the copy machine.

“Were you looking at my sister’s tits?” he asks me quietly.

“Shut up, ‘Mikey.’”

For the next three hours, Deacon and I cruise around in the Sabre and poster the town. Armed with a staple gun and three rolls of packing tape, we hit every telephone pole, streetlight, and phone booth in Port Arthur. Dave at Cumberland Stereo lets us put a poster up in the store. We also put posters up in Comix Plus, Colosimo’s Music, and the Calabria. Then we go to the South End.

For a city of just over a hundred thousand people, Thunder Bay sprawls out for over three hundred square kilometers with no clear urban plan. In a rare moment of lucidity, my OAC History teacher, Mr. Hildebrandt, told us the story about how Thunder Bay got its name. Apparently, in the late sixties, when the powers-that-be amalgamated Port Arthur and Fort William, they took suggestions about what they should name this new, booming metropolis. Thunder Bay made the short list, because that's apparently what the Ojibwe called this area: *Animikie*, which I think means *thunder*. The most popular name, though, was actually Lakehead, which kind of makes sense because we're at the top of Lake Superior. But *then*, some genius thought it'd be a good idea to put both Lakehead and *The* Lakehead as options on the referendum ballot. The two names split the Lakehead vote, which would've otherwise won, and it was the loser name that they put on the sign. Loser name for a loser town. That's Thunder Bay.

We come back to the north side and finish up in front of Mackenzie King. Already the sun's starting to go down. Deacon and I take a minute to admire our handiwork. Our breath is visible in the cold air.

"Fuck," Deacon says, putting the staple gun under his arm and rubbing his hands together. "I should've worn gloves."

"Did Rita tell you about that kegger tonight?" I ask. Rita's always trying to get us to get drunk with university kids. She calls it networking.

"Yeah," Deacon says. He points the staple gun at the nearest telephone poll and fires off a couple rounds. "I think I'm doing something with Ruth instead."

"Hmm," I say, mildly intrigued. Since I've known him, Deacon hasn't had a real girlfriend. Just a series of awkward misfires. "How's that going?"

He shrugs. "I dunno. She's cool."

I listen for a moment as Deacon pulls the trigger again.

"So what was the deal with Soda today?" I ask. "For real."

"I don't know. I saw Mark Zaborniak at Robin's Donuts this morning and he said Soda was out partying with Emily last night. Said they were both pretty hammered."

"Emily Gardner? I thought they broke up, or whatever."

"No, Emily *McCormack*."

He fires another round and I see a staple ricochet off a pole and fall through the fading light.

"Aren't Emily McCormack and Emily Gardner best friends? You know, that whole 'Emily Squared' thing they used to do? I thought they were inseparable."

"Yeah," Deacon says, holstering the gun in his jacket pocket. "They were."

I don't need to look for the house number when I get to Banning Street that night. There's no mistaking a keg party. Already there are a few people standing on the front lawn wearing heavy knit sweaters and drinking out of plastic cups. On the porch, some guy with a ponytail is trying to work out the chords to 'No Woman, No Cry' on an acoustic guitar. He looks cold. I smile when he looks up from his fingering, and he eyes me with something between indifference and open hostility.

"If you're going to drink, you have to pay Steve twenty bucks," he says, re-adjusting the strap on his guitar. For a hippie shindig, this seems like a pretty capitalist venture.

"Okay," I say, as cheerfully as I can. "Where is he?"

But by then he's moved on to 'Buffalo Soldier' and instead of answering me, he's enthusiastically singing to no one in particular.

I go inside and leave my shoes in the giant pile by the door. From the front hall, I can see the place is pretty packed with people I don't recognize. The stereo is blaring *Blood Sugar Sex Magik*, and the house has this damp, living smell, like the inside of an old cooler. I head for the kitchen, the nexus of all house parties, in hopes that I'll find Lovely Rita, but she's nowhere to be seen. I do, however, find the keg, and as there's currently no lineup, I pull a plastic cup out of its sleeve and pour myself a beer. I'll have to pay Steve his twenty dollars when I see him.

Armed with a beverage, I go in search of Rita and get a feel for my surroundings. Most parties I go to are still in the houses of my friends' absent parents, where I spend an inordinate amount of time feeling nervous around Royal Doulton figurines and dangerously pale-coloured carpeting. Here, the only breakable decorations are a lava lamp and a neon Molson Canadian sign. Where there is carpet on the floor, it's already stained. The walls are decorated with posters: Pink Floyd, Led Zeppelin, *A Clockwork Orange*. There's an enormous Canadian flag hung like a curtain in the front room and a stolen construction sign on the bathroom door that says *No Dumping*.

I'm on my way up the stairs when I run into Matty Wheeler and his enormous dreadlocks. I guess now that he plays in a band with university guys, it makes sense that he's hanging out at university keggers.

"Hey, bu-uddy," he says, sounding a little too much like Pauly Shore. "What are you doing here? Is Soda here too?"

I hate how relieved I am to see him. On principle, I usually can't stand him and his tribe of musical beardos, but right now he's the only friendly port in a sea of strangers. I tell him I'm looking for Lovely Rita. He knows who she is—everybody does—but he hasn't seen her tonight.

"I'm just about to smoke a bowl in the basement. Want to come with?"

I hesitate. The truth is, I've smoked pot only a few times in my life, and I'm starting to suspect that it's all just a big scam. The only physiological effect I've experienced is sleepiness, and I'm not such a big fan of sucking some wet end another guy just had his lips all over. Of course, that said, I've got nothing better to do.

"Yeah. Sure."

"All right, brother. Follow me."

He puts his arm around me and steers me back down the stairs. We head through the kitchen, and on the way, Matty stops and interrupts this guy with big teeth and weirdly purple gums. He's talking to a blonde girl who's really pretty in a bored and angry kind of way, like how some runway models always look so pissed-off about nothing in particular.

"Dude," Matty says to Purple Gums, "I'm going to conduct some business in the basement. You should come." He looks at Angry Face. "You too, little sister."

They fall in behind Matty and I follow them. We all go down a very rickety set of stairs. At the bottom, the room opens up into what looks like a rehearsal space, with a few amps, a drum kit, and a set of bongos. Suddenly, I realize I'm in the lion's den: Honeydew Headquarters.

"Is this where you guys practise?" I ask.

"No, Sherlock, it's our interpretive dance studio," says Purple Gums.

"Oh hey, sorry, dudes," Matty says, packing the bowl. "I'm just no good with, y'know, *formalities*. This is Pete. Pete, that's Steve, our trumpet player, and that's Kim."

"Our groupie," Steve says. Kim looks in the opposite direction and shakes her head.

"Oh, *Steve*," I say, feeling a little guilty about the beer in my hand. "I've got twenty bucks for the keg."

"Nope. Wrong Steve." He seems inexplicably put out. "Fucking people have been trying to give me money all night."

"Must be awful," Kim says.

"That's *Sudbury* Steve," Matty gestures toward Purple Gums. "You want Kim's brother, *Townie* Steve."

"Townie Steve." I turn to Kim. "Does that mean you're also a townie?"

Sudbury Steve rolls his eyes.

Kim aims her index finger and thumb at me like a gun, and winks. "Born and raised, dude."

We stand in a loose circle and watch as Matty lights the bowl and sucks on the glass pipe a couple times. A thick cloud of smoke rolls out of his mouth, and then, miraculously, travels back up into his nostrils.

"Ni-ice," Sudbury Steve says. "Irish Waterfall."

Matty exhales. "So yeah," he says, passing the pipe to Steve, "this is our new *space*. We even have an eight-track set up so we can just roll tape and record our sessions. Last weekend we got fucked up on 'shrooms and jammed for *three hours straight*. It was beautiful."

"Bet the neighbours loved it," Kim says.

"Oh, fuck the neighbours," says Sudbury Steve, passing the pipe to Kim. "That guy's a crackhead."

"Well at least he doesn't kick puppy dogs," she says and takes a haul.

"Fuck you. That thing is a Doberman, and it was trying to bite me."

"It's a *chocolate lab*. Her name is Cocoa."

After Kim finishes, she passes me the pipe. I take a couple drags, but I don't feel like I'm getting very much. "I think maybe it's out."

Kim takes it back and inspects it. "Looks okay," she says. She puts it back in my hands, then gently directs my fingers with her own. There's something a little intimate about the way she doesn't break eye contact. "Just take your thumb off this hole when you inhale."

I do as she says. I take a good suck and suddenly a flaming fist of smoke punches me in the back of my throat. I start hacking. In seconds I'm a red-faced, watery-eyed mess.

"Easy, champ," she says, patting and rubbing my back.

I hear Sudbury Steve cough out the word *loser* and I decide that I don't like him very much.

"I'm going to take him upstairs and get him another beer," she says, referring to me. "I think he could use one."

As we walk back up the stairs to the light and noise of the kitchen above, I think I can hear Matty and Steve laughing, but by the time we get to the top step, I don't remember what they're laughing about.

We stand in line at the keg for a little while, and Kim seems to know everyone. I watch her talk and smile at people I've never met. She looks less intimidating when she smiles. And her laugh is really musical. *What song is that*? She introduces me to somebody—Jamie? I think his name is? I wave at him, but he seems really far away. Everyone seems really far away. All I can do is concentrate on her. And then I can't even do that. *What song is that*? I wander into the living room and watch the stereo make music. It's the greatest song that anyone has ever written. Ever.

There's a beer in front of my face.

"How we doing, Pete?"

"This is the greatest song that anyone has ever written."

When I say it out loud, it doesn't seem to have the same kind of gravity as it does in my head. I feel a little dizzy and take a few steps toward the music.

"You look a little pale," Kim says. "Want to sit somewhere quiet for a bit?"

I don't remember agreeing, but she gives me her hand and I take it. It feels warm and small, but she has an incredible grip. Maybe her hand is metal underneath the skin, like Luke Skywalker. Or, no. *The Terminator.* A small, blonde Terminator is leading me up the stairs. She opens the door to somebody's bedroom, then sits down on the bed inside. I lower my ass down slowly beside her and hold my beer with two hands in front of me so I don't spill.

"Whose room is this?" I ask.

"Steve's," Kim replies, pointing at a map of Sudbury on the wall.

"Oh yeah," I remember. I take a sip of my beer. "Are you ... *dating* that guy?"

"Something like that."

"Weird. I don't think I like him very much."

She finishes the rest of her beer, then takes mine and puts it on the nightstand.

"I think the feeling's about to be mutual," she says. She leans in and kisses me.

The first thing I notice is how she smells—like dewberry soap, that purple stuff girls get from the Body Shop. It's nice. She pushes me backward onto the bed and crawls up toward my face. I can feel her breasts against my ribcage. For a while, we're just mouths. Just lips and tongues. And then she kisses my neck, just under my jawbone, and *that's* all we are. When she works her way up to my ear, I can feel the humid rhythm of her breathing, but I can hear it, too, and that sound blocks out the rest of the world.

I'm not entirely sure why she's doing this, or whether it's a very good idea, but I don't want her to stop. And then, about thirty seconds later, she does. Very abruptly. She seems to be listening for something, and I realize there might have been a noise outside the door. It's hard to say because until very recently, her tongue had been probing the inside of my ear. What I do hear is the doorknob turning, and the sudden increase in volume as the sound of the party infiltrates the room. Then I hear something else.

I hear Kim saying, "Hi, Steve."

There are moments where your destruction is so inevitable that time seems to slow down so you can fully comprehend how fucked you are. This might be one of those moments. Or maybe I'm just really stoned. Either way, it feels like an eternity or two pass before I realize that Kim is not acknowledging her boyfriend, but her brother, Townie Steve. Her brother who is accompanied by Lovely Rita.

"Thought I might find you in here," Townie says to Kim. "Who's your new friend?"

"Pete?" Rita says, laughing. "How long have you been here?"

"I don't even *know* ..." I tell her honestly. Then I try to make my eyes focus on Steve. "*You're* Steve?"

He nods.

"Hi, Steve. I owe you twenty dollars."

There's more laughter. I'm pretty sure it's mine.

SIDE B
Almost Crimes

There's an interesting difference between the laughter of teenage boys and the laughter of teenage girls. When boys laugh, especially that sort of Beavis-and-Butthead-style sniggering, it always seems unintentional. It squirts out of them like an unguarded fart. When girls laugh, no matter if it's a giggle or a cackle, it always seems a little calculated. Like they've come to a decision about something. Their laughter is a verdict. When I'm covering a class and some of the guys start laughing, I worry about what they did. When the girls laugh, I worry about what they're going to do.

At quarter after three, I'm standing at the door of a grade nine French class, trying to keep the students from sneaking out before the bell rings. It's like facing the slow advance of a zombie horde. Everyone wants to be as close to the door as possible so they don't waste a second of their Thursday night. When the bell finally sounds, they speed up so they're more like those zombies in *28 Days Later*. I'm nearly trampled.

"Who are these little hooligans?"

I hear Ruth's voice behind me. I tap the poster of a smiling Eiffel Tower cartoon that reads *Bienvenue à la classe de français!*

"Ah, très bon. Parlez-vous français?"

"You were in my grade eleven French class. I barely passed."

"*Trop mauvais.* Maybe you should've spent more time studying the textbook and less time studying the teacher."

"Touché."

"Nicely done. Mademoiselle Gauthier would be so proud. Is this her class?"

"No. Carruthers's."

"Hm. Oh hey, don't forget—you've got that department meeting after school today."

"I know. *And* I agreed to supervise the dance tonight."

"Seriously? You're a glutton for punishment, my friend." Ruth has this way of being sympathetic in a way that doesn't really make you feel any better. "You know it's the Halloween Dance tonight, right? It's going to be Slutty Angel, Slutty Maid—half-naked teenyboppers all night long."

"Ugh." I hadn't thought about that.

"Skip it," Ruth insists. "Say you're sick."

"Can't," I say, and before she objects, I remind her that some of us don't have a permanent position quite yet.

"Well, skip the meeting, at least."

"Can't do that either. Kovalski's making a guest appearance. Checking in on us."

"God," she says, "*that* guy."

Stan Kovalski was a vice-principal at Churchill when Ruth worked there last year. They were transferred around the same time. Ironically, it was Kovalski's unflagging commitment to incompetence that made Ruth want to transfer in the first place.

"He'll be gone soon enough." It's my turn to be sympathetic.

Kovalski is what you call a Career VP, and his career is almost over. Photocopy room gossip says he's going to retire at the end of the school year. It's kind of sad. He climbed his way to the top of the minors, but never got called up to the big leagues.

"Personally, I don't need any more responsibility," I've heard him say in the staff cafeteria. "I'm right where they need me."

Of course, this is crap for two reasons: one, his job sucks; and two, he sucks at his job. Being vice-principal means a lot more headache for only a little more pay. It's a lousy stepping stone on the path toward bigger and better things, and you can forgive most VPs for doing a shit job because they don't do it for very long. Kovalski had been a vice-principal for *eleven* years, in *five* different schools. I'd feel sorry for the guy if he weren't so goddamn useless. So far, he had spent his brief tenure at Mackenzie King attending workshops, massaging parents, and offering fun-sized Butterfingers to aspiring young drug dealers.

"Any word who's going to replace him?" I ask.

"Doesn't matter. *Anyone* would be better."

"Careful," I say. "The devil you know ..."

On my way to the department meeting I do the math in my head and decide I don't quite have the time for a much-needed smoke break. For the same reason I can't skip the dance supervision, I can't risk being late, even though I know full well Gail won't start until Ellis arrives. Ellis has been late to every meeting and no one bats an eye, but of course, he's also sixty-something and pretty close to retirement, so it's not like he's going to get fired. Knowing him, I'm kind of surprised he shows up at all.

I remember the first meeting in September, when I could already see a cynical glaze hardening over his eyeballs. I was the new kid, so I sat up straight, paid attention, and asked questions. This strategy quickly hurled me into a soul-crushing vortex of impenetrable buzzwords and statistics. When I came out on the other side, I had somehow volunteered to attend a day-long seminar entitled *Engaging Intelligences*, during which about thirty teachers were locked in a conference room with a turtlenecked presenter who possessed the enthusiasm of a kindergarten teacher and the comb-over of a cult leader. Through the cloudy lenses of his Transitions, he eyed us coolly, then proceeded to tell us that everything we had ever learned about teaching was wrong.

"Surprised?" he asked us. A few Dedicated Teachers sat near the front of the room and took careful notes. Others leaned back and ate the free crullers. "I was a little surprised too, when I realized that kids don't learn with their *heads*." He paused and tapped his head for dramatic effect. "They learn with their *hearts*." He then put his hairy-knuckled hand on his chest, as though he was about to pledge allegiance to some invisible flag. Dedicated Teachers smiled approvingly.

He continued to romance us with the idea that the current methodology was outdated and didn't respect students' emotional intelligence. He spent a couple hours engaging in conceptual foreplay—Maslow's Hierarchy of Needs, Valid Assessment, Backward Design. At last, he began thrusting into his central premise. Throughout the presentation, his voice rose in pitch as he described in agonizing hypotheticals the challenges that young students face. His pace became more and more frenetic, until finally, he showered us with his solution: "learning strategies designed to engage today's high school student in community-based learning," described at length in a series of DVDs that were available for purchase through his website. In the end, I couldn't help but feel a little used.

Since then, I've adopted a new strategy. As Gail speaks, I focus my energy on the box of donut holes as it's passed around, and psychically prevent people from taking the coconut ones before they come to me. Sometimes it works. If Gail polls the room for a volunteer, I frown and tap my pen thoughtfully on my agenda, as if to say *If only it was another day ...*

While we sit and wait for Ellis, I notice that Candice Chang, our incredibly pregnant Ancient Civilizations teacher, is conspicuously absent, which seems to suggest that she's had her baby and that the stranger sitting at our table is her replacement.

The unexplained female looks about my age, which is in itself pretty rare, but more than that, she's beautiful. I don't mean supermodel gorgeous, but I also don't mean office pretty. She's beautiful in exactly the way I find women beautiful, as if someone had rifled around in my subconscious and yanked her out. She's got these jungle cat green eyes and faint freckles. Her dark hair is tied back in a bun, and she's wearing a slightly beat-up leather jacket that makes her look a little like a photojournalist recently back from some remote and possibly dangerous assignment. How I didn't notice her the moment I entered the room baffles me. All of the sudden, she was just there, quiet and exotic.

Eventually, Ellis shuffles in, reeking of cigarettes. He apologizes for what he calls his "tardiness," and Gail starts the meeting.

"Well, I should start by introducing Molly. This is Molly Pearson."

"Hi, Molly," we all sing in unison.

She grins self-consciously and waves, like she's the guest of honour in a kindergarten class. Gail continues. "Molly's coming to us from ... Victoria?" She looks for help.

"Vancouver," Molly says. Everyone nods, as though her geographic origins have been scrutinized and met with approval. "I have some family here in town, so I thought I'd give it a shot. It's ... nice."

I can already tell she's disappointed. Thunder Bay has that effect on people. "Molly is taking over for Candice, who, if you haven't already heard, had a baby girl last night!"

Everyone around the table erupts into the expected chorus of pleasant surprise and asks for details Gail doesn't have. Personally, I'm more interested in the other new arrival, and it's pretty clear I'm not the only one.

"This is your first time teaching, then?"

Danny Pound gets an angle on Molly while I'm still just absorbing her existence. He's in his mid-forties and recently went through his second divorce, so I guess he doesn't want to waste any time.

"Actually," Molly replies, "I volunteered for a year in Kenya before I—"

"Ah, don't worry," he interrupts, not letting the facts interfere with his opening gambit. "I'm sure you won't do any worse than Curtis here." He laughs and slaps me on the back, as if to suggest we share some sort of playful camaraderie. We don't. "Just kidding, buddy," he says to me without taking his eyes off Molly.

"I'm Pete," I explain, feeling a little like the straight man in Pound's lame comedy act. "I'm also supply teaching."

She looks like she's about to say something to me, but Gail calls everyone to order and starts working her way through the agenda.

"Okay, so Stan's going to join us in a few minutes—he's just meeting with a parent right now. In the meantime, we need to talk about textbooks. Does everybody have enough right now? I noticed we're a little short on *Western Civilizations* ..."

One of the great things about meeting a beautiful woman for the first time is you get to witness all these different ways she's beautiful. From across the table, I get a front-row seat for how Molly's beautiful when she sips her coffee, how she's beautiful when she laughs politely at a bad joke, even how she's beautiful when she frowns. And as the meeting continues, there seems to be more and more to frown about.

After textbook talk, item number two on the agenda is provincial assessment. As if on cue, Kovalski materializes, and Gail starts distributing large booklets full of tiny numbers. He recognizes his new hire, shakes her hand, and sits down. Then, like seasoned middle management, he doesn't ask any questions and takes charge.

"Okay, good," he says, looking around the table, "you've all got the stats."

He proceeds to rattle off a semi-prepared presentation about the importance of statistics and what student success and failure could mean with regard to accountability and funding. Somewhere between *scope and sequence* and *valid assessment*, my mind has completely refocused on how I'm going to get Molly to go for a beer with me. That's probably why I don't actually hear the announcement when he makes it. I just feel it, the way you can feel weather change before the storm actually hits. The news reverberates off the other teachers in my department, and as I tune back in, I'm able to pick out the different reactions. Ellis rolls his eyes. Pound is indignant. Gail is vibrating with dogmatic enthusiasm.

"Are you saying," Pound says, "that we're going *back* to standardized exams?"

Stan holds up his palms in a gesture of peace. "Based on the success of the provincial literacy and numeracy tests, the Board is greenlighting a pilot program to make all culminating assessment more consistent."

"And by 'consistent' you mean 'the same,'" Ellis says.

"Teachers will still create summative assessments, but yes, starting next semester, all students enrolled in Ontario high schools will write a sealed exam from the board based on provincial curriculum."

People start talking at once.

"Wait, *what's* being standardized?"

"Can we even *see* the exams beforehand?"

"—a wonderful opportunity."

"I just redesigned my whole unit on—"

"—like I'm back in the sixties."

"Stan," Pound booms, "we have to go to all these workshops about *multiple* intelligences, *differentiated* instruction, and now the province is implementing *standardized* exams?"

Kovalski works his mouth into an grin. The wingspan of his moustache prepares for flight. "Come on, guys," he says weakly, "don't shoot the messenger."

I can see why he's planning to retire.

After the meeting I start heading back toward History Storage. Molly has disappeared in the opposite direction and I find myself walking beside Ellis for a little while.

"So what do you think, Ellis?" I ask.

"About what, Peter?"

"You know. This whole standardized exam thing."

"Bah." He dismisses the idea with a wave of his hand. "The pendulum swings back and forth. You watch. This won't last too long."

Ellis Kohler is the oldest member of our department and kind of the reason I have a job here. He was my associate when I was a student teacher, and his mentoring style mainly consisted of leaving me to sink or swim while he drank coffee in the staff cafeteria. I guess he thought I did something right, though. He gave me a pretty stellar reference, and here I am.

Ellis refuses to retire, but in a lot of ways, he checked out years ago. He doesn't use email, data projectors, or even computers for that matter, and no one ever calls him on it. While the rest of us are pulling out all the stops to compete with the internet, Ellis just teaches out of the textbook. Or sometimes, off the top of his head.

I can't wait until I can get away with being a crazy old man.

On my way back to the school later that night, I find myself wishing I had brought a mickey of vodka to sneak in. I'm twenty-seven years old and nervous about going to a high school dance. When I walk into the building, a bearded, middle-aged Superman is sitting on a chair near coat check with his legs propped up on a folding table and an issue of *Cosmopolitan* resting on his flabby blue stomach. When he sees me, he puts the magazine down and stands up.

"Lookin' good, Man of Steel," I say.

Jim Lodge pats his belly and smiles. "I know I shouldn't invite comparisons, but the wife *loves* it. Seriously. When I go home tonight, it's going to be all '*Up, up, and away!*'"

Dolores Lodge, Jim's wife, was my grade five teacher. This is information I don't need to know.

"Where's your costume?"

"Guess I'm just going as a high school teacher."

The tucked-in shirt, the sweater vest, and the khakis do feel a bit like a costume. There's no way I'd dress like this outside of work. I wonder if the real Superman has trouble putting on those schleppy glasses and that suit all the time. He must worry he's starting to turn into Clark Kent.

Jim gives me the lay of the land and a few words of advice. My shift is for the second half of the night, and I'm essentially on supervision detail. There are a couple other teachers, and a cop, so I shouldn't have to do too much heavy lifting. In fact, for the next little while, he expects it will be relatively tame. That last hour, though, things can apparently get a little nuts.

"Let Officer Dan handle the really drunk kids—that's what we pay him for. You're probably going to have to break up a few dance-floor makeout sessions," he warns me. "Kissing's okay, a little ass-groping's okay too, but we generally draw the line at hands in pants. Got it?"

I nod, suddenly terrified.

"You'll be fine. Get in there and have some fun!"

I walk away from Jim's red-and-blue bulges feeling a little nauseated. On my way to the gym, I hope and pray I can find another teacher to buddy up with; otherwise, it's going to be a long, awkward two hours of looking like a creepy old wallflower.

"Hey, stranger!" Vicky Greene appears beside me dressed in a skin-tight cat costume and, unlike Jim, she wears her spandex pretty well. Like a figure skater or a bike messenger, she's just on the socially acceptable side of obscene. I can see every curve of her Pilates-fit thirty-something-year-old body. She loops her arm around mine so that as we walk, I can feel her hip rubbing against my thigh. *Up, up and away.*

"Where's your costume?" she scolds me.

"I didn't think we were supposed to wear costumes."

Seriously, am I the only authority figure who's not dressed like an idiot? Even Officer Dan is wearing a cape and devil horns over his uniform.

"Where's your holiday spirit? This is the one night of the year you get to be someone else for a little while. Do something you might not usually do."

As we get closer to the dark mouth of the gymnasium, I feel the heart-shuddering bass and smell that nostalgic, chemical smell of dry ice. In the hall outside, it seems like every teenager is also being someone else for a while. I see Gene Simmons in full Demon regalia bending over to get a drink from the water fountain. Freddy Krueger and Michael Myers sit cross-legged on the floor and argue about the Conn Smythe Trophy. A girl in a dog costume suddenly materializes and tells Vicky how much she loves her cat suit. As they talk, various monsters and superheroes walk past me on their way to the bathroom.

Given the chance to be someone else for a while, I'm not sure who it would be. Some days, I wish I could be one of these kids again. If I could start over, knowing what I know now, I'd be so much better at being a teenager. Most days, though, I'm just happy that whole mess is behind me. I think that, ultimately, I'd like to be me, but just not the me I am right now. Maybe the me I'll be in a few years. These days I'm just a little too in-between things. It's been a long time since I felt like I had my shit together—almost two years since Catherine, and Filthy Witness, and everything that happened in Toronto.

And so, arm in arm, I walk with a married woman into a teenage Sodom and Gomorrah. Almost immediately, I'm accosted by Slutty Red Riding Hood.

"He-e-ey! Mr. Curtis! You were my supply teacher last week!"

"Hi," I say.

It takes me a moment to place her, mainly because she's far more naked than she was in Biology class. Her pale cleavage spills dangerously out of a laced bodice, and her legs, wrapped in thigh-high stockings, sprout from a tiny ruffled skirt. Her red sheer cloak is more a nod to the *idea* of clothing than it is an actual article.

She leans in closer and pulls my tie out of my sweater vest to squint at it. "What are you supposed to be?" she asks. Her breath is sweet and very alcoholic. I look over to Vicky, who raises a pretend bottle to her lips in a little drinking motion.

"Um, a high school teacher?"

"Oh my god!" Red Riding Hood giggles. "That's adorargh—"

I'd like to flatter myself and believe that the word she's attempting to say is *adorable*. Unfortunately, what comes instead is the partially digested contents of her dinner and what looks to be some kind of berry-flavoured wine cooler. All of which lands on the front of my teacher costume.

By the time Vicky returns with Officer Dan, a crowd is starting to form. Officer Dan attends to Red, whose fairy tale has ended in a weepy mess on the gym floor, and Vicky escorts me to the one and only male staff washroom on the other side of the school.

"Do you need any help?" she shouts through the door.

"No!"

I really don't. I'm naked to the waist and rinsing my shirt in the sink. My sweater vest is ruined in a very awful and very smelly way. I shove it into the trash like a bad memory and try not to get any vomit on my hands. I try my best to wring the shirt out, but it's still soaking and cold when I ease it back over my shoulders. Where I've wiped down the front of my pants with wet paper towels, it looks like I've pissed myself.

Vicky is waiting when I walk out. She gushes with amused sympathy.

"Oh, you poor thing. You should just go. I'll tell Jim."

I agree, but then Vicky asks a crucial question.

"Do you know how you're getting home?"

I had planned on getting home the same way I came: on foot and in dry clothes. This no longer seems like an option.

"I'll just call a cab," I tell her, knowing full well she won't let me.

"You can't take a cab. Let me drive you. Officer Dan's here until the end of the night. They can make do without us."

I squint down the hallway and see Thunder Bay's finest prodding Superman in the stomach with a plastic pitchfork. I wonder whether Red Riding Hood will make it home safe.

"Really, it's no big deal."

"It *is* a big deal." She laughs a little. "Look at you! You're a mess."

Several depressing likelihoods race through my mind. First, I think the odds are pretty good that Vicky has either Shawn Mullins or Third Eye Blind in the CD player of her 2002 PT Cruiser, and I'm going have to hear at least seven minutes of it before we get to my apartment. That's, like, two songs. Second, I think the odds are equally good that she's going to invite herself into my apartment for a drink, and I'll oblige, because she came to my rescue and now I kind of owe her one. Finally, if I were a betting man, I'd say that by the time she gets me out of my wet clothes—which she inevitably will—and by the time she takes off her costume—which she inevitably will—I'm going to be in *way* over my head. So, yeah. I am kind of a mess.

"Sure," I finally tell her. "You let Jim know what's going on, and I'll go grab my coat from the staff room. Meet you back here in five minutes?"

"Deal."

Vicky bounces off toward the gym. On her way, she looks back and smiles at me, and for a moment, I do feel like I'm someone else—someone who doesn't care about full contract, superintendents, or husbands. Someone who has the moral flexibility to let Vicky Greene take him home. Then the moment passes, and I'm back to me. Boring Old Me.

When I get my heavy coat on over my wet clothes, the damp soaks into my skin until it reaches my bones. Boring Old Me pushes his feet through one of the side doors and out into the premature Thunder Bay winter. Twenty minutes later, when I'm home, shivering and thawing out, I can't stop thinking about what it would've been like to peel that cat suit right off her. If she showed up at my door right now, I'd let her in, no questions asked. Sometimes doing the right thing is all about timing.

SIDE A
Rescue Us from Boredom

For someone who's part of a rhythm section, Deacon's got a pretty shitty sense of time. He was supposed to meet me in front of his locker and give me a ride home, but I've been sitting here for twenty minutes and there's still no sign of him. I'm about to give up and walk, when Mr. Murdock stops in front of me.

"Mister Starkey," he says, looking down. "How are we this afternoon?"

"Uh, good. Really good."

Mr. Murdock is one of those nickname guys. Everyone's Champ, Sport, or Cap'n. Ever since grade eleven, when he found out I play drums, I've been either Ringo Starr or Richard Starkey or some combination of the two.

"So. Young minstrel. Any *rilly big shews* on the horizon?"

I'm thrilled to have an answer. "Yeah, actually, we're playing Whiskey Jack's tonight."

"Ah. Whiskey Jack's. The Toppermost of the Poppermost." I have no idea what he's talking about, but I smile and nod my head like I do. "Well, break a leg. I suppose one of these days I'll have to come out and see you play."

"For sure!" I gush like a twelve-year-old girl at a Beatles concert. "We'd be honoured."

Jesus. Did I really just tell him we'd be *honoured*? Murdock smiles and continues down the hall, but I'm going to feel like an idiot the whole way home.

After supper, Deacon appears at my door, all bristly haired and chipper and wearing a *Countdown to Ecstasy* t-shirt, which I hope he changes before we go on stage.

"Sorry about earlier," he says as we walk down to the basement. "Had an oral exam in French. Bunch of us had to stay after school and finish it."

"An oral exam? With Mademoiselle Gauthier?" There's a joke there, but I don't make it.

"It's not Mademoiselle Gauthier anymore. It's Madame Greene."

"What the fuck? She got married?"

"Yeah. To some vice-principal at Churchill. I think he used to play for the Flyers or something."

"Seriously? A hockey guy?"

"Yeah. Like *you* had a chance."

We heave Deacon's enormous Trace Elliot cabinet up the stairs and then out into the Sabre.

"Oh, hey," Deacon says as we catch our breath, "Rita said not to pack your drums tonight. Just bring breakables."

"Shit."

While it's nice not to lug my own gear, I always hate it when I have to use someone else's drum kit. Even after I adjust the height and the angle of everything, it still feels weird. My balance is always off and I never play quite as well. We go back to the basement, and I grab what I need. Snare, pedal, cymbals, sticks—all the things that can break. All the things drummers don't share.

It's cold out, but the Sabre warms up quickly. The front dash smells like hot dust and there's a faint memory of cigarettes in the upholstery. Deacon pushes a tape into the player, and music blares at us. He turns it down, but just a bit.

"You're going to kill your ears listening to ... whatever this is."

"*Aja*? Dude. This is classic Dan."

"It's classic something."

As Deacon pulls out of my driveway, we listen to a seemingly endless guitar solo that sounds suspiciously like jazz. Then Deacon asks me about History class.

"How'd the bonspiel go today?"

"Hard to say. I think Hildebrandt was winning."

Before I had him as teacher, I heard all these rumours that Hildebrandt had once suffered some kind of nervous breakdown and either got suspended or sent to the loony bin for a semester—that part's always a little vague. In September, he seemed fine. I mean, his class was pretty boring, but he was just like any other middle-aged teacher—balding, jowly, slowly fading into the chalkboard. Then, a couple weeks ago, he started to space out when the class got noisy. At first I thought it was some kind of classroom management strategy, like I-can-wait-just-as-long-as-you-can, but on Tuesday he stared at the same spot on the back wall for almost *five* straight minutes. Then it got even weirder. He started curling. He crouched down and threw imaginary curling rocks down the centre aisle of the classroom, again and again.

Today, I tell Deacon, he changed positions from skip to sweeper. With impressive determination, he cleared the path for phantom rocks for nearly twenty minutes. Some students trickled out, and others stayed to watch the show.

"So when are the nice men in white coats going to take him away?"

"Not for a while, I hope. The longer he stays crazy, the less *Western Civilizations* I'll have to read."

We're able to get a half-decent parking spot outside of Jack's. When I hop out of the car and get my feet on the sidewalk, I feel a giddy energy. Later on, it will turn into panicky butterflies, and I'll seriously consider the logistics of climbing out the bathroom window, but when we're just loading in I feel like I'm part of something that's about to happen. Something exciting.

We try the front door, but it's still locked. I'm about to suggest to Deacon that we try the back when I notice he's gesturing to a couple of figures walking down the sidewalk. One is Soda. The other guy, I'm not sure about. He's bundled up in a blue lumber jacket and an orange hunting cap. I recognize him, but I can't place him.

"Hey. You guys know Andy, right?" Soda says once he's in proximity. "He's going to lend me his amp tonight so we won't have to worry about the Peavey crapping out."

Andy Thaler. Thaler the Wailer.

"Hey, Andy," I say, holding out my hand. "I'm Pete."

He grins broadly, cigarette clamped in the corner of his mouth, then gives me a big, swinging handshake. His fingers are rough with guitar-player calluses.

"Oh, I know *you*, man," he says. "My trumpet player wants to kick your ass." His cigarette bounces up and down as he talks.

For a second, I'm not sure what to say. Deacon looks at me, a little worried.

"Don't sweat it," Thaler says. He laughs, and then slaps my shoulder. "That guy's all talk. Steve's a good musician, but he can be a bit of a dick sometimes."

"You coming to the show tonight?" Deacon asks.

"For sure, dude. Got a couple buddies coming too. You know Wheels and Townie? Actually, Townie said he's going to review the show for his zine."

"Cool."

To be honest, I don't really care if Townie reviews us in *Bigmouth Strikes Again!*, but I *am* interested in whether or not his sister is coming to the show. I'm kind of hoping Thaler volunteers that information, but Soda changes the subject before he can.

"Uh, so ..." I can tell by the look on Soda's Cheshire Cat face that he knows something Deacon and I don't. "Guess who's playing drums for the Super Friendz tonight?"

"Phil Collins!" Deacon blurts out.

"No," Soda says, screwing up his eyes. "Not fucking Phil Collins. Why would Phil Collins play drums for the Super Friendz?"

"Because Phil Collins is a fantastic, completely underrated drummer. Have you ever listened to *Selling England By The Pound*? It's amazing."

"*It's not Phil Collins.* Guess again."

"Karen Carpenter?"

"Jesus," I say, exasperated with both of them. "Just tell us already."

Soda takes a drag on his cigarette and points at me. He smiles as if he knows I'm going to like the answer. Then he exhales. "Chris Murphy."

"Chris Murphy from Sloan, Chris Murphy?"

"Yep. We just helped him and those other guys load in before they all took off to the Calabria for dinner."

"Weird. I didn't even know he played drums," I say.

Whiskey Jack's manager, Frank, opens the front door and we start bringing our gear inside. We don't talk about it, but I'm pretty sure Deacon and Soda are thinking the same thing I am. Besides playing bass, and apparently now drums, Chris Murphy also runs a record label. A record label that signs bands that are just getting started. Bands like Giant Killer. So all of a sudden, tonight just became kind of important.

An hour before we're about to go on, there's still only a handful of people milling around the bar. I get that sinking feeling that everyone's bailed. I try to think of all the other things going on tonight, all the competing social events. I know that Shelley Vallenti is having a party, but most of the people who would go to that wouldn't come to our show anyhow. There's some Tom Cruise vampire movie opening at the Cumberland, but I can't imagine people would stand us up for that. Would they?

The Super Friendz and their star drummer are still out eating dinner, so after our sound check—on *Chris Murphy's* blue oyster pearl Ludwigs—I help Rita set up our merch table, which really just consists of a handful of t-shirts, stickers, and little buttons that Rita made with her button maker.

"Where the fuck is everybody?" I finally ask.

She stops and sizes up my distress.

"It's early," she says. "People will come. We advertised the shit out of this show." She looks around at the near-empty bar, then says, "Look. You've got two jobs tonight: play the drums and talk to Chris Murphy. Make sure he watches your set. In the meantime, go get Soda and Deacon and get them out of here for about half an hour. Now scoot!"

I do as I'm told. I grab the rest of the band, and we take off down the street. In the last hour the weather has gone from cold to vindictive, and I can feel the air fit to my face like a mask of ice. As we head toward Red River Road, groups of people wander away from us in tiny apathetic herds. I resent everybody who isn't walking toward our show.

Soda suddenly decides he's hungry and ducks into Mr. Sub. Deacon and I follow. We sit in a hard plastic booth and watch Soda inhale a meatball sandwich. I can't imagine eating right now. Already my stomach is reconsidering the whole dinner arrangement I made with it earlier.

"Think we should play 'Necessary Evil' tonight?" I ask. "It's a little Sloanier than our other songs. Might be good, considering who's in the audience."

Soda pulls a plastic mickey out of his coat, spins off the cap, and pours some Silent Sam into his Coke.

"Guy doesn't want to hear another version of his band," Soda says. "Don't mess with the set list. It's fine." He sucks down the rest of his drink.

Eventually, when we've killed off enough time, we start to walk back to Jack's and run right into Matty Wheeler walking the opposite way.

"Hey, Wheels," Soda says.

"Oh, hey, dudes," he says. For a future member of our audience, he seems oddly surprised to see us. "What's happening?"

"We're just heading back to the bar," I explain. "We're on pretty soon."

"Oh *shi-i-t*," he says. "Is that tonight?"

Soda nods.

"Ah, man, I totally thought it was tomorrow. I'm sorry, I can't make it tonight." Soda jumps on the awkward silence before I even realize it's happening.

"That's cool. We'll catch you next time."

"Absolutely," Matty says walking backward and pointing both index fingers in our direction. "One hundred percent. Break a leg!"

We watch him wander down the street like a bad omen.

"Well," Deacon says, "there goes one third of our confirmed audience."

We go around to the back of the bar, and Soda produces the mickey again. We each take a couple turns knocking back a shot, grimacing, and stomping our feet into a layer of packed snow. If we're lucky, we'll be able to sneak a beer later on.

"All right, boys," Soda says, tossing the plastic bottle over a nearby fence, "I'll see you on stage." He pushes through the back door, and as it opens, I listen for crowd sound. I don't hear anything.

Deacon looks at me and shrugs. "I'm going to see if Ruth's in there. I forgot to put her name on the guest list." And then he's gone too.

I wait for a minute out there and brace myself for the likelihood that the bar will be as empty as we left it. I tell myself all the reasons why it won't matter. I tell myself we could just as easily put on a great show for ten people as we could for a hundred, and I almost manage to convince myself.

But when I go inside, the bar has transformed. It's been less than an hour, but already the house lights are down and the coloured stage lights are up. A fog of cigarette smoke hovers near the ceiling. The soundguy is blaring Metallica's *Kill 'Em All* over the PA, but I can barely hear it. It takes me a moment to realize why. The place is packed and buzzing. The miracle of people has happened.

A few moments later, I spot her. Kim is sitting at a table with Townie, Thaler, and a couple other people who aren't, thankfully, Sudbury Steve. With her hair tied back and the curve of her neck visible, she's even prettier than I remember. There's an empty chair beside her, and I've got just enough vodka flowing through my veins to say hello. There's nothing stopping me.

"Hey, Pete! You watch *X-Files* last week?"

Nothing except Twatkins.

"Ever notice how you never see where Mulder sleeps? I think it's because he sleeps in Scully's *bedroom*. Except, I don't think they do much sleeping, if you know what I mean."

I sentenced myself to this conversational prison earlier this week when I told Toby Watkins—a sausage-lipped kid in my Science in Society class—that he should "come check us out on Friday." Now, there's no escape in sight.

"I also heard David Duchovony's a sex addict, and it's in his contract that he can't have an on-screen romance with Gillian Anderson because it might trigger his animalistic urges, and he might be forced to, you know, ravish her."

That's the word he actually uses. *Ravish.*

After a science fiction eternity, Lovely Rita finally rescues me.

"Sorry to interrupt," she says to Toby. "I have to borrow Pete here for a minute."

"Thank you," I say when she pulls me away. "I really need to say hi to somebody." I look over in the direction of Kim, and for the first time that evening we make eye contact. She looks away first.

"Nuh-uh," Rita says when she realizes who I'm looking at. "No pretty, unavailable girls for you right now. You need to talk to Chris Murphy. Get him to watch your show. He's over there with Frank. Wouldn't hurt to talk to Frank a little, while you're at it."

She pushes me in their general direction, and a moment later I'm hovering next to two people having a conversation that doesn't involve me at all. I smile and nod in hopes that maybe they'll think I've been there all along. Eventually, Frank fixes his humourless gaze on me. He's heavyset and dressed all in black with a black beard to match. He looks like he'd be better suited behind the wheel of a transport truck. Or a pirate ship.

"You're with the opener tonight, right?" he asks me. "The—what is it—the Giants?"

"Giant Killer. Yeah," I tell him. "Yeah, I am."

"Okay. You guys should be ready to go on in ten minutes."

It's not like I wasn't expecting the moment to arrive, but when he lays it out like that, it suddenly feels real. And reality feels like someone just filled my underwear with snow.

Frank turns back to Chris, who has been watching us patiently.

"Well, I should let you talk to your fan club here," he says, gesturing in my direction. "I hope things work out for April. It'd be nice to have you guys back. All ages or not."

Frank slips away into the crowd, and suddenly I'm face to face with a guy whose band is on every mixed tape I've made since I was fifteen.

"Hey," he says, chewing gum and looking at me over his glasses. "I'm Chris."

He's skinnier than I would've expected. He's got a bit of bed-head, and he's wearing a too-tight yellow t-shirt you could spit peas through. It reads *I was the Centaur of Attention.* At Mackenzie King, he'd be an easy target for the Pussies, but here, he's a rock star.

I introduce myself then quickly realize I have no idea what I should say to him. *Will you sign our band and take us on tour?* might seem a bit forward.

"So ... I'm using your drums tonight," I finally tell him. "Anything I should know about them?" It's a lame excuse for conversation.

"Well, you should probably know how to play them."

I laugh stupidly and tell him I do.

"Then you'll be fine. Nice turnout, by the way."

I can see him look past me for a polite way out of this conversation, and I figure I'd better cut to the chase before I become his Twatkins.

"Hey, do you think you're going to stick around and watch the show?"

"Wouldn't miss it," he says. *Wouldn't miss it.* His exact words. "I'm just going to grab a sweater out of the van, but I'll be right back. Give 'em hell."

He slips through a crowd of people who all say *Hi, Chris* like they know him, and he smiles and waves at them politely as he backs out the door.

From across the room, I see Deacon pointing his finger at me and then jerking his thumb toward the stage. It's time to go on. I signal back, but make one more run to the washroom to take a final, nervous piss. For a minute, everything smells like disinfectant and urine, and as always I momentarily consider squeezing out of the bathroom window. I walk the gauntlet from the back of the bar toward the stage while Soda and Deacon are up there, switching on their amps and raising their guitar straps over their shoulders. Already a few people in the crowd are sounding off.

Yeah, Sodapop!

Giant Killer!

Woo-hoo!

I'm halfway to the stage when I feel a twinge shoot up my hindquarters. Unmistakably, someone's just pinched my ass. I turn around and see Kim sitting at her table, cigarette dangling from two fingers, a curl of smoke leaving one side of her smile. She raises a glass of beer in my direction, and I grin back like a little boy. Then I make my way up onto the stage.

It's kind of pointless to talk about what it's like to play drums at a rock show. I read somewhere that Levon Helm said it's like having the best seat in the house. For me, though, it always feels like I'm strapping myself into an electric chair. I sit down on the stool, look at the crowd, and promptly forget everything I've ever learned. All the angles and surfaces of the skins and cymbals look suddenly alien under the stage lights. My arms are useless. Dead weight. I feel like a fraud. I certainly don't deserve to be the Centaur of Attention. I hear Chris Murphy's joke in my head: *You should probably know how to play them.* It's not so funny now.

When we play live, Deacon does most of the talking on stage. The Banter, he calls it. He usually starts off with some dumb line like *Warning: People in the first few rows will get wet*, or *You wanted the best? You got us instead. The hottest band in Port Arthur!* He must be feeling a little nervous, because tonight he just thanks everyone for coming out and then looks back at me and nods. It's my cue to count in, and I do it even though I have no idea what comes next. For a second, there's only terror and free fall, but then, somehow, the parachute of muscle memory opens up, and I watch my hands play the drums. The sound through the monitors is terrible, but no one in the crowd seems to mind the house speakers. No one's got their fingers in their ears, in any case. Then Soda walks up to the microphone.

I guess the thing that sets us apart from your average shitty high school band is this: Soda can actually sing. He doesn't do that power-saw screaming, but he's not into that mumbly shoe-gazing stuff either. There's this weird, fugitive quality to his voice. Just when you think you've figured out who he sounds like, it slips away from you.

"*Officer, you can read my rights / Cuff my hands and take me downtown ...*"

His lyrics aren't half bad for someone who claims he's read one book his entire life. Of course, he has read a lot of record sleeves.

"*Pull the shade and shine the light / interrogate me until I break down ...*"

We tighten up and lock in by the second chorus, and if Deacon and Soda are making mistakes, I can't hear them.

"*There is a cage inside my chest / I'm under cardiac arrest ...*"

By the time we start the second song the dance floor is standing room only. I see Evie and Ruth near the front. Ruth is wearing a Giant Killer t-shirt that Lovely Rita designed and Deacon probably gave her. A few guys with stringy hair and moth-eaten cardigans nod their heads in time. For the most part, I try to keep my eyes on the drums.

Some people talk about stage fright as something that they get before a show, something that goes away the moment they walk on stage. I wish that's how it worked with me. I heard the drummer from Fat Like Dad keeps an empty beer pitcher beside his kit so he can puke in it. Apparently he barfs out all of his nerves after the first song, and then he's rock solid for the rest. They've kind of made it part of the show.

For me, though, the nerves never go away. Part of it's like that nightmare when you show up to school and realize you're not wearing any clothes. You feel all naked and vulnerable. But the other part is that, when you're playing live, it kind of forces you to live in the moment. People spend most of their time thinking about the past or worrying about the future, and they do it because it's safe. Good or bad, it can't get at you for the time being. When you play live, you're completely stuck in the present. All you can do is hope your timing is dead on. Now. Now. Right now.

By the end of our set, Soda is shirtless and in the middle of the crowd, lying on the beer-splashed floor of the bar and playing his guitar spastically on his back. Someone has drawn a lightning bolt on his chest in magic marker. Deacon is standing on top of his amp, trying to keep his balance, and trying not to put the headstock of his bass through the ceiling. Three girls I don't even know have commandeered the microphone and are singing a slightly out of tune version of our final song, a cover of Neil Young's 'Hey, Hey, My, My.' I'm hammering away at the crash and snare, just trying to keep it all together. The crowd is sweaty and pulsing like one giant organism. A few meaty-looking guys who haven't figured out that moshing died with Kurt Cobain keep slamming into each other. I try hard not to take any of this enthusiasm too personally. Kids have an innate need to fuck shit up. We just provide the soundtrack.

The show ends in crescendo of cymbal noise and feedback, and as Soda pulls the strings from his Telly, it's clear there will be no encore. And really, there doesn't need to be. It's been our best show yet, and all the right people were here to see it.

After the cheering subsides, the soundguy moves forward in his Metallica catalogue and turns up the volume on *Ride the Lightning*. We're being evicted from the stage to make room for the out-of-town talent. Still, Deacon and Soda take their time to wander out into the crowd, to get their hands shaken, their backs slapped, and to soak up a little flattery. I stay on the stage, putting my stuff away. I'm drenched in sweat, and there's blood on my hands from when I grazed my knuckle on a cymbal. Part of me wants to go out there and swim around in all that good will, but there's another part of me that needs a few minutes to come down. Plus, seeking out congratulations is really just a way of tempting hubris. I like my praise when I least expect it.

"Nice show, *asshole*!"

I hear Evie's voice as I crouch behind Chris Murphy's drum kit, wiggling my kick pedal off the bass drum. When I look up, she's standing beside Ruth at the edge of the stage. Her arms are crossed, she's tapping her foot, and she's either mad, pretending to be, or a little of both.

"What's up?" I shout over the house music.

"What's up is you promised us a show. I want answers, Curtis. Don't toy with our emotions this way." She's only half joking.

"Okay. All right," I say, pushing my gear with my foot into the corner behind the drums. "Let's go talk to Rita."

They follow me over to the merch table where Lovely Rita's still on duty.

"We should've made more t-shirts," is the first thing she says when she sees me. "We would've made a killing." I can barely hear her over James Hetfield singing 'Fight Fire with Fire.'

"Rita, these guys are from Martha Dumptruck. They want to set up a show with us. Can you talk to them? I need to finish packing up."

She eyes the girls skeptically. "Sure thing. Nice show, by the way. You guys killed it."

I leave them to figure out details and head back toward the stage. As I do, I scan the room for signs of Kim. I'm riding a pretty serious high of adrenalin and optimism when I run into Matty Wheeler for the second time that night.

"Wheels! Hey, I thought you weren't going to make it tonight."

He looks at me and grins sheepishly. "Well, I felt bad about missing your big show, so I cancelled my other plans and hoofed it back."

In that instant, I re-evaluate him. Maybe Matty Wheeler isn't so flaky after all. Maybe being really, really good at devil sticks doesn't automatically make someone a total idiot.

"Thanks, man. Hey, did you like our Neil Young cover?" Neil Young seemed like some safe common ground. Hippies like Neil Young.

"Well, that's just it," he says, looking down at his mukluks. "When I got back to the bar, I saw this guy climbing out of a van, and he looked really familiar. So I talked to him for a bit, and he turned out to be that guy from Sloan—you know, they had that 'Underwhelmed' video a couple years back?"

"Sure. Chris Murphy."

"Right! Well, we get chatting, and turns out that guy knows so-o-o much about *The White Album*. I mean, *wow*. We could've talked for *hours*."

Suddenly I'm not sure if I like where this story is going.

"Anyway, I totally lost track of time, and when we headed back into Jack's, you guys had just finished. No worries, though, right? It looks like you had an *amazing* turnout."

I resist the urge to grab Matty by his filthy dreadlocks and bang his head off my knee.

"Well, I need a beer. Oh, hey—" he starts to slink toward the bar "—I gave that guy outside—Chris?—a Bunsen Honeydew demo tape. You should too. I think he has a record label or something. He'd probably be really into your music."

When I get back to the stage I see Deacon standing beside his heavy amp, waiting for a little help. The collar of his shirt is still dark with sweat, and he's got a little satisfied smile on his face, like he just got laid and nobody else knows it. I help him lift the amp off the stage and manoeuvre it through the crowd. When we get outside, everything is covered with two clean inches of snow. It squeaks a little under the weight of our boots. Soda's already outside, smoking and talking to some pretty, green-haired girl I don't recognize. Where Soda finds these girls is a mystery to me. It's not like he ever tries to pick them up. They're just suddenly there, touching his arm, laughing at his jokes, giving him phone numbers. After Green Hair goes back inside, he walks over and helps us lift the amp into the back of the Sabre. When we slam the hatch shut, chunks of ice slide musically down the back window and then disappear into the snow below.

"Are you guys sticking around?" I ask.

"For sure," Deacon says.

Soda flicks his cigarette butt into oblivion. "I hate to say it, but my new friend Jillian just offered me a ride home, and I think it would be *impolite* of me to refuse."

"Got it," I say.

I'm a little disappointed. I want to keep the night going, maybe get ourselves invited to some kind of after party. There were always rumours about where the bands stayed when they came through town. Apparently, Frank owned this flophouse in the East End, but I had also heard that Ariss Donaldson's hippie parents had some kind of rock 'n' roll bed and breakfast down Highway 11/17. But without Soda, I wasn't going to see the inside of either of those places.

Rita's always trying to get me to talk to the out-of-town-band guys, but I don't think she really gets it. Those guys in the Super Friendz are adults. They pay rent, go on tour, and sleep on the dirty floor of their van. Deacon and I reek of teenager. Our hair is too clean, our clothes smell too nice, and we're too full of our moms' cooking. Soda's the only one of us with any kind of real credibility. He's spent the last four or five years being the only adult in his house. He's the guy who cashes his dad's disability cheque to make sure the Hydro bill gets paid. On some level, people seem to get that.

"I should go grab the rest of my stuff off the stage," I say.

I walk back into the damp heat of the bar to the opening bongs of 'For Whom the Bell Tolls,' and it reminds me that I have precious little time to accidentally run into Kim. The house music is loud enough as it is, but once the band starts, any conversational attempts on my part will be reduced to the utilitarian shouting usually reserved for trench warfare.

Hurrying, I hop back up on the stage, pack up what's left of my gear, and do a quick survey of the room. Through the crowd, I think I catch a glimpse of Kim's jacket, but before I can chase her down, Rita appears like a cock-blocking angel.

"So, I think we can kill two birds with one stone," she tells me. "Townie wants to set up a show for you guys next month, and he's willing to put those girls—Martha Dumptruck—on the bill. Okay?"

"Sure. Sounds good."

I scan the bar over Rita's shoulder. There's no sign of her. James Hetfield growls.

"Hey, Pete," Rita waves her hand in front of my face. "Could you at least listen to me when I'm doing you a favour?"

I look at Rita and realize I'm acting like a dick. "Sorry."

"She's gone, by the way."

"Who's gone?"

"Kim. Townie had to take her home. She was pretty drunk, and Frank was starting to give her the stink eye."

And there it is. For whom does the bell toll? Turns out it tolls for me.

I mule my gear past Rita and through the door. Back outside, I'm cruelly flanked by couples. Deacon and Ruth debate the merit of Kim Deal's bass playing, while Soda's green-haired chauffeur—Jillian, I presume—ties her scarf around his neck. Suddenly, I'm just a fifth wheel that's rolled to a dead stop on the sidewalk.

"Somebody going to help me with this?" I feel very tired.

Deacon disengages from Ruth and unlocks one of the side doors. I chuck my stuff on the back seat. Through the wall of the bar, I can already hear the muffled notes of guitar players tuning and Chris Murphy testing the drum levels. *Boom. Boom. Thud. Crack.*

"That Kim chick was looking for you," Soda says before he goes back to playing with the zipper on Jillian's winter coat.

"Yeah," Deacon confirms. "She was *wasted*. She climbed up on the hood of the Sabre. Her brother had to pull her down. She left a message on the windshield for you."

I walk around to the front of the car and expect to see a piece of paper flapping under the wiper blade like a parking ticket, but instead, I see something written in new snow on the windshield itself. A number. 7 6 7 8 5 1 2. It takes me a second to process that it's a phone number.

"She said you've got two days to call her," Ruth explains. "She's kind of ... intense."

"She's kind of a crazy bitch is what she is," Deacon says.

"Yeah," I say, repeating the number in my head. Memorizing it. "She kind of is, isn't she?"

SIDE B
The Laws Have Changed

I put the phone down on the receiver and claw at my skull through my hair. "Crazy *bitch*."

"Who?" Ruth asks.

"This parent." I motion toward the telephone as if it still possesses the disembodied spirit of Dylan Beaucage's mother. "She's pissed off because I won't meet with her during my dinner break tonight."

"Hm. You'd think that one of the five hours you're available would be sufficient."

"Yeah. You'd think."

Ruth leans back in her chair and taps a pile of papers with her pen. "What's a nicer way to say *Your essay is utterly devoid of critical thought and demonstrates little to no understanding of the conventions of language?*"

"I don't know ... leave out the word *utterly*?"

She makes a few more notes on the page in green ink—green, not red, because someone told us in teacher's college that red ink is psychologically damaging to children—and then pushes the stack of marking away from her in disgust. "What's the point of teaching English if you can't say what you mean?"

"Yeah, and what's the point of teaching history if you can't say what happened?"

"*Your daughter can't shut up for more than ten seconds at a time*. Why can't I put *that* on a report card?"

"*Your son has a reasonable understanding of course concepts, and is proficient at pocket pool.* That could be helpful information for a parent."

I look at the clock, then dig tonight's schedule out of my binder.

"What time do you have to be down in the 'Lyons' Den'?" I try to pronounce the name with sufficient irony.

"In about half an hour. I've got a full dance card as of four o'clock."

"Shitty. Well, I guess I'll see you there. I have to go use the staff bathroom downstairs."

"What's wrong with the boys' room up here?"

"They closed it. Someone barfed in the sink and clogged it up."

"You guys are animals."

I run into Molly just as I'm leaving the washroom.

"Ready for a long night?" I ask, praying I've remembered to zip up my fly.

"Ugh," she says. "I kind of hate these things."

"A few of us are going to go to this new Italian place for the dinner break. Want to come?"

"Thanks," she says, "but I can't tonight."

While trying not to be too pushy, I've made a point of keeping Molly informed of any staff outing I could stomach myself: the Welcome Back mixer, after-work drinks, and last month's Halloween party where Danny Pound got so drunk he pissed in Tanis Jansen's sauna. So far, all my invitations have been met with cheerful and apologetic unavailability.

When Molly and I reach the gym, she smiles politely and wishes me a good night. I give her a little wave and watch her walk away across the free-throw line.

Although no one actually uses the name, our gym is now officially called the Lyons' Den. The school board shelled out for the new facility in 1998 when they discovered that the old one—where I attended my first high school dance, kissed my first kiss, and was subjected to endless laps and burpees by my beer-gutted grade nine phys. ed. teacher—was apparently riddled with asbestos. Since then, the administration has used the Lyons' Den to hold parent–teacher interviews, rather than having parents wander through the labyrinthine hallways in search of non-sequential room numbers. If anyone ever wanted to take out Mackenzie King's teaching staff in one fell swoop, this would be their chance. Around the wide circumference of the gym, I can see more than sixty of my colleagues in alphabetical order, displaced from their classrooms and chalkboards, looking small and vulnerable in orange plastic chairs and wobbly student desks.

On the other side of the gym I can see a woman sitting across from a small placard labelled *Mr. P. Curtis*. A quick glance at my watch tells me she's a few minutes early, but it doesn't matter. You don't keep your public waiting.

Students think these interviews are about them. They think their moms and dads come in to get the straight dope on how they failed a quiz or don't participate in class discussion. The fact is, parent–teacher interviews are bi-annual opportunities for parents to size up their kid's teachers to see what kind of person is spending seventy minutes a day in a room with their child.

"Hi there," I say, taking my seat and trying to sound a little winded. "Sorry I'm running late."

"Oh, no problem," she says, "I'm probably just early."

For an evening out at a high school, Mrs. Adams (*Oh please, call me Sondra*) looks a little too polished, like a beautician you might see working behind the cosmetics counter at Sears. She's draped in a fur-trimmed mauve coat and a fuzzy, expensive-looking scarf loops around her neck. Her perfume is a mess of artificial flowers. The introductions are cheerful, but then Sondra leans forward and makes a let's-get-down-to-business face.

"So. How's Tracey doing in your Civics class?"

Tracey, who has perfect attendance and has never received a mark lower than eighty percent, is doing A-okay in my Civics class. I imagine Tracey has always done A-okay in all her classes and will continue to do A-okay when she graduates with honours and a scholarship a couple years from now. Sondra's got nothing to worry about.

Most of the parents who come out to these interviews are the ones who don't really need to. They're the parents who make a decent living and who force their kids to care about school because they can afford to send them to university afterward. They're the ones who make sure their kids have a lunch, who write notes when their kids are sick, and who come out to watch them play football, or sing in the school choir, or whatever.

I'm not saying that rich kids don't have their problems. Both of Chuck Turrie's parents are lawyers and he still got kicked off the hockey team and spent three months in rehab for OxyContin addiction. The difference is that some kids invent their bullshit and other kids inherit it. The kids who are really fucking up are usually fucking up because their parents are fucked up.

At the end of our allotted seven minutes, Sondra and I shake hands and wish each other the best.

"Call me if Tracey ever gives you any trouble," she tells me, but we both know I'll never have to.

I take a moment to catch my breath. Across the gym, Ruth seems to be a popular destination. She's got grade nines this semester, so already a group of anxious-looking forty-somethings is hanging around her desk like they're trying to get backstage at a Josh Groban concert.

About fifteen seats to Ruth's left, Vicky is also attracting attention. As always, her cleavage seems to have the gravitational pull of two perky suns. I watch her leaning over her little desk and speaking confidentially to someone's dad, who is, in turn, leaning forward himself and laughing along. The same someone's mom sits and watches them, arms and legs crossed. Even from the other side of the gym, I can tell there's going to be a fight on the drive home.

Since I ditched her at the Halloween dance, Vicky had gone on a flirting rampage with every Y chromosome who happens to be in the building. I'm sure sooner or later she'll find someone else to push her self-destruct button, and I guess I'm a little relieved. Still, it would've been a pretty fun button to push.

A dozen or so parents come and go before I notice a familiar name on my schedule. Marshall Heyen-Miller is this smart, funny kid who almost makes that shitty Civics class bearable, but I actually met his mom, Dr. Karen Miller, years before when she taught me seventeenth-century literature at Lakehead. She gave me an A on my final paper about John Donne, and we kind of bonded over our shared love of Tom Verlaine. So, when it's time for our appointment, I'm a little disappointed to see the shadow of a stranger darken my desk. A thick-haired stranger with a carefully groomed mustache who, like Sondra Adams, seems a little overdressed for the evening.

"Hi," he says, "I'm Marshall's father, Michael Heyen."

I stand up to shake hands. He's a good bit taller than I am, with broad shoulders made broader by his sport coat. He extends his wrist to reveal a watch that would cost me a month's salary. He grips my hand a little harder than I grip his, and then he gives me his card: *Michael D. Heyen, MBA, PhD, Professor of Economics*. This is a first. We take our seats and get down to business.

"I'm sorry my wife couldn't make it tonight. She had to take our other son to a concert."

"Oh. Who's playing tonight?"

"Well, actually," he says, leaning back in his chair and crossing his legs,

"Jonathan is. Youth Symphony. He's turning out to be quite a musician."

"Oh. Well, that's great."

For a moment, he chews on my statement like a piece of uncooked meat. "I suppose it is. So how's that other son of mine doing in—what is it? Civics?"

I provide the same basic information I've given everyone else tonight: Marshall's marks, his behaviour in class, and even what we'll be studying in the months to come. It's all pretty straightforward. Marshall's doing well, so I figure his dad should be happy. Still, as I talk I can't shake the feeling that, instead of listening to me, he's silently measuring me for a coffin.

"So, did you have any questions or concerns about Marshall's progress so far?"

He hesitates leisurely. He frowns a little and flares his nostrils as though someone farted a few desks down. "Well, I wouldn't say I had any concerns so far about Marshall's progress. I have to say I was a little concerned to hear that you were *lamenting* the re-election of George W. Bush earlier this month."

He's caught me off guard. "Well, I wasn't really—"

"I mean, I'm no fan of the Bush Administration *per se*, but we have to teach our kids to respect the democratic process. We can't just go around *indoctrinating* them, can we?"

"Of course not, but I didn't—"

"There's no need to get defensive, Peter, I'm sure your intentions are good, but ..."

What follows is a lecture on the need for objectivity in public education that far exceeds Dr. Heyen's seven-minute appointment. As he pontificates, he seems completely oblivious to my 5:24 and my 5:31 who have lined up behind him, and who have started to compare their watches to the gym clock.

Finally, Heyen lands on the topic of the school board's recent plans to standardize exams, which has been hotly editorialized in both the *Chronicle-Journal* and the *Source*.

"... and frankly, I think it's a great idea. I don't think this kind of standardized testing is viable for, say, something as specialized as a university course, but when it comes to a provincial education, it only makes sense. Tax dollars pay for a specific curriculum, and the public should know if they're getting what they paid for. Are you guys delivering the goods or not?"

When he finally stands to leave, I consider calling him *Mister* Heyen, only because I want to hear him correct me ("Actually, it's *Doctor* Heyen"), but I don't bother. What I do instead is shake his hand and say, "Well, good talking with you, Professor." These are literally the only words I've said in the past ten minutes. If he hears the irony in my voice, he doesn't acknowledge it.

By the time I get to Ruby's, everyone's finished eating, and the lasagna they've ordered for me is getting cold. The "few of us going out for dinner" idea that failed to hit the mark with Molly was actually just the usual dinner with Deacon and Ruth. It was a schemey way to turn a staff outing into a double date with my pals, but with that plan foiled, I'm forced to reattach myself as the third wheel on Ruth and Deacon's bicycle built for two.

"I still can't get used to you with a beard," I tell Deacon.

"You're probably just threatened by my masculinity."

"How was your pizza?"

"Meh," Ruth says, see-sawing her hand. "I guess it's hard to totally screw up pizza."

Three months ago, you couldn't get into this place. Now the only other patron is dressed in a Mr. Sub uniform and slurping up a bowl of soup. This is the shelf life of the Thunder Bay restaurant. I give this place another six months. Tops.

"So what took you so long?" Deacon asks.

"I had this parent lecture me on 'objectivity' and 'accountability' and all this crazy shit about standardized testing. Totally put me off-schedule." I take a bite of lasagna.

"Well, get used to it," Ruth says. "Come next semester, that's all we're going to hear about. You know all those lessons you developed on social justice?"

"You mean 'You've Got to Fight for Your Right to Participate'?

"Can't use them any more."

"What?"

Admittedly, Ruth's love of bearing bad news and my love of being indignant are the hook and loop of our velcro.

"Yep. Your girlfriend Molly isn't going to be able to play her Protest Song of the Day, either."

"Seriously? Why?"

"School board's investing in all this revamped curriculum shit. We're going to have to overhaul everything and teach to standardized assessments. Plus, the vice-principals are going to start randomly checking in on our classes to see if we're on schedule."

"*Jesus*. What is this? A fucking police state? Kovalski's going to just randomly show up in my classroom to make sure I'm teaching the right bullshit?"

Deacon and Ruth look at each other.

"Well, I guess that's the one silver lining with all this. Apparently, Kovalski's going to retire a semester early to avoid all this crap."

"Fucking *A*." I high-five her across the table. "Any word on who the new guy's going to be?"

"That's actually the best part," Deacon chimes in. He's been fully briefed on Ruth's Kovalski hatred and has a pretty good idea about what happens at his old alma mater.

"Well, don't keep me in suspense."

Ruth smiles. "Howlin' Mad Murdock."

I put my fork down next to the lukewarm lasagna and wilted spinach salad. I've suddenly lost my appetite.

SIDE A
Today I Hate Everyone

"What the hell? You said you were hungry."

Kim's all wide-eyed and indignant.

"I *am* hungry," I say, looking at the enormous slab of pizza in front of me, "but I didn't mean you should swipe someone's order from Mrs. Vanelli's."

Apparently, my girlfriend is a kleptomaniac. Or wait. Let me rephrase that. Apparently, I'm "just hanging out" with a kleptomaniac. We're not using the "g" word. Not yet.

While Kim "isn't into proprietary labels," she *is* into having sex with me. A lot. The first time we did it coincided nicely with our first date. I suggested we go out and see *Interview with the Vampire*, but she said that vampires were "faggy." Plus, she didn't want to do anything with me in public until she "sorted things out" with Sudbury Steve. I wasn't about to pull on that thread. Instead, we wound up sitting on either side of a popcorn bowl watching *Sleepless in Seattle* at her mom's place in Current River. It wasn't until she paused the movie and reappeared with a small bottle of Dr. McGillicuddy's Fireball that I realized we had the place to ourselves.

"Sorry about the chick drink," she said as she twisted off the cap and handed me the bottle. "My mom's still weird about me drinking in the house, so we're kind of limited to what I've got stashed in my closet."

As I took a sip of the room-temperature, cinnamon-flavoured whiskey, I could hear Young MC giving me advice in my head. Quickly, I took stock of the very few moves I knew how to bust, and opted for the classic Yawn and Stretch. True, it wasn't very original, but it got results. Unfortunately, the result it got that particular time was Kim looking at me sideways and saying, "Seriously?" I quickly rerouted my arm to land on the couch cushions and not her shoulder.

It didn't make sense. She kissed me in her boyfriend's bedroom, grabbed my ass in a bar, but now she wouldn't let me put my arm around her in her own house? And also, when was this shitty movie ever going to end? Okay, I get it Tom Hanks. Your wife is dead, you're lonely, and all of a sudden, a bunch of women—including Meg Ryan—want to bone you. Boo-fucking-hoo.

When the credits finally rolled, I figured I'd be out on the sidewalk sooner than later, so I did my best to stall.

"What'd you think?" I asked, like we had just watched *Citizen Kane* and not some crappy rom-com.

Kim's response was to pull her shirt over her head and throw it on the floor. For a moment, I just looked at it, confused, as though it had some sort of subtext I wasn't getting.

"I think I need to get the memory of that terrible movie out of my head," she said. When I looked back, her bra fell away to reveal the unexpected whiteness of her breasts. "What do *you* think?"

She didn't wait for me to answer. Her tongue worked my mouth while her fingers worked my belt buckle. Guess I wouldn't have to hang myself with a celibate rope after all.

"Ribbed? Studded?" she asked. "Piña Colada flavoured?"

Already I knew I was out of my league. I mean, it's not like I hadn't had sex before. When Margie Nelson and I were dating in grade eleven we did it a few times, but I always suspected she wasn't having as much fun as I was. Kim made it abundantly clear that she was having a good time, and although I think that had a lot more to do with her than it had to do with me, I was more than happy to help.

Afterward, she stretched out on the floor and caught her breath. I sat with my sweaty back against her mom's couch and experienced the unusual sensation of Berber carpet on my bare ass. I stared at the front entrance way, listened for the sound of a doorknob turning, and felt very, very naked.

Kim rolled over and fished a pack of du Mauriers out of her jeans, which were lying in a heap nearby. She lit up and blew a plume of smoke over our heads.

"Want one?" she asked, shaking the carton in my direction.

I took a cigarette, and like I had seen Soda do a hundred times before, flicked the lighter and sucked the flame inside. Immediately, I doubled over coughing.

"You're not really good at that, are you?"

I really hoped she was talking about smoking.

Three weeks and seven conjugal visits later, Kim continues to make it abundantly clear that I'm still on probation. So now, if someone were to ask me to define our relationship—and I keep hoping someone does—I'd have to say, "Who us? We're just fucking." Which, I guess, is kind of awesome.

Before I scarf down Kim's ill-gotten pizza, I do a quick look around the food court. Even on a Saturday afternoon, Intercity Mall is really one of the saddest places in the world. Frazzled Christmas shoppers. Teenage moms with babies named after *90210* characters. Mall employees on break and eating alone. Old people.

I eat too fast and know I'll get heartburn later, but I don't care. I chug the watery fountain pop she also stole and punctuate my meal with a burp. Kim crinkles her nose, and I'm on the verge of apology when she gulps down the rest of my Coke and belches so loud that at least three people look in our direction.

Where has this girl been all my life?

"Okay. Can we hurry up and finish this Christmas shopping *nightmare*? This place is lousy with teenagers."

"Aren't you a teenager?" I ask.

"I'm a first-year university student. Totally different species."

"So what does that make me?"

"You were just in the cradle I robbed." She stands up while I'm still dusting crumbs off my coat. "Come on. Let's go. If I have to hear 'Tears Are Not Enough' one more time, I'm going to stab myself in the eardrum with a candy cane."

We start making our way to Music City where, at the very least, they'll be playing a slightly better selection of shitty Christmas music, but we don't get more than fifteen feet before I spot Mr. Murdock coming our way.

Usually, seeing a teacher outside of school is super weird for all involved. They always seem so uncomfortable, like it's their responsibility to be nice to you but they secretly resent it. With Murdock, it's different.

"Hey," I say to him, trying to be cool, "don't you need a hall pass or something?"

"Mister Starkey, as I live and breathe. And this is," he says, directing his attention to Kim, "Missus Starkey, I presume?"

Who us? We're just fucking.

"This is my friend Kim."

"So, Kim, are you also a minstrel like our friend Ringo here?" Kim smiles and shakes her head. "I see. Not the musician, but the muse."

"Something like that," she says.

"So what have the Starkeys been up to this afternoon?"

A memory from earlier today blooms into full colour—Kim straddling me, her breasts bouncing under her bra, sweaty strands of blonde hair clinging to her cheekbones.

"Christmas shopping," I blurt out.

"Okay then." He looks at my bags. "Radio Shack for Dad ... Laura Secord for Mum ... and—what's this?—something from Black's for your favourite art teacher? How *thoughtful*."

"That's mine," Kim says. "I just bought a thirty-five-millimetre SLR for a photography course I'm taking next semester."

"Pentax or Kodak?"

"Nikon, actually."

"I see. *Brave* girl. Well," he looks at his watch and sighs, "best be going. Still have some errands to run." He offers Kim his hand and she shakes it. "Nice to meet a fellow shutterbug. Ringo?"

"Yeah?"

"Take good care of Annie Leibovitz here. Buy her something nice for Christmas."

"Will do." In fact, I already had.

As Murdock strolls away, I realize I didn't tell him about our show tonight at End of the Century. It would be pretty awesome if one of these days he actually showed up to see us play.

A few minutes later, we're flipping our way through the albums at Music City. I'm hypnotized by the cassettes in the Alternative section: Afghan Whigs—*Gentlemen*; Alice in Chains—*Jar of Flies*; Bad Religion—*Recipe for Hate*. Kim's browsing the Classic Rock CDs because her dad recently sent her a Discman as part of his ongoing campaign to buy her love. It makes me think that my folks could stand to put a few more dollars toward my love. I hate the idea of buying new albums in an outdated format. I feel like I'm just going wind up buying them twice. I wish technology would go ahead and sort itself out. Maybe everything will just stop at CDs, although Deacon was telling me just the other day that these new Japanese mini-discs are going to be huge in a couple years.

"So," Kim says without looking up from AC/DC and Aerosmith, "your teacher seems kind of cool. I like his accent."

"Yeah. I think he grew up in England." Beck—*Mellow Gold*; Cowboy Junkies—*Pale Sun Crescent Moon*; Dinosaur Jr.—*Without a Sound* ...

"How old do you think he is? Twenty-seven? Twenty-eight?"

"Uh, I think more like mid-thirties." Flaming Lips—*Transmissions from the Satellite Heart*; Green Day—*Dookie* ... "He's got a daughter in elementary school."

Eventually, I bring Pavement's *Crooked Rain, Crooked Rain* over to the counter, and the cashier, a tiny replica of John Lennon circa 1971, detaches the enormous anti-theft casing and rings it through.

"That'll be sixteen ninety-nine."

I slip a twenty out of my wallet. Through the store speakers, I can hear Bruce Springsteen promise Clarence Clemons that Santa's going to bring him a new saxophone.

When Kim's hatred for the mall reaches a critical mass, she drives me home in her Mom's 1988 Chevy Cavalier, or, as she calls it, the Divorcemobile. I talk about tonight's show as we idle in the driveway.

"Do you know what time your brother wants us there for sound check?"

"Nope," she says, "that's out of my jurisdiction."

"Do you think," I ask the question I've been afraid to ask all afternoon, "you're coming tonight?"

"No promises, Pete. I'm a busy girl this holiday season."

"Okay. Fair enough." I smile and lean over to kiss her goodbye, but she pulls away. I look at her, a little confused.

"That's not what we're about," she says.

I get out of the car and watch her drive away. Then I spend the next few hours replaying the day in my head, trying to figure out what I did wrong.

End of the Century is a sketchy little club on Donald Street. Like a lot of bars in Thunder Bay, it's changed its name and ownership a few times, and Soda claims it's a money-laundering front for some Italian or Vietnamese crime syndicate. It's basically the place people play when they can't book anything better. The stage is weirdly high and the sound is weirdly terrible. The latest renovation features a chain-link fence motif inside, which I'm guessing the owners thought looked sort of industrial, but the effect is more Beaver Lumber than Nine Inch Nails. The only real upside is that none of the bar staff seem in a hurry to check ID.

After we finish loading in, we find Townie sitting around a table with Rita and the Marthas. When the three of us grab a seat, Townie presents us with a pitcher of beer and a problem.

"Okay, so first of all, don't worry," he says.

Immediately, I start to worry.

"The manager added another band to the bill, but you're still getting paid the same, and you're still the headlining act."

Soda frowns. "So it's Martha Dumptruck—"

"The Killjoys ..."

"The Killjoys, and then us."

"Yep."

"Why did those guys want the middle spot?"

"Don't know. They mentioned something about having to drive to Winnipeg afterward."

Soda shrugs and pours himself a glass of beer. "Whatever. It's still our show."

After sound check, we hop down from the stage as the new arrivals shamble their way out of the back corner. They're baggy shirted and frizzy haired. They look tired, as if this wasn't their idea, as if Thunder Bay is the last place they want to be tonight.

I pour what's left of Townie's pitcher into my glass and grab a seat beside Rita at the merch table. On stage, the Killjoys go through the motions of a song I don't recognize.

"So," Rita says, "is your girlfriend coming tonight?"

"She's not my girlfriend."

By the time Martha Dumptruck finish checking, it's getting late, and there's already a healthy crowd forming in front of the stage. Deacon's up there to support Ruth, who looks terrified standing behind a Rickenbacker that's almost bigger than she is. The others just look excited, like they're bursting to play.

"Can we, like, just start now?" Evie asks into the microphone. Friendly laughter ricochets around the room.

It seems like the soundguy gives them the okay, because their drummer, this tough, Joan Jett-looking chick, counts to four and they hammer into their first song. They're way heavier than I expected, and they're good. Evie sings lead and Ruth hits all the harmonies. They've got this other guitar player who plays these fuzzed-out solos on a gorgeous sunburst Fender Strat I'm sure Soda would trade his left arm for. Together, they sort of sound like the Go-Gos fronting Black Sabbath. In all honesty, I'm a little surprised. I mean, I know Evie can play, and it's not like I don't think women can rock—Kim Gordon, Liz Phair, PJ Harvey. It's just that I didn't think they'd be *so* good.

I watch for a while longer; then I drain the rest of my glass and stand up. "Mind the store?" I ask Rita. She nods.

When the door to the bathroom swings shut behind me, Martha Dumptruck's third song suddenly sounds like they're playing it underwater.

"Hey!" Soda's voice rings out from the row of urinals. "Didn't you read the sign?"

"Huh?"

"It says *Men* on the door."

"Fuck off," I say through a smile.

"Hey, you hear about Hildebrandt?"

"No. Why?" I step up, leaving one urinal between us.

"Well, *apparently* he disappeared from his period four class in the middle of a lesson. Just walked out mid-sentence. Mark Zaborniak said everyone waited fifteen minutes and then took off."

Soda zips up and walks over to the sink.

"Shit," I say. "I'm surprised they haven't locked him up already. Hey, I saw Howlin' Mad Murdock today."

"Where?" I hear him pump the soap dispenser and run the water.

"I was at the mall. Went with Kim."

"So where's your girlfriend tonight?"

"She's not my girlfriend."

"Nope," he clacks the button on the hand dryer and talks over the noise. "Doesn't seem like it. At least tell me you're getting some."

"I'm getting some."

"Nice. Oh hey, one more thing ..."

"Yeah?" I button my jeans and turn around, only to realize he's already left. The fucker.

Martha Dumptruck unplug, smiling as their applause finally dies off, and the crowd heads for the bar. Mike Rotten, who usually doesn't have anything nice to say unless it's about the Sex Pistols, continues to clap a relentless meter shouting "Encore! Fuckin' *encore*!" He's pretty wasted.

In the limbo between bands, Rita wanders off to schmooze with some older guy with a shaved head and earrings. Deacon, having completed his boyfriendly duties, takes over the merch table, and I'm just about to see if I can get in on Soda's pool game when Townie sees me and waves me over to his table. He's sitting alone, and while I'm not particularly interested in any kind of hurt-my-little-sister-and-I-kill-you conversation, it's hard to deny the golden column of beer condensating in front of him. When I sit down, he fills my empty plastic cup.

"Thanks, man," I say. "They sounded pretty good, didn't they?"

"Yeah ... I don't know ..." He looks at his beer like there's a fly in it. "I'm kind of done with the whole female vocalist, loud-quiet-loud thing. I mean, I like the Breeders as much as the next guy, but come on ..."

Townie's review of our last show in *Bigmouth Strikes Again!* was, in fact, pretty kind, but he did accuse us of being too derivative of the Replacements (none of us had actually heard the Replacements, but I went out and bought *Pleased To Meet Me* the next day). I guess that's just what Townie does.

"So how come none of your roommates showed up tonight?"

"Who? The Honey-Dudes? Fucking *at home* watching the Leafs game. God. Those guys walk around like the second coming of Pink Floyd, but deep down they're all small-town rednecks."

I don't know if Townie is officially "out" or not. Kim talks about his "jerk-off obsession" with Jordan Catalano like it's common knowledge, but I'm not so sure it is. Maybe it's different once you get to university, but admitting you're gay in a Thunder Bay high school is almost as dangerous as admitting you don't like hockey.

"How'd you wind up living with a bunch of guys from Sudbury?"

"Kyle's from Sioux Lookout."

"You know what I mean."

"I'm not sure, man. It was kind of a bad scene when my parents split up. I wanted to move out, but they thought I was too young to live on my own. So they agreed to pay for residence. Made some friends there. This year I rented a house with them. Had I known they were going to start a *jam band* ..." He lets the conclusion hang in the air like it's self-evident. It kind of is.

"Ever think you'd want to move back home?"

He raises an eyebrow. "What home? My dad got a job in Vancouver and now we barely ever hear from him. My mom and Kim—you've met my sister, right? They've got this tiny place in Current River ..."

He keeps talking but I kind of lose track of what he's saying. I'm on my fourth or fifth beer, and the room's starting to swim a little. Plus, if I'm not mistaken, he just asked if I *met* his sister. Of course I'd *met* his sister.

And then it dawns on me. Townie has no idea I've been dating Kim for nearly a month. Even though I'd spent all this time with her, even though I'd gone out and bought her a two-hundred-dollar camera lens for Christmas, she hasn't even *mentioned* my name in polite conversation.

"Hey, is your sister coming tonight?" I ask. It's a clumsy segue.

"I don't think so. I think she had other plans."

"What could be more important than this?" Also clumsy.

"I don't know. I think she was going to go winter camping with Wilson and Janie, you know—that whole outdoorsy crew. They're crazy. Who wants to go camping when it's twenty below?"

Wilson and Janie. That whole crew. Who were these people?

A couple university students I don't recognize sit down at our table and start talking to Townie. He doesn't introduce me and after a couple minutes seems to forget I'm even sitting there. I look at my watch and realize it's almost eleven o'clock. Behind me, I can hear the sudden fade of the house music, and the anticipatory hum of amplifiers takes its place. The lead singer from the out-of-town band says something I can't quite make out into the microphone, and people laugh. From our table, I can see the crowd multiplying exponentially in front of the stage.

This is the crowd that was supposed to be our crowd. Everyone who's drinking is just drunk enough, and everyone who isn't is still excited to have the night ahead of them. Maybe they'd meet a girl or a boy from another high school, or smoke a joint with the band behind the bar. I finally get why the Killjoys wanted to play in the middle. Because that's where the action is. Right in the heart of the evening. By the time we get on, people will be looking at their watches, thinking about curfew or where they're going next. We won't be headliners; we'll be sloppy seconds—sloppy thirds, in fact. We'll be playing the crowd out.

I sit and watch the band for a few songs. They're okay, but all the noise and heat starts to seem a little oppressive, and I've got this weird feeling in my stomach, like I'm heading into a rollercoaster loop. Before I even realize I've done it, I stand up. My chair tips dangerously behind me, almost falls, then doesn't.

"Hey—sorry—" I say to Townie. "Thanks for the beer." His new friends stare at me like I've just materialized out of nowhere. He nods, and I walk outside to breathe some cool air. Something's shifted irreversibly in my guts, and there's a telltale watering in my mouth that means trouble's coming. I run around to the alley where Deacon parked the

Sabre and stop by a pile of black garbage bags. I feel my stomach close like a fist and empty its contents through my esophagus. Townie's beer and what's left of his sister's stolen pizza boil a hole in the snow. I steady myself against the wall of the bar and wait one minute, then another, until a second wave of nausea hits. At this point, there's not much left but bile. Eventually, I stand up, lean against the building, and spit stringy orange gobs onto the ground. I'm suddenly exhausted. I rummage around in my jacket pocket for candy or a piece of gum, but all I can find is Kim's BIC, and a crumpled, nearly empty pack of du Mauriers.

"For practice," she had said.

I light the tip and take a drag. Immediately, I start to hack until I think I'm going to throw up a third time. Eventually, though, my breathing evens out, and I stand and smoke a few feet away from the puke, until I'm down to the filter. It's cold, but I jam my hands in my pockets and start walking down the street. Through the foggy window of a Robin's Donuts, I can see a smear of old men in peaked caps drinking coffee. I go past a strip mall dark with storefront vacancies. *For Sale. For Lease.* There's a Mike's Milk so I go inside. The light is fluorescent, like a hospital or a high school. By the time I get to the front with a pack of Trident, I realize I gave Rita the rest of my money for the float. The woman behind the counter scowls at me under hairsprayed bangs that reach out from her forehead like a bleached claw. I feel like I've seen her around, like maybe she was a senior when I was in grade nine, but she has an age-disguising fatness that could put her anywhere between twenty and forty. Even though I know there's nothing there, I make a show of searching my pockets, as if it would somehow validate her time and mine.

"Sorry," I eventually tell her.

She doesn't say anything but stares at me until I put the gum back and leave, as though her eyes were emitting some sort of reverse-tractor beam, pushing me out of her store. Outside, in a fog of my own smoky puke-breath, I realize I should probably head back. As I get closer to End of the Century, I start to pass people on the sidewalk—my audience, on its way home. One by one, they make their excuses.

Mark Zaborniak pauses with one leg already inside the backseat of an idling minivan. "Sorry dude, my ride's leaving. Have a good show."

Danny Grove apologizes through a balaclava. "I've got to work an early shift tomorrow."

Brandy Sawchuck shrugs. "Twelve o'clock curfew."

Rotten is shitfaced. "I need to go pass out. Tell that Evie chick I think she's hot."

Martha Dumptruck's Joan Jett drummer and guitar player walk past me and avoid eye contact.

When I get to the door, it sounds like the Killjoys have finished, which means I have to get up on stage and summon the energy to play to whoever's left. I'm about to go inside and confirm this when the front door swings open and clocks me in the nose. I lose my balance and trip backward onto the sidewalk. Until this exact moment, I had always thought "seeing stars" was just an expression, but there they are—a whole constellation twinkling in front of my eyes. When they clear, I see Toby Watkins's fish face grinning down at me.

"Have a nice trip?" He laughs, and a little snort escapes.

I'm exhausted, my mouth tastes like a sour asshole, and my jeans are soaked. Nothing is funny.

I get to my feet and notice he's got his arm around the waist of an exact female version of himself, minus the moustache and dandruff. Well, minus the dandruff. It's like seeing some ugly, Robert Crumb rendering of Mickey and Minnie Mouse out on a date. They're even wearing matching Killjoys t-shirts under half-zipped winter coats.

"What the *fuck*, Twatkins!"

My voice comes out thick and mean, but it makes me feel good.

Toby cringes a little. "I don't like that name, Pete."

He doesn't look at me or his girlfriend when he says it, but I keep looking right at him. A shiver of adrenalin unhinges my mouth from my brain, and I get this wild thrill of cruelty, like I'm about to squish a bug.

"Yeah?" I say, taking a step toward him. "Well, you should probably take that up with your stupid fucking parents, shouldn't you, *Twatkins*?"

I half-expect him to freak out, or lunge at me, or something, but he just watches some spot on the ground with this hangdog expression that only makes him look more pathetic. Minnie Mouse stares daggers at me.

"Come on," she says to him. "Let's go."

I watch them leave; then I turn to go into the bar. Rita's waiting in the doorway and watching me with this weird look in her eye.

"You guys are on in a couple minutes," she says.

She goes back inside and the door swings shut behind her. I follow with a vague sense of horror, like I'm about to attend my own funeral.

SIDE B

Where Have All the Good People Gone?

"Someone die?"

Dylan Beaucage poses the question as he comes in late for the third time this week. "What's with the suit?"

"Well, Dylan, sometimes a guy just wants to look his prettiest," I tell him.

"Fag," he mumbles, just loud enough so I can hear him. He sits down at his desk and checks his phone.

As much as I'd like to, I don't send him down to see the vice-principal. I have a job interview later today, and I don't want the people in charge thinking I can't handle my class. I swear, though, if I ever get a full contract, I'm going to send kids down just for looking at me funny.

At lunch, right after I've tucked into a chicken burger, Ruth sits down across from me and hands me a piece of paper.

"You may remember some of this bullshit from teacher's college," she says.

I read through a list of vaguely Orwellian terminology. *Backward design. Cooperative grouping. Context variables.* There's about fifteen terms in all, and each one has a little check box beside it.

"What's this?"

"That, my friend, is a checklist of buzzwords that Trimble wants to hear during your interview today."

"Seriously? How did you get it?"

"Swiped it off his desk when I went in to talk about my schedule next semester. There were a bunch of them there. He didn't notice anything."

"So, what do you think my chances are?" I ask her.

"To get the job?"

I nod.

"I think it's a no-brainer. Two positions and two incumbents? I think you and *Ms. Pearson—*" she winks when she says Molly's name "—have it pretty much locked down."

When fourth period rolls around, I find myself outside the principal's office sitting in one of the chairs usually reserved for delinquent students.

"In trouble again, Pete?" one of the secretaries jokes.

"No, ma'am," I say. Although I have to admit I am feeling a bit pre-firing-squad.

Out of nowhere, two miraculous legs appear before me, and I look up to see Molly transformed into a living, breathing sexy librarian archetype, complete with the skirt, blouse, and a pair of glasses I've never seen her wear before. Her hair is tied up in a bun and I half expect her to shake it loose in slow motion, like we're in some glam rock music video. I sure wish she would.

She leans over, squeezes my arm, and whispers, "The last question is about a 'defining event' and how it shaped you as a teacher."

"Thanks," I say, but I'm barely processing her advice. I'm too blissed out on the smell of her orange blossom perfume and the fact that her breasts are hovering mere inches from my face.

"Merry Christmas." She smiles back at me as she walks away, and I immediately wish I'd given her a copy of Trimble's checklist.

Eventually, the door to the office, decorated with a politically correct wreath that wishes everyone "Happy Holidays," opens and my department head walks out.

"Hi, Peter," Gail says with a reasonable facsimile of a smile. "We're ready for you."

When I walk into the office, two men in suits are seated at a round table—not the principal's desk but a table for meetings and interviews like this one. The first man is Principal Wayne Trimble, a demure, thin-faced man in his late fifties. When I was a student, our principal was this six-foot monster named Barry Hawkes, who scared the shit out of just about everyone. There was always a rumour that he kept a strap in his desk in hopes that corporal punishment would once again come back in style. Since I've started teaching, I kind of miss the Hawk. We could use a little more authoritarian terror around here.

The other man is someone I haven't spoken to in ten years. For a moment I'm almost happy to see him, like when you see your ex-girlfriend unexpectedly and for just a second you can remember the good times before they're eclipsed by the bad. In that moment, I forget to hate his guts, but when I hear that arrogant, fruity voice, all the old feelings come flooding back.

"Mister Starkey. Nice to see you again."

He looks older, but there's still a boyishness to his face. He's put on a bit of weight and tied his hair back in a sad little ponytail to disguise a developing bald spot. I try to remember if he's always worn that earring.

"Er, no, Ken," Wayne corrects him, "this is Peter *Curtis*. He's been doing an LTO for Sue Ramsey this semester."

"Oh, don't worry. I know Ringo. He and I go way back." He smiles a toothy grin and, in turn, I twist my face into mask of professional civility.

Wayne seems a little confused, but we all take our seats and begin. "Right. So, Peter," he says, "we thought it might be best if Ken sat in on these interviews since he'll be taking over next semester when Stan retires."

"Great. I think it's never too early to start developing a *professional learning community,*" I say with a smile.

That's one.

Wayne nods thoughtfully and checks something off on a piece of paper. Gail sees him doing it and makes a note of her own. Good. I was nervous before, but now I just feel focused and clear. All of a sudden, I really want this job. I want to take it and shove it in Murdock's forty-four-year-old face. And here's how I'm going to do it: every time they ask me a question, I'm going to pack my answer so full of bullshit that by the end of the interview, Trimble's going to have a buzzword boner big enough to knock over the table.

"Peter, to start off, could you describe what strategies you use to manage misbehaving students?"

I'm reminded of Dylan Beaucage, stoned and weaving out of my class yesterday, giving me the finger as he did it.

"I think that, almost always, disruptive behaviour is a symptom of a greater issue that is rooted in the student's *context variables*, like learning style, culture, or socio-economic background."

I suppose it's true. But what's also true is that, sometimes, kids are just dicks. And everyone at this table knows it for a fact. Still, that's two. I keep going. "I try to establish clear expectations for classroom behaviour and offer *differentiated instruction* that respects the student's *multiple intelligences*."

And there's three and four.

Buzzwords are funny things. Every once in a while I hear them materialize in emails or at staff meetings. Suddenly, people start dropping this new terminology like it had always been a part of their vocabulary. Everyone else just pretends to know what they mean. To ask for clarification would be to ask why the emperor's wang is blowing in the wind.

"Peter, what have you done in terms of professional growth since you've started here this semester?"

"Wayne, I like to consider myself a *lifelong learner*—" that's five "—and I've recently applied to take my Special Education qualifications. I've also just started reading this great book called *A Passion for History: Helping Students Discover Yesterday, Today.*

Not true. *A Passion for History* has been sitting on my shelf since I graduated from teacher's college, and the only way I'm taking a Spec Ed AQ this summer is if I *don't* get this job and need to beef up my CV, but no one's going to call my bluff. I parry, thrust, and blow some Bloom's Taxonomy in their eyes to blind them. This is how you prove your mettle in the tower of ivory. Meanwhile, I'll be showing *Christmas with the Kranks* in class tomorrow because we're four days away from vacation, and everyone stopped paying attention about a week ago.

Not once do they ask why I wanted to be a teacher. Not once do I have to risk saying something honest. It's only after I dropkick Gail's question about teamwork with *cooperative grouping* and *collaborative learning* that Murdock finally asks a tough one.

"Speaking of 'teamwork,' Ringo, how's your mate Jesse doing?" He's salting an old wound and he knows it. "I heard his song on the radio the other day—you know, '*Contrary to popular belief* ... '"

He keeps singsonging his way through the first verse until I cut him off with the title.

"Common Cold Heart."

"Right! *Love* that song. '*There's no cure for the common cold heart* ... '"

"I know that song," Wayne says, to the surprise of everyone. "My son was playing that CD in the car the other day. Jesse Maracle. He's from Thunder Bay?"

"He is. In fact, he went to this very high school. *And*, if I remember correctly," Murdock gestures deferentially toward me, "he and Mister Starkey used to play in a *band* together."

Wayne's eyebrows climb his forehead. Gail shrugs and looks over her notes again.

"Wow," Wayne says. "Too bad you weren't able to hitch your wagon to that star, huh?"

"Well, that was a long time ago," I tell him, smiling. "I don't think I was cut out for showbiz." And I'm not sure, but I think he even believes me. Over the years, I've perfected this cheerful lie.

"Right. Well," Wayne gets the train back on the tracks, "I think Gail's going to ask one last question ... Gail?"

Gail asks the question that Molly warned me about, the one that has me describe my "defining moment." I talk about working with disadvantaged kids in Scarborough when I was a student teacher. It's a great cherry to put on top of this bullshit sundae, but the truth is, I never had any kind of "defining moment." There was no revelation. I wasn't "called" to the profession. The only reason I became a teacher was because nothing better came along. That, and the whole summers-off thing.

Afterward, we all shake hands and smile, and they tell me they'll let me know as soon as they can. And then, on my way out of the office, I walk past Doug Hildebrandt like he's the Ghost of Christmas Past. He floats by and his vacant eyes don't seem to recognize me. I'm almost ready to believe that I'm hallucinating, but when I reach the door to the office, I look back and see my old art teacher shake hands with my old, but very corporeal, history teacher.

"Weird. Didn't he ... retire, or something?" I ask one of the secretaries.

"Or something," she says without looking up from her paperwork.

At the end of the day, I orchestrate a major coup. Molly, now a fellow veteran of the interview process, agrees to join me for an after-work beer.

"What the hell?" she says. "It's Friday, and after all that, I could use a drink."

Molly's never been to the Phoenix before, so I have the privilege of introducing her to Thunder Bay's most popular watering hole for the over-twenty-five, under-forty crowd. The walls of the bar are covered with these giant murals of rock dinosaurs—Jimi, Janis, Jerry. We grab a table underneath Neil Young.

"Canadian-content section?" Molly asks.

I remember once I complained to Deacon that they should have more local colour on the wall, but really, who else was there? Paul Schaffer? No one needs to see a six-foot-tall rendering of his shiny dome. Now I live in fear that I'll walk in here one day and see an enormous Soda grinning down at me from the back wall. I'd have to find a new place to drink, and since Whiskey Jack's went out of business, my options are limited.

After we've made our way through the better part of a pint, Molly asks me how my interview went.

"Okay, I guess. What did you think of Murdock?"

"He seemed nice enough. He kept calling me *Vancouver*."

"Yeah, he's really into nicknames."

"So ... what do you think our chances are?"

"It's a no-brainer," I say after I finish my beer. "There are two positions and two incumbents. Seriously, who else are they going to hire?" The image of Hildebrandt flickers in my memory and I dismiss it. "We're easily the most talented, the most qualified, and the most ... *attractive* people for the job. They'd be idiots not to hire us."

"Here's to that." She drains the rest of her drink and waves two fingers at our waitress. "I hate all this interview stuff. Kissing ass. Updating my resume. I just want to teach."

She stops talking as our waitress brings us two more beers. She takes a sip and a strand of dark hair falls in front of her face.

"I just see all these lost kids out there, and I want to help them. So many teachers talk a good game, but then they've got no follow-through. They just want to sound good in front of the hiring committee."

"Totally." A little guilt passes through me. Silently, I resolve to be a better person.

As we drink, we talk about the usual stuff—the safe little anecdotes single people carry around with them instead of pictures of their kids. A funny story about meeting a celebrity. A weird job. Favourite movies. It's starting to feel like a real date, and we both know it.

"So," I point up at Neil, who looms haggardly above us, "what kind of music are you into?"

"Uh-oh," she says, leaning back in her chair. "Is it that time already?"

"What time?"

"Music Talk Time."

"Sure. I mean, why not?"

She sighs. "Okay. Let's say I like the Rolling Stones—"

"Awesome! I love the Stones."

"Yeah, 'awesome,' but the next thing you're going to ask is if I like *Sticky Fingers* better than *Exile on Main Street*."

"*Exile*, obviously. Did you know they recorded that album in France to avoid a drug-possession charge?"

"See? That's just it. Guys always do this. You say you're a fan of something and then they start quizzing you on it. '*Did you know ...* ?' or '*Have you ever heard ...* ' Just because I *like* a band, it doesn't mean I wrote my doctorate on them."

"Oh."

Then she smiles. "And yeah, I did know it was recorded in France, but it was to avoid tax laws, not a drug charge."

It's becoming a very real possibility that I'm going to fall in love with this girl.

"You know what I miss?" she asks. "Mixed tapes. *God.* I used to make mixed tapes all the time."

"You can still burn CDs."

"Yeah, but it's not the same. CDs take all the guesswork out of it. I miss the physical editing—trying to time it right so you don't get too much dead air and you don't cut off the start of the song. You know, after high school I backpacked across Europe with a Walkman and just two mixed tapes. I knew every click and pause between every song." She takes a sip of beer and looks wistfully over my shoulder.

"Okay. I need to pee," she announces. "If our waitress comes by, do you want to order us some nachos? I'll buy, as long as they're vegetarian."

"Deal."

She's been gone for only a couple minutes when a swarm of angry bees spontaneously materializes in my pocket. I'd managed to put off buying a cell phone for ages while my friends clipped what looked like small walkie-talkies and field radios to their belts, but my parents finally bought me one for Christmas last year. They reasoned that if I was going to be supply teaching, I'd need to be constantly available. In reality, it was just another opportunity for my mom to perfect the art of calling me at the wrong time. The pizza delivery guy arrives—she calls. I start watching a movie—she calls. I'm having a drink with a pretty girl—she definitely calls. At least by now I've figured out how to set it to vibrate, so it doesn't sound like I'm hosting a rave in my pants every time the ringer goes off. I'm surprised, though, when I pull it out and check the display, that it doesn't read *June Curtis*. Instead, it reads *William Lyon Mackenzie King*. I get a little jolt when I realize it might be about the job.

"Hello?"

"He-e-e-ey!" It's a woman's voice. It's familiar but I can't quite place it.

"Hello?"

"It's me."

I hate it when people identify themselves on the phone with a personal pronoun. When I don't respond, "Me" takes a hint and clarifies. "It's Vicky!"

"Oh. Hey." Weird. She's never called me on the phone before.

"I tried you earlier, but you didn't pick up."

"Oh. Uh, sorry. I'm not so great with cell phones."

"Well, I stayed late at school to watch the basketball game, and I got your number from the staff directory. Hope that's okay."

"Sure." It's totally *not* okay, but I'd like to end this conversation before Molly gets back from the bathroom.

"What's up?"

"Well, I just got off the phone with Jamie. He's on his way to watch the Leafs game at Boston Pizza." It's also kind of weird to hear her say her husband's name. "*Apparently*, he was just at some board meeting with your old pal Ken Murdock, and he got the inside scoop on the current round of hirings."

"Oh, really?" I try to feign nonchalance but can't quite pull it off.

"Yeah, *really*," she imitates me. "Come on. Don't act like you're not *dying* to find out."

"Okay. You got me. Totally dying."

"Well, good news, Golden Boy. You got the job. You're full time starting in February."

"Holy shit!"

"'Holy shit' is right!" She imitates me again. "So when are we going to celebrate?"

"Soon." Never. "Hey, did you hear who else got hired?"

"You mean did your little friend in the tight skirt get hired? Well, knowing Trimble and Murdock they probably *wanted* to, but no. They hired Hildebrandt. He has the most experience, so it was kind of a no-brainer."

Goddammit. I wish people would get together and establish clear criteria for what constitutes a no-brainer these days.

"Well, I'm going to get going. Don't forget—you owe me a drink sometime. And you said 'soon.'"

I concede her point and hang up. When Molly comes back, her hair is out of its bun, and I can't help but wonder what lucky soul in the women's washroom got see it fall down her shoulders.

"So?" she asks. "What's the good news?"

"Huh?" Impossibly, she knows.

"Did you order us some nachos yet or what?"

"Oh. No. Not yet. The waitress didn't come around."

"*Jeez*, Curtis. Take some initiative already."

She waves down our waitress and not long after, a feast appears in front of us. We pull at the nachos and they come apart reluctantly, tailed by long strings of elasticky cheese, but when we bite down they taste microwaved and unsatisfying. We pick away at our mediocre snack in a temporary, hungry silence. The waitress suggests another two glasses of the same to wash down the food, and we don't argue. By the time we reduce the plate to tortilla shrapnel, we're both a little drunk and Molly's ready to leave. I haven't said one word about the job.

It's cold outside, but not as cold as it has been. As we walk down Algoma Street, bundled up in our coats and lit by streetlight, I want to keep talking, but I don't know what to say.

"This was a good night," Molly decides. "I really hope they hire both of us."

"Yeah," I croak. "Me too."

"And they will, right? They'd be idiots not to."

"*Complete* fucking idiots." I'm starting to feel like a terrible, evil person, but instead of telling Molly what I know, the question I'm most afraid to ask finds its way out of my mouth. "So—worst case scenario. What if you don't get the job? What happens then?"

"Well," she thinks about it in silence as we walk, "realistically, I guess I'd have to move back to Vancouver. My parents said I could stay with them until I found a job."

"Oh." I'm too drunk to hide the disappointment in my voice.

"I miss the mountains, Pete. And the ocean. And I hate all this fucking snow. I guess, if I'm going to be unemployed, I'd rather be unemployed in Vancouver than Thunder Bay." She kicks a chunk of ice and it skitters ahead of us on the sidewalk. "No offence."

We keep talking about nothing in particular, and every time there's a pause in the conversation, I think about telling her what Vicky said. Maybe it'd be easier to hear it from me than from Gail or Wayne or fucking Murdock. Maybe not. I just know that, as soon as I tell her, that's the end of everything. And I don't want it to be the end of everything. Not yet.

"Well," she says, as we stop in front of an unremarkable brick bungalow. "This is me."

An awkward moment passes between us that, in the future, I'll probably pinpoint as the moment I missed my shot. I think she senses I'm waiting for something too, because she says, "I'd invite you in for another drink, but Charlie's a really light sleeper."

Charlie? I get this awful, panicky feeling that I've completely misread the entire situation, that this was never a date and that inside her house there's some drowsy, shirtless dude sleeping on the side of the bed I was hoping would be mine tonight.

"Charlie's your ... roommate?" I ask optimistically, expecting her to correct me with *boyfriend* or *husband*. She doesn't use either.

"Daughter," she says instead. "She's four. My aunt's staying over tonight to look after her."

"Oh. Crazy."

"I wasn't trying to keep her a secret or anything. It's just nice not to be Somebody's Mom for a little while."

"Right. Totally."

There's an uncomfortable pause at the end of which Molly gives me a measured look. "Well. I can tell by your face that I'm Somebody's Mom again, so I should probably just say goodnight."

She turns abruptly and hurries up the concrete steps to her front door. I'm not entirely sure what I said or didn't say, but the transformation is complete; I am now an asshole.

"Molly," I call after her, a little too drunk and a little too loud.

"*Sshh!*" Molly puts her finger to her lips and then points up at the window of what I can only assume is her daughter's bedroom. Then she's through the door and I'm alone.

"Dude!" Deacon yells. "What's happening?"

I'm not quite halfway home when Deacon calls. All the warm, buzzy blood in my veins has turned to mud, and I was looking forward to a quiet evening of feeling sorry for myself.

"How'd your hot date go?" There's a lot of crowd noise in the background and he sounds pretty drunk.

"Well, I'm on the phone with you, so I'd say not that well."

"Bummer!"

"Where are you? It sounds ... loud."

"Duggy's. It's *crazy* here! Everyone's home for Christmas. Brandy Sawchuck ... Mazz Moore ... Grover and Rotten said they might come by ..."

The Dugout is the local sports bar in town where high school went to die. Or, more accurately, where high school went to play foosball and drink cheap draft.

"Farkas brought Whee—I mean, Matty. He was pushing him around in a Santa hat and handing out dimebags of medicinal weed. Oh, *and* Brad McLaren showed up and tried to buy me a beer! He kept asking if I thought 'Jesse' was coming. As *if*."

As if.

"Hey—I've got someone who wants to talk to you ..."

"Hey, Pete!"

It's lovely to hear Rita's voice.

"What are you doing in town?" I ask. "Shouldn't you be at some industry party, playing beer pong with Avril Lavigne?"

"I still like to visit you northerners now and then. You know, rub shoulders with the common people," she says. "Remember my humble beginnings."

"*She met Geddy Lee*!" I hear Deacon shout ludicrously in the background.

Even after everything that happened with Soda, I still saw Rita now and then until she finished her BA. After that, she moved to Toronto and immediately made herself invaluable to a series of boutique record labels, each one more fashionable than the last. I still get the occasional email from her.

"So are you coming out tonight or what?"

"I don't know ... It's been kind of a weird night. I was just on my way home."

"Eff that. It's eleven thirty!" she says. "I'm ordering us a pitcher. Get your ass over here!"

Then she hangs up.

I'm not sure why seeing my friends has started to feel like an obligation. Maybe it's just something that happens as you get older. Maybe that's why my parents never seemed to make any new friends after they turned fifty. One day, they just met their quota.

I'm about fifteen minutes from the bar and ten from home. I feel the old exhaustion working its way into my back, my shoulders, my eyes, but with a Herculean effort I cut down a side street and head toward the Dugout.

How much longer can I do this? I wonder. How much longer can I keep living in the past? As I watch the machinery of my feet below, it occurs to me that I'm still wearing my Hush Puppies and my interview suit. I'll definitely be a little overdressed for Duggy's, but fuck it. If I'm going to travel back in time, I might as well arrive in style.

SIDE A

It Falls Apart

"And let me remind everyone that 'Those who cannot remember History are condemned to repeat it.'"

"God," Rotten moans across the aisle to me, "does he have to say that *every* time he hands back a test?"

"Those who can remember stupid sayings are condemned to repeat them," I tell him.

Rotten snorts.

Looking at the stack of paper he's cradling in his arm, I suspect that Hildebrandt spent a good chunk of his Christmas vacation marking our test on the Industrial Revolution. How the difference between a spinning mule and a spinning jenny is ever going to be useful to me in the future is a mystery, but at the very least, memorizing a bunch of historical terms is a lot easier than the voodoo magic of math and science.

"I'll hand the tests back in no particular order," Hildebrandt promises and then immediately slams mine down on my desk. I search his face to see if, despite what he just said, it's some kind of bad sign, but his eyes are distant and impassive. I try to imagine a time when Hildebrandt didn't look ugly and old, but I can't do it. Under his glasses, the skin around his eyes is loose and the colour of a bruise. Jowls tug at his cheeks. Feathers of hair rest tenuously over his blotchy scalp. I'd kind of feel sorry for him, if he wasn't so terrible.

It's my nightmare to wind up like Hildebrandt—rhyming off the same tired facts year after year, trotting out the same tired anecdotes. He's like some kind of assembly line worker in a kid factory. It's no wonder he's so fucking nuts. I want a job where I can change things up. Throw a wrench in the works. If the whole music thing doesn't work out, I think I'd want to be a lawyer. Fight the system from the inside out. My marks aren't half bad, so who knows?

When I turn my test over, I see I've managed a seventy-one percent. It's respectable, but I kind of expected to do better. Admittedly, there were a few questions I blanked on, but even still, something doesn't quite add up. For starters, I'm *pretty* sure James Watt invented the steam engine, but Hildebrandt put a big red X beside my answer. And as much as I wanted to write "A fluty prog rock band from the seventies," I explained quite admirably that Jethro Tull was the guy who invented the horse-drawn seed drill. Hildebrandt gave me a zero on that one too. In fact, there are a bunch of questions I thought I had right but he marked wrong.

"When you're done looking through your test, read Chapter Eight in your textbook, then answer the first six questions," Hildebrandt instructs us. "*Quietly*, please."

He sits down at his desk and shakes open a copy of the *Chronicle-Journal*, his daily constitutional. Tim Puurula once tried to tease Hildebrandt about doing his "personal reading" in class, a line he borrowed from the history teacher himself. Over his glasses, Hildebrandt told Tim that news was history in the making and gave him two detentions for impertinence.

"*Rotten*," I whisper across the aisle, "what'd you get?"

"Ninety-two," he says.

"Bullshit!"

"Ten bucks." He puts out his hand. Rotten's always betting people ten bucks.

"Just let me see it."

He holds up his paper and I lean into a fog of fresh Cheetos and armpit tang to see that he has in fact clocked an incredible ninety-two percent. Usually, he pulls sixties, or maybe the occasional seventy. The last time he got a better mark than I did, I'd been off sick for three days with the stomach flu and Hildebrandt dropped a pop quiz the day I returned. Even then, it was still kind of close. Something's definitely up.

I'm a little torn, because I don't want to rock the boat. Seventy-one is a decent mark, and I don't want to seem like a grade grubber. So, instead of slinking up, hat in hand to Hildebrandt's desk and asking for special treatment, I try to make it a public problem.

"Uh, Mr. Hildebrandt?" I ask. There's no use putting my hand up. He can't see me through the Arts & Entertainment section. "I think there's something weird about the way you marked my test."

Behind a wall of newsprint he says, "There's nothing 'weird' about the tests, Peter. Please get back to your reading."

I hate it when teachers just dismiss you like that. I look around helplessly, polling the faces for dirty looks or allies. That's when I notice that everybody's looking at their tests with more than purely academic interest.

I'm not saying I started it, because I didn't. Someone else would have said something eventually. I just happened to notice it first. Soon, people are comparing their tests and pointing emphatically at their papers. Jeannie Drew, an apple-cheeked sweetheart of an overachiever, is at the front of the room, standing over Hildebrandt's desk and attempting to direct his attention. Her sandy curls bounce diplomatically. Jason Sebesta hovers next in line with his test rolled up like a billy club in his fist. Hildebrandt continues to read his paper seemingly unconcerned. Over my shoulder, I notice Padma Singh using a calculator to figure out what this test will do to her ninety-something average and her chances for premed. Mazz Moore, a squinty stoner who sits at the back, stops carving his name into the file cabinet beside his desk long enough to high-five Kyle Beaton on a job well done.

I look back to Hildebrandt and see that Jeannie has given up. As she walks back to her desk she directs a disappointed shrug to Brandy Sawchuck. Sebesta has taken Jeannie's place, interrogating Hildebrandt with his palms down on the teacher's desk, his head cocked between his bulky shoulders, bad cop to her good. Still, Hildebrandt reads his paper and avoids eye contact. There's a weird tension in the class. The academics are at a rolling boil, while slackers are stirring the pot. A balled up piece of paper bounces off Jason's shoulder and he stomps in the general direction of his assailant. Brandy Sawchuck is scolding Kyle Beaton for flying his test like a paper airplane. I just keep my mouth shut and watch. Unexpectedly, it's Padma who brings things to a head.

"Mr. Hildebrandt, this is bullshit!"

Everyone in the class is immediately silent. Padma, who's usually the poster girl for student obedience, stands up at her desk and stares through Hildebrandt's newspaper shield. Her voice is an iron bell.

"You must collect these tests, and you must grade them again. *Properly*."

The kids I'd expect to shout her down hesitate, possibly because picking on Mackenzie King's only Indian student might smack of racism, or conversely, because Padma's expensive Mumbai English rings with all the authority of the British Empire. Maybe they're just waiting to see what happens. What does happen is a whole lot of nothing, an eternal silence that is finally broken by the crackle of Hildebrandt turning a newspaper page.

"Mr. Hildebrandt!" Padma says again. This time it's an accusation, a command, a condemnation all rolled into one.

Finally, Hildebrandt folds the *Chronicle-Journal*, opens a desk drawer and puts the paper inside. He stands up and walks to the front of the class. Still, he doesn't look at anyone. His eyes seem lost in strategy, as though he's only now understood that his class is on the verge of mutiny and he must act. He crouches down, and for a second, I wonder if he's going to plead his case, or attempt to reason with us on our level. Instead, he puts his foot in an invisible hack, squares his shoulders with an invisible broom, and lets loose with an imaginary curling rock down the centre aisle of the classroom.

"Hurry hard," he whispers urgently. "*Hurry hard.*"

"So, like, what? You spent the rest of the class watching him hallucinate?"

Kim speeds the Divorcemobile toward Mackenzie King so recklessly that, were I not still in a constant state of trying to prove how cool and laid back I was about everything, I would make her pull over and let me out so I could call the cops. It's official. My feelings for her have become a danger to myself and others.

"Not the *whole* period," I reply. "Most people took off, and—*Jesus*, watch that—"

Kim blows through a four-way stop as another car lurches to a standstill and the driver leans on the horn.

"Yeah, fuck you too ..." A moment passes. "Okay ... *and* ... ?"

"And, uh, this girl—Jeannie—she went down to the office and came back with the vice-principal, and we got the rest of the period off. Apparently, the Hawk escorted him to his car at the end of the day."

Kim rolls into the student parking lot in fourth gear and hurtles into the first available spot. We're thrown forward and then back into our seats.

"So. You finally drove him crazy. Nicely done."

"Well, I don't think we *drove* him anywhere. He arrived at crazy months ago. We just sort of opened the door and let him out."

"Speaking of which ..." She ratchets the parking brake into position and steps out of the car. She looks across the street to the yellow lights burning in the school. "I can't believe you talked me into this. I swore I'd never set *foot* inside another high school."

"Oh, come on. It's a rock show. There'll be lots of different people there, like students, and parents, and teachers ..." She raises an eyebrow and I realize I'm not making it any better. "Well, it's not like I'm taking you to the prom."

"I should fucking hope not."

We walk through the parking lot, across the street and through the front doors. It's a little depressing being at school when you don't have to be, but even still, the Battle of the Bands usually has a good turnout, and there are a lot of people buzzing around in the front hall. It's not long before Deacon finds us.

"Heard you broke Hildebrandt's brain."

"I didn't—he was already—"

"Apparently it was more of a group effort," Kim explains.

"Oh. Like a lynch mob?"

I change the subject. "So is Ruth excited for the show?"

The real reason for coming tonight was to support Martha Dumptruck, but as one of last year's Citywide Champions, I kind of felt a certain responsibility to make an appearance. The rules stated we weren't allowed to compete this year, but I was still a little surprised when no one asked us to perform a song, or even help out with the judging.

"Richard Starkey! And you brought Annie Leibovitz!" Mr. Murdock is all smiles and wears an Odds *Bedbugs* t-shirt under a black blazer. For the first time I notice that there's a little impression in his earlobe where an earring must have once dangled. "Annie, how did that SLR work out for you?" Even though he's clearly forgotten her name, he engages Kim in a five-minute conversation about lenses, every minute of which becomes exponentially more technical and boring. I smile and nod stupidly, until Deacon takes me aside.

"Who's Annie Leibovitz?" he asks.

"No idea. Is Soda coming tonight?"

Deacon shrugs. "Does Soda show up to anything anymore?"

He's got a point. With the exception of a couple half-hearted band practices, I had barely seen him since that awful End of the Century show last month.

"Well, Annie ..." A few feet away I can hear Murdock's voice swell to a note of finality. "I should probably go collect my offspring and find ourselves a seat. *Ali, honey—*" he yells into the crowd "—don't drink all the orange pop, Sweet Pea. No, I said *one* glass—" And then he's gone.

"That guy is so weird," Kim says as the three of us make our way to the auditorium.

The Andrew Wyndham Memorial Auditorium is a wonder of modern theatre, the likes of which are usually reserved for community auditoriums or Catholic schools. Andrew Wyndham was this rich kid in the seventies who died of something—Lyme disease or not wearing a seatbelt or, I don't know, being a teenager in the seventies—and his parents donated a pile of money to the Drama Department because, apparently, Andrew had wanted to become an actor. I imagine if he wanted to be a football player we would've got a stadium.

We make our way inside and grab some empty seats. Deacon sits on my left and Kim takes the outside seat, just in case she has to "flee in absolute horror." Soon enough the room darkens and the spotlight shines on a lone microphone. There's a temporary awkward silence. Then, from behind us, an unfamiliar sound surges down the aisle. A battle cry. An air-raid siren. Roger Daltry at the end of "Won't Get Fooled Again." Todd Farkas flies past us, running down the aisle with his arms outstretched like an airplane. His goatee is a concentric circle around the perfect O of his open mouth. His oversized Cat in the Hat hat bounces as he leaps up the stage steps two at a time, and his oversized novelty sunglasses flash in the spotlight. When he reaches the microphone stand, he takes a deep bow, and his hat falls off to reveal springy curls recently dyed green and gold—the school colours. Everybody cheers on cue.

"*Hello, Mackenzie King*!" he bellows into the microphone.

The final syllables are swallowed up by a tsunami of shrieking feedback, and the clapping and cheering stops as approximately three hundred friends and family members simultaneously clutch at their ears. I turn around to see Mazz Moore calmly adjusting levels in the sound booth. He grins under a bird's nest of hair and finally gives Farkas the thumbs up.

"How's everybody doing tonight?" The crowd cheers cautiously, and the feedback threatens to swell again, but Mazz quickly wrangles it under control.

"Welcome to the Twelfth Annual Mackenzie King Battle of the Bands!"

The cheering doubles in strength, and Farkas is now unstoppable. "Aw, man," he says, "we got a *sweet* show tonight. Lots of homegrown talent from right here at Mackenzie King."

More cheering.

"Okay! All right. Let's get to it. Our first act tonight describe themselves as cross between Jimi Hendrix, Led Zeppelin, and the Red Hot Chili Peppers."

Deacon turns to me and rolls his eyes.

"Barf," Kim decides.

It's not because either of them dislike the "influences" Farkas has just listed off—I mean, who doesn't like Zeppelin? It's just because they're all safe and meaningless references. Why not say the Beatles? Why not say Classic Rock? Why not say "their influences include breathing oxygen and having listened to the radio at least once or twice in their lives"?

"Please give it up for *Holden Minefield*!"

As Farkas runs off into the wings, the curtains behind him open on a four-piece band, poised and ready. I recognize one of the guitar players from my Science in Society class. The drummer counts in and they launch into the first of three solo-heavy and hookless songs.

Drawing first in a battle of the bands is basically drawing the short straw. People need a little bit of time to warm up to the fact that they're being sonically assaulted, and the first few songs don't always stick. Plus, the soundguy is still working out the bugs, so if it's someone like Mazz—and inevitably it's someone like Mazz—it takes at least two or three songs just to get the levels right. By the time Farkas is back centre stage, everyone has forgotten all about Holden Minefield, partly because they were forgettable and partly because, in the fifteen minutes he's had backstage, Farkas has managed a costume change. He reappears wearing a vampire cape and long black wig. He eyes the crowd from behind a cloaked forearm.

"*Bevare*, ladies and gentlemen!" he vamps into the mic. "I varn you that our next act is very scary! Ah ah ah!"

His Count is way more Sesame Street than it is Bram Stoker, and I'm sure that whatever metal band is waiting behind the curtain is seething with gothic angst.

"*Spawned* from the *darkest pit of evil—*"

"*You mean your asshole*?" somebody shouts. Angry forty-somethings in front of us crane their necks to see who. Ten bucks says it's Rotten.

"—please velcome *Open Casket*! Ah ah ah!"

Farkas swoops away and the curtains part to reveal four young men who look like the result of a cloning experiment gone just slightly wrong. They all have the same long black hair and black t-shirts, and the same sallow, acned faces, but one is short, one is tall, one is fat, and one is incredibly thin. I recognize the short one from a Media class I took in grade eleven, but I don't think he lasted the semester. The fat one plays a few dreary chords on his B.C. Rich Warlock, and then they're off and running with their double bass drum pedal, their five-string bass, their white-noise distortion pedals, and their muppety monster vocals. I suppose you have to give them a little credit. Metal guys never win these things. Most of the audience watches them like they're some obnoxiously loud joke with no punchline, and still they soldier on, feet planted, necks hinging, hair swirling, completely lost in the ecstasy of their own sound. To commit so fully to an aesthetic enjoyed by so few is, in its own way, kind of admirable. After an abrasive fifteen minutes—the maximum time each band is allowed—Open Casket end their set with manic guitarmonies and a final note that stomps down like the foot of some giant demon.

"Holy shit. That was terrible," Kim says.

"Yeah," Deacon agrees, "but come on—you have to admit those guys can play. That solo at the end was *insane*."

Kim blows an unimpressed raspberry.

"What? You don't like guitar solos?" Deacon asks over me.

"No, I don't like guitar solos," Kim replies. "I don't like guitar solos, or choreographed fight scenes, or those video games—y'know—where you chase each other around a castle with guns? If I wanted to watch guys getting off on other guys, I'd rent gay porn."

Deacon's eyes go wide, and he's about to retaliate when Todd Farkas appears in a studded leather jacket and idiotic green mohawk wig and shouts down what has become a fairly chatty crowd.

"*Oi!* That's enough out of you lot!"

He proceeds to mumble incoherently through a weak cockney accent, squeezing in *blimey* and *bleedin'* and, incongruously, *slap and tickle* before he introduces Marathon of Hop, Mike Rotten's most offensively named punk band to date.

Like Count von Count introducing a metal band, Farkas's costume falls a little short of the cultural mark. As Marathon of Hop speeds through a series of fast, nasally pop songs, I'm a little surprised to find that Rotten, premier advocate for all things anarchistic in the U.K., has joined forces with a bunch of California-style neo-punks. Well-fed, jocky, and with hair carefully sculpted into liberty spikes or dyed like a lady's leopard-skin handbag, Rotten's goons pogo and posture on stage the way they've seen their favourite bands do on MuchMusic. How any self-respecting—or self-loathing—Pistols fan could suffer the suburban whining of mallrat punk is completely beyond me, but I guess that even nihilists have to make compromises.

They end their set with a cover of the Clash's 'Police and Thieves,' but even that manages to sounds bratty and ironic. Just before the curtains sweep them from sight, Rotten sneers, "Ever get the feeling you've been cheated?" I can't help but wonder if he's asking the crowd or himself.

And then comes the moment we've been waiting for. When Farkas reappears on stage, he's wearing a woman's wig and a floral-print dress like my grandmother used to wear. Deacon elbows me with the giddy pride of a hockey mom, and in a castrated voice, Farkas introduces Martha Dumptruck.

"*Seriously*?" Kim asks, disgusted. "That's what he thinks their most distinguishing feature is? Their *gender*? Like there's no difference between their rock band and, like, Wilson Phillips?"

Of course, as the band is revealed, Kim must realize she's been duped, even though she doesn't show it. All four members of Martha Dumptruck are dressed just as Farkas was—floral dresses, black orthopedic-looking shoes, and gaudy costume jewelry. Evie's wearing something on her head that looks more like a doily than a hat, and Ruth's got her hair up in curlers. In these ridiculous outfits, they launch fearlessly into their first song and make all the boys who came before them look like pussies. Ruth's bass pulses with authority, and between verses Evie launches off the drum riser, her fake bifocals swinging from a chain around her neck. The drummer and the other guitar player are spot-on. They're tight and ferocious. By the end of the first song, all four of them are sweating, their dresses are torn, and their updos are in shambles.

"Phew," Evie charms, "it's hot up here!"

"You're hot up there!" someone yells. Again, probably Rotten.

"Easy, tiger," she says, delighted. "We're Martha Dumptruck. This next song is called 'Bell Jar Superstar.'"

From Evie's opening riff, the song has a kind of immediate awesomeness that has the people around us nodding in pleasant surprise. Then, unexpectedly, it's Ruth who steps up to the microphone and starts singing. And, also unexpectedly, she's amazing. Over the PA, her voice sounds sweet and weary, like a tiny bird coated in rust. I look over and Deacon is grinning like a fool.

By the end of their last song, almost half the crowd is on its feet cheering and whistling. I'm convinced. Martha Dumptruck shall inherit the Earth.

"Well, I'd hate to follow that," Deacon says.

"We *did* follow that. Last month."

"Yeah. And look what happened. Man, we've got to practise more. Write some new songs. Step up our game."

"I know. Soda's been busy."

"Doing what?"

I shrug. "I don't know. Busy."

There's only a couple acts left, but it doesn't take a "local record producer," a retired music teacher, or the mustachioed sales clerk from Colosimo's Music—this year's venerable panel—to know that Martha Dumptruck have this battle in the bag. The crowd is just settling down when Farkas finally slouches across the stage for another lame introduction. This time he's wearing a tie-dye shirt, a peace-symbol pendant, bell-bottoms, a headband, and little round glasses.

"He-e-ey, man ..." He addresses the audience like he's knocking on Tommy Chong's door. "Hey, listen ... listen ... I've got some good stuff here for you." A few people in the crowd hoot. "This next band will really broaden your *mind* ..." More cheers. "They're about to get really *high*—" he pauses for effect "—on my list of favourite bands. Please welcome my *personal* friends, *Bunsen Honeydew*!"

I look at Deacon. His face is mobilized by disgust.

"What the *fuck*? Who in the band besides *Wheeler*—" he spits his name like a curse word "—even goes to this school?"

He's got a point. The rules are pretty clear on the fact that there needs to be at least two people in the band who currently attend Mackenzie King to compete. Thaler graduated last year, and the rest are from out of town. As the curtain opens and the band eases into their first groovy number, I see how they did it. They brought in a ringer. Jay Olejnik, one of the stoners who commune daily on the far side of the football field, is swaying in front of a set of bongos. Occasionally, he reaches out and taps one, not particularly in time. He and Sudbury Steve nod to one another like a couple of old pros.

"Well, I think that's my cue to use the little girls' room," Kim says before she disappears up the dark aisle.

After about a minute or so of innocuous, folky jamming, Matty walks up to the microphone. His head is a crown of dreadlocks as he addresses his people.

"Hey, everyone. I'm Matty."

He pauses for a moment, confident in the cheers that eventually follow the very mention of his name.

"Y'know, I think music is better if you can dance to it. Don't you?" There's more cheering, and the band grooves along behind him. The last few months of playing house parties, Whiskey Jack's, and the University Pub have endowed him with the breezy banter of an experienced showman. "Why doesn't everyone come on up to the front, and we can have ourselves a good time?"

On command, about nine or ten of the school's female hippie contingent—all friends of Matty—run boldly down the aisle with their homemade skirts and long, straight hair. When they arrive in front of the stage, they bounce around each other, their hands weaving toward the sky like stop-motion flowers. They laugh a little self-consciously, but also seem proud of themselves, as though they've shaken the heavy shackles of complacency.

Matty starts singing something about a sea serpent named Jarret, and the song takes off. The bearded drummer feels out a competent rhythm with the tall, skinny bass player. Sudbury Steve blows some thoughtful notes on his horn. Thaler the Wailer lives up to his name. And Jay Olejnik pretends to play the bongos. After a few minutes the song seems to reach its conclusion, but no one stops playing; they just get a little quieter. It's a good trick. Matty talks to the crowd as the band chugs behind him, maintaining a kind of musical momentum.

"Not bad, not bad ..."

From the back, a girl screams, "I love you, Wheels!"

"Thanks. I love you too." More screaming. "Here, let me show you how much I love you ..."

Matty walks back behind the drum riser and returns a moment later carrying a cardboard box the size of a small television. He puts his hand inside, and it resurfaces with a few snack-sized bags of Doritos. "We like to call this next song 'Munchies from Outer Space.'"

With that, he begins to toss the bags into the crowd. Some are caught by the hippie girls, while others slide across the floor. Upon seeing this, some of the bolder boys rush to the front and scoop them up. Like unwashed sirens, the hippie girls pull the Dorito-eaters into the circle of public display and they give in, smiling at the attention. Matty rains more chip bags into the crowd, the band gets a little louder, and I can feel an undeniable shift in the landscape as more and more people get up out of their seats.

Soon, Matty's repeating some lyric about "sunny weather" and "keeping it together," and the reverie has spilled up the aisles. It's a full-blown party. Woodstock before the brown acid. Jeannie Drew and Brandy Sawchuck have clasped arms and swing each other around in delighted circles. Even Mr. Murdock stands with his hands in his pockets and does a slouchy, head-bobbing shuffle. Most of our immediate neighbours have left their seats while Deacon and I stay conspicuously seated. A middle-aged mom in a fanny pack points at us and arcs her thumb toward the crowd, encouraging us to "Join in the fun!" We stare straight ahead and refuse to acknowledge her.

Bunsen Honeydew have bought the crowd's love with a little charisma and a lot of Doritos, and while I think the music is terrible, I have to admit that they're really good at making it. Plus, it turns out that there're a lot of people who seem to like terrible music, including the judges, who keep smiling at one another. Even though I'm not competing, I'm starting to feel like a sore loser. I wonder where Kim is.

'Munchies from Outer Space' winds down, but like their first song, it doesn't really end; it just mutates into something a little trippier. One by one, most of the instruments fall away, but Thaler's Gibson continues to creep out a rhythm drenched in spacey delay, until it becomes the only sound, the focal point.

"We've got one more for you folks—" the crowd continues to bounce in anticipation as Thaler plays "—but it's kind of a tricky one. I think we're going to need a little help from a very special guest ..."

I can see the curtain leg flutter. A concealed figure is waiting behind it.

"Please welcome to the stage ..." Matty drags the suspense for all it's worth. "... the winner of last year's Citywide Battle of the Bands ..."

I look at Deacon. He looks back, as confused as I am.

"Jesse ... 'Sodapop' ... Koskinen!"

The crowd erupts and Soda walks out onto the stage with a cheese-eating grin. He casually flares out a few notes from his Telecaster.

"So-daah!" a girl from the back of the room screams.

I look at Deacon again, but this time he doesn't look back at me. His eyes are fixed on the stage in disbelief and vibrating with betrayal.

Soda arrives beside Matty, who slaps him on the back and leans away from the microphone to say something. Soda laughs a silent, conspiratorial laugh under the music, and with that laugh, the contest is over. No one's saying it, but everybody knows it. Soda's appearance on stage is like the old Miss America stepping out to crown the new Miss America.

Matty cues his drummer, who lays down some slinky four-four time under Thaler's guitar. Sudbury Steve drops a few somber notes, and finally Soda joins in with a little rhythm. The melody's familiar, but I can't quite place it. I imagine Deacon knows exactly what it is, but I'm afraid to disrupt his catatonic rage. Everyone's still bobbing up and down, but not in the silly, self-conscious way they were before. They're all watching the band, waiting for their next move.

"We'd like to dedicate this one to the teachers ..." Soda tells them. "And Mr. Hawkes. This one's for you, too. Okay. Here we go ..."

Soda and Matty sing together into the microphone. They tell the crowd that they don't need no education. Nor do they need no thought control. If the music wasn't immediately recognizable to most, the lyrics are, and a delighted roar goes up from the crowd as though everyone simultaneously realized that this is their Favourite Song Ever. Soda and Matty shout at the teachers to leave them kids alone. They tell the teachers that, all in all, they're just bricks in the wall. The staff supervisors sing along, seemingly without a shred of irony or self-awareness.

Bunsen Honeydew and their new guest guitar player shake and shimmy through another verse and chorus, and the crowd is happy to come along for the ride. They've gone a little past the allotted fifteen minutes, but nobody—except maybe the other bands—really seems to care. Soda and Thaler end the song with an epic guitar solo that duels and intertwines and falls back on itself. Even Kim might have liked it, if she was actually watching the show. I wonder where she is.

Once the curtain closes and the insistent cheering and hollering for an encore dies down, Kim collapses into the seat beside me, breathless and sweaty.

"Sorry. Got caught in a dance party. Couldn't be helped. Your friend Soda is *amazing*."

Deacon stands up.

"I'm going to go see if I can find Ruth."

"Aw. You're not going to watch the last band?" Kim asks. "Isn't that what you musicians are supposed to do? Support the scene?"

Deacon fires a warning look and doesn't respond. He steps over us into the aisle and heads up toward the doors.

"Dude's got to *relax*," she says.

By the time Farkas gets back behind the microphone, about a third of the crowd has left, and another third is leaving. Farkas hasn't even bothered to put on any thematic outfits this time. He just introduces the final band by their forgettable name, and the curtains open on three small grade ten students doggedly performing unremarkable originals. I feel a little bad for them when the bass player invites everyone to "keep the party going" in a voice that cracks with inexperience, but not so bad that I accept his invitation, or even stay until the end of their set.

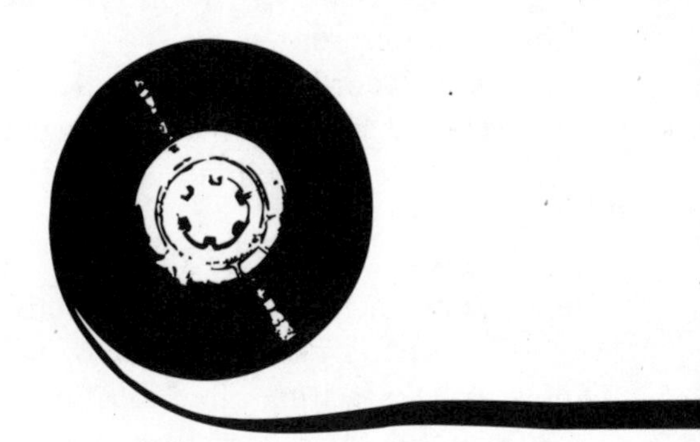

SIDE B
Combat Baby

"Thanks, but I kind of need to get going."

Since the disastrous end of our would-be date, and since she found out I got the job and she didn't, Molly has reinstated her old policy regarding extracurricular activities and me. "I have a lot of packing to do."

I can't imagine she's brought too many of her worldly possessions for a five-month employment experiment in northern Ontario, and I know her flight doesn't leave for another few weeks, but I'm not about to poke holes in her story. It seems pretty clear she's made up her mind about me. The weird thing is, I don't really care that she has a kid. Granted, it's not exactly first on my list of qualities that I look for in a romantic partner, but I think I could handle it.

Maybe.

There's a whole dynamic to dating a mom that I'm just not sure about. How do you make friends with a four-year-old? And who gets to explain why Mommy's friend is still hanging around the next morning wearing Mommy's bathrobe? More importantly, what happens if Daddy suddenly shows up? How am I supposed to compete with that? Still, I'd like to give it a shot.

We walk together a little ways down the hall, but after a civil goodbye, Molly takes the first available exit to the parking lot. I don't follow. Instead, I'm immediately ambushed by two representatives of Students' Council. They've been buttering me up all week, so I should have seen this coming.

"Hey, Mr. Curtis, you were in Battle of the Bands when you were in high school, right?" This is Kirsten, an impossibly tall senior wearing a Three Gut Records t-shirt.

"Didn't your band *win* a Battle of the Bands once?" This is Steph, a bespectacled and bohemian-looking kid from my grade ten class.

I imagine they're both getting their information straight from Jim Lodge.

"Mr. Curtis, you'd be a perfect judge! And we totally need someone else—someone who knows about music."

The truth is, I should probably start doing more extracurricular stuff now that I'm getting hired full-time, and my options are kind of limited. I'm not exactly sporty enough to help coach the football team, or smart enough to help out with Reach for the Top. I'm definitely not stupid enough to supervise another school dance grind-a-thon. Plus, the whole Battle of the Bands thing *is* kind of up my alley.

"You said yes?" The next day, Ruth disapproves. "When's the first audition?"

"First audition? I'm a judge. I show up and I judge."

"Sorry, my friend." Ruth leans down and crunches holes into a class set of handouts. "I did this last year at Churchill. They sucked me in with talk of my glory days as a bass player, but really, all those kids need is a warm body with a teaching certificate. Next thing you know, there'll be first-round auditions, final-round auditions, lyric sheet approvals, dress rehearsal, sound check. You didn't agree to do Citywide did you?"

"I said I'd think about it."

"Don't." She punches holes into another set of assignments. "Unless you want it to drag on for another month."

"I thought Lodge did all that stuff. He's Student Council Supervisor, isn't he?"

"My guess is that Jim takes a pretty deistic approach to school events. He needs a staff supervisor for all the menial stuff. And then later, he'll probably bring in a couple ringers for the actual judging. Thunder Bay music-industry types. You know—some guy with a ponytail who did sound for April Wine back in the eighties. That's what happened at Churchill, anyway."

It's not until a week later, during the second round of rehearsals, that I fully comprehend Ruth's warning. It's quarter to seven, I have a bagful of Great Depression essays I should be marking, and yet here I am listening to a prepubescent guitar player solo enthusiastically and inaccurately on an old Ibanez. The lead singer runs his fingers through his longish hair and prepares to belt out what seems like the song's millionth chorus: "I-I-I am suf-fer-iiiin' ..." The irony is palpable.

"Don't these guys have some kind of time limit?" I ask Steph over the suffering.

"Uh ..." She looks over to Kirsten. Kirsten looks back at me and shrugs. The band finishes, and the three of us clap politely.

"Okay, thank you ... *Katharsis*," Steph reads off her clipboard. "We'll let you know soon. Could you tell Dave his band is on next?"

They unplug and slink back into Rehearsal Room One where the other hopefuls are congregated. There are no windows here in Rehearsal Room Two, but I know that the sun has already set.

"All right," I announce, "we need to give these guys a signal to stop after we get the general idea. Some of these songs are going on ten minutes." I look around at the crowded arsenal of instruments—xylophone, timpani, tuba—when I notice the heavy Chinese cymbal hung a few feet away from me. I go to the percussion rack and help myself to a mallet. When the next band comes out, I'm so psyched about my plan, I explain it to them immediately.

"Okay, guys," I say, "we're running a little behind, so after three minutes, I'm going to bang on that gong over there so you know it's time to stop."

"Nice," the guitar player—Dave—nods.

"Totally Bonhamesque," the drummer agrees.

I like these guys already. Dave plugs a well-loved Firebird into the school amp, and it hums with promise. He strums it a couple times to check the tuning, then nods to the other players.

"This one's a cover," he says into the mic.

And then something kind of strange happens. Dave starts playing his introductory riff, and I have one of those moments where I totally recognize the song but can't place it. When the drummer and bass player kick in, Steph and Kirsten are already leagues ahead of me.

"Oh, I *love* this one!" Kirsten gushes. "Someone told me this song is about Thunder Bay."

"Have you seen the video for it on Much?" Steph asks her. "The singer is *so* hot. I think he's dating Emily Haines from Metric."

"*Contrary to popular belief / The heart's not a muscle, it's a barrier reef / and it's home to a hundred species of grief ...*"

When Dave starts singing the lyrics, it twigs, and I know I won't be able to listen for much longer. It's not that I don't like this song. The truth is, I hate how much I love it.

"*Just like a road that leads back to the start / There's no cure for the common cold heart ...*"

I look at my wristwatch. Dave's band hasn't been playing for more than a minute and a half, but I stand up, sidestep my way through the other instruments, and smash the giant cymbal. It bellows out, louder and longer than I expected. The song disintegrates and Dave looks at me with a little hurt in his eyes.

"Was that three minutes?" he asks into the microphone. "We didn't even get to the second chorus ..."

I glance at Steph and Kirsten, who also look a little confused.

"Thanks," I say. "We'll let you know."

There's an uncomfortable silence as we wait for the band to unplug and pack up. I feel terrible all the way through it. Dave's band wasn't half bad, and there's no way they could have known.

"Who's next?" I ask.

"Jonathan Heyen-Miller," Kirsten says. "The guy with the banjo."

The guy with the banjo walks in with a reusable shopping bag overflowing with electronic gear. As he sets up, I explain to him the whole deal with the gong, but I'm not as excited about it as I was before.

"Sure," he says when I stop talking, "sounds like fun."

I'm not convinced he's really listening. He's all elbows, bent over an effects pedal, plugging in his cord, and adjusting the knobs. He's a good-looking kid in an unconventional sort of way—tall and skinny, with strategically messy hair. Eventually, he looks up and seems to realize we're waiting for him to start. He takes off his thick-rimmed Buddy Holly glasses, adjusts his keffiyeh so it doesn't interfere with his strap, and squints in my direction.

"Aren't you my brother's Civics teacher?" he asks into the microphone.

"Oh, yeah," I remember, "you're Marshall's brother."

"Do you teach music as well?" he booms.

"No, just history." Unmiked, my voice sounds weak, unauthoritative. Instinctively, I clear my throat.

"Oh." He raises his eyebrow in a faint gesture of disapproval, and for a minute, he reminds me a little of his father, Dr. Michael D. Heyen, MBA, PhD, and Professor of Economics.

When he begins to play, his confidence is unnerving. The other acts so far have been a little tentative and inexperienced, uncomfortable under our scrutiny, but Jonathan's fingers move with an easy boldness and his foot taps out perfect time, like he's played in front of countless crowds. Like we're not even here. His music is a glassy pointillism at first, minimalist and clean, and I'm reminded that when you take away all the backwoods sodomy, there is something really beautiful about the banjo.

After he builds a good rhythm, Jonathan steps on his pedal once, and then again to loop it. He starts to sing, and while his voice isn't as trained as his hands, it's got this fragile quality that complements his playing. He finishes a verse, loops in some layers of vocal harmony, and continues with a second. The song is a little precious, but not without its charm.

"Usually," he says into the mic, as the music circles around him, "I'd add in some minor chords on the Micro Korg here. Maybe a little violin. I figured it was just an audition, so ..."

And then, as if to compensate, he begins to add more layers of banjo. Soon, he's looping in pentatonic scales and percussive thumbing. What started out a simple melody has transformed into a swirling monsoon of self-indulgence. It's been almost three minutes since Jonathan started, and the mallet is weighing heavy in my hand. I look over to Steph and Kirsten, who seem enraptured by what they'll surely describe later as "completely brilliant," and decide I've had enough. I jump up and hurry through the crowd of instruments. I swing the mallet back and then bring it home.

Lost in his genius, the banjo player is startled by the brassy explosion. He stops playing and steps on his effects pedal a couple times to stop the loops. The song dies abruptly. Steph glares at me with unveiled teenage annoyance, but it's the look on Jonathan's face that I find the most disconcerting. His expression changes from mild irritation, to wide-eyed anticipation, and finally to smirking glee, as he watches something just behind me. I turn around to figure out what he's looking at and discover that, in my eagerness to end the song, I've managed to topple the gong somehow, and its metal frame has fallen over and sliced right through the school-crested skin of the marching band's bass drum.

Jonathan lets out a solitary low whistle. "Nice one."

I curse, hopefully under my breath, and get up to assess the damage. Steph, Kirsten, and some nosy parkers from Rehearsal Room One gather around the damaged drum. I've already started composing the email I'll have to send to the head of the Music Department when Lois Kimball herself walks into the room with a conductor's impeccable timing.

"Hi, Peter," she says. "Thought I'd just come and check on—" In a flash, her cheerful façade fades. "How did *that* happen?"

"Lois, this was my fault," I say. "I'm really sorry. I'll totally pay for it."

But Lois has something else on her mind.

"You Students' Council people," she begins. "Every year, you come into the music room and use our equipment. You don't put anything away. You *break* things. This—" suddenly there's a tambourine in her hand "—do you have any idea how much this tambourine costs?"

For the record I do. I have the same one at home.

"This is a *sixty-dollar* tambourine, and I found some ... some *joker* in Rehearsal Room One banging it off the head of another student!"

"Like I said, Lois, I'm really sorry, but I'm not really a part of Students' Council, I just came to judge the—"

"And now *this*!" I cringe as she points toward my fresh damage. "This is a *custom-made*, twenty-four-inch bass drum skin. Do you have any idea how much *this* costs?"

I'd say about two or three hundred dollars.

"Our department doesn't have the budget for this!"

As I promise again to pay for my mistake, and as Lois continues to scold me, Steph, Kirsten, Jonathan, and a few members of a gloomily clad emo band watch our conversation like the world's most awkward tennis match.

Eventually, Lois leaves, mumbling something about having to speak to Mr. Trimble, and once again, I'm the only adult in a room full of uncomfortable silence.

"Okay!" I say clapping my hands together in a sudden gesture of forced enthusiasm. "Who's next? Blank Society? Great! Let's hear it."

The auditions finally end around quarter to eight. There's a bit of a bottleneck in departure when the singer from Katharsis gets a nosebleed. As I'm the only one with keys, I have to wait until it's under control before I can lock up. After the debacle with Lois, I'm not taking any chances. A few other students stay, either out of politeness or because they're waiting to get a ride from the nosebleeder. We stand around and make small talk as he stems the flow with coarse brown paper towel.

"So ... Mr. Curtis," a bass player from one of the earlier bands says, "do you play any instruments?"

Steph and Kirsten, the only students with any apparent knowledge about my musical past, are long gone.

"I used to play the drums," I admit.

"Oh. Cool. Anything else?"

"Nope. Just drums."

"Oh. Cool," the bass player says again. "I guess it's good just to focus on one instrument. You ever play in a band?"

"Not really." I'm just about done with this line of questioning.

"What kind of music do you listen to?"

That one catches me a little off guard. What kind of music do I listen to now? I know I'm not really old, but when I think about music these days, I start to feel my age. I still love music, but God, do you ever love music the way you did when you were a teenager? When you're fifteen, you've got all these fucked-up feelings and no place to put them, so you pour them into music. You find a song or a voice that says exactly what you want to say, only better and louder. And maybe that voice doesn't really have all the answers, but for a little while, you believe in it. You trust it. Now that I'm almost thirty, I've got more than enough places to put all my fucked-up feelings. I don't need some twenty-year-old guitar player speaking for me. I don't trust that voice anymore. I outlived Kurt Cobain.

"I've really been into Hank Williams lately," I tell the bass player, "and Johnny Cash."

He looks at me the way I imagine he looks at his parents. Admittedly, I'm one of those Johnny Cash fans who can only sing along with 'Folsom Prison Blues' (the part about shooting a guy to see him die, specifically), but nothing scares off a teenager faster than country and western. The interrogation coagulates just around the same time as the nosebleed, and I herd the kids out of the building.

It's pitch black already. I haven't had any dinner yet. As I walk, I weigh my options. While I know there's some leftover stir fry in my fridge, I'm pretty confident I'll wind up ordering pizza for one and eating it in front of the television. I think about grabbing a movie on the way home. It's been a long day, one that cost me a little more than I made, but I feel like I've finally escaped.

Video Hutch is one of those independent video rental places that's become accidentally hip since all the Blockbuster franchises descended upon the city like a plague of blue-and-yellow locusts. Video Hutch employees don't wear dorky shirts or nametags, and the owners use the somewhat alienating system of alphabetizing by director instead of title. How it's survived in a cultural wasteland like Thunder Bay is beyond me, but I'm glad it has.

"Jim Jaramusch fan?"

I don't recognize the woman behind the counter who's reading the back of my movie pick, *Down By Law*.

"Kind of. I liked what I saw of *Dead Man*."

"Oh, yeah," she remembers. "Johnny Depp? And that *score* by Neil Young?" She gives an enthusiastic whistle. "What's not to like?"

She's cute, in an unintentional slacker kind of way. Sandy brown hair and pale blue eyes. She's wearing an old Pixies t-shirt, and I wonder if she's a grad student at Lakehead. She's vaguely familiar, but if I ask her if we've met before, it'll come off as a pick-up line. Of course, I *want* to pick her up, but I don't want her to *think* I'm picking her up. Maybe I could ask her about school. Maybe I could tell her how much I like Neil Young and the Pixies. Maybe I could invite her out for a beer at the Phoenix, and then after a couple hours of conversation she'd wind up spending the night at my messy apartment, brushing her teeth with her finger, and sleeping in a borrowed t-shirt. Better yet, maybe she'd take me home to student housing and I'd fall asleep on a futon surrounded by fat, half-melted candles, dead roses, and an oversized Klimt poster. I'm just about to ask her what program she's in when the bell on the door chimes and I hear a voice say, "Hey, it's Mr. Curtis ..."

One of my keeners from second period walks in with her mom, and I realize I'm thwarted. I pay for my rental, smile a goodbye to the Video Store Girl, and narrowly avoid an impromptu parent–teacher interview. My basement apartment might be an empty, lonely place, but soon there would be pizza, Jim Jaramusch, and most importantly, no kids.

SIDE A
Salesmen, Cheats, and Liars

"Sorry. No kids tonight. Licensed show."

Frank's looking at me like he's never seen me before in his life. It probably wouldn't help to tell him I play drums in Giant Killer. He probably wouldn't remember us, and to be honest, I'm not really sure there is a Giant Killer anymore.

"Come on, Frank. We're on the list." I point to a lined sheet of paper he's got next to the cashbox. Already I can tell that this evening isn't going to go the way I expected it to.

"*She's* on the list." He points at Kim. "And she's nineteen. *You* don't even have a driver's licence."

Kim pulls me aside and lets the people behind us pay their ten dollars and slip past me into the bar. We walk back into the cold air outside. "Okay, here's what we're going to do—"

"You know, we could just rent a movie or something." To be honest, I wasn't all that keen on watching Bunsen Honeydew open up for some Toronto band anyway, especially if Soda was going to make another surprise appearance. "I haven't seen *True Lies* yet. If it isn't any good—" I rub her shoulder a little and smile "—we could always find something else to do."

"I can't," she says, shaking my hand off. "I promised Matty I'd get live shots for their album artwork. I'm a photographer, Pete. This is what I *do*."

She says it with a tone that suggests I have no respect for her art, even though earlier today she asked me with a straight face if I had learned the drums because guitar was too hard.

"Well, what am *I* supposed to do?"

"Well, if you'd *listen*, I was about to *tell you*. Go wait out by the back."

"You know they lock that door now, right? Ever since Gordie Miller snuck in and stole that case of—"

"I know, I know. Give me about ten minutes. If Janey's working in the kitchen, I should be able to sneak you in."

"What happens if you can't?"

"If I can't, then come back and meet me at eleven thirty. I'll be right here. Standing in this very spot." She points at her wine-coloured Doc Martins.

"Ugh. It's so complicated. I wish we had, like, walkie-talkies or something."

"Well, we don't. So sit tight." She kisses my cheek. "Happy Valentine's Day."

I start to walk around to the back of the bar when I run into Rita, red-faced and bundled up against the cold.

"Hey!" she says. "Can't get in?"

"No," I say, suddenly optimistic. "Any chance you can pull a few strings?"

"Sorry, dude," she says. "Apparently Liquor Control fined the shit out of Frank last week, so he's really cracking down."

"It's so stupid. We packed the place a couple months ago, and now I'm not even allowed inside."

"Aw. Don't worry." Rita pats my head. "You'll be able to play with the big kids soon enough."

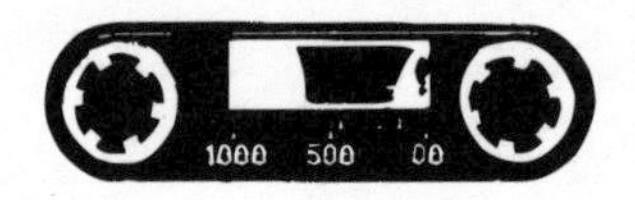

Behind Jack's, I pull my toque down over my ears and kick at little balls of ice on the ground. The door swings open too early, and a skinny guy in an apron throws out two black bags of garbage and eyes me warily. I fumble in my jacket for cigarettes, just so I look like I have something to do. He turns back inside and the door slams shut. I light my cigarette and wait. I don't worry so much when ten minutes come and go—since I've known her, Kim's never once been on time—but when nearly twenty minutes have passed and I hear the first few muffled chords of the unfortunately familiar 'Munchies From Outer Space,' I know I'm beat.

I might not have cared all that much if it wasn't for the fact that I hadn't really seen Kim for the last two weeks. First, she got "totally clobbered" by a bunch of papers due for school; then her dad paid for her to go with a couple friends to the Dominican during Reading Week. When she came back brown with the promise of tan lines, I thought Valentine's Day would be a pretty good excuse to regain some romantic momentum. My parents had gone to Kenora for the weekend, and I was planning on lighting a bunch of candles and making her dinner. Then she suddenly remembered she had promised to photograph Bunsen Honeydew, and I got relegated to being her plus one. Now, I'm not even that.

I make my way up Cumberland, and once I cross Park Street, I walk backward to protect my face against the razor wind. In the distance, I can see Trevor Beaucage, Brandy Sawchuck, and a couple other legal-aged stragglers file into the bar. Even Mr. Murdock is among the elect. He seems weighted down in a very adult-looking peacoat, and he holds the door open for a short, red-haired woman who's probably his wife. When they go inside, I turn around to face the cold.

"Uh, hello?"

In the back room I can hear the rattle of someone shaking up an aerosol can. The whole store reeks of spray paint.

"Where are your new releases?" I call out.

Eventually, a familiar figure appears. She's wearing a baggy Harley-Davidson t-shirt tucked into a pair of acid wash jeans. Her big, blonde hair is pulled back in a scrunchie, and she's admiring a freshly stenciled sign that says *Be Kind Rewind*. She doesn't bother looking up when she answers me.

"We don't separate current releases and older releases," she recites. "We organize the films by director." When she finally puts down the sign, she squints at me and snaps her gum. "Hey, aren't you Mikey's friend?"

I hadn't seen Deacon's sister for at least a couple of months.

"Yeah. I thought you worked at the Business Depot."

Deandra starts stacking returned videotapes on the countertop. "Well, Business Depot money isn't great, so I work here, too. Fuckin' graveyard shift. Won't make it to the bars before midnight tonight."

"That sucks."

"Yeah. Well. What are you looking for?"

"Uh, *True Lies*?"

She blows a small purple bubble and chews it back into her mouth.

"Seriously?" she says. "I mean, I know Valentine's Day is bullshit and all, but this is how you're going to spend it? Watching *True Lies*? That's fuckin' *sad*, dude."

There's nothing worse than being pitied by a pretty girl, especially if you spent a good portion of your freshman year imagining her naked. I puff my chest a little.

"Maybe I'll be watching it *with* someone."

Deandra smirks. "I *highly* doubt that, but look—" She unlatches the little door at the side of the counter and comes over to my side. I follow her across the store as she decodes the baffling library. "If you're going to lower yourself to renting a movie tonight, at least get something ... appropriate." She crouches down and traces her finger along the video spines. She finds what she's looking for, and on her way back behind the counter, drops it into my hands.

Four minutes later, I'm out the door and wondering just how she's convinced me to leave with some ancient artifact called *Roman Holiday*. It's not like I have anything against old movies. I just think they could be improved with a little colour and actors who don't walk around wearing suits all day. In any case, the issue is quickly resolved when the movie suddenly disappears from my hands.

"Hey, I didn't know they sold gay porn here."

I hadn't seen Brad McLaren all that much at school, even though he's in my fourth-period law class this semester. The few times he has shown up he just gives me the stink-eye from under the brim of his Montreal Canadiens ball cap. He passes the tape over his shoulder to Dave Greatorex, who menaces beside him like an escaped gorilla. I can smell the alcohol coming off both of them like aftershave.

"*Roman Holiday*, hmm?" Greatorex muses. "Wouldn't have guessed you were into Italian queers, Curtis. You like those hairy-chested wops, huh, *paisan*?"

"You know, I don't want to point out the obvious," I say before my brain can stop me, "but *you're* the ones renting a movie together on Valentine's Day. So, really, if we're going to point the gay finger somewhere—"

And that's when Greatorex breaks my nose.

"I'm tired of your *fuckin' mouth*, Curtis."

Once again, things aren't working out the way I expected them to tonight. First of all, I just assumed there'd be a little more back and forth with the Pussies, a little more gentlemanly repartee during which

I could talk them down or make a run for it. I'm pretty fast when I want to be. Also, I never imagined that Greatorex would just haul off and sucker-punch me. I'd never been punched in the face before, and I always expected it to be kind of like in a video game, where you can take a few hits before your opponent does any real damage. Apparently, this is not the case. Instead, there's a dull thud of meat and bone, a stabbing in my sinuses, and a blinding blur as my eyes tear up. I swoon back and forth like an inflatable clown, and he clocks me again in the jaw, which doesn't hurt quite as much, but sends me sprawling. My toque leaves my head, and I find myself down in the salty beige snow of the Video Hutch parking lot.

McLaren's voice is suddenly inches from my ear.

"Where's your bogan boyfriend, Curtsey? He leave you all alone tonight?"

Greatorex puts his boot on my throat and pushes down on my Adam's apple like it's a gas pedal. The hard rubber tread bites into my collarbone, and I can imagine a small *Size 12* imprinting itself into my neck.

"How's that feel? You like that, Curtsey? I heard you faggots were into this kind of shit—auto-erotic-whatever-you-call-it."

"Asphyxiation?" Brad offers.

"Yeah. That. You're probably getting off on this aren't you? You're *loving* this ..."

I can still hear him, but his malicious cooing gets further and further away. Brad's talking too. The nasally timbre of his voice is advocating for other forms of abuse. I feel the pressure on my neck diminish a little, and while I'm grateful for the oxygen, I know that whatever's coming next can't be good.

Then I hear the beautiful music of a *deus ex machina*. Deandra's voice. I can't quite make out what she's saying, but I have a feeling it has something to do with me.

"Fuck you, slut. Call the cops," Greatorex says.

I hear the music again, on the move now, with added percussion: the familiar rattling of a spray can.

"You do it and I'll kick your ass. I don't care if you're a girl, I'll—"

Suddenly, Greatorex's bluff is silenced by the shushing of atomized paint.

"*What the fuck*?" There's a hysterical edge to his voice. "*That's my dad's truck*!"

In an instant I'm free. The sprinkling of loose snow from their boots as they give chase is celebratory confetti. I turn over and watch them all clomp around the corner of the building chasing after her. I worry for a silent second about what they might do if they catch her, but by the time I get my feet under me, there's a wild slam and the sound of Pussies pounding on a locked door.

"You bitch!"

"Fucking cunt!"

As they continue their assault against the back door, Deandra appears through the front, grabs me by the wrist and yanks me inside. She locks the door, kills the light, and turns the *Come In, We're Open* sign to *Sorry, We're Closed*. For a moment, there's only the sound of my broken, hitching breath. The wall-mounted television silently broadcasts chiaroscuro images of Johnny Depp in a John Bull hat and face paint from a remote VCR.

"What if they break the windows?" I croak, consonants sticking in my throat—*Uht ih dey reak duh indows?*—and then proceed to double over in a coughing fit.

She waits patiently until I finish and then points to another sign that says *Smile! You're On Camera!*

"They can't be *that* fuckin' stupid," she says.

I shrug. I want to tell her that I've never fully plumbed the depths of their stupidity, but I ration my air instead. Through the glass we watch the simian form of Greatorex slouch out of the shadows and around the corner with Brad trailing behind. He puts a cupped hand to the window and peers into the near-darkness of the store. We crouch down, out of sight behind the collected works of Martin Scorsese and Ridley Scott. Greatorex hammers once on the window. It warbles a little, but doesn't break.

"You're a dead man, Curtis." His menace is muffled by the glass.

We wait a few moments and then peek around the video shelves. The two of them stand behind the enormous blue-and-white Ford inspecting the damage.

"Motherfucker!" he shouts. He kicks his own tire and then shoves Brad to the ground. He gets in the cab and starts the engine. Brad pushes himself up to his feet and races to the passenger door. They fishtail out of the parking lot, then accelerate down the street, a dripping black-paint cock and balls adorning the truck's tailgate. My face is still raw and aching, but I can't help but crack a smile.

The front of my jacket has soaked up most of the blood from my nose, but Deandra has me perched on a stool, one hand pinching my nostrils, the other holding a plastic bag full of broken icicle on my nose.

"Keep your head back," she says. "I am *not* cleaning your fuckin' blood off the floor, so don't make a mess."

The night continues to defy my expectations. I sit and watch the rest of the black-and-white movie on the store TV while she cashes out. It all seems very surreal. Things don't go so well for Johnny Depp at the end.

"Okay." She appears before me as the credits roll. "Let's see what we got."

She gently removes the plastic bag and lifts my nostril-pinching hand by its wrist.

"Well, I hope you weren't planning on doing any modeling soon, because you look like shit."

"Thanks," I tell her. She puts away my stool, and I stand around stupidly as she slides into a Ski-Doo jacket. "It would've been a lot worse if you hadn't ... I mean, like ... that was awesome. Thank you."

"All in a day's work. Speaking of which—" she looks at her watch and exhales. "Jesus fuck."

"What time is it?" I remember that, a million years ago, I agreed to meet somebody somewhere.

"It's time for you to go. *Chop chop.* No more convalescing."

Outside, the cold air feels good on my face. Numbing. Deandra's keys jingle, and on the ground I find my toque, matted with snow, and *Roman Holiday* in its plastic case. I hold up the latter up and show her, like it's a good omen, a relic from better times.

"Are you going to be okay?" she asks.

"Yes. Definitely. Wait. What time did you say it was?"

She sighs. "Well, it's still Valentine's Day. For another half hour, anyhow."

I realize I'm screwed.

Deandra jams her hands in her pockets and starts walking backward away from me. "Hey, if you see Mikey at school, tell him I'm coming over for supper on Tuesday."

"Okay. I will. Happy Valentine's Day."

I start jogging, and despite the ache of my face, I make pretty good time until I cut across the Holsum Bakery parking lot—which has turned into a giant skating rink—and go down hard. I get back up on all fours, teetering like Bambi, and press on. When I finally arrive at "this very spot," the place where Kim's Docs were planted mere hours before, she isn't there. Seconds later, the bells of Trinity United tell me that it's midnight, and I'm half an hour late.

Through the windows I can see that there's still a pretty sizeable crowd in the bar. It's possible that the band went on late, or she decided to wait for me inside. If I can't get in, I can at least wait for potential emissaries to come out. I watch a little group of people leave, but there's nobody I recognize. I reach into the inside pocket of my coat for another cigarette. I've started buying my own packs of du Maurier now. Health Canada Warning: Pretty Girls Make Graves.

"Ponyboy?" A hand comes down on my back. "*Jesus*. What happened to your *face*?" Soda stands there, guitar case in hand.

"Dave Greatorex."

There's a dark flash in his eyes. "That guy's a piece of shit. You okay?"

"Yeah. Hey, do you know if Kim's still in there?"

I don't like the sympathetic look he gives me when he answers. "I think she left a little while ago."

"She went home?" I offer the explanation I want to hear.

"No. She took off with the Bunsen Honeydew guys. They were going to party with the headliners at that band house out Highway 11/17. You know, the one Ariss Donaldson's parents run?"

The ground shifts a little under my feet, and for the second time tonight I feel clobbered. I play it off like it's no big deal, like Kim and I were having a see-you-if-I-see-you kind of night.

"How come you didn't go?" I ask him.

"I don't know. Not really my scene."

"Where you headed now?"

"Home." He switches the case from one hand to the other. "You should come over."

"Dude. *Look* at my face."

"Nothing a couple beers won't fix."

It'd been ages since I'd hung out at Soda's place, and a couple beers sounded pretty good right about now. "Yeah. Okay."

We start walking, and Soda points at my cigarette.

"Why don't you give me one of those things, and I'll show you how to do it properly. You smoke like a cancer patient."

"Fuck you. Smoke your own." But I give him one anyway. And just like that, we're cool again. No teary-eyed hugs or pledges of eternal friendship. Just cigarettes and the promise of beer.

"Play a little Floyd tonight?" I nod toward the guitar.

He flicks his BIC and a little cumulus drifts away. "Yeah. Matty got me up for a few songs."

"A *few* songs? What—do you practise with them now?" I try to sound casual, but the question is deadly serious.

"Not really. I just sort of wing it." I don't press the issue. For a moment there's only the sound of our running shoes squeaking on the packed snow. I worry that I've disrupted our new equilibrium.

"Dude, it's not like the three of us are married to each other," Soda says finally.

"I know. It's cool."

Then Soda sighs. It's the kind of deep, preparatory sigh that people sigh before they're about to bear some bad news. "Bunsen Honeydew got the opening slot for Sloan. In April."

"*What?*" How many times can a guy get sucker-punched in one night? "That's fucking *bullshit*."

"Maybe it's bullshit. *But—*" the gravity in his eyes lightens a little "—the bar wanted one more local band to open things up. I got Matty to suggest us."

"And?"

Soda makes a no-big-deal face. "It's ours if we want it."

"Of *course* we want it, but you're going to have to talk to Deacon." Soda doesn't say anything, and my words hang in the cold air.

As far as I knew, Deacon was still pretty pissed off about whatever part Soda had played in Martha Dumptruck's second-place finish in last month's Battle of the Bands. When Soda eventually suggested he should join his girlfriend's band if he was going to "keep PMSing," Deacon threatened to do just that. "At least," he said, "there'd be fewer dicks." Then we didn't practise for three weeks, and Soda and Deacon avoided each other at school like wounded lovers while I waited around for them to reconcile.

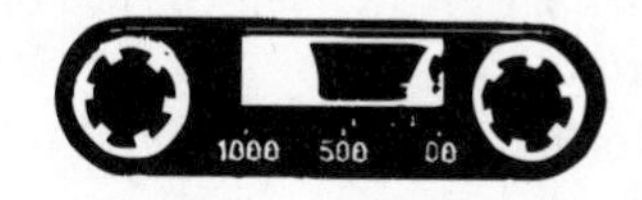

Soda's house is a slightly crooked, one-and-a-half-storey fire trap on Secord Street, kept erect by a load-bearing exoskeleton of once-white vinyl siding. It's next door to a hair salon called Contours that went out of business a couple years ago. The chain-link fence that separates Soda's house from the salon and from his neighbour on the other side (an Italian widow who always wears black and intermittently accuses him of stealing her mail) has been bashed nearly horizontal. Absurdly, the little front gate still stands sentinel, and even though we could walk past it, Soda always makes a show of holding it open and ushering me through.

"Mauri says he's going to fix the fence this weekend."

It's an old running joke. Mauri has been saying that as long as I can remember.

Four concrete steps that don't quite touch the ground lead up to a screened-in porch. Over time, the porch has become less of an antechamber and more of a chaotic storage facility for empty beer cases, a rotting turquoise armchair that never quite made it to the dump, and the shrouded corpse of a Broil King barbecue. By this time of year, the steps are just an icy booby-trap for mailmen, newspaper carriers, and door-to-door salesmen. We squeeze past Mauri's pickup and take the side door. The landing is littered with boots and shoes and serves as a no man's land between the upstairs and the basement, which Soda claimed when he was thirteen and has since used to live as separately as possible from his father.

We go down the stairs, and I wonder how the smell of damp never sticks to Soda. His room is a wide, unfinished cell with two by four bars, a concrete floor, and bare light bulbs. He's managed to outfit it with a bunch of stuff he's picked up over the years. Soda's never had any steady work, but his cousin brings him along on landscaping jobs when he needs an extra set of hands. Last year he sold a bunch of hash he got from this Vietnamese kid who always drove a Mercedes to school. Most of the money he's made over the years has gone into his black-on-black Telecaster and his eternally fritzing Peavey Bandit, but he's also got about five mattresses stacked Princess and the Pea style, an exhausted futon on which I've crashed more than once, a functional record player and tape deck, a TV, a VCR, and even a mini-fridge. Pictures of his favourite singers and bands, cut from the covers of music mags, are tacked to undrywalled framing or duct taped onto bulging plastic vapour barrier. *True Grunge: How Neil Stays Forever Young. Nirvana: Corporate Magazines Still Suck.*

Soda's prize possessions, though, are two milk crates full of old records that used to belong to his mom. He rescued them from the curb one morning when he was twelve. Mauri never really talks about Soda's mom, but every October nineteenth, he apparently gets a little extra wasted and pitches a bunch of her stuff. Soda figures the nineteenth is either her birthday or the day she died, but he doesn't want to ask. Over the years, Soda's rescued a jeans jacket, a mood ring, an eight-by-ten graduation photo, and the records. Sixty or so well-worn vinyl records. There's a lot of your standard fare in there, like those red and blue Beatles compilations, *Hot Rocks*, and *Rumors*, but there are some real finds too. Sam Cooke's *Twistin' the Night Away*. Patti Smith's *Horses*. Van Morrison's *Tupelo Honey*. The Diodes self-titled first album. Neil Young and Crazy Horse's *Rust Never Sleeps*. These were the records that taught Soda how to sing. There were even some country and western albums—Johnny Cash, Patsy Cline, Waylon Jennings—that I kind of snickered at initially, but when Soda started sneaking them on mixed tapes he made for me, they were actually kind of cool. Plus, I was always jealous that, unlike the *kachunks* of my compilations, the songs on Soda's tapes were bookended by the creak of the record player's arm and the soft, dusty crackle of the needle touching down.

On the floor beside his bed, I notice the dog-eared copy of S.E. Hinton's *The Outsiders*. I pick it up and thumb open the cover. A blue stamp reads *Property of McIntyre Public School* and underneath, a list of names ends in a blockily printed *Jesse Koskinen*. It's still the only book I've ever seen him read.

As Soda pulls opens the door to his mini-fridge and clinks out a couple cold beers, a small animal darts out from under the futon, runs past me, then stares at me defiantly from the other side of the room.

"What the fuck is that?"

Soda turns around, looks in the direction I'm pointing, and swears under his breath. The grey-and-white kitten walks across the floor, rubs its whiskers on Soda's pant leg, and lets out a screeching meow twice its size.

"My dad found this guy eating out of our garbage a week ago and let him in the house. Said he missed having a cat around, but now he never remembers to feed the fuckin' thing."

The kitten does a circle of my legs and then looks up at Soda accusingly with big green eyes. I bend down to pet him, but he runs to the other side of the room. "What's his name?"

The cat strolls over to a stack of empty pizza boxes near the stairs and sniffs at a grease stain.

"Pepperoni," he decides. "We better go topside. See if we can find him some food."

We climb back up the basement stairs, then a few more past the landing into the kitchen. Pepperoni follows at a distance. A prayer on the wall reads *Bless This Mess*. The sink is full of dishes, and the stove top is a Jackson Pollock of dried spaghetti sauce. A half-empty case of Crystal beer sits open next to the fridge.

While Soda goes spelunking in the pantry, I can hear a river of white noise rushing out of the living room. When I poke my head in, the television is a snowy beacon in an otherwise dark room. By its light, I find the remote control on the coffee table and turn it off.

"Hey ..." a groggy voice surges to life. "I was watching that."

A shadow pushes itself off an easy chair in the corner of the room. It lurches forward, suddenly illuminated by the light from the kitchen. I haven't really seen Mauri for a couple years, and he looks like he's aged a decade. His blond hair is now white and his moustache is murky against a few days of silvery beard growth. He steadies himself with both hands against the arm of a couch. Shoulders gargoyled, he stares at me without recognition.

"The fuck you doin' in my house?" His voice is a hoarse whisper of restrained rage, like Clint Eastwood behind a .44 Magnum.

"Uh, it's Pete, Mr. Koskinen. Pete Curtis." My face throbs, twice shy.

"I don't know a ... ?" He confers with himself, then directs another question at me. "You think you can just come into my house and turn off my television when I'm watching it?"

He takes another shambling step toward me, taller now than he seemed a moment ago. I'm relieved when Soda jogs in between us.

"Hey! Dad! It's just me and Pete. We didn't know you were watching that." He holds the remote out to him. "Here you go."

It's in his hand for a second before Mauri flings it against the wall. The batteries eject on impact and clatter against unseen furniture.

"Don't you suppose to tell me what I can do in my own goddamn house. This is *my* house."

Soda lets Mauri rattle off a few more incoherent accusations before talking him down. "No one's telling you what to do, Dad. We're just going downstairs."

We retreat through the kitchen and I watch Pepperoni attacking his food, pushing the little cereal bowl around the linoleum floor as he eats. We head down the stairs and Soda stops on the landing. There's a sudden heaviness.

"I don't think tonight's a good night to hang out, Pete. Sorry."

I realize he's showing me the door.

"That's cool. I get it."

"Yeah." His eyes won't meet mine.

In a short, awkward silence, punctuated only by Mauri cursing the blank screen of the television, I swing my arms back into my coat and tie up my shoes.

"Look," I say. "Tell Matty we'll do the show. I'll talk to Deacon. He can be very forgiving when it comes to Sloan."

Soda nods. I open the door and leave.

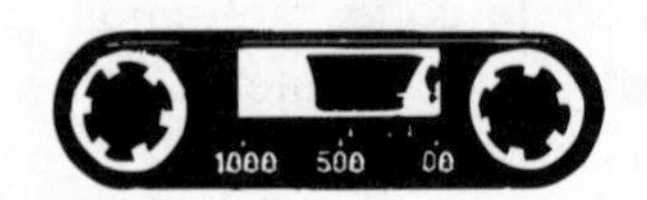

Against hope, I've constructed a dim fantasy that involves me walking up the sidewalk to my house only to find Kim sitting on the front steps—cold, repentant, head leaning on her hand. She'll look up at me with her big blue, shimmering eyes, see my ruined face, and burst into tears. She'll provide some perfectly understandable explanation for her departure, which doesn't involve servicing *any* members of *any* rock bands, and then we'll have really intense make-up sex.

Instead, I fall asleep on the couch, surrounded by unlit candles, just after Gregory Peck gets his hand cut off in the Mouth of Truth. A gift-wrapped negligee sits on the coffee table with a card that reads *Happy Valentine's Day.*

SIDE B
Romantic Rights

"Happy Valentine's Day, Mr. Curtis!"

Bethany Atkinson pulls a pencil from my 94FM coffee mug and taps it playfully on my desk. With her strawberry-blonde curls and her straight teeth a year or two out of braces, she's exactly the kind of girl who didn't look twice at me in high school.

"Any big plans tonight? With your ... girlfriend?" she fishes.

"Nope. Not really."

In my head, I can hear Sting advising against this kind of student proximity. Bethany's a nice kid, but these little chats before my new Ancient Civilizations class have started to make me feel uncomfortable. I guess it's bound to happen if you're a young(ish) teacher and you don't look like Gabe Kaplan in *Welcome Back Kotter.* Still, you can't be too careful.

After delivering a fairly painless lesson on Ancient Rome, I find Ruth in the staff cafeteria chewing on a bleak-looking salad. I order a tuna melt and sit down beside her.

"Okay, question: I've got a couple of no-shows in Ancient Civ. Who do I talk to about that?"

"Well," Ruth talks through the iceberg lettuce bouncing under her nose before she chews and swallows. "If you talk to the office, they'll tell you to call home. But if you call *home—*" she punctuates this second option with a raised fork "—they'll probably just tell you their kid isn't taking your course and that you should talk to the office."

"So ... ?"

"So, I'd let it sort itself out. This salad sucks." She pushes the plate away from her in disgust. "What are their names?"

"Uh, Alexandra Carter and Sasha ... something."

Ruth shrugs and takes her plate over to the wash bin.

"Sasha Mersault?" A couple seats down, Len Salwowski is negotiating a chicken burger with one arm in a sling. "I taught Sasha music, oh, about three semesters ago. She didn't show up for the first two weeks."

"Any idea why not?"

"She told me why not. She said the first couple weeks of class are 'bullshit,' so she doesn't come. Her words. Her parents seemed to be in agreement."

"Yikes. What happened to the good old days when Ed Rooney chased you all over Chicago for missing nine classes?"

Ruth reappears with a carton of fries and chimes in. "With our board, Ferris would have to miss sixty *consecutive* classes before he got expelled. And even then they'd just move him to another school."

"*Sixty* classes?"

"Who's Ed Rooney?" Len asks.

"Sometimes," Ruth says, sipping her Diet Coke, "the office will keep a student on the roster even after that. As long as the kid's enrolled, the school gets funding."

I have to laugh. It's a pretty good scam.

"So," Len says, changing the subject, "I'm getting a finder's fee for your big debut tonight, right? Ten percent?"

He's joking, I think, but it's not a completely unreasonable request. About two weeks ago, Salwowski knocked on the door of History Storage with his one good arm. Apparently, he had taken a header on a patch of ice a few days before, and the resultant broken bone constituted the third strike against Silverwolf, a weddings-parties-anything band, that had also lost its lead singer to vocal cord polyps and its keyboard player to a Floridian retirement earlier in the month. Salwowski had tried filling in on singing duties, but when he couldn't play guitar anymore he knew that Silverwolf was finished. They still had one show booked, though, a standing Valentine's Day gig at a bar called Shenanigans, and he told the owner, an old friend, that he'd try to hunt up a replacement act. Unfortunately, most of his contacts in the "biz," as he called it, had dried up. That's when he remembered that Ruth Kipling, the new English teacher, got an A+ in his choral music class back in the nineties, *and* that she once played in a band.

"It's decent money," he promised. "My wife and I were going to use it to fly to Mexico this year, but that's off. Now, we'll have to spend the Break with her brother's family in Beardmore. Ice fishing."

Ruth was flattered, but claimed she was too out of practice. And besides, she hadn't played in a band for years.

"Too bad," he said. "If you can think of anybody who can fake their way through 'Love Me Tender' and wants to make three grand, let me know."

When he shut the door, I stared saucers at Ruth. Three grand was more money than I had *ever* made with Giant Killer or Filthy Witness. Clearly those old guys knew what they were doing. Later that night, Deacon came over to watch a movie, and I mentioned Salwowski's proposal. That's when he told me that his wife still played guitar "like, every goddamn night." Within the hour we had cornered Ruth with the guitar tab and lyrics for a bunch of Valentine's Day-appropriate schmaltz.

Ruth protested, but eventually Deacon convinced her by promising that they could use their share to go anywhere she wanted on the March Break. She called Salwowski the next day, and he put us in touch with the bar manager.

"I was pushing for one of those all-expenses-paid tropical resort trips, with palm trees and a swim-up bar," Deacon told me. "Of course, just to spite me she's decided we're going to New York City which is probably just as fucking cold as Thunder Bay in March. Maybe colder."

I set up my drums in their basement and the three of us rehearsed every day after work for a week and a half straight. We learned 'Forever Young,' 'Nothing Compares 2 U,' and 'Never Tear Us Apart.' We learned 'Stairway to Fucking Heaven.' It was like endlessly reliving the last twenty minutes of a high school dance. We learned some more up-tempo numbers too, but the theme remained the same. 'Hello, I Love You.' 'Baby Love.' 'Tainted Love.' 'Love Cats.' 'All You Need Is Love.' 'Crazy Little Thing Called Love.' I never realized how much I hated love.

It had been almost a year since I'd even played the drums, but luckily, fifteen years of muscle memory takes a while to atrophy, and I got my chops back after a few practices. Deacon and I fell back into step pretty quickly, too. He was still a solid player, but his back-up singing had gotten a little rusty.

"Hey," I told him, "you should use your diaphragm."

"Your mom should've used her diaphragm."

It was just like old times.

Still, there was no doubt—as far as Deacon and I were concerned—that Ruth was the real talent. I remembered seeing her play with Martha Dumptruck years ago and thinking she was a good singer, but the last ten years had given her voice this cracked, whiskey-and-cigarettes quality that made me wonder if she'd been secretly moonlighting in honkytonks.

We tossed around a few band names but had trouble deciding on one.

"What about Hit Remedy?" I suggested. I'd been saving that one up for a while, but no one seemed all that impressed.

"Like Zit Remedy from *Degrassi*?" Ruth said.

"Why do fake band names always sound so phony?" Deacon asked.

"*All* band names sound phony until they're real," Ruth said. "Would you believe that Red Hot Chili Peppers was a legitimate name if you didn't know they existed? Or Death From Above 1979?"

We ran through a string of other possibilities. Nearly every musician worth his or her salt has a couple band names under glass for just such an occasion.

"How about the William Lyon Mackenzie Kings"?

"Too long."

"What about T-Rex Murphy?"

"Too punny."

"Phasers On Stun?"

"Too nerdy."

"Kid Charlemagne!"

Finally, Ruth put things in perspective. "Look, we're going about this all wrong. We're not some ambitious art-punk band. We're a cornball cover band playing a Valentine's Dance for a bunch of forty-somethings. We need a cornball name."

"Yeah, like Marvin Berry and the Starlighters," I said.

"Who?"

"Marvin Berry and the Starlighters. From *Back to the Future*. You know, the Enchantment Under the Sea Dance?"

"Now *that's* a great fake band name."

Deacon thought about it for a second and then made a final suggestion. "Ruth Kipling and her Gentlemen Callers."

"Holy shit. That's perfect."

"Wait. Why does my name have to be in the title?"

"You're the star, babe. Can't help that."

On my way to class, Vicky Greene stops me in the hall and says she's got something for me. Students stream around us like we're two sticks standing in a river, and her hand is warm as it presses something into my palm.

"See you tonight, Drummer Boy. Don't forget—you still owe me a drink."

"You're coming to Shenanigans?"

"Of course! It's a Valentine's Day tradition."

She smiles and disappears back into the current. I open my hand and look at what she put there. In slightly smeared block letters, a pink Sweetheart reads *Wink Wink*.

I get to my room before the bell and let the kids in. The gods of timetabling have cursed me with Civics yet again, but I have to admit, teaching it the second time around is definitely a little easier. It's not quite the nightmare of weekend planning and marking it was last semester. Some days, I actually feel like I'm kind of good at my job. Like today, I'm teaching this lesson on democracy versus authoritarianism. I've got Clash lyrics projected up on the overhead, I've got music blaring out of the English Department's thirty-dollar portable stereo, and I'm bobbing my head along to Topper's drumming, which is probably why I don't hear the knock on my classroom door, or notice Murdock until he's looking over my shoulder. A couple kids giggle. I turn around and wrench a stupid, welcoming grin to my face.

"Hey!" he shouts to the students over the music. "You guys won't mind if I borrow your teacher for a minute, will you?"

Thirty-two heads shake no.

"You can keep him," someone shouts out of the darkness.

"Brilliant."

His sudden presence in my room is grating, but as I follow him out into the hall, it occurs to me that I might be in trouble for something. I'm not sure what.

"The Clash, huh? 'Know Your Rights'? *Love* that tune."

"What's up?" I'm not interested in rock talk.

"Well, what's 'up,' Ringo, is I've just been touching base with the other Civics teachers—y'know, Gail, Mary, Doug, the whole lot—and it seems like they're all on schedule with the standardized agenda. Second week—examine political parties of Canada. Liberals, NDP, Progressive Conservatives—seems pretty straightforward. But here you are, kind of doing your own thing now, aren't you?"

Inspired by the spirit of Joe Strummer, I want to say something tough and smart. Something Murdock might have said himself when he was still a classroom teacher. Instead, I just stand there and pretend that his advice is well intended.

"Look, mate, I know what it's like, but sometimes you've got to toe the line for a paycheque. Trimble and the school board are really into these new 'standard practices,' and you need to be too. At least—" he looks at me meaningfully "—while you're still on ninety-day probation."

Joe Strummer rolls over in his grave as Murdock squeezes my balls just a little tighter. "I mean, if Trimble thought you weren't on board, you'd be *buggered*."

Having little other option, I nod stupidly.

"Okay. Glad we're agreed." He turns away and starts walking down the hall. As he does, I hear him sing another Clash song to himself: 'Clampdown.'

After the bell, I make my way down a flight of stairs to a little bathroom on the bottom floor that has only one sink, one stall, and two urinals. It's a little out of the way, but it's my shitter of choice when I've got the time. It's closer than the staff john, and kids usually steer clear of it. Granted, it is a little sketchy looking. Exposed pipes hang out of the ceiling like internal organs, and after someone ripped the mirror down off the wall, the school never bothered replacing it. Still, I like the fact that I can usually take a dump in private, and because it hasn't had a new coat of paint in almost twenty years, the stall provides an interesting historical record. There's politics (*Clinton inhaled*), romance *(Tina Lessinger takes it up the ass*), and culture (*SLAYER RULES*). Weirdly enough, it's also a veritable Louvre of cock drawings: cocks going into vaginas, cocks going into bums, sad cocks, smiling cocks, cocks fountaining semen willy-nilly. But the best graffiti is what's scratched into the back of the stall door. There's a thoughtfulness to this vandalism, as though the young men responsible for it appreciated that they were providing material for the ages. From my U-shaped throne, I review some old favourites. In black marker, someone reminds me to *Question everything!* In blue pen, someone else asks *Why?* The proclamation to *END TYRYNY* has been amended to *END the TYRYNY of spelling*. Finally, my eyes wander to the bottom of the door where, less cleverly, four-inch block letters spell out a simple message: *FUCK MURDOCK*. I feel a little better after reading it, until I start to wonder how long it'll be before someone scratches my name into the paint.

That evening, a portable billboard in the Shenanigans parking lot invites us to the *8th Annual Cupid Bash*. I can't help but picture a mob of angry singles beating the little cherub until he bursts open and bleeds cinnamon hearts. When we walk inside, the half-assed majesty of the bar reveals itself to us. Between sponsored neon signs for Molson and Labatt, red-and-white streamers swoop lazily above us. Metallic paper hearts and cupid silhouettes appear sporadically on doors and counters. In the corner, there's a pretend wedding arch of pink and white balloons and a sign that cheerfully announces future participants as *Just Married.* Every tabletop has been outfitted with a tablecloth, a dish of foil-wrapped candies, and one long-stemmed rose in a beer bottle. The manager, a goateed, stocky guy in his late forties, appears from the back of the bar with his arms outstretched.

"All right, the *band* is here. The *talent*! You must be Ruth—" he shakes her hand "—and you must be the Gentlemen."

"Gentlemen *Callers*," Deacon corrects him.

"Gentlemen Callers. Right. I'm *Aries*."

We take turns shaking his hand and saying our names. He repeats his each time, as if we hadn't just been a part of the same conversation.

"Michael."

"Aries!"

"Peter."

"Aries!"

Aries loves Valentine's Day and Aries loves life.

"Hey, maybe you guys can let me come up on stage with you later. I'll play the tambourine. Or the cowbell. '*More cowbell!*' You know? Like on *Saturday Night Live*? '*More cowbell!*' Love that."

Never have I met a more enthusiastic bar manager. In fact, for all the years that I played in Thunder Bay and Toronto bars, I don't think I'd ever met the manager until I tracked him down at the end of the night in some fluorescent-lit back room where he'd glare at me until I asked for our tiny cut of the door. Instead, Aries pays us up front with an envelope full of crisp green twenty-dollar bills, then directs us to a dressing room complete with bottled water and a vegetable-and-hummus platter.

"Drinks are on the house. Just tell Solly, our bartender, what you want. Uh, what else? Todd, our soundguy, should be here in about an hour, so if you want to set up now that's cool, or you could order something from the kitchen while you're waiting. Our cook Jorge makes really great empanadas, if that's your thing."

Eventually Aries leaves us to stare at each other and wonder aloud if he's made some kind of mistake.

"I don't know about you," I tell my bandmates, "but I'm getting a free beer before he realizes we're not famous or important."

Load-in and set-up take a little while, but every time we're about to shoulder something heavy—Deacon's bass amp or the rolling coffin that houses my drum hardware—Aries suddenly appears and insists on helping out. When the soundguy arrives, he is neither stoned nor surly and demonstrates a rare attention to detail during sound check. After, we spend about ten minutes sitting in our dressing room before we feel stupid and anti-social and decide to sit at the bar and make friends with Solly and Jorge. Slowly but surely, Shenanigans begins to fill up with thirty- and forty-somethings.

"Sure beats huddling around a mickey behind Jack's," Deacon says.

"Or hoping that ten of your friends show up so you're not playing to the back of the room," Ruth says.

As I watch the crowd mingle to the sounds of Shania Twain, I worry we won't go over quite as well as our predecessors. The guys in Silverwolf, I'm sure, were pretty crack musicians and far better at crowd-pleasing banter and bad jokes than we could ever be. I order another beer from Solly to drown the butterflies.

I'm a little surprised when Aries reappears and gently suggests we start making our way toward the stage. I know the arrangement is that we'd play two one-hour sets starting at nine o'clock, but the concept of a show actually starting on time is completely novel. What's more, we don't have to stall and wait for more people to show up. The bar is at capacity. I've never played in front of this many people, and as I walk through the crowd toward the stage, I wished we were playing our own songs and not a bunch of covers. I sit down behind the drums, pick up my sticks, and once again, see the crowd through stage lights.

"Happy Valentine's Day!" Deacon says cheerfully into the mic. "This is Ruth Kipling—" he pauses abruptly for unexpected cheering "—and we're the Gentleman Callers!"

Egged on by all the unearned enthusiasm, we break into our most thematically appropriate song of the evening—Sam Cooke's 'Cupid.' Without any coaxing, the crowd is on the floor, dancing, swinging each other around, getting a good return on their babysitting investment. When we finish, they erupt like we're the Beatles on Ed Sullivan. Deacon looks back at me with an astonished grin and pulls a *What the fuck?* face.

Four songs deep into the first set, we are rock gods. We slow it down a little, because it is, after all, a Valentine's dance. Ruth does a really pretty acoustic version of 'Forever Young' by Alphaville, and when she's finished, some guy sporting a salt-and-pepper mullet repeatedly demands Def Leppard. When we just *happen* to have "Love Bites" in our back pocket, he celebrates with the *joie de vivre* of one recently laid in a Pontiac Fiero. He slow dances close to the stage with his hands all over a small, embarrassed-looking woman in high-waisted mom jeans. When the song ends, the guy disappears, only to return soon after balancing three shots of Jägermeister "for the best fucking band in town." I realize, as I down the mediciney syrup, that I've never felt like such a superstar or like such a shill.

There are some familiar faces in the crowd. Despite her pleadings to the contrary, Ruth's adorable parents have made an appearance and stand quietly back near the bar, smiling proudly whenever the crowd cheers, frowning only when someone yells at Ruth to "take it off." Deacon's sister Deandra is back there too, with her second husband, Tommy. They stand arm in arm wearing matching leather jackets and Sorels.

Vicky's on the dance floor, as promised, bouncing around in a tiny skirt. Her husband is nowhere to be seen. I try not to make eye contact, but inevitably do.

We finish our first set with Glass Tiger's 'Don't Forget Me (When I'm Gone)' and promise our new fans that we'll definitely return after a short break. Aries is quick to grab the microphone as we get off the stage and insist that the crowd reward our hard work with yet another round of applause. As I make my way to the washroom, I can hear him announce that they will be serving free champagne and taking Polaroids at the fake wedding booth. A woman in a sequined crop top and stirrup pants, who's clearly old enough to be my mother, plants a sweaty hand on my forearm and pulls me toward her.

"Wanna get married?" she yells boozily over the din. I smile like her joke is hilarious. "Y'know, it's nice to see some young blood up on the stage."

"Thanks. It's a fun night." I start to walk away, but she grabs my arm again. My bladder screams in protest.

"What are you guys called?"

"Uh, Ruth Kipling and her Gentlemen Callers."

"Gentlemen Callers? Honey, you can call me anytime." As her laughter disintegrates into a phlegmy death rattle, I smile and escape. I make a weaving beeline for the urinal and drain myself of three pints and the Jäger shot. As I zip up my fly, it occurs to me that I'm fairly drunk and dying for a cigarette.

Aries cranks the house music—'Mambo Number Five'—and I slip through the shockingly bright kitchen, wave at Jorge, and duck out the back door. The back of the bar is lit by a buzzing fluorescent tube, and as I blow smoke it travels in and out of shadow. Once Soda tried to teach me to blow smoke rings, but I never really got the hang of it. They always came out as billowy blobs.

The little clock on my cell phone says that it's quarter after ten. It's probably too late to call, but I dial her number anyway. It rings a couple times, then a mechanical voice tells me to leave a message.

"Hey, Molly," I say, trying not to slur my words, "Ruth and I are playing this lame Valentine's show at Shenanigans, and it would be really fun if you came out. I mean, if you're still in town. Which, I think, you probably aren't. But if you are, you should come." I punch the red button before I make a more gigantic ass of myself. At least I'll have something to regret in the morning.

It's funny. When I was younger and I stepped away from the crowd, I almost always hoped that some pretty girl would notice me standing alone and come talk to me. Now that I'm a little older, I find that I just want to be left alone. So of course, Vicky Greene shows up with two plastic champagne flutes. Her top half is all puffy winter coat and her bottom half is all legs.

"You really should be buying one of these for me." She holds out a glass and I take it. "You still owe me a drink."

"Aren't they free?"

"That's beside the point."

We make a clicky *cheers*, and I suck down half my glass in one go. It's sickeningly sweet.

"Can I bum a smoke?"

I reach into my pocket and pull out a fresh cigarette. She puts it between her lips and when I flick my lighter, she pushes her hair behind her ear and leans in like an old pro.

"I didn't know you smoked."

She exhales like she's been holding her breath for a very long time. "Nobody actually *smokes* anymore, Pete. Everyone's just in various stages of quitting."

She has a point. I had planned on quitting for New Year's, but never got around to it. It would've been my third attempt.

"I thought Jamie was coming tonight."

She looks sideways at me and then contemplates the red ember between her knuckles. "You know, so did I. I really believed him this time. Jamie's been telling me he's going to come to this thing for years now, and every February he finds some reason not to. Yesterday, he suddenly decides he needs to see his parents in *Dryden* for the weekend. Says his mom is sick again."

She says *Dryden* like the word tastes bitter, and in the pale light, her eyes shine and shift behind water. I imagine her ten years ago, prettier than any teacher should be, recently married to a local hockey hero turned teacher turned vice-principal. She must have felt like she had climbed above all the bullshit, like there was no way life could reach up and drag her back down to grocery stores lineups and bad sitcoms and putting off kids for a career. And now she's out here with me—some guy who used jerk off to her staff photo in the 1993 *Lyons' Pryde*—and I barely even give her the time of day.

"Are you guys going to play any Matchbox Twenty tonight?" she asks.

"Uh, no. Sorry. We don't know any."

"Oh. How about the Cars?"

I smile. "Let me see what I can do."

She smiles too.

We finish our champagne and go back inside through the kitchen. When we pass the bar I order a beer and something for the lady.

"White wine spritzer?" she asks the bartender.

We cheers again, a proper clink, and as I drink I see Ruth and Deacon standing close to the stage talking to a woman wearing a lot of scarves—Matty Wheeler's mother, I think. Ruth notices me with *Madame Greene* and gives me a little frown. She holds up her wrist and taps an invisible watch. I nod okay.

"Got to get back to it," I tell her.

"The Cars," she reminds me.

The second set seems to go by a lot faster than the first. The crowd is still enthusiastic, but it's clear that our novelty has worn off a little. We get another round of shots—Jack Daniels this time, from Aries—when we play 'Honky Tonk Woman.'

"More cowbell!" he yells into the microphone, and everyone cheers.

People seem to like our minimalist treatment of 'Stairway to Heaven' and we get a final burst of frenetic dancing when we play 'Love Shack,' but the dance floor is already starting to clear (babysitters charge time-and-a-half after eleven) when we end with 'Drive' by the Cars. By request.

"Well, you sure made me wait for it," Vicky tells me when I find her afterward. She's sitting alone at a table with another white wine spritzer.

The sun's coming up when I take Roach's Taxi home from Vicky's house in Fort William. I sit in the back and try not to make conversation with the driver.

"Mind if I smoke?" he eventually asks me.

"Not if you don't," I tell him.

I reach into my pocket for my pack, but instead I find the fake wedding photo. Vicky and I stand awkwardly still like the weird-looking farm couple in that American Gothic painting, but without the pitchfork. I pull apart the Polaroid into very small pieces.

The cabbie cracks his window to let the smoke out, and the morning air feels cold and good on my face. I crank my own window down and throw the evidence into the air like rice at a wedding.

"Hey, man," the cabbie says, "I could get fined for littering."

"You could get fined for smoking, too," I tell him.

An unfamiliar melody sounds in my pocket. I fish out my cell phone and, sure enough, I've managed to miss three calls: *Molly Pearson, 10:41 pm; Molly Pearson 11:02 pm; Molly Pearson, 11:36 pm.* There aren't any messages.

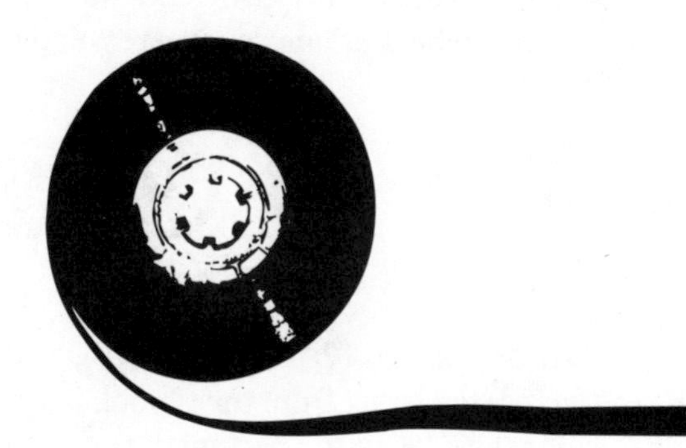

SIDE A
The Party Rages On

"Dude, I called you, like three times."

"Well, maybe you should've left a message." I'm starting to hate it when she calls me *dude*.

"I'm not leaving a *private* message for you on your *parents'* answering machine. I'm just *not*. You need to get your own phone line."

Of all Kim's many talents, the one I like the least is her knack for shifting blame. Let it be known—Kim never is, never was, and will never be at fault. For anything. It was the same deal after the whole Valentine's debacle. *I* was the one who didn't show up at Jack's, so what was she supposed to do? Wait around all night? How was *she* supposed to know that I was busy getting into some stupid fight?

I tried to give her the cold shoulder and broke down after two days. I made myself crazy thinking about what her eyes look like when she's unbuckling my belt, what her breasts feel like when she presses against me, and how her mouth sort of curls up in the corners, even when she's angry. I couldn't stand the thought of giving that up. Or letting someone else have it.

And anyway, it's not supposed to be easy. I mean, if it was all happily ever after, if there was no boy-loses-girl stuff, it would be boring. Things are supposed to get a little screwed up before they get better. Or at least, that's what I tried telling Soda when she bailed on me again last weekend.

"That's bullshit," he said as we watched *The Wedge* and drank beer in his basement. "You just want her because you can't have her."

"What do you mean 'I can't have her'? I *have* her all the time."

"Right. She's on a real short leash."

"Dude, she's my girlfriend, not a cocker spaniel."

"Maybe. But one day you're going to call and she's not going to come."

After lunch, Kim pulls the Divorcemobile into the Mike's Milk across the street from the school. Dirty snow and chocolate bar wrappers line the edge of the parking lot.

"I'm going to buy smokes, so I'll drop you off here."

I know for a fact she's still got three quarters of a pack minus the one I stole after we ate.

"No sweat," I say, pushing out of the car. "I'll call you later."

I had been hoping for a nooner, but Kim said she got her period, so I had to settle for Taco Time instead.

"Hey," she shouts out the window. "Happy birthday."

I give her a little salute and start walking.

So far, I'd say the age of majority has been a bit of a bust. The fact that you can decide who runs the country but can't buy beer is a cruel joke. At least when you turn sixteen you can get your licence—not that I have—but it's an option. The problem with becoming an adult is that nothing really good comes with it.

I guess my parents did buy me a swanky watch, but it looks super expensive and makes me a little nervous. My dad was kind of disappointed when I decided I didn't want to wear it to school today. He told me that part of being an adult means not always dressing like a hobo. So really, I got a lecture wrapped in a gift. Awesome. In any case, it's a better present than the one I got from Mother Nature.

I get pimples now and then, but it's rare that I get one this big. Already this morning, I've noticed my parents staring at the bright red dot on my forehead like they're worried someone's trying to assassinate me from a distance. Without warning, it birthed itself fully formed from my forehead, like Athena from the head of Zeus. I tried to pop it, but all I managed to do was create an angry, swollen lump that was going to make me feel self-conscious for the rest of the day. Our bodies betray us in the end, but we do our fair share of betraying them long before that happens. Luckily, the thing's high enough on my head that I can cover it with a hat. I know the whole wearing-toques-inside thing is getting a little trendy, but it's also the most practical way to hide my shame.

As I walk up the front steps of the school, I hear the bell ring, but I know Mr. Murdock won't care if I'm late. OAC Art has been pretty awesome so far. I'm not sure how much I've learned about watercolours, charcoal, or sculpture—all promised in the course description—but it's been fun listening to Howlin' Mad go off on whatever tangent he happens to be on that afternoon. Last week, he spent an entire class talking about David Lynch movies and then two more classes showing us *Blue Velvet*. This week he was all about Andy Warhol, Edie Sedgwick, and the Exploding Plastic Something-Or-Other. I'm not sure what it has to do with the curriculum, but I don't care. I'd rather hear about that stuff than secondary colours and crosshatching. When I get to class, he's already blaring *The Velvet Underground and Nico*.

"Mister Starkey!" he says over the music as I walk into the Art Cave. He motions upward to the speakers he's wired into the ceiling. "Moe Tucker. Played drums standing up. Didn't use cymbals."

I smile and nod in agreement, as if I know exactly what he's talking about, then take my seat on the stool next to Todd Lupinski, one of the headbangers from Open Casket, who's spent the last three classes sketching a disturbingly anatomical depiction of a man being flayed alive by tiny demons.

"Malachi," Murdock calls over to Todd. "You're a nihilist. What do you think of the Velvet Underground?"

"I think they suck, sir."

"Ah," he says with a squinty look of approval. "A man who knows his own mind."

I adjust my toque and take a pencil out of my backpack.

Room 242—the Art Cave—is an enormous, windowless studio—four times the size of any other classroom in the building. It was originally built as part of a tech wing that was added when it was clear Mackenzie King could no longer survive as a strictly collegiate school. At any given time, the room is a chaos of wall-sized, half-finished paintings, melted-looking sculptures, and whatever crazy shit Murdock has deemed necessary to import. Some of his trophies include a V8 engine, which he apparently rescued from the wreck of his 1987 Trans Am, a life-sized model skeleton he christened "Geddy," and a blown-up, framed photograph of a younger Ken Murdock shaking hands with a younger Bono (yes, *the* Bono). In the back, there's an old potter's wheel and a kiln that hasn't baked any glaze since our class started. Past that, he's partitioned off an area he calls his "Quarters," where he occasionally invites the particularly inspired or discouraged student for a "little chat." Though I haven't seen it myself, there's apparently an old pullout couch back there, which has led many to speculate that Murdock uses it to either nap at lunch, bed pretty seniors, or pass out after an evening of artistic frenzy.

Today's lesson is a continuation of yesterday's. New York, the Factory, Lou Reed, Chelsea Girls. He talks a little about printmaking, and in a spontaneous burst of enthusiasm just before the bell, tells everyone we're going to start silkscreening on Monday. I doubt it'll actually happen. It's not that he doesn't mean it at the time, but Murdock throws a lot of ideas at the wall. I've learned to wait and see what sticks. Once in grade nine he promised us a trip to Kingfisher Lake so we could paint landscapes "the way they were meant to be painted: outdoors!" For weeks, I waited for the field trip permission forms to materialize and fantasized about sharing a cabin with Alyssa Becker, the hot hippie girl with patchwork pants who painted watercolours every day and listened to what I could only imagine was *American Beauty* on her Walkman. It never happened.

Murdock's own fifteen minutes of fame went down in the early eighties. Not long after he moved to Canada, he painted that portrait of Terry Fox called *Marathon*—the one they still use when they do Run for the Cure fundraisers in high schools. He did some other stuff too, but nothing really successful. One time, my dad pointed out one of Murdock's paintings in this big Canadian art compendium he won at a shag. I can't imagine why you'd want to become a teacher after making it kind of big in the art scene, but Murdock seems happy and does things on his own terms. If I ever fuck up so badly that I have to resort to becoming a high school teacher, I'd want to be like him.

The *last* person I'd want to wind up like is my fourth-period law teacher. His name's Mr. Kohler, but everyone calls him the Führer. In a lot of ways, the Führer's classroom is the exact opposite of Murdock's. It's bleak with fluorescent lights and walls the colour of a hospital waiting room. He hasn't put anything up on the walls except a framed copy of the Canadian Charter of Rights and Freedoms, and a yellowing piece of chart paper that lists, in red marker, *Classroom Rules of Conduct.* Some of his laws include No profanity. No chewing gum. No listening to Walkmans. No speaking out of turn. You get the idea. Not a lot of laughs in OAC Law.

Signing up for the course seemed like an obvious choice when I decided I wanted to be a lawyer, but I had no idea I'd have to finish out my day falling asleep to the sounds of some old German guy reading straight out of a textbook. He also wears the same sweater every day, which has the effect of making every class seem like a tiny part of one long and fantastically tedious lesson.

Although it's on the other side of the school, I manage to get to Kohler's room before the bell rings. Even still, I'm one of the last to arrive.

People tend not to be late for this class, because people tend not to like getting berated in front their peers. Unfortunately, before my ass can even hit the seat, the Führer's pointing at my head and then back to rule number seven on his poster.

"You're indoors now, Mr. Curtis. Please. Take off your hat and stay awhile."

Fuck. Of all the bullshit, arbitrary rules I hate, the one I hate most is the Hat Rule. Other teachers have backed off on the policy, probably recognizing it for what it is—an archaic tradition from a long-dead era—but Kohler's the type that'll enforce a rule until it's off the books. Reluctantly, and now with the class's undivided attention, I pull the hat from my head and reveal my disfigurement.

"Jesus *Christ*, Curtis. Can you see out of that thing?" Brad McLaren asks. A couple of his Pussy buddies snort.

It's been real fun having McLaren in this class. When he's not doing his best to publicly humiliate me, I can feel his eyes on the back of my head, plotting my death. For a while, I thought maybe the whole thing with Greatorex's truck would just blow over. Nope. A couple weeks ago, when everyone was busy doing group work, I got called down to guidance to talk to Mrs. Leedy about this pre-law scholarship at U of T. When I came back, my coat was missing. It showed up a couple days later duct taped to my locker door, all cut to ribbons and smelling like piss. There was a note pinned to it that read *YOU'RE DEAD FAGGOT.* Deacon drove me to the Sally Ann, and I found this cool blue parka like Han Solo wore in *Empire Strikes Back* for twelve bucks. My parents just assumed I was trying to be hip, and that the two-hundred-dollar Sierra Designs coat they had bought as a Christmas present last year was still hanging safely in my closet. Still, it didn't solve the problem of my imminent demise.

Kohler rounds out my afternoon with an agonizingly dry lecture on constitutional law, and I start to wonder if law school will be as boring as law class.

"Are you still listening, Mr. Curtis?" he asks when my eyes get a little droopy.

"Hanging on your every word, sir."

"Then maybe you could explain the Oakes test to the class?"

I sigh. Even the Führer seems incapable of directing his question to anywhere but the middle of my forehead.

"Canadian courts use the Oakes test to determine whether a law violates one of our fundamental freedoms in the Charter. Like how your law violates my freedom to wear a hat."

"Ah. Good, Mr. Curtis. But of course, that test only works in a *free* and *democratic* society. The high school classroom is not such a place."

No shit.

After the bell finally rings, I make my way to my locker. I grab the Zumpano tape that Evie lent me and drop off my history textbook. Kohler assigned some chapter questions, but as I've adopted an official Fuck Homework policy for my birthday weekend, none of my academic materials would be leaving the school today. I truck down the languages wing, past Wyndam Aud, and past the main office on my way to the exit. I'm in a hurry to get out of there, and I almost don't notice Soda through the big glass windows of the office, talking to, or rather, being talked at by the vice-principal. I slow down a little and try to get his attention, but he doesn't see me. He's looking directly at Fat Fuck and even from this side of the glass, I can tell something's up. The look on Soda's face is pretty familiar. He had that look in grade six just before he nearly crushed John Tisdale's larynx for calling him a wagon burner. Like his whole face becomes a middle finger. For a second, I wonder if I'm about to watch Soda punch the bifocals off Fat Fuck's chubby mug, but then the two of them go into the VP's office. I keep walking to my locker. I try not to think too much of it, but when I make it outside and walk through the staff parking lot, I notice a cop car sitting empty in the visitor's spot, radiating official menace.

I head home by myself. When you're alone on your birthday, you kind of feel extra alone. I was hoping to catch a ride with Deacon, but he said he had some errands to run for his mom after school. I was also hoping to spend my night hanging out with Kim, but inconveniently, her dad's in town this weekend and dinner with the Doctor is a command performance. I asked if she wanted me to come along for moral support, but she said, "Hell no."

Deacon calls me after supper and says we should grab Soda and play some laser tag at R.O.N.'s Virtual World. Admittedly, I think I'm a little old to be running around with a fake gun, surrounded by shitty glow-in-the-dark space murals, but I figure it's better than spending the night watching TV with my parents. Plus if Soda was coming, it was entirely possible that we'd all smoke a joint first and the whole thing would be hilarious. It's been a relief to see Deacon and Soda getting along again.

A little after nine, the Sabre rolls up my driveway. I see it through the window and grab my coat and gloves.

"We picking Soda up?" I ask Deacon as I climb in the passenger seat.

"Can't get ahold of him."

"Weird. Do you want to swing by his place?"

Deacon yawns. "I guess. Mind if I stop by Rita's first to pick up posters for the Sloan show?"

Rita lives in a student rental with two third-year girls, Anna and Hannah. They both have short hair and round glasses, and they drape their seemingly shapeless figures with baggy jeans and fleece hiking sweaters. They're always eating bowls of oatmeal, no matter what time of day it is. I can never remember which one is which, and I suppose I have no real reason to. The few times I've met them, I could never tell if they were shy or just quietly annoyed by my presence. Soda thinks they're lesbians. Or Communists. I dread ringing Rita's doorbell because they inevitably answer the door together, blink like twin owls, and never remember who I am.

Waiting in post-doorbell purgatory, I turn around and look past Deacon's shoulder.

"Lot of cars parked around here," I say. "Someone's having a party."

When the door opens, it's not Anna or Hannah. It's not even Rita. It's Evie. And she's shouting something at me.

Like funerals, surprise parties are gatherings in your honour that give you zero say over the guest list. At least at your funeral, you don't have to mingle. I guess I really shouldn't complain. Clearly, Rita has gone to great lengths to corral a *This Is Your Life's* worth of acquaintances into her shabby little house. I've never belonged to a gang or a clique—unless you count the band—so seeing all these people under one roof is a little disorienting. It also makes me realize that my friendships—much like Dante's vision of the afterlife—are divided into concentric circles: a hell of other people. The innermost consists of close friends. People I talk to and do stuff with on a regular basis. People like Deacon and Rita. People like Evie, and I guess Ruth, now that she and Deacon seem joined at the hip. Even people like Mike Rotten who's already twiddling the knobs on the stereo and complaining about the EQ.

Then there's the circle of friends by special interest. People who are into the same stuff I'm into, or do the same stuff I do. Jacques pumped gas with me in the summer at the Husky and keeps telling me he's going to teach me to hotwire cars. Trevor Barry introduced me to rap music early on—MC Miker G and Deejay Sven, to be specific—but nowadays he's all about Wu-Tang and wears a lot of Adidas. Danny Grove and Mark Zaborniak are into a lot of the same bands I'm into, so I see them out at shows now and then.

Further out, there are acquaintances and friends of friends. People who all might wish me a happy birthday but are here primarily because Rita bought a keg. People like Jay Olejnik, Brandy Sawchuck, Todd Farkas, and the recently reconciled Emilies that Soda used to date.

Finally, on the periphery, there are the people whose names I won't know in ten years. People who I'll remember only as the Guy Who Brought a Flare Gun to School or the Girl Who Got Caught Having Sex Behind the Bleachers. People I might recognize in the halls and wave at without committing to conversation.

All of these people have taken over Rita's little house, drinking out of plastic cups, smoking cigarettes on the porch, scaring Anna and Hannah into their bedrooms, but as I weave through the crowd, I realize that there are two notable absences tonight: my best friend and my girlfriend.

"Some party," I shout to Rita when I shoulder my way into the kitchen.

"Just keeping the talent happy," she says.

"The talent is happy. Now the talent needs to get drunk."

"Do it," she says. "And hey, Martha Dumptruck are setting up their gear in the basement if you guys want to throw down some impromptu Giant Killer."

I do want to. That's exactly the kind of thing I would want to do. But.

"That's going be tricky without Soda."

"He'll show. It's your birthday."

"Yeah, probably." I study a plastic shot glass with a picture of Snoopy playing the guitar. "It's weird that Kim's not here, though, right?"

Something flickers in Rita's eyes. It's not surprise. "Deacon tried to get ahold of her. He left her a couple messages."

"She's having dinner with her dad tonight. Said she couldn't get out of it."

Rita shrugs and changes the subject. "Who wants jello shooters?" she asks the kitchen, holding up a tray of little paper cups. Locusts descend.

By the time Soda shows, I'm well on my way to shitfaced. I've been the Three Man twice in Three Man, the Asshole once in Asshole, and a Liar a bunch of times in Liar's Dice. I notice him out of the corner of my eye, just as I finish my last roll-off and lose the game to Farkas.

He arrives with Thaler in tow, and I find them priming the keg in the kitchen. As I watch them together, I get a weird sinking feeling. There's nothing wrong with Thaler—he's a good guy. It's just that the two of them seem to hang out a lot these days. I guess it makes sense. They're closer in age. They can get into bars. They both play guitar. They're both tall, too. Thaler's got that same quality Soda's got, like the world is just a little too small for him. They duck when they go through doorframes, drape over couches when they sit down. They're like adults pissing in elementary school urinals. With the game over, I head back into the kitchen for a refill.

"Well, ho-lee shit," Soda says when he sees me, "if it isn't the birthday boy."

He's drunk. I mean, I'm pretty hammered too, but Soda doesn't get drunk like most people get drunk. He can knock back a twenty-sixer of whatever and still walk a straight line. He has to work pretty hard to get wasted, and when he finally does, it's a significant transformation.

"Hey, man! Glad you're here," I say.

"Course I'm here. You think I'd miss your fuckin' birthday party?" He grabs my shoulder and pulls me toward him. "You think I'm some kind of an asshole or something?" His breath is one hundred proof vodka.

"No, dude. I'm just saying that it's nice you made it."

"Well, sorry I didn't hold your fuckin' hand as you blew out the candles, buddy. Had some celebrating of my own to do. Not everything's about the fact your mom shit you out eighteen years ago."

It's good that Soda's here. It is. But now that he's here, I feel like I'll spend half the night talking him down. Soda's one of those paranoid drunks. He thinks that Everyone Is Out to Fuck with Him and he Refuses to Take Any Shit. Calming him down is like lion taming. Or harder. With lion taming, you've got a whip and a chair. You can back that lion into its cage and slam the door. Taming the drunken Soda is more of a finesse job. And there's no cage. You're constantly placating him, but if you're too obvious about it, he'll suspect you of patronizing him, and all of a sudden believe that you, like Everyone, are Out to Fuck with Him. It's exhausting.

"So what were you celebrating?" I ask.

"My fuckin' emancipation!" Soda looks over at Thaler, holds his wrists together and then breaks free from invisible shackles. Thaler laughs at an inside joke I don't get.

"I saw you in the office with Sundell," I tell him. "What was up with that?"

"What's up with that is I got fuckin' expelled. That's what's fuckin' up with that."

"What—you mean suspended?" No one actually gets expelled anymore.

"You got shit in your ears? That Fat Fuck broke into my locker—fuckin' *illegally*—and found a bunch of shit I got from Nguyen and accused me of 'trafficking.' They suspended me *indefinitely*—at least until the end of the semester—and because I'm over eighteen they don't have to let me back in. So I when I say 'expelled,' I fuckin' mean *expelled*."

"Maybe you could finish out the year at Churchill and still graduate."

"Fuck that." He drains the plastic cup in his hand and lets out a wet belch. "I'm done. Cops were there and shit."

"Are they going to charge you?"

He shrugs. "Probably not. I mean, they fuckin' better not."

The night is getting weird, and then it gets even weirder. As I'm patiently listening to Soda describe his plans to dismember both the Hawk and Fat Fuck, I see Townie materialize by the refrigerator like he just crawled out of the vegetable crisper. He leans into a conversation with Farkas and the Guy Who Accidentally Set His Hair On Fire In Chemistry Class, and when he tilts his head back and laughs at something hilarious and out of earshot, I can't help but wonder: if he's here, where's Kim? At that moment Soda cauterizes the wounds of the entire Mackenzie King administration so he can refill his beer, and I take the opportunity to interrogate my girlfriend's brother.

He's snorting again at Farkas when I sidle up to him. It takes him a minute to register I'm even there.

"Hey, Townie."

"Oh. Hey, Pete. Happy birthday."

"Thanks, man. So ... how was dinner with the Doctor?"

"Who?"

Farkas and Hair On Fire are looking at me like I've got three heads. I stumble to make sense.

"Uh, you know, 'The Doctor.' That's what Kim calls your dad. I thought you guys were having dinner with him tonight."

"Dude, my dad's in Atlanta banging some chick he met heli-skiing last month."

"Your dad's such a player," Farkas says.

"*Pla-ya!*" Fire Hair hollers.

I have this unpleasant buzzing sensation in the base of my skull, like I just backed into a wasp's nest.

"So, you and Kim weren't supposed to have dinner with him tonight."

"No, man." Townie looks at me strangely. "I thought Kim would be *here* tonight."

"Okay. Cool. Well, I've got to ..." I trail off and walk away, knowing that their eyes will be on the back of my head until they shrug and dismiss me. I push through the crowd to Rita's room.

Make a phone call. I've got to make a phone call.

She had written it in the snow, and all the way home from the show that night, I had repeated it like a mantra. 7 6 7 8 5 1 2. 7 6 7 8 5 1 2. 7 6 7 8 5 1 2.

Under my toque, I can feel my pimple throbbing in time with my heart as I jab at the buttons on Rita's bedroom telephone. It rings five times before her answering machine picks up and I hear her message.

"*It's a shame I'm not here,*" her voice sings to the tune of a Lemonheads song. "*Leave a message and I'll call you when I reappear.*" The song disintegrates into self-conscious laughter, and the beep sounds. I hang up and dial again, interrogating the keypad with each of the seven digits: *Where. The. Fuck. Are. You. Kim. Kivela?* I hear five rings, then the message again. I put the phone back in its cradle and then surprise myself by throwing the whole mess across the room. It stops short of hitting the wall, caught on the cord like a dog choking on its leash.

SIDE B

Nightime/Anything (It's Alright)

There's a part of me that wants to throw my cell phone against the wall every time it goes off. I miss the pre-cellular days, when you had no other choice but to leave your phone at home. Now, every call hunts you down like a heat-seeking missile.

"Seriously?" I say, chewing on the last of my Mexi-fries. "You want me to go to a shag?"

I'd been enjoying a quiet dinner alone at my favourite taco establishment when Ruth called.

"It's for my cousin Sharon," she says. "I promised my mom I'd 'represent the family.'"

"Why don't your parents 'represent the family'?"

I sip root beer through a straw.

"Because they're in Florida for the winter. Michael's in Toronto for this stupid web design thing, and everyone else my age has kids and goes to bed at ten o'clock. Come on. I'll buy your drinks *and* drive you home."

"Fine. But I'm warning you. I'm going to have to drink a lot."

A shag, at least in the northern Ontario vernacular, is the combination of both a wedding shower and a stag night. They're wedding fundraisers disguised as parties, and they're usually held in some sadly decorated community centre where they sell shitty beer, play shitty music, and at some point in the evening serve beef on a bun. People sit at long folding tables and complain about how you can't smoke at these things anymore. Eventually, when the crowd's downed enough beer, the DJ will crank up some 'Old Time Rock and Roll'. Besides the beer, you're expected to buy raffle tickets for donated door prizes, which usually consist of slow cookers, fishing trips, and unconventional meats. Once I went to a shag that offered a freezer full of moose steaks as the grand prize.

A couple hours later, I find myself seated next to Ruth at a long wooden table. People move around us in the dim hall like a shadow play. I recognize a few faces from high school—Tim Puurula, Jeannie Drew, the Guy Who Got Caught Masturbating in the Boys' Locker Room—and depending on how drunk I get, I might even say hi to some of them.

"All this bad music is making me thirsty," I say meaningfully in Ruth's direction.

She rolls her eyes. "Well, why don't I get you some drink tickets?" She stands up and wanders off in the direction of the bar.

The truth is, I'm glad I've got an excuse to do something tonight. It definitely beats sitting around debating whether or not I should return Vicky's latest phone message.

"I've got the house to myself a-a-all weekend. Just thought you'd like to know. Call me anytime."

Since the show last month, we've slept together a total of three times. That first time was in her guest bedroom. I have a vague recollection of a mauve bedspread depicting some fairly majestic stallions running through a riverbed, and a photograph of the Sleeping Giant hanging on the wall. The second, and what I *swore* would be the last time, happened at my place. She knocked on my door, and when I opened it, she said something like *It's cold out here. Maybe you could warm me up?* It just seemed so surreal, like some kind of cliché porno movie. How could I turn her down? The third time, a staff meeting ran late, so she offered me a ride home. Stupidly, I accepted. We didn't get two blocks before she had both unbuckled and unzipped me with her free hand. Older women—they don't waste any time. She drove us to this secluded place down by the train yard, and we did it in the back of her PT Cruiser. I had to listen to her Nickelback CD the entire time.

I'm not sure if three times technically constitutes an affair—I'd like to think of it as three isolated errors in judgement—but either way, as I watch Ruth's cousin and her fiancé work the room, my conscience is winning the wrestling match it's been having with my libido since this all started. I can't help but imagine what Vicky and Jamie's shag must have been like. Baggy overalls. *MuchMusic Dance Mix '92.* Betty Boo 'Doin' the Do.' And their whole lives ahead of them.

I try to remember the last time I felt optimistic about my love life. Or even the last time I had sex that didn't feel like a bad idea the next day. Back when I was living in Toronto, I thought things might actually work out with Catherine. She was beautiful and dressed really cool and knew about all these bands before anyone else did. She worked for this weekly called *Pulse* and got us our first and only feature article, titled "Filthy Witness Pleads the Fifth" (even though I'm pretty sure we answered all of her questions). I still have a copy of it somewhere. I moved into her one-bedroom apartment on Clinton Street, and she'd come out to our shows and drink our free beer. Then, when things with the record label fell through, so did things with us. I couldn't help but wonder if the two were related.

Ruth returns after a while with a handful of tickets and two plastic cups of beer. She gives me the tickets and one of the cups.

"So," she says as she sits down, "we might have another show lined up."

"How's that?"

"Matty Wheeler's mom." She points behind herself in the general direction of a middle-aged woman dressed like Stevie Nicks. "She was at the Shenanigans show. She told Matty that you're in a new band, and he wants us to play his birthday."

"What ... the *Bunsen Burner?*"

"It's the tenth anniversary of everything, so apparently the city's getting involved. Might be kind of cool."

I'm not convinced. Since the accident, Matty's birthday had become an annual event that I went to great lengths to avoid. They rent out the Polish Legion for an open mic jam session and produce what I can only imagine is some of the worst psychedelia, folk, and prog rock ever heard by human ears. As I search my brain for a reasonable excuse, I'm interrupted by the bride to be.

"*Ruthie!* I'm so glad you're here!" Ruth's cousin Sharon approaches her with shoulders hunched and arms out, like she's about to pounce. She's a good five years older than we are, heavyset with a round face and hair bleached matrimonial blonde. Ruth disappears inside her bear hug, and I can make out the hilarious discomfort on her face over Sharon's meaty shoulder. "And *Michael!* I haven't seen you in *ages*!" Suddenly, I'm subjected to the same ursine attack. I feel like Luke Skywalker in the trash compactor.

"Sharon," Ruth corrects her, buoyant with schadenfreude, "that's not Michael. That's my friend Peter."

"Oh gosh. I'm sorry, Peter! I'm just a *little* tipsy."

A moment later, a broad-shouldered man with a shaved head appears beside her. "This is my fiancé, Ray. Ray, you remember my cousin Ruthie—you know, the teacher? And this is her friend Peter."

Ray shakes my hand like there's a handshaking competition no one told me about.

"Pleasure's mine. You both teachers?"

We nod and identify ourselves by our subject: English. History.

"You know, I love the History Channel and all that, but *Canadian* History—*yeesh*! So boring." He takes a sip of his beer.

I shrug and smile. "I think a lot of the kids would agree with you."

"All that stuff about the Fur Trade and Quebec and boohooing about the Indians. I heard they make Louis Riel out to be some kind of *hero* now." His face grimaces in disgust.

"Well," I offer, "Riel was a pretty controversial—"

"And *English*," he continues, gathering steam. "All that fruity Shakespeare stuff? Half these kids can't write a goddamn sentence and you confuse them with five-hundred-year-old nonsense?"

"Actually—" Ruth tries to interject.

"You know what my English teacher did?" He pauses for effect and takes another sip of beer. "I'll never forget. He got halfway through *Hamlet*—and of course we were all screwing around 'cause we didn't care—and he said, 'Hell with it.' We spent the rest of the semester analyzing the lyrics of *rock songs*. Pink Floyd, Aerosmith, Rush. It was great. And now, every time I hear 'Closer To The Heart' on the radio I actually know what it means. Did you know the drummer wrote all the lyrics? And that he was inspired by Ayn Rand?"

I can't say I did.

"Now that's useful stuff. Kids would appreciate that kind of stuff." He looks at me straight on and says, "*That's* the kind of stuff you should teach. Not King Richard or whatever."

I want to remind him that I'm the one who teaches boring Canadian History, but I don't think he'd hear me. Instead, I shrug noncommittally and decide it's time to pull the rip cord on this conversation.

"Well, my glass is getting dangerously empty," I say and shake the plastic beer cup as if to demonstrate its potential threat. "Anybody want something from the bar?"

The bride and groom-to-be politely refuse, and Ruth reminds me, not without ire, that she's the designated driver tonight.

"Well, good luck, you two. And congratulations."

I leave Ruth to represent the family and make my way through the crowd to the window where a steel girder of a man is serving drinks. His sleeves are rolled up to reveal an unrecognizable smear of tattoo under his forearm hair. He doesn't say anything, but watches as I fish a chain of drink tickets out of my jeans.

"Uh, could I get a rye and ginger?"

The bartender turns around and gets a bottle of Canadian Club out of the fridge behind him. "Want a double? Costs two tickets."

I'm drinking on Ruth, so it's all the same to me. Plus, I don't want to look like a pussy in front of this guy. "Sure. I could use one."

"A double, huh?" I hear a voice say behind me. "Let me guess. You must be the groom."

I turn around and find myself knowing the face but not the name. I *wish* I knew her name. Pale blue eyes. Beach-sand hair. Pretty without trying to be pretty. Where do I know her from? And why the *fuck* can't I think of her name?

"Groom ... ? Oh, *god* no," I say. "I mean—unless you're—shit, sorry—are you related to somebody?"

"Well, I'm definitely related to *somebody*, but no, no one in the wedding party."

Suddenly, it comes to me. I can't remember her name because I never knew it in the first place. I actually snap my fingers in recognition. "Video Store Girl."

"Jim Jaramusch Guy," she snaps back.

"Pete." I hold out my hand with what must seem like weird formality, but she shakes it and smiles this crooked smile that completely reorganizes my priorities.

"Alex." There's a laugh as she says it, as if that crooked smile had crept into her name as well.

"Sorry—I couldn't place you at first. You know, that whole thing where you don't recognize people out of context."

"Prosopagnosia."

"Sorry?"

"Prosopagnosia. That's what it's called when you can't remember people by what they look like."

"Oh. Okay."

"It's usually a sign of acute brain damage."

"Uh ..."

Is she fucking with me?

"I'm fucking with you. Next time just picture me next to a faded poster of *Bridget Jones's Diary* and you'll be fine."

I can't help but notice she said *next time*.

"So, Pete, what brings you to the social event of the season?"

"Well—"

Just then, Avril Lavigne's adolescent lament, which for the better part of this conversation has been describing the unfair treatment of a Sk8r Boi, dies a sudden death. The house lights pour down like a bucket of cold water, and I hear Sharon's voice through the PA.

"Oh. Sure. Could you ... oh, it's on? *Now*?"

She taps a microphone, and I locate her somewhere near the front of the room. She and her fiancé are standing in front of a folding table, over which door and raffle prizes have been spread.

"Hi, everyone! Uh, we're going to give a way a couple prizes now, and then it'll be time for some food!"

Shit. I feel like someone's hit the pause button a few minutes into a romantic comedy. As Sharon brays out the winning numbers for a set of frying pans—"donated by the wonderful folks at Stokes. Hey! That rhymes"—Alex and I shrug and grin helplessly at each other. When Sharon announces that she's giving away a set of "beautiful brand-new camping chairs" and starts fumbling around in a shoebox full of ticket stubs, I imagine Alex will take her leave. She could do it easily enough, and it would be completely understandable under the circumstances. She could give me a little smile and a wave that said *See you later* and then disappear back to wherever her friends are sitting. But she doesn't. She sticks it out. That's something, at least.

After an eternity of bad lighting and bad public address, Sharon finally wraps it up. "We'll be back in an hour, so stick around."

Someone wheels out a cart topped with limp-looking cold cuts, fleshy roast beef, processed cheese, and powdery kaiser rolls. The lights go back down, and the music comes back up halfway through a soul-eroding Maroon 5 song.

With all this extra time, you'd think I would've come up with some witty banter, or at the very least a good excuse to keep talking. In the six or so minutes we stood in shag limbo, I must have thought of *something* decent to say, right?

"So ..." I gesture toward the food cart. "Beef on a bun?"

It's official. I'm dying alone.

"Uh, no, thanks. I'm a vegetarian."

"So ... just bun, then?"

She laughs, and I realize whatever kind of moment we were having before has passed.

"No, I'm good. But you go ahead. It was nice to see you out here in—" she looks around and names the place hesitantly "—the real world."

Suddenly she's gone. And while I may be partly to blame, at this particular moment I'm choosing instead to blame Ruth. Ruth, for convincing me to come here tonight, and Ruth, for being related to that idiot Sharon who just stepped all over my chances like a downtown Tokyo Godzilla. Some people are just happier than they deserve to be.

"Who's your new friend?" Ruth asks when I collapse into my seat and put my forehead on the table.

"Alex Something-Something," I grumble. "Fu-*uck*. I *hate* how you can't smoke at these things anymore."

Ruth ignores me. "She's pretty cute. You should go back and talk to her."

I sit up and shrug.

"You should," she says again.

Normally, Ruth wouldn't encourage me to get involved with two women at once. Of course, she wouldn't encourage me to sleep with a married woman either, which is exactly why I haven't told her about Vicky.

"She looks kind of familiar."

"She works at Video Hutch."

"That's not it. Michael downloads everything. I haven't been to a video rental place in years."

"Well, maybe you just have prosopagnosia."

"What?"

"Never mind. God, I need a smoke. I'm going outside."

As I walk through the crowd, I survey the room for Alex while trying to look like I'm not surveying the room for Alex. I fail miserably, I'm sure, at both endeavours, and finally push through the front doors to find a group of four other outcasts shivering around their cigarettes. I recognize the closest to me as Tim Puurula. Last I heard, he got a job working at the *Chronicle*. I light a cigarette and ask him if he's doing a story for the Local Events page.

"Nah. The groom's my cousin. You?"

"I'm friends with the bride's cousin."

"Oh."

We smoke in silence until the Guy Who Got Caught Masturbating in the Boys' Locker Room slams through the doors and clinks open a Zippo.

"Hey," he says, pointing at me with two fingers and a cigarette, "aren't you the Guy Who Used to Play in a Band with Jesse Maracle?"

He offers me his hand and, begrudgingly, I shake it. I guess we all have our crosses to bear.

The night progresses unremarkably until 'Rock the Casbah.'

There's no denying the following fact: I'm an awkward man-dancer. You might think that as a drummer I've got some coordination of my limbs and a decent sense of rhythm, but somehow it just doesn't translate into good dancing. A lot has been said about the white man's inability to dance, and I'm of the opinion that most of it is fairly accurate. I think white women are equally guilty, but they seem to overcompensate with an enthusiasm and inhibition that I could never muster. I mean, I can bob my head as enthusiastically as the next guy at a rock show, but as soon as I'm in a crowd of people, and the music is getting piped in by a DJ, I'm lost. So, as it stands, I maintain a steadfast No Dancing rule.

There is, of course, a combination of two factors that will cause me to waive the rule, and both of these factors need to be in play in order for me to cut a rug. *One*, I need to be comfortably drunk—not sloppy drunk—just buzzy; and *two*, the DJ needs to play 'Rock the Casbah.'

I'm not sure what it is about 'Rock the Casbah' that unleashes my inner MJ—maybe the fact that, like Rush's 'Closer to the Heart,' it was written by a drummer, or maybe the fact that something so funky is being performed by four pale Englishmen inspires me to embrace my own pale greatness; but in any case, when I hear that song, and I've had a few rye and gingers, I'm an unstoppable dancing machine. As a result, I'm performing some awful, exaggerated version of the twist (one of the old stand-bys in my limited repertoire) and singing about Sharif (even though I'm not entirely sure who Sharif is) when I feel someone tap me on the shoulder.

At first I assume it's Ruth. I tried to get her to come up and dance with me, but she opted out. For all her complaining about friends who don't last past ten o'clock, she's been doing a lot of yawning at nine thirty.

But when I turn around, mid-twist, I realize it's Alex.

"Nice moves," she observes.

I immediately stop dancing and realize I'm the only one left on the dance floor. "Hey," I say, trying to gather some semblance of cool. "Don't I know you from somewhere?"

"Big Clash fan, huh?"

There's this great Martin Amis line in *The Rachel Papers,* something about how not enjoying the middle-period Beatles is like not enjoying life itself. I try to conjure it and make it about the Clash, but fail. "Everything up to *Cut the Crap*," I tell her.

“Well, there’s a band playing at the Phoenix that’s supposed to sound a bit like the Clash. Want to go?”

Do I want to go? With her? I’d go see a Hootie and the Blowfish tribute band with her. Of course, she can’t know this. Eagerness is death.

“Depends,” I say. “When is it?” I expect her to say in a few days, or next week.

“In about an hour. My friends don’t want to go, but I’ve heard really good things.”

Well, I guess that calls my eagerness bluff.

“Uh, okay. Yeah. I think so. I just need to let someone know I’m leaving.”

“Oh,” she says, “are you ... *here* ... with someone?”

The unmistakable disappointment in her voice has got be one of the sweetest sounds I’ve ever heard.

“My friend’s wife,” hoping it sounds reassuring and not tawdry. Of course, all things considered lately, I add, “I’m just here for moral support.”

“Oh. Okay cool. Meet you by the front door in five minutes?”

When I approach Ruth, she shakes her head in disapproval and smiles at the same time. It must be hard being friends with a cad.

“No,” she anticipates my question (incorrectly, I might add), “I am not driving you to that woman’s apartment so you can have sex with her.”

“We’re going to see a rock show,” I tell her, summoning a look that hopefully conveys offended chastity. “And we’re going to walk.”

“You know, you’re the worst date I’ve ever had.”

“Oh please. Didn’t Deacon take you to R.O.N.’s Virtual World on your first date?”

“So what? I liked laser tag.”

“Bullshit. Nobody ever liked laser tag. Especially not seventeen-year-old girls.”

“And yet you’re still the worst.”

When I get to the front door, I worry for approximately forty-three seconds that she’s bailed, until she shows up, cute under a fuzzy coat and hat.

The Phoenix is downtown on Red River, so it’s going to be a bit of a hike. As soon as I get out into the cold air, I’m dying for a cigarette, but I’m not going to light up until I can figure out if she’s anti-smoker, or even worse, one of those self-righteous I-quit-so-why-can’t-you ex-smokers. I get through about ten minutes of small talk: *So what’s this band we’re going to see? What’s it like working at Video Hutch? Did she remember when Video Hutch had that cigarette machine?* But she reveals no clues about her stance on nicotine addiction, and I’m getting antsy, so I cave.

"Mind if I smoke?"

"No. I don't mind."

"Want one?" I hold the pack out to her.

"Better not. I'm trying to quit."

I borrow Vicky's line—the one about how people don't actually smoke anymore, they're just in various stages of quitting—but I feel bad as soon as it leaves my mouth. It gets a laugh, but a few moments later my phone's message reminder beeps like a tell-tale heart. *Call me anytime.* It's a fine hole I've dug. I feel guilty when I call her. I feel guilty when I don't call her. I feel guilty just talking to another woman.

We walk a little while in silence. It's actually kind of a nice night. It's snowing a little bit, and the temperature has warmed up. Alex seems comfortable with the silence, but as usual, I scramble to fill it.

"So, Video Store Girl," I say, "what did you do before you were an employee of Video Hutch?"

"We-e-ll," she prefaces, as though it's a long, complicated story and she's trying to decide which version she should tell. "I was going to school in Montreal, but it didn't quite work out."

"How come 'it didn't quite work out'?"

"Honestly, it's not much of a story. There was a guy. There were some drugs. There was a lot of dancing and not a lot of attending classes." *Some* drugs? Christ, and here I was worrying about smoking in front of her. "What can I say? It was Montreal. It was fun. It's the exact opposite of here."

"Yeah. Tell me about it."

And of course, it's then, right then, that our little chat turns into a real conversation. Sure, we've already established that we have a few common interests—bands, movies, leaving shags early—but nothing unites people like a common enemy. And in our case, it's a mutual hatred for our hometown. The floodgates open.

"Seriously. Is there one decent bar in town that hasn't burned down?"

"And why are they called Persians anyhow? They're definitely not imported from ... Persia ..."

"Oh, fuck the Hoito. And fuck their Finnish pancakes. I'm not standing in line for an hour on Sunday for a pile of crepes."

When I lived in Toronto, I defended Thunder Bay to the death, the way you might defend the family moron to outsiders. But one of the greatest privileges of being among family is you can finally talk shit about your favourite idiot.

We finally get to the Phoenix, and I can see the windows are steamy with crowd heat. I want to keep walking. I'm having a good time and I don't want to share her with anyone else. I know the minute we go in that bar, she's going to run into people she knows, or I'll run into people I know, and we'll be forced to separate and make that annoying bar small talk where people shout things in your ear while you nod and pretend you've understood what they've said.

I hesitate at the door, then feel her woolly, wet mitt grab my cold hand.

"It'll be good," she says. "I promise."

And I believe her.

We go in and the door guy holds up five fingers for five dollars. Alex lets go of my hand and digs a ten out of her pocket to pay for both of us. I try to give her a bunch of loonies, but she mimes refusal. The band is just setting up and the house music is still impossibly loud. Metallica. *Always* Metallica. It's standing room only, so we hang near the back corner where we can just see the stage over a canopy of Bad News Bear haircuts and ironic trucker hats. Alex holds up a finger—*one minute*—and disappears. While I wait, I notice a couple people I know toward the front of the room—old campaigners like Danny Grove and Mark Zaborniak—thicker, balder Ghosts of Rock Shows Past. Mike Rotten is also here. It's a rare sighting. He has two little girls and it's a miracle when Evie lets him out of the house at all. Still, I don't want to talk to him. Not any of them. Not right now.

I feel a little self-conscious being alone in a room full of people until I see Alex working her way back through the crowd, two bottles of Moosehead held aloft.

"Thanks," I shout. "That was fast!"

"I know the bartender!" she shouts back.

She hands me a bottle and I tip it to my mouth. I wonder if she's going to grab my hand again, or if I should grab hers. We stand shoulder to shoulder and drink our beer, insulated by crowd noise. I watch the band as they silently tune their guitars and tweak the knobs on their gear. The bass player says something into the guitar player's ear. The guitar player smiles and nods. The keyboard player bobs his head along to the house music.

If there's a signal, I don't see it, but the sound of James Hetfield et al. suddenly implodes. The crowd pushes closer to the stage with a slight cultishness, and all that's left is the hum of the amps and the occasional encouraging *Woo-hoo!*

"Who are these guys again?" I ask. The truth is, I don't really care. I just want to talk to her again before we're separated by walls of sound, but the band starts up before she can answer me.

They don't introduce themselves. They just play. Slowly at first, building to something bigger, until bigger finally breaks and it feels like the entire bar is caught in an ebb and flow of sonic pulse. I can feel the bass all the way in my balls, and the kick drum beats in my chest like a second heart that's stronger than my own.

Alex is right. They're good. In fact, it's been a while since I've heard a band this good. I'm a little surprised they weren't already on my radar, but that's what happens when you move back to Thunder Bay. The *way* in which they're good is hard to say. Music reviews always seem as nebulous as those descriptions on pricey bottles of wine: *A masterful blend of the finest musicians from the Southwestern Ontario region, the band layers a heady nose of Fugazi and early Clash, with savoury whispers of Bon Scott-era AC/DC and a rich, lingering finish of unoaked Springsteen. Enjoy on a frosty March evening with a video store employee who may or may not be your next sexual partner.*

The band hurtles through five songs before they're stalled by technical difficulties. While the guitar player pounds on his amp head in an attempt to fonzie out the music, Alex comes clean.

"Okay. *Truth*," she says during the unexpected intermission, as if we've silently agreed to start a game of Truth or Dare and she's picked the first option. "We actually met a couple years ago. I saw you play drums with Filthy Witness in Montreal. And I thought you were kind of cute."

Wait. Who'd she see? She thought I was what?

"You guys opened for Hot Hot Heat at Casa Del Popolo. You were pretty good."

She says *pretty good* and not *great* or *amazing*, but I'll take it. It's probably the truth. I remember that show, because it was the only time I'd ever played in Montreal. Our bass player set up this tour that was supposed to go all the way out East, but our van broke down in Drummondville, and we had to cancel Moncton, Charlottetown, and Halifax. I wish I remembered her.

"I bought a t-shirt from you at the merch table. You gave me a deal because I said I only had ten dollars—which, by the way, was kind of a lie. I was saving the rest of my money for beer."

I look at the empty bottle I've been holding stupidly for the past few minutes. "I'd say we're square."

She may be the first person in Thunder Bay to ever acknowledge my musical past and not say the words *Jesse Maracle*. I want to ask her more, but just then the guitarist's amplifier crackles back to life, and the drummer shouts out the name of another song and counts in. The crowd cheers and claims their victory over bad wiring. Song by song, things keep getting better. By the end of the set, Alex's hand makes slow circles in the small of my back as the lead singer—now inexplicably stripped down to his briefs—howls into the microphone.

No one stays long after the band finishes. We follow the herd as it leaves the damp sauna of the Phoenix and spills out into the cool relief of the night. I stop to light a cigarette and notice Danny and Mike enthusiastically recapping the show a few feet away. In a minute or two, they'd see me, and I'd be stuck in a conversational vortex, probably about how *Revenge of the Sith* has to be better than *Attack of the Clones*. Alex would die of boredom.

"Want to get out of here?" I ask. She nods. Part of me wants to also ask, "Where to next?" but nothing jinxes getting laid like the planning of it. Without discussion, we start walking west up Red River Road, which just happens to be in the direction of my apartment.

For a little while, we're back at small talk—"Great show." "Where are they from again?" "So many people out tonight"—and just when I worry we've lost the rhythm of our conversation, she starts telling me about Montreal. The whole deal. How when she first got there, she bought a second-hand Raleigh and spent a solid week just riding through all the cool neighbourhoods, stopping at cafés and book stores. In my head, I could see her, hair tied back out of her face, scarf in the wind, tires humming on the cobblestone. Why are Ontario cyclists all about mushroom-shaped helmets, spandex, and toe clips? In Montreal, a girl on a bicycle is a poem; here, she's a safety manual.

She doesn't say much about her art school. I imagine it's because she didn't go there all that often. She does talk about the job she got on Rue St. Denis, at a place that was a vegetarian restaurant during the day and a dance club at night.

"But not one of those shitty techno clubs. It was strictly Stax, Soul, and Motown. *So* good."

Apparently, she hooked up with her manager, this older guy named Joe—short for Joaquim—fuck, even Montreal *names* are cooler—and after a couple months of jumping the line at every club in town, imbibing pharmaceutical grade coke and MDMA, and falling "into what I *thought* was love," she started to tailspin. She had burned through her savings and couldn't afford rent. She was failing all her courses, and the school contacted her parents. "*So* embarrassing." Her roommate kicked her out, her mom stopped paying tuition, and she dropped out of school and moved in with Joe for a few months until he started fucking another Rue St. Denis waitress.

"You figure out pretty quickly how shitty someone is when you live with him. Turns out Joe was *thoroughly* shitty. So I figured it was time to come home."

She exhales like she's been holding her breath a long time, and I realize she's been talking for almost ten minutes straight.

"Sorry," she grimaces. "I go on a bit."

We walk along in silence for a few moments. We're almost at the top of Red River, and there are impending decisions to make regarding the destination of this journey.

"What about you?" she asks. "What about your big city misadventure? You know—Toronto, rock band, meeting pretty girls at merch tables ..."

I shrug. "Well, I wound up going to university here in town—which sucked—did a year in Toronto at teacher's college—which also sucked but a little less. Then I worked part time in a museum, played music when I could, and sank further and further into debt."

"What happened with the band?"

"I don't know. I guess I got tired of toiling in obscurity."

"Whatever. I heard you guys were supposed to get signed to Makeshift Records. That's kind of a big deal."

"It was, until the guys who ran it realized the label hadn't turned a profit since 1998 and decided to 'scale back their whole operation.' At least, that's what they told us. Who knows?"

"So you broke up over that?"

"Not exactly. I got offered a job back here and I took it."

I always hate that part of the story. I know what it sounds like. It sounds like I came home with my tail between my legs. The truth is, I never really clicked with the guys I played with in Toronto. Not the way I did with Soda and Deacon. I hated all the schmoozing and the lame parties and the promises no one ever kept. There was no sense fooling myself. I just wasn't cut out for the whole Queen Street West scene.

"So that was that?"

"Pretty much. My old Law teacher got me an interview, which is weird because I always thought he hated me."

"So—wait. You're a *high school* teacher?"

"Yep. At Mackenzie King."

"Weird. I just can't see it. Do you miss playing music?"

"Yeah. A little. I miss some of the people I used to play with," I tell her. But just before I parachute the name *Jesse Maracle* into the conversation in a sad attempt to impress her, Alex slows to a halt at the corner of Summit Avenue.

"Well, Pete," she says, "I live a couple blocks down there, so I think—unfortunately—this is where we say goodnight."

Goodnight? How could the night be any good at all if she leaves now? I try to stall, to keep the conversation going, to buy me a little more time.

"Are you living with your parents?" I ask.

"With my mom, just for now. My folks are divorced."

"Shitty."

"Yeah. My mom caught my dad with some nineteen-year-old."

"What, *recently*?"

"No. About ten years ago."

"Still, though ..." It's getting colder now that we've stopped moving, and I can tell she isn't catching any of my conversational throws, so I run a Hail Mary: "Hey—do you want to come over to my apartment, instead? I've got *Westway to the World* on DVD."

She smiles her priority-shifting smile. "If we go to your apartment, it won't be to watch *Westway to the World*. And as much as I'd like to, I'm still kind of figuring things out right now."

I nod stupidly. She stands on her tiptoes, delivers a consolation kiss on my cheek, then starts to walk backward away from me.

"You know where to find me, right?" she asks.

"Yep. Next to a faded poster of *Bridget Jones's Diary*."

I wait until she's out of sight and light another cigarette. The way home seems impossibly long, and the cold is starting to press down on my throat like a metal thumb. I walk for a few minutes before my phone rings. I don't remember giving Alex my number, but still, I hope against all odds that it's her. She's changed her mind. Her mom is out of town and she wants me to spend the night. But when I look at the caller ID, it's not Alex. It's Vicky, and I know why she's calling.

I want to say that I'll do the right thing. I want to say that I'll let the phone ring itself out, walk home, and sleep off all the rye and beer I drank tonight. If there's any chance that something could happen with Alex, I want to draw a clean, straight line right to it. But, the truth is, I have a very pragmatic libido, and it knows that a bird in the hand is worth more than one that's "still kind of figuring things out." I take a deep breath, press the green button, and hold the phone to my ear.

SIDE A
Worried Now

I know why she's calling, but she refuses to say it over the phone. She won't acknowledge my imminent dumping, because to acknowledge it would make it so, and then I'd be well within my rights to call her That Bitch Who Broke Up with Me over the Phone.

"We need to talk about some stuff" is all she'll say.

"Okay, so you ditch me on my birthday, you *barely* return my calls for the last week and a half, and now you want *me* to change *my* plans so I can meet you at Hillcrest Park to 'talk'? Well, sorry. I'm a little busy today."

"Fine, if you're going to be a child about it—" She starts to say something else, but then changes her mind and hangs up.

Part of this is a power play. I want to keep fighting indefinitely because, as long as we're still fighting, we're still together. I don't want to know that she's slept with Matty or Sudbury Steve, or some sensitive douchebag she met in her Gender Studies class. As soon as we have this "talk," all my perfectly good anger is going to be eclipsed by crippling sadness, and I just don't feel like dealing with that right now. Right now, she's just my pain-in-the-ass girlfriend, and we're in a fight. I'd take angry over sad any day.

The other part of this, though, is that I actually *am* pretty busy. Was she seriously going to break up with me the same day Giant Killer was opening for fucking Sloan? I already feel like one giant raw nerve. Soda's insisting that we play this new song and I'm not feeling really confident about the time changes. Plus, I'm going to have to play on the Bunsen Honeydew drum kit, which has all these ridiculous rototoms and weird cymbals because Kyle, their drummer, thinks he's the love child of Neil Peart and Mickey Hart. I wanted to have another practice this afternoon—one last cram session just so I felt more ready—but Deacon and Soda agreed that it wasn't a good idea.

"It fucks up your *chi* to practise on the same day you play," Soda explained. "It's like jerking off when you're about to get laid."

In a way, Soda getting kicked out of school is one of the best things that could have happened to the band. I half expected him to go off the deep end, but lately he's been crazy focused on music. All he does while we're at school is sleep in, sit in his bedroom, listen to music, and write new songs. They're really good songs too—he played me this one yesterday called 'Common Cold Heart.' It's not finished yet, but I can tell it's going to be amazing.

I look at my watch after Kim bangs the phone down in my ear and realize that Rita and the guys will be over in about an hour to pack up the Sabre, and then it's another three hours or so until game time. Already my bowels feel like they're migrating out my asshole.

I hear the door slam shut. My dad is yelling about something. He works Saturdays and always comes home grumpy and smelling of Zellers—that weird mix of plastic, carpet glue, and cheap retail. I'm heading for the kitchen to grab a Coke when he accosts me with an envelope.

"Doesn't anybody pick up the mail in this house?" he asks. He serves me the envelope like it's a subpoena. "Might be important."

I take it out of his hand and read the return address. *University of Toronto Admissions.* Jesus *Christ*. As if I needed more anxiety today. I feel very close to throwing up.

My dad unpins the *Manager* tag from his chest. "You going to open it?"

"Yeah ..." I say. "Maybe on my own, though."

"Suit yourself," he says and goes to change out of his work clothes. I go back to my bedroom, throw the letter on the bed, and just stare at it for a few minutes.

All in all, I applied to three universities. I was just going apply to one, but it cost the same to do three and Mrs. Leedy said I should play it safe. Of course, as soon as I did that, I started seeing three different potential futures. The future I wanted the most was at U of T. Their brochures were the glossiest, and the girls inside them were easily the prettiest. I wanted to major in Poli Sci and minor in getting drunk at the Horseshoe

Tavern. York was my second-place future. It was a little further away from downtown, the campus looked kind of sterile, and the girls, well, I guess there are always pictures of pretty girls in campus brochures, but I suspected the York girls were ringers. One of the models appeared twice in two separate gangs of laughing, learning study-buddies, and I'm sure that didn't happen by accident. Lakehead, obviously, was my last place. It was my safety. I didn't bother looking at the brochure, because I already knew what that school was about. Brutal grey architecture, a man-made lake full of gently rusting bicycles, and miserable snowsuits scurrying from one class to another through the perpetual blizzard of Thunder Bay winter. Even worse, I'd have to live at home with my parents for another three years.

And now, it seems my fate could be determined by the contents of a small white rectangle that looks disconcertingly slim. Bad news, I've heard, comes in thin envelopes. Maybe I should wait until tomorrow to open it. Maybe bad news is even worse for your *chi* than practising the day of a show. I tear it open anyway. It's not an acceptance letter or a rejection. It's a scholarship offer.

"Dear Peter Curtis," it starts. "We are pleased to offer you a Pre-Law Admissions Scholarship for the University of Toronto. This scholarship exempts you from tuition fees and student fees for the first year of your Bachelor of Arts degree."

I let out a happy holler and know that my parents will be barging into my room in a matter of seconds.

The band arrives a little later than I expect. Deacon, Soda, and Rita spill into the kitchen in mid-conversation.

"Well, maybe if you actually fed him, he wouldn't try to escape all the time," Rita tells Soda.

"Yeah, dude," Deacon says. "How he's still alive is a fucking mystery."

"Hey, look—if you want him, he's all yours." Finally, Soda addresses me. "Sorry we're late. Fucking Pepperoni got out again. Deacon and Rita had to help me find him."

"Poor thing was eating a dead seagull," Rita says.

"Well, he probably killed that seagull," Soda replies. "That cat is fucking vicious."

We all file down the stairs and start packing. Soda's Telly, Deacon's P-Bass, and all my breakables go into their cases. Pedals and cords are shoved into bags. Amps and cabinets go up the stairs and into the back of the station wagon.

On the way to the show, everyone talks like it's business as usual, but underneath, there's this low hum of electricity, like when you stand too close to a power conductor.

"Ever notice on *Friends* that Rachel's nipples are always hard? Like *always*," Deacon says.

"I don't watch *Friends*." This is Soda.

"How do you not watch *Friends*?" This is me.

"I don't know. I watch *Seinfeld*." Soda.

"It is possible to watch *both* shows, you realize." This is Rita.

I want to talk about other things. I want to talk about how I'm so nervous about the show and so fucked up about Kim and so happy about getting a scholarship, but it's all this weird, swirling deluge. I worry that if I take one finger out of the dike, everything else will come bursting out in some kind of permanently embarrassing way. I figure it's better just to keep it all contained and talk about TV.

When we get to the Odeon, Sloan's silver tour bus is parked outside, but there's no sign of its occupants. The Odeon used to be this big old movie theatre. The new owners cleared the seats, built a stage, painted everything black, and turned the concession stand into a sound booth. Now it's a bar that's so big it's never full and usually open only on Saturday nights for fundraisers and CD release parties for local bands. Most bigger acts usually play at the university or the Fort William Gardens, but seeing as Sloan is a little too big for the pub, and they don't draw the over-forty crowd required to fill the Gardens (my dad took me to see Kim Mitchell there in '88—*rah rah olé*), the theatre is an unlikely fit.

Outside, perpendicular to the bus, a lineup is already forming. We spend a few minutes trying to convince the brick shithouse of a bouncer at the back door that we're not just trying to sneak in. Eventually the promoter, a thirty-year-old guy dressed head to toe in Adidas appears and tells the shithouse that we're okay.

"Just load in your stuff and leave it by the stage."

We do as we're told and then lean against the stage while we await further instruction. Without anyone in it, the room seems enormous. There's even a balcony if people want to watch us from a safe distance. Eventually, the Adidas guy reappears and asks us to follow him. He takes the four of us across the room, through a set of doors, and up a flight of stairs into an office that I assume was once the projectionist booth.

Adidas surveys the room and lets loose with a weary sigh. Then he introduces himself as JP. He shakes hands with me and Soda, but just nods at Deacon and Rita, like he's reached his handshaking quota for the time being. I don't want to judge a book by its cover or anything, but I can't really say there's anything about him that suggests legitimate businessman. With his shaved head and thick neck, JP looks more like an aging boxer than a bar manager.

He inspects us up and down and frowns. "Okay. You guys are more than half an hour late. Your sound check was supposed to be at six thirty."

We glance at one another, eyebrows raised in confusion. As far as I knew, no one actually told us when to arrive. We just sort of guessed. Soundmen are not a particularly punctual species, but traditionally, sound check starts at seven o'clock.

"Sorry about that. We weren't really sure when to come, and then—" I stick a thumb toward Soda "—his cat got out."

JP rubs the back of his head and it makes a sandpapery sound. I expect him to say something like, "Goddamn cats," or at the very worst, "Don't let it happen again," but instead he stares at us for a while with these cold, dead eyes and says, "I'm trying to run an event here, and you've put me behind. I'm docking your pay by a hundred bucks."

Again, we look at each other, our faces all screwed up. What the hell was going on? Rita speaks first, as our manager, trying to head the other guys off at the pass with a little diplomacy.

"Okay. Hold on. Let's talk about this—" but before she can continue, Soda runs roughshod over her strategy.

"How the hell are we supposed to do a six-thirty sound check? We're sharing equipment with the other band, and they're not even here yet."

"This isn't about the other band. This is about you."

"You're only paying us two hundred bucks to begin with. Have you seen the lineup out there? You guys are going to make *thousands* of dollars tonight."

JP smirks at Soda.

"You think that lineup out there is for you? You guys should be paying *me* to play tonight. Consider yourself lucky."

We're not really in any position to argue. In fact, JP Adidas could kick us off the bill, pocket our cut, and it wouldn't put a dent in his bar sales.

"This is *such* bullshit," Soda says, with a hollow little laugh.

"Chalk it up to a learning experience," JP pontificates. "I've worked for a lot of big names and let me tell you, this is how it is. If you plan on staying in this business, you've got to learn to be *professional.*"

"You know you're wearing sweatpants, right?" Deacon asks him.

JP picks up his leather jacket off the desk chair, as if to announce he's done with the conversation, but then adds some final words of wisdom.

"Just be grateful that you learned this so early in your—" He looks at the band and I can almost hear him name us in his head: Skinny, Shorty, Indian Chief. "—in your *musical careers*."

I can see Indian Chief wrestling to keep his mouth shut, so I hustle him out the door and down the stairs, with Deacon hot on my heels. Soda gets a few feet ahead of me and ducks into a bathroom. I follow. He pounds a couple decent-sized dents into a paper towel dispenser before I grab his arm.

"Hey! Easy!"

Deacon walks in a second later. "You're going to mess up your strumming hand doing that," he says, surveying the damage.

Soda backs up against the wall and takes a deep breath. "I'm fine. I just—*fuck*. I hate guys like that."

"Like what? Guys who wear sweatpants?" Deacon asks.

"I'm going out for a smoke. Can you start setting up my amp if the other guys show?"

Deacon nods, and Soda's out the door.

In the next two hours, three notable things take place.

First, Bunsen Honeydew finally arrive and set up their gear. The soundguy, this bone-thin gargoyle with a ponytail down his back like a piece of nautical rope, tells us we're only getting a line check because we were late. It doesn't make any sense, but we don't bother fighting him. It's never a good idea to piss off your soundman. Instead, we sit and drink our two-dollar Cokes and watch as Kyle fusses with his ludicrous drum kit, and as Matty brags to anyone who will listen that they're going on tour at the end of May ("About ten or twelve dates. No big deal.").

Second, I see Kim. While Bunsen Honeydew sound check, Deacon and I decide to leave Rita and inspect the downstairs band room Matty had pointed out earlier ("We've played here a couple times before. Have you met JP? He's hilarious. Bought us all Jägerbombs last time."). Really, it's just a big storage closet with a couple metal folding chairs and a filthy couch. After the thrill wears off, we go back upstairs and there she is. My girlfriend. She's standing with her brother, drinking a beer. When she sees me, she whispers something in Townie's ear and then vanishes. Townie locates me, stares a couple daggers, then takes off after her. Because *I'm* the asshole.

The third and final notable incident occurs after Bunsen Honeydew's sound check, when Matty corners me outside the bathroom.

"Dude, check it out ..." He sticks out his tongue to show me what's on it—a tiny light-blue tab of paper. "Things are about to get fucking *in-sa-a-ane*."

"Are you sure that's a good idea?" I realize I sound like an enormous square, but seriously, dropping acid would be the last thing I'd want to do before getting in front of hundreds of people.

"Trust me, brother. It's a *great* idea," he assures me.

When I sit back down with Deacon and Rita, I'm a little alarmed that Soda hasn't materialized. JP's henchman soundguy appears at our table reeking of cigarette smoke and tells us we better be on that stage at ten o'clock sharp. He leaves and I look toward the back door, as if Soda will suddenly burst through it, stage lit and dry iced. He doesn't, and we're on in exactly thirty-six minutes.

"He'll be here," Rita says, reading my mind. "You guys go get ready. I'll set up the merch table."

"I'm not sure ..."

She shrugs and says, almost sadly, "Where else would he go?"

There're two full pint glasses of water in my jittery hands and the sides are already wet from little spills. I put one down beside Soda's amp. The other, I put down next to the monstrosity that is the Bunsen Honeydew drum kit. Slowly, and feeling very much like I'm on display, I twist and pull and adjust and readjust until the drums take a slightly more familiar form. The way the stage lights are, I can't really see the crowd very well, but I'm sure that somewhere in the audience Kyle is watching me tinker with his babies and seething through his beard. Stage left, Deacon is crouched in front of his amp, making minor adjustments, twiddling knobs. Then he stands, steps on a pedal with a clacking sound, and tunes his bass. I can hear the ugly, elastic twang of his metal roundwounds. I put a freshly sharpied set list underneath one of the legs of the floor tom and read over it one last time.

"How much longer do you think we can stall for?" I shout to Deacon over the house music (Metallica, 'Nothing Else Matters').

By way of answer, I hear the gargoyle's voice come through the monitors. "*All right, I'm going to need to hear some drum levels.*"

Reluctantly, I sit down at the kit, keeping my eye on the back door.

"*Bass drum?*"

I start pounding with my right foot. *Boom. Boom. Boom. Boom.* Still no Soda.

"*Okay. Snare?*"

Crack. Crack. Crack. Crack. Still no Soda.

"*Okay. Play the rest of the kit?*"

For about ten seconds, I make a racket that, I'm sure, annoys pretty much everyone in the bar. When I finish, I'm left in line-check purgatory for a couple minutes until I hear the sound gargoyle ask Deacon to play his bass. Deacon thumps through a few bars until we hear an irritable "Okay, that's fine."

Then comes the question we've been dreading.

"*Guitar?*"

"Uh," Deacon says into his mic, "he's not—"

And then, as if he's been waiting there the entire time, Soda plugs his Telecaster into Thaler's Fender Twin and strums a few bars.

"Never mind," Deacon mumbles.

"So-daah!" I can hear someone in the audience—a girl—yell his name.

"Nice fucking timing," I say from behind the drums.

"*Check the vocals.*"

Soda taps the mic. "Check one. Sibilance. Sibilance."

"Sodapop!" another voice—another girl—yells.

Deacon taps the other mic. "Check check. Syphilis. Sipowicz."

The house music implodes in on itself and the room is impossibly quiet, save for the hornet's nest of amplifiers. Deacon looks at Soda and he nods. He looks back at me and I do the same. We're starting. My first four stick clicks sound tiny and insignificant.

'Necessary Evil.' We play our first song to an empty pool of light on the dance floor. It's okay—a little shaky, maybe. First songs usually are. As my eyes adjust to the darkness, I can see the outline of approximately four hundred people ignoring us.

'Glass Knuckles.' Even though we play it all right, the end of our second song is still only met with a smattering of polite applause. Soda's maintaining a certain level of swagger, and Deacon's bantering away to the crowd, inviting people to come up to the front, but personally, I'm losing what little nerve I have. This is the curse of the opening act at a big show like this. You're an obstacle in the way of the main event. People expect you to suck, and so you suck.

'Thirty Helens Agree.' Halfway through the third song, I can feel all my insecurities converging. It's like I'm disconnected from my own arms and just watching them play the drums. I worry that if I even *think* the wrong thing, they'll just stop on their own accord. Worse is the knowledge that Kim and her brother are watching us go down in flames. Townie will probably write about it in his stupid zine.

But then, during the breakdown of 'Helens,' the quiet part where it's just me stomping on the bass drum and Deacon pedaling on the G, a few figures bravely creep out of the darkness. Evie. Ruth. Rotten. It's something, and when we drop back into the chorus, I try to play as if they're the only people in the room. By the end of the song, Danny Grove and Mark Zaborniak have joined them.

'One Jenny Too Many.' We go right into the next song to build our momentum. There are more familiar faces. Jay Olejnik, Brandy Sawchuck, and Todd Farkas materialize, and everyone sheepishly moves closer to the stage. A small crowd grows behind them. Kim and Townie materialize on the periphery, and a sad flash goes through my chest when she looks up at me.

When we play one of Soda's new ones ('Unbreakable Hearts' Club'), things start to snowball. People I don't recognize fill out the crowd, along with people I do recognize but didn't expect to see tonight. Toby Watkins and his doppelgänger girlfriend. Rita's lesbian and/or communist roommates. Even Howlin' Mad Murdock, dressed in a t-shirt and blazer, stands in the crowd, a glass of beer sweating in his hand.

Afterward, when the applause and cheering get swallowed up in the house music, I'm sweaty and relieved and flooded with endorphins. In the end, it was a good show. I want to be as happy as I think I should be, but there's something strangely anticlimatic about the moment. Once all the fear and excitement is gone, it leaves a hole for all the Kim-related sadness to seep in. Now there's no excuse. No hiding from her. She's out there, and she's going to break my heart.

"Uh, guys? We have a bit of a problem here."

By the time Deacon and I head down to the band room, Soda's already waiting for us at the door. Beads of sweat still cling to his forehead and he smells like Right Guard. I can see around his shoulder that Matty is sitting on the dirty floor, hugging his knees to his chest. He's shirtless, muttering to himself, and his eyes are blank and pink. In the back corner of the room, Andy, Kyle, and Sudbury Steve are huddled and talking in low, strained voices. I put down my snare and slide my cymbal bag off my shoulders.

"Matty's pretty fucked up," Soda explains. "They don't think he can play." I can only hear snatches of their conversation.

"... there's no way ..."

"... a thousand dollars, though ..."

"... instrumental, or ... ?"

Here's the thing. Unless you're Jerry Garcia or Jim Morrison, you might want to lay off dropping vast quantities of acid before a big show. Actually, seeing as though Jim Morrison's dead, I guess he's not exactly the best example. Don't get me wrong. I don't want to sound like an after-school special or anything. I thought the episodes of *Degrassi Junior High* where Shane takes acid and then falls off a bridge were hilarious. Soda's done acid a bunch of times, and I know Kim has, too. If I were a little ballsier, I'd probably give it a shot, but seeing Matty—who's now tasting each of the couch cushions with the tip of his tongue—firmly retraces the drug line I draw at marijuana.

"What are they going to do?" I gesture toward the rest of the band.

Soda shrugs, but I think we both have a pretty good idea of what's going to happen next. It's Thaler the Wailer who finally pops the question. He walks over to us, looks at me and Deacon for a second, and then propositions Soda.

"We need you to fill in for Matty."

Soda looks at him. "You want me to sing? I just sang an entire set."

"Come on, man. You know all the covers. 'Friend of the Devil.' 'Riders on the Storm,' 'Back in the USSR.' I'll write down the lyrics for the originals—they're really simple, and you know how they go."

Soda turns to us. "I'm only going to do this if it's cool with you guys."

I can tell by the look on Deacon's face that it's decidedly not cool, but the fact that Soda's asking permission makes it somehow impossible to say no. Plus, desperate times and all that junk. Without a lot of enthusiasm, we both nod our heads.

He tells the rest of the band, and a few moments later they're all walking out the door together.

"All right," Sudbury Steve claps his hands together. "Here goes nothing."

"Oh," Thaler says offhandedly, "can you guys babysit Matty while we're on?" He doesn't wait for an answer.

"Fuck," Deacon says quietly.

"*Fuckuckuckuckuck* ..." Matty parrots.

A floor above, I can hear Thaler introduce Soda as their "special guest singer," and there's a couple seconds of confusion that dovetail into a lot of cheering and hollering. It takes about two songs for Ruth and Rita to find us in the band room.

"What the shit is Soda doing up there singing 'Scarlet Begonias'?" Rita asks.

"You're so *beautiful*," Matty tells her. "Your *face* is like the *moon* ..."

Things are quickly self-evident.

"Oh, for fuck's sake," Rita mutters. "And—*Jesus*, why aren't you guys helping him? Where's his shirt? It's freezing down here." She takes my parka off the coat rack and wraps it around Matty's shoulders.

"*So warm* ..." he says, sliding his arms through the holes.

"Great," I grumble. "Now my jacket's going to smell like patchouli and armpits."

Rita and Ruth stick around, partly to keep us company and partly because they don't like Bunsen Honeydew. After a little while, they offer to relieve me and Deacon from babysitting duty so we can watch the end of Soda's set. Deacon opts to stay, but I decide to go take a look. Matty's pretty out of it, but he seems calm enough. As I leave, he's leaning his head against the wall and watching the concrete floor like it's a television set.

When I get upstairs there's a pretty solid crowd in front of the stage. It's about the same size as ours—maybe a little bigger—but with a lot more interpretive dance. I keep to the back to avoid getting hit by a twirling skirt or beaded necklace. Soda's halfway through 'Munchies From Outer Space,' and while it's still an undeniably terrible song, his version is at least a little more listenable.

"Wasn't this guy your lead singer, too?" someone asks when the song ends.

"Yep," I say, keeping my eyes on the stage. I can see Soda skimming through the lyrics of the next song. "Their regular singer's too stoned to play. He's just filling in."

"Oh yeah. Sort of like Joe Strummer taking over for Shane MacGowan in '91."

Jesus, who just *knows* this kind of stuff? That's when I look over and realize that, for the second time this year, I'm having a conversation with Chris Murphy from Sloan. Of course. Chris Murphy from Sloan knows this kind of stuff.

"Well, killer pipes," he says, "but I liked your set better."

"Really? Thanks!"

Despite my telepathic efforts to keep the band quiet, Soda starts into another song. 'Hydroponica.' I wait for the instrumental part in the middle before I make conversation again.

"I'm Pete," I tell Chris.

"Chris." No shit.

"We met before when you came through with the Super Friendz."

"I remember. *Giant Killer.*" He says our name with theatrical menace, the way a six-year-old boy might say *dinosaur* or a fifteen-year-old boy might say *Slayer*. Immediately, I wish we had gone with Kid Charlemagne. "You guys have this sort of Teenage-Head-meets-Crazy-Horse thing going on."

I have no idea what he's talking about. "Is that a good thing?"

"For sure it's a good thing. I'm into it. Do you guys have any plans to tour?"

So. This is how it all starts. Our band was going to get signed, go on tour with Sloan, and rule the entire universe. When Kim eventually dumped me, the fragments of my broken heart would be glued back together by a long line of indie rock groupies who, while generally not as cleavaged or hot-panted as their hard rock counterparts, would make up for it in kind with charming shyness, cat's eye glasses, and basic literacy skills.

"I'm going to give you my number," he says when 'Hydroponica' finally finishes. "Maybe we could do a couple dates when we come back through Ontario this summer, and—"

"*Pete*!" Ruth suddenly appears in front of me, breathless, pulling on my sleeve. I don't understand it. Why is Ruth interrupting Chris Murphy from Sloan?

"Pete, it's Matty."

I don't care. I don't care. Fucking Matty was *not* going to fuck this all up again.

"He just start freaking out—scratching at his face—then he took off and ran outside. We all chased after him but—" She catches her breath, and I notice her eyes are wet with tears.

God-fucking-damn it. Fucking Matty was going to fuck this up again.

Chris Murphy from Sloan looks concerned, and his words break the spell. "You should probably go help your friend."

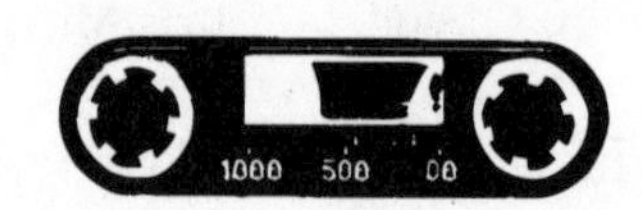

Outside on the main drag, there's already a crowd gathering. Bad news travels fast. People stand around in the frozen slush and stomp their feet. I follow Ruth to Rita and Deacon. Matty's about twenty feet away, lying on the road. The alternating red and blue lights from a cop car reflect off his face and make him look ghoulish. The blood coming out of his nose looks black. His bushy dreadlocks spring from his head like a cartoon explosion. One of the cops, a middle-aged woman—crouches beside him with her ear to his mouth. The other one, a young guy with a goatee, stands a little ways down the road and talks to some kids beside a pick-up truck. The truck that hit Matty.

"The ambulance is on its way," Rita tells me. "We're supposed to stay back and give him air. He just fucking *took off*." I've never seen Rita cry before.

I suddenly need a cigarette. Is it bad form to smoke while someone you know might be dying in the middle of the street? I look around and notice a few other people smoking. One of them is Mr. Murdock, so I figure it's okay. Rita lets me step back a few feet to light up. As I move, I get a better view of the pick-up and realize that I've seen it before. The enormous blue-and-white Ford is half on the curb, and the headlights are looking at each other cross-eyed from either side of a lamppost. I walk past my friends and go a little further up the street to get a clearer view of the driver and his passenger, who lean against a recently repainted tailgate. Dave Greatorex has an ugly-looking cut on his forehead, and Brad McLaren is wide eyed and holds his Montreal Canadiens cap in front of him by the brim. They're talking to the cop with the goatee, and Greatorex is waving his hands around emphatically. When I walk a few steps closer I catch the end of what he's saying.

"... just playing a joke. Give him a scare."

The cop says something inaudible.

"That's what I'm *saying*." Greatorex's hockey rink voice cuts through the night and a couple people look in his direction. "We thought he *was* somebody else. He was fuckin' stumbling around in the middle of the road ... he didn't get out of the way ..."

I look back at Matty's body, still wrapped in my Han Solo parka. It's suddenly very clear to me just who they were trying to scare.

I hear the ambulance for what seems like a long while before it arrives. When it does show up, it's a carnival ride of noise and light. It seems funny that something so deadly serious can arrive so cheerfully. The paramedics spill out and work with cool precision to get Matty onto the stretcher and then into the back of the van. Only after the sirens finally Doppler themselves out of earshot do I notice Kim. She's standing around with Townie and Jay Olejnik. Her face is a mess of mascara, and I know I should go to her, maybe even hold her hand. She's technically still my girlfriend, after all, and I don't need to be afraid of her tonight. Not after all this. Even Mr. Murdock goes over and talks to her. *Annie*, he's probably saying to her, *where's Ringo tonight? Shouldn't he be out here with you?* It seems like a good moment to make an appearance, and I'm about to when I notice something strange.

People comfort each other in times of crisis, so it's pretty understandable when Murdock puts his hand on Kim's shoulder and smiles at her. But then, as they keep talking, there's this tiny gesture—honestly, if I didn't think it was so weird to see a teacher smoking, I probably would've missed it. Kim reaches down and takes his cigarette in her fingers without breaking eye contact. Kim's pretty bold, and it's not like she hasn't stolen a smoke before, but when Murdock doesn't react, when he lets it leave his fingers as if she's done it a hundred times before, it hits me like a truck.

Kim isn't sleeping with Sudbury Steve, or another musician, or even some guy she met in one of her classes. She's sleeping with my OAC Art teacher. She's sleeping with Mr. Murdock.

SIDE B

Rebellion (Lies)

"Yep. Murdock is totally fucking you," Ruth says. She shoots back the rest of the cold coffee left in her thermos lid and brushes the crumbs off her skirt.

"Murdock? I thought this was the department head's job."

"Yeah, but Murdock's the VP in charge of timetabling for next semester. Plus, I don't think even Gail is cruel enough to give you three Civics classes in a row."

I tack the piece of paper to the bulletin board with one pushpin and then stab it repeatedly with another.

"I don't know what you did to that guy in a former life, Pete, but he's definitely got it in for you."

The office doesn't have any more work for me today, so I'm just packing up to go home. Ruth opens the door to leave for her next class, then stops at the threshold. "Hey," she says, "don't forget we've got that thing tonight."

"What 'thing'?"

Ruth rolls her eyes in disgust. "I knew you'd forget. You're worse than Deacon."

"Let's not get crazy here. *Nobody's* worse than Deacon."

She ignores me. "The dinner party. At Sharon and Ray's."

I stare blankly.

"My cousin Sharon? You went to their shag?"

"Shit," I say. It all comes back to me. "Why would I agree to that?"

"Well, you did, and you're coming. Don't try to get out of it now."

"Is it just the five of us? Won't that be kind of weird? That's about as fifth wheel as you can get."

"I think there'll be others."

I smell a rat. A lady rat, to be precise. "This isn't some kind of fix-up, is it?"

"No," Ruth says.

"Because the last thing I need is to get stuck sitting next to someone with a 'great personality'—" I use air quotes for emphasis "—who complains about her divorce all night or starts quizzing me on whether or not I like kids."

"I get it."

"I mean, I'm sorry, but the viability of one's eggs is just *not* good dinner conversation."

"*Okay*! All right! No fix-ups."

"Good," I say, leaning forward a little in my chair, "'cause I'm kind of just getting out of a ... situation ... right now."

"Oh," Ruth pauses a moment. "So you're not boning the superintendent's wife any more?"

Deacon.

"I know all about your little 'situation,' Pete," she says before she closes the door.

The fact is, I hadn't really talked to Vicky for a couple weeks. Even earlier today, I kept an eye out for her on my way to class, but no dice. I used to see her like clockwork in the hallway before Ancient Civ, but I'm starting to think she's changed her route, along with our ... situation.

Two Sundays ago, she showed up at my apartment and kissed me backward onto my unmade bed without saying a word. Afterward, as she was cinching up her jeans, she told me her marriage was over. Jamie was moving out. I wanted to be sympathetic, but all I could think about was how long it would be until her husband showed up banging on my door. Or worse yet, how long until he found a way to transfer me up north to Nip-Rock High. Vicky assured me my fears were unwarranted, that our secret was still a secret.

"I tried to call him last Sunday when he was supposed to be at his parents' place," she explained. "I couldn't get the remote to work with the new DVD player. I had just rented *Love Actually* and I *really* wanted to watch it. He wasn't picking up his cell, so finally just I dialed his parents' landline, even though I *hate* talking to his mother on the phone."

It turned out that her husband was not the infuriatingly dedicated mama's boy she believed him to be. For almost two years he had not been visiting his parents in Dryden every two or three weeks, but rather a twenty-six-year-old phys. ed. teacher named Natalie who lived in Marathon.

"They met *online*," she added bitterly. "Who meets *online*? Losers. Shut-ins. People with too many cats."

"Actually," I said, "online dating is becoming a pretty legitimate—" My defence of the internet ended abruptly when I saw the murder in her eyes. "Sorry."

She sighed and tugged a tank top over her skinny frame. "It's okay. It was bound to happen sooner or later."

When you're having an affair, you tell yourself that every time is the last time. At least, that's what I did. But when the last time comes, it always comes too soon. Vicky is old enough to play a hot mom on TV. She has those weird, stripy highlights women over thirty colour into their hair, and she thinks alternative is a real genre of music. We have absolutely nothing in common except adultery and teaching high school. And yet, when she was standing in my bedroom that night, buttoning up a very professional-looking blouse and seeming very out of place next to my clip-framed album covers and cheap Ikea bookshelves, I knew I still wanted it to happen again.

After that, she stopped calling me. We never talked about it, but when I saw her at work, I could tell by the sad little smile she gave me that things were probably done. She didn't really need me to self-destruct anymore. What's weird, though, is that over the last few days, she seemed to be overtly avoiding me. I've caught her a couple times in the photocopy room, and I've tried to be friendly—you know, just let her know there's no hard feelings—but both times she made an excuse and disappeared.

Stupidly, I finally broke down and told Deacon about the whole situation over a couple beers—Vicky, Jamie, the phys. ed. teacher from Marathon. Now that it was over, I had to tell someone. Apparently, so did Deacon.

When the three of us arrive at Sharon and Ray's place, I realize we're not alone. Sharon introduces me to "one of the girls from work," a thin, big-eyebrowed woman named Carol, and just as I start to feel a little apprehensive, she introduces me to Nick, her chubby, cherub-faced husband. Nick is pleased to meet everyone. Carol seems relatively indifferent. Once everyone finishes the very grown-up business of shaking hands, Sharon offers to take us on the "grand tour." Carol and Nick choose to stay and catch up with Ray. Apparently they've seen it.

Sharon and Ray have one of those big places up in Cherry Ridge that was built in the late eighties. They bought it a couple years ago and since then had ripped out and renovated most of the interior. As we walk, Sharon proudly explains that Ray's done most of the work himself. He owns a small contracting business, and it looks like he knows what he's doing—cathedral ceilings, marble countertops, swooping *Gone with the Wind* staircase. It's the kind of house I could afford to live in only if I married rich.

On our way upstairs to see Sharon's favourite feature (it turns out to be a shower with a glass door and a hydra of built-in shower heads), we pass a series of framed photographs that could be called *Sharon and Ray: A Sears Portrait Retrospective*. Deacon nudges me, just before our hostess slows down to carbon-date each image.

"We get these done every couple years," Sharon explains. "Ray knows the photographer."

When we get back downstairs, we find Ray, Carol, and Nick standing in the kitchen. Ray has a bottle of Coors Light in his hand, while Carol is sniffing at a glass of red wine.

"Can I offer you something?" Ray says. "We've got beer, rye, vodka—I just opened a bottle of Chateauneuf ..."

Deacon and I each take a Silver Bullet.

"Just one—" Ruth says to Deacon. "You're driving."

Deacon shrugs. When Ruth turns away, Ray gives him a covert wink. *Short leash, huh, buddy?*

The living room has one of those swanky raised fireplaces. I stand with a flaming orange log unsettlingly close to my face and try to follow Ray and Nick's conversation about the Leafs. Eventually, Sharon says something about checking on the chicken, and Ray redirects the conversation away from hockey. At first, I think it's a good thing.

"Hey, Shar," he says, "do you mind if I take the boys downstairs before we eat? I want to show them something."

"*Sure*, hon." There's something suspiciously complicit in the tone of her voice. I half expect her to pull a big open-mouthed wink. "Maybe the girls could help me in the kitchen."

I feel a little weird about this very 1950s division of gender. Despite my best efforts, I always find most "Men Only" stuff kind of lame. As we head down into the finished basement, I wonder on what field of masculinity I'll inevitably disappoint our host. Will I be forced to grimace down some stupidly expensive scotch? Or hack on an imported cigar? Maybe I'll luck out and Ray will turn out to be a model train aficionado. Those I could get behind.

It turns out to be none of these things.

"Nicky's seen this before," Ray says, "but I thought you guys might get a kick out of it."

We round the corner past a cold storage and wine cellar, where Ray opens a door on which a sign warns *Beatles Parking Only, All Others Will Need Help.*

"Holy ..." I hear Deacon say.

Suddenly I find myself in what has to be the *most* tricked-out rehearsal studio I've ever seen in my entire life. First of all, he's got this beautiful set of clear-finish Gretsch USA Customs, along with a full arsenal of cymbals, percussion, and a fucking *gong* behind it. Beside that he's got a rack of synthesizers, and a bunch of crazy shit I don't know anything about except for the fact that they're expensive as hell. He's also got a real deal Hammond B3 *and* a Leslie speaker. On the far wall, a rack of seven or eight guitars and basses stand like erect penises.

Ray and Nick watch us, beaming like a couple dads letting their kids run wild in a toy store. I'm no gearhead, but I can tell Ray's got at least twenty thousand dollars' worth of stuff in here, easy. Deacon, who *is* a gearhead, has already camped out in front of a wall of amps—Fender, Marshall, Trace Elliot. He seems particularly taken with a big Traynor.

"You want to try it out?" Ray asks.

He lifts a polished MusicMan StingRay out of the rack.

"Holy!" Deacon says again and takes the bass with two hands.

"That's a rosewood fretboard, there. The body's ash. Neck's maple. It's got dual humbuckers, and I've got a set of flatwounds on it right now. Sounds fat as hell. Plugger in!"

Deacon's eyes find the ceiling. "I better not," he says. "It'll be pretty loud."

"Ah, hell," Ray dismisses him. "I soundproofed the shit out of this room. See these?" He raps on the wall with his knuckles. "Acoustic panels. And behind that, you got high-density concrete. Between them I've got a layer of rockwool. I could wail on those drums for hours and Sharon wouldn't hear a mouse fart."

Suitably impressed, we all nod our heads.

"Here, let me get you a patch cord," Ray tells Deacon.

"You know what?" Deacon gazes lovingly at the bass, then holds it back out to Ray. "Let's do it next time. If I get started, I might not want to stop."

There's a little pause, and I notice Ray gives Nick a look.

"Well," he finally says, "to be completely honest, Deacon, that's sort of what I brought you boys down here to talk about."

The tone of his voice confirms my earlier suspicions. This *was* a fix-up after all.

Nick, who's been pretty quiet this entire time, suddenly chimes in. "Sharon says you guys used to back up Jesse Maracle."

Ray flashes a *shut-up* look at Nick. "So, yeah. Nick and I have been practising a bunch down here. You know, rocking out on some covers with a drum machine, but writing some of our own tunes, too."

Let it be known: I *hate* it when people call songs "tunes."

"In any case," Ray continues, "we thought you might like to, shit, I don't know, come jam sometime. See what happens."

The thing is, I know already that I have no interest in "jamming" with these two. Ray's not a bad guy, and Nick seems okay, but the truth of it is, we're just not on the same wavelength. We're not going to make beautiful music together. That's just the way it is. Of course, that said, it's going to be hard to find a way out of this that doesn't sound like I'm calling them a pair of assholes.

Thankfully, there's a knock at the door. It's Sharon.

"You boys and your toys," she says, pleased as punch to be scolding us. "You'd spend all night down here if I didn't come get you. Dinner's on the table, so come on up."

When she leaves, Deacon shrugs a little *What can you do?* toward our would-be bandmates. I'm hoping we can leave things a little fuzzy, but Ray presses the issue.

"So what do you guys think? Jam sesh? Next weekend?"

"Well," I hear myself say, "the Gentlemen Callers have a show coming up in June—" Deacon looks at me sideways. *We do?* "—so let's table it until then. Cool?"

I leave twenty thousand dollars' worth of musical equipment in my wake before Ray can respond. I can tell he's not completely happy. He wants to pin us down, but I'm not going to let that happen. Maybe next time he'll know enough to get us a little drunker first. Deacon would've had his hands all over that StingRay after a couple more beers.

When we get back upstairs, the spread is pretty formal. Sharon's busted out the cloth napkins and wine glasses, and she's making rounds with a bottle of expensive-looking white wine. Ray gives a toast about old friends and new, then we all dig in. The dinner conversation begins.

Everyone except Ruth and Deacon agree that the chicken is great. Sharon is so sorry that she forgot her cousin and husband are vegetarians, and loads them up with the lion's share of pasta salad. Ruth says it's no big deal, really. I'm constantly afraid that Ray's going to want to chat a little more about "jamming" on his "tunes," but thankfully, he steers clear of the subject. I guess he's keeping it in the clubhouse for now. Instead, he circles back around to the hockey season, but when Deacon and I don't bite, he starts in on teaching.

"So what do you guys make of these new 'standard practices' I keep reading about in the paper?" Ray asks.

"They're a pain in the ass," Ruth says after another mouthful of pasta salad.

"Well," Ray says, smiling sagely at his chicken, "I guess no one likes being told what to do."

For a brief moment, there's just the sound of cutlery scraping against porcelain, and I wonder if Ruth is going to let it go. She isn't.

"It's not that at all." She takes a sip from her wine glass and puts it back down on the table. "You just can't expect every class to be taught the exact same way."

"Hey, what's good for the goose ..." Ray reinforces his position.

"Standard practices aren't good for anybody," Ruth fires back. "They just kill anything we do in class that's interesting or creative."

That last bit should strike a chord with Ray. Wasn't it just last month that he talked about how boring school was, and how the best thing he ever learned in English class was how Neil Peart had a boner for Objectivist authors?

"Ah, hell, you know, being creative is great and all, but kids need more than that touchy-feely crap. You can't be out there playing jazz on the taxpayer's dime. Don't forget, Ruthie, I'm the guy who pays your salary."

'Ruthie' puts down her fork with a clatter and I ready myself for the inevitable shitstorm.

Nick's hand drifts across the table for wine, like a tumbleweed at high noon. Sharon smiles some more, but she looks uncomfortable. "Does anyone want seconds? There's lots of everything ..."

Just in time, Deacon successfully changes the subject. "So ... how are the wedding plans coming?"

Sharon, sensing both an ally and an opportunity to turn things around, clutches her fiancé's arm and explains to Deacon that, as an early wedding present, he's building them a brand-new camp out on One Island Lake. She imagines her future summer home in a filibuster that details two fireplaces (fieldstone), a deck (wraparound), a sauna and boathouse (western red cedar), paint colours (Dark Truffle and Kenya), living room upholstery (microsuede), and other excruciating particulars.

Later, even a much-hyped lemon meringue pie fails to neutralize the toxicity of the evening, and we soon say our farewells with all the thespian stiffness of fourth-graders in a school recital.

"Dinner was delicious."

"Thanks. That was really fun."

"Yes. We should do it again. Soon."

Neither Ray or Nick mention anything about getting together to "jam" on their "tunes." I suspect the crisis has been averted. On the way home, we tell Ruth about Ray's masterbatorium.

"Completely soundproofed? God. Are they really that terrible?"

"We didn't stick around to find out."

"Hey, Pete," Deacon eyes me in the rearview. "What did you mean about the Gentleman Callers playing in June? That was just bullshit, right?"

When Ruth turns around to hear my answer, the look on her face makes the decision for me.

"You know what? Fuck it. Let's play the Bunsen Burner."

Ruth smiles. "It's not called that this year. Since the city's involved, Matty's mom made it all legit. Now it's the Wheeler Foundation Fundraiser for Spinal Cord Research."

"Just rolls off the tongue."

"And it's not at the Polish Legion either. It's going to be this big outdoor concert dealie down by the Marina."

"Well," I say, "it looks like spinal cord research is moving up in the world."

The next day at school, I see Vicky. Twice. The first time is in the morning. She passes me as she comes out of the staff caf with a cup of coffee that lurches like a miniature wave pool. She doesn't seem to notice me. Later, I see her just before I get to my second-period class. She appears at the other end of the hall, then stops and stares at me like a deer that's just wandered out of the woods and into oncoming traffic. I give a little wave, but she looks away and keeps walking. I feel a little bit sad and a little bit free.

Kids start filing in and taking their seats, pulling their binders out of their bags, chatting with their seating partners, checking their cell phones. I review my notes and remember that I've actually got a pretty decent lesson on Aztec ruins, so I pick up a piece of chalk and tell students to take out a sheet of lined paper. Just then, as I'm writing the word *Mesoamerican* on the blackboard and silently congratulating myself on having climbed out the Sarlacc's Pit of ill-advised romance, Video Store Girl walks in. She sits down in an empty desk and unzips her backpack, as if she's been in my class all along.

"Alex?"

"Hey, good job," she says, smiling. "You remembered my name. See? You don't have brain damage after all."

"Uh, what are you doing here?"

Before she has a chance to answer, Jonathan Heyen-Miller walks in and spots her.

"*Alex*?" he says, crossing directly in front of me. "Are you in this class now? That's amazing!"

I looked for her. In spite of what was happening with Vicky, I stopped by Video Hutch no fewer than six times in the past month. I had never rented so many movies in such a short period of time. *The Bourne Supremacy. Dodgeball. Mean Girls. Mystic River. The Day After Tomorrow.* And, for some reason, *White Chicks.* Finally, I swallowed my pride and asked the tattooed kid behind the counter when Alex was working next. He looked at me like I was old and square and told me Alex had quit a couple weeks ago. And now here she was, sitting in my Ancient Civilizations class.

"Alex, can I see you out in the hall for a sec?"

"Sure thing, *Mister Curtis.*"

When she says my name like that, something feels very wrong. I shut the door of my classroom and look at her. She's still smiling.

"So, what are you doing here?" I ask, keeping my voice down.

"Well, I had planned on studying Ancient Civilizations. And your note on the blackboard says something about the Aztecs, so I'm thinking ..."

"I mean what are you doing in a *high school*?"

"I'm a high school student." She takes the attendance folder out of my hand, opens it and points to a name on the class list. "See? Right there. Alexandra Carter."

She *had* been in my class all along. On paper, at least.

"But—" I try to make sense of it "—you were an art student. You went to an art school in Montreal and rode your bicycle and lived with some guy with a weird French name I can't remember right now."

"Joaquim. And it was an arts high school. And I never graduated. Look, I need two more credits to get my diploma. The guidance counsellor put me in grade twelve Art because I can just hand in a bunch of the paintings I did in Montreal. She put me in your class because, well, apparently it's a bird course."

"But ... we went to a bar ... together. You bought me a *beer*."

"Why are you yelling?"

"I'm whispering!"

"You're whisper-yelling. Calm down."

Bethany Atkinson, arriving late, gives us both a strange look as she passes us and goes inside the classroom.

"First of all," she explains, "I'm twenty years old, and I imagine you're twenty-something—"

"—eight."

"Twenty-eight. So there. We're both old enough to buy alcohol in the province of Ontario. No problem. Secondly—" she looks around and says the next part quietly "—nothing happened. With us, I mean."

"I can't—" I try to articulate what I'm thinking, but nothing comes out. I brush past Alex and go back into the classroom.

"Folks, I'm sorry," I tell everyone. "Something's come up. Could you please start reading chapter four in your textbook?" As one, the class lets out an irritable groan. I raise my voice over all the grousing. "I'll be in the office for a few minutes. Sit tight."

I scurry down the hallway. I'm not sure exactly what I'm going to do, but somehow, I had to get her transferred out of my class. When I get to the office, I ask Kathy who I should speak to about a student named Alexandra Carter. She gives me a strange smile, and for second, I can't help but wonder if I'm completely transparent. "You should probably talk to Ken about her," she tells me. Before I can object, she picks up the phone and dials his extension. "You busy? Pete Curtis wants to talk to you about Alex."

No, he doesn't. Murdock's the last person I want to talk to about this. And even if he wasn't, I've just left all my students alone to ask squidgy questions about an attractive twenty-year-old student. How much more rope would he need to hang me?

"You can go in, Pete," Kathy says. "He's not doing anything important in there."

I find Murdock in his office staring at a computer, toggling between the screens of some unfamiliar software. Maybe he's finding new ways to ruin my next semester, like assigning me after school detention supervision five days a week.

"Mister Starkey," he says without looking up. "What can I do you for?"

I try to build a case. "Well, I was wondering what the deal is with

Alexandra Carter. She skips out for half the semester, then waltzes into my classroom today like she owns the place."

There. That's a perfectly legitimate question. Even Murdock must know you can't just blow off half a semester, no matter how attractive and mature you might be.

"Well, the *deal*, Ringo—" he studies me for a moment "—is that Alex has been out of school for a couple years, and she's back to get her diploma because she's too smart to wait tables for the rest of her life. So you're going to cut her a little slack because she's a great kid and ... well—" he hesitates for a moment, as though he's not sure I need to know the next part "—because she's my daughter."

I can hear Murdock's voice hurtling out from ten years ago, just before the Mackenzie King Battle of the Bands: "*Ali, honey—don't drink all the orange pop, Sweet Pea ...*"

When I go back to my class, I try not to look directly at her. Instead, I stand at the front of the room, with my dress shirt tucked in and my khakis pleated, and try to ignore her. She, in turn, slouches in her NoMeansNo t-shirt and ignores me right back.

How was it that only a few weeks ago we were on the same frequency? Now she was Brave New Waves and I might as well be John Tesh. I muddle through what's left of my lesson and make a point not to watch Alex leave when the bell rings. I walk through the empty hallways and past the detritus left by teenagers. An orphaned pen. A crunched can of pop next to, but not inside, a garbage can. An uneaten sandwich in a ziplock bag on the ground. I wait until I'm off school property before I light a cigarette.

SIDE A

The First Day of Spring

When I leave the hospital, there's a big sign that says *No Smoking Within Twenty Feet of Entrance.* It hasn't stopped a lot of people. They stand out in the May sunshine with their coats over their hospital gowns, their hands gripping the polls of their IV carts, and their lungs filled with rich tobacco. I light up and keep walking toward the bus stop.

I thought maybe when Kim and I broke up, I'd quit smoking. I told myself it was a way of taking control of my life, but the real reason was that every time I lit up, I couldn't help but think of lying naked on the floor of her living room. For those first couple weeks, I'd either get depressed and smoke or smoke and get depressed. So in a grand gesture, I threw the rest of my du Mauriers in a trash can. Sixteen hours later, I bought a fresh pack.

Hospitals always smell so gross, and the lighting is so depressing. It was really fucked up seeing Matty like that—head screwed into a halo, tube in his neck, hooked up to a respirator. I'm not going to pretend—like a lot of people at my school seem to pretend—that Matty was my best buddy, or say, "*Oh*, it's such a *tragic* thing to happen to such a *gifted* young man," like Sundell did at the school assembly. I think Matty was a mediocre singer, a lousy guitar player, and he did way too many drugs.

I think it's bullshit that since the accident all everyone talks about is his "lost potential." That said, he's my friend. Or at least, he's in my circle of friends. I guess it's only right I visit him.

Still, there's this weird culture of celebrity around people who almost die. With Matty, they didn't allow visitors for a couple weeks. When they finally did, it was like a dam burst. Going to see Matty stretched out in a hospital bed and shitting himself became the hottest thing to do in Thunder Bay. Goths, Bangers, Skaters, Pussies, everybody did it. Even teachers. Deacon said they ran into Madame Greene, and that she was wearing these really tight jeans and a low-cut shirt. I couldn't help but wonder if quadriplegics can still get it up.

I waited until things cooled off a little before I went. I didn't want people thinking I was just another disaster groupie, and plus, I was kind of hoping to go with Soda, but he wound up going with the Bunsen Honeydew guys. In any case, it took me forty-five minutes to bus over to Port Arthur General, and when I finally found his room, Matty was asleep. The nerve of some people.

"Matty will be happy to know you stopped by," his mom told me. She was dressed in these really flowy clothes and scarves, sort of like a gypsy. She acted cheerful, but I could tell she was tired and sad. I put the flowers my mom insisted I buy next to the billions of other bouquets and arrangements and gift baskets that cluttered his small room and looked for the exit.

About two blocks from the bus stop, I notice a 1991 Chevy Cavalier driving toward me. The Divorcemobile. It slows down and pulls over. I see Kim lean across the seat and crank down the passenger side window.

"Hey," she says as I pass by.

I keep walking and she reverses her car to catch up with me. "Hey!" she says again. I stop. Car beats pedestrian, every time. One of these days, I'm going to have to fucking well learn how to drive.

"What?"

She turns off the engine. "Did you see Matty?"

"Yep."

"How is he?"

"Asleep."

"I went and saw him a few days ago. I promised I'd bring him a copy of the new *Rolling Stone* with Tom Petty on the cover, but they were sold out, so I got him the new *Spin*. It's got a thing on PJ Harvey. I'm not sure if he even likes PJ Harvey."

A car swerves around her and honks. Technically, she's in a no-stopping zone, and someone wants her to know it.

"Why are you telling me all this?"

She slides over to the passenger seat and looks up at me. I remember we had sex on that seat once. It reclines all the way back.

"Ken says you're not going to class. That you haven't gone for almost three weeks."

"*Ken* says?"

"Yeah. Ken. That's his name. He's a person and he's got a name."

"Sure. He's also got a wife and a kid."

An exasperated sigh inflates her cheeks. She slides back behind the wheel. "Just go to class." She turns the key in the ignition and starts to pull away. "Don't fuck up your last year of high school just because of me."

Even when it's about me, it's really just about her.

So far, I hadn't told anyone that Kim had dumped me for my OAC Art teacher. Even just saying it in my head made me sick to my stomach, so I imagine saying it out loud would be mortifying. As far as my friends were concerned, Kim was just a colossal bitch and I deserved better. I wish I believed it. Instead, I just felt outleagued, like I showed up to play baseball with a wiffle bat. Murdock has fifteen years on me, at least. How could I compete with fifteen years of living in England and Toronto and going to cool parties and saying clever British things to quasi-famous people? How could I compete with fifteen years of sexual experience? He probably has silk robes and special oils and kinky stuff like handcuffs and blindfolds, and—I don't know—big, long feathers. What kind of experience did I have? Besides Kim, I had slept with one other person, unless you count the time I dryhumped Elisa Gowling behind a stack of gym mats at a grade eight dance. Which I don't.

What's worse, I keep worrying which of my sexual embarrassments Kim has already shared with Murdock. The time my equipment didn't exactly work? Or how about the time we tried to do it in the shower and I slipped and smashed my head on the faucet? *God.* It's no wonder so many exes wind up hating each other. You let someone know who you really are, and then, when it's all over, you live in fear that they'll reveal you to the world.

Two buses later, I get home and find that Lovely Rita's left a message for me. When I call her back, she tells me she's heard about this guy who's coming through town. He's got a portable studio and records bands on the cheap.

"You guys need to put some of those songs to tape," she says, "and not those shitty four-track recordings you never seem to finish. Something decent."

I agree. I never did get Chris Murphy's phone number after the accident, but it couldn't hurt to send him a demo.

"I'll wrangle Soda and Deacon. Just make sure you've got nothing going on next weekend."

I scoff a little at this. "Don't worry. I never do anything anymore. The social highlight of this weekend was going to visit Matty in the hospital—and he was asleep."

"Yeah ..." she says quietly.

She's been beating herself up a lot over the accident. Like it was her fault Matty had a bad trip. Like it was her fault Greatorex and McLaren tried to run Matty—me—down.

"Have you heard any more about what's happening with those douchebags who hit him?" I ask.

As far as I knew, Dave Greatorex had been charged with dangerous driving causing bodily harm, and there was going to be some kind of court date in the next couple of weeks.

"The latest is that he could get ten years," Rita says. "I still can't believe they didn't nail that other little shit, too. He could have at least tried to stop him."

Brad wasn't charged with anything. Instead he's been enjoying his new status as Mackenzie King's social leper. I guess he found out pretty quickly that most people—even his fellow Pussies—just tolerated him because he was Greatorex's sidekick. Now that he's an accessory to the vehicular crippling of the school's most popular stoner, Brad eats a lot of lunches alone.

The next day in Law class, everyone's buzzing. Kohler tries to calm us down and get us working on some chapter questions, but in the end, it's futile. Apparently, Murdock's wife had burst into my Art class (I *wish* I had been there) and started pointing out female students like she was picking them off from a bell tower.

"Was it her?" she demanded to know. "Her? *Her?*"

She thought he was sleeping with one of his students.

Robin Samchek, a diminutive Middle Earther, revealed that he witnessed the whole spectacle, and was now experiencing a kind of rapt attention that was, for him, previously unknown.

"... and then Mrs. Murdock called him—" he looks around the room nervously and whispers the next part "*—a fucking pedophile!*"

Mazz Moore slaps his knee and whoops. "Holy *shit*!" Even Brad listens from his desk and smiles, happy just to be a part of something.

"Yeah," Robin continues, propelled by everyone's enthusiasm, "and then Mrs. Murdock dropped to the ground. Like, *boom*. Mr. Murdock tried to help her up, but she told him, '*Get away!*'" He shakes his palms in front of his face as if to demonstrate. "So then, Mr. Murdock went back into his Quarters? You know? And I guess he made a phone call, because a couple minutes later, Mr. Sundell and Mr. Doyle showed up and helped Mrs. Murdock out of the classroom. She was still crying a lot."

Kim catches up with me on my way home as I'm crossing the Mike's Milk parking lot. She jumps out of her car just after she almost hits me with it.

"What the fuck did you tell her?"

"Nothing. I wouldn't do that."

"You're a liar."

"Yeah," I say, with a wry smile. "*I'm* a liar."

The truth is, I *am* a liar. I mean, yeah, I didn't tell Murdock's wife about Murdock and Kim. But when I said I wouldn't do that—that part's a lie. It's exactly the kind of thing I would do.

"You can't just go around fucking with people's lives," she says just before she slams her door and her tires spit little stones at me. She's pretty smart, so I'm sure the irony of her statement will come to her in time.

I'm not sure who ratted out Kim and Murdock—*if* anyone ratted them out at all. It's entirely possible that Mrs. Murdock found a pair of Kim's turquoise bikini briefs, or spotted Murdock climbing out of the Divorcemobile one evening when he was supposed to be working late. All I know is that I didn't say shit.

But I almost did.

I called from one of those payphones around the corner from the main office. A couple times. The first time, I came into school early, during my spare. No one answered, so I tried again period three, when I was supposed to be in Murdock's class. This was last Thursday. I felt kind of badass at first, like I was a secret agent or a spy or something. When I came up with the idea, I imagined I'd be calling from some street corner downtown (in this fantasy, I was probably also wearing a trench coat), but I realized if she had caller ID, the school was probably the best place to call from.

I got this weird, reckless thrill when I heard the phone ringing on the other end. I had a whole speech prepared: *'Mrs. Murdock? You don't know me, but ...'* It was full of all these self-righteous statements like *I believe in the importance of honesty*, and *I just thought you had the right to know*. I never once thought about whether or not she *wanted* to know.

I almost started to hyperventilate when someone finally picked up the receiver, and I suddenly realized that I never really believed anyone would answer.

"Hello?"

It wasn't Mrs. Murdock. It was a little girl. She sounded about nine or ten. Her nose was stuffed up like she was home from school with a cold.

"Hel-*lo-o* ..." she said again, nasally and impatiently.

"Uh, hi," I said, not sounding at all like a secret agent. "Could—could I talk to your mom, please?"

"Are you a telemarketer?" the girl asked.

"Nope. Not a telemarketer."

"Okay ..." she said skeptically, "but if you *are* a telemarketer, my mom's going to yell at you ..."

There was a rustling sound as someone—Mrs. Murdock, I assumed—took the receiver and shooed the girl away. She sounded faintly amused when she finally said, "Hello?"

I hung up the phone; I couldn't do it.

I leaned against the payphone divider for a full minute, frozen with—I don't know. Fear, maybe? Shame? The hall was pretty empty, but I felt like the few people walking by—a couple of grade nine girls, that kid from Rotten's band with the liberty spikes—knew exactly what I was doing.

Like they knew exactly what a shitty person I had become. I jammed my hands in my pockets and started walking. Eventually, I found myself in that sketchy bathroom in the basement that no one ever uses. I locked myself in the stall and sat down on the seat. I tried to fight it—if anyone caught me crying, that would be the end of me—but then I thought about Matty lying in the hospital room with a tube in his throat. I thought about Soda living in the basement of that shitty house with his shitty, drunk dad. I thought about Mrs. Murdock and her daughter. I thought about Kim. I even thought about that piece of shit Brad McLaren, and how even though he wasn't going to jail, he had a whole different kind of sentence, just for being as weak-willed as I am.

I stayed in there until I was sure my face had gone back to normal. It's no wonder boys try not to cry in public. When girls cry, they look vulnerable and their eyes get all shiny and you want to hug them. Guys just wind up looking like puckered assholes. Before I left, I took out my house key and carved *FUCK MURDOCK* into the back of the stall door in big block letters.

Now, without someone to drive me, the way home seems infinitely long. I know that, on top of all the big sadnesses, the little sadness of having to walk everywhere now probably seems kind of petty, but it still sucks nonetheless. It's just barely springtime, and while the sun feels good on my face, the air still stings the tips of my ears. When I get home, my mom's making dinner in the kitchen.

"Hey. How was school?"

Mom started being extra nice when she found out Kim dumped me. She met Kim a couple of times. I don't think she really liked her all that much.

"Fine," I tell her and hang up my coat in the hallway.

"Anything eventful?"

"Nah. Not really." I sit down at the kitchen table. Maybe I'll tell her about Mrs. Murdock tomorrow. I don't feel like getting into it right now.

"Want a cup of tea?"

"No, thanks."

"Jesse stopped by earlier."

Soda? "Why? Did he forgot it was a school day?"

My mom sighs. "You know, it's a real shame. I always thought he was smarter than that. And Matty? The *Chronicle-Journal* said he had taken LSD the night he got hit. I hope you never get involved with any of that stuff."

"Nope."

"Well, Jesse left a bunch of records for you. He had two crates, so I asked him to put them in your room. They're probably full of mildew. I don't know what you're going to play them on. That old record player in the basement hasn't worked since we moved."

When I open the door to my bedroom, there are two red milk crates full of records in the middle of the floor. Sam Cooke. Joni Mitchell. Patti Smith. Van Morrison. Soda's records. His mom's records. Why was he leaving them here? That's when the phone starts ringing.

"Can you get that?" my mom hollers. "My hands are full of chicken guts."

Still staring at the records, I pick up the phone. "Hello?"

"Pete?" It's Rita.

"Hey."

"Hey. Listen. Do you know where Soda is?"

"Right now? No idea. Apparently, he was at my house this afternoon. He left a bunch of records here."

"Well, here's the thing." I know already that whatever Rita's about to tell me isn't good news. "I called Soda's house a bunch of times yesterday about recording. Finally, his dad answered—*that* guy's a piece of work. He said that Soda—and I quote—'fucked off somewheres.' He said his furniture's still there, but all of Soda's stuff is gone."

I can't take my eyes off those records. "Did he know where Soda went?"

"I asked him, but he just rattled off a bunch of bullshit about Soda being a 'goddamn freeloader.' I think he was kind of drunk."

"Sounds like Mauri."

"There's one other thing." Again, I get that bad feeling. "I didn't think of it until just a few minutes ago. It's kind of why I called. I saw Andy Thaler eating lunch at the pub during exams. We talked about Matty for a bit, and then he said something weird. He talked about the Bunsen Honeydew tour. In the present tense. Like it was still happening."

"So ... what are you saying?"

"Well, it's the end of the month. Most of the university students have left town."

"*And* ... ?"

"And ... I think maybe Soda went with them."

SIDE B

Let It Die

"Guess who's coming to town?" Ruth says as she bursts into History Storage.

I put down my green pen next to a pile of shockingly terrible essays on Ancient Egypt and sigh.

"Shouldn't you be bumming out grade elevens with some kind of dystopian literature right now?" I ask her blearily. "*Nineteen Eighty-Four? The Handmaid's Tale? Barney's Version?*"

She stares at me, one eyebrow cocked.

"Okay. Who's coming to town?"

"I was just in the library when I saw this. Thought you might like to give it a read." She slams down the Entertainment section of today's *Chronicle-Journal* on top of "Ra: Sun God, or just the Sun?"

I see his picture before I actually read the headline. He looks pretty much the same. His hair's a little shorter, and his clothes look more expensive, but expensive in a way that's not supposed to look expensive. Expensive like the second-hand "vintage" Guns N' Roses t-shirts you can find in Kensington Market for thirty bucks a pop. I wonder if he has a stylist or something now.

"It says he's playing at Matty's fundraiser. *Our* show. We're *opening* for Jesse fucking Maracle."

I can't tell if she's excited happy or excited angry.

"*Hometown Hero Returns to His Roots,*" I read. "They've got the hype machine rolling early for this one. Bet a lot of people show up."

"How can you be so blasé about this? It's been *ten years*!"

"You're right," I tell her. "It's been ten years. I guess I'm just kind of over it."

Ruth shakes her head and leaves me alone with the newspaper. The truth is, I'm not over shit. The only reason I seem "blasé" about anything is because Tim Puurula, investigative reporter extraordinaire, called me up a couple days ago, wanting to know if he could ask me a few questions about Jesse Maracle. You know, to promote the fundraiser. I didn't clue in right away. I just figured Tim was digging around in Matty's illustrious musical heritage and drumming up a little human interest.

"Sure," I told him. "Shoot."

"Okay. So, I guess, first of all, what's it like playing with your old friend again? I mean, it's been what? Nine? Ten years?"

That's when I realized something was up.

"Sorry?"

"I heard you guys hadn't spoken to each other in a long time. What was it like reconnecting?"

"Uh, I'm not totally following you, Tim."

"Okay—the press release we got said that Jesse was going to play a set with some of his old bandmates from Thunder Bay. That's you right? You guys played together in—what was it—Giant Killer?"

"Honestly, this is the first I've heard about it."

There was a pause on the other end and a rustling of papers.

"You sure?" he asked finally. "I understand if you guys want to keep it a surprise or something. Let me read you the email from Jesse's publicist—"

"Tim. It's not us. Maybe try calling Andy Thaler."

More rustling.

"I'm sorry, Pete. I just assumed—*shit.* I'm sorry."

When my parents retired last year, they bought a place out on Lakeshore Drive so they could be on the water. Now, at least once every couple weeks, my dad shows up with two or three cardboard boxes filled with old notebooks, photographs, and Star Wars figurines. All the stuff that I thought was too important to throw out, but not important enough to store myself.

This week, with a sort of eerie synchronicity, my dad dropped off some of my own musical history. Inside an unassuming Pizza Pop box (Pepperoni and Bacon—a classic) I found a treasure trove of old cassette tapes. And, inside an empty tape case, a chunk of old hash.

A few of the tapes were survivors of garage sales—I always tried to unload them so I could buy CDs—but a lot were just blank tapes in various degrees of blankness.

Some were gifts from people I barely remembered, filled with song compilations of bands I also barely remembered. Some were named, with titles referencing inside jokes I didn't get anymore, like *Look a Talking Cow, That Person Called You,* or *Songs About Aubergine.* Some had cover art clipped from ancient *National Geographics* and *Family Livings* that were, by the 1990s, ripe with irony. Ponderous monkeys. Beehived ladies serving Jell-o moulds. A Sony ad that read *This could be the tape deck you leave your great-grandson.* When you're eighteen, the idea of being out of date is hilarious.

One particular prize was a copy of the four-track tape Giant Killer recorded the summer after we won that battle of the bands. A lo-fi piece of shit that sounded like Soda's singing in one room, while his guitar and the rest of the band were squished into another. We called it *We Are the Champions.* It's terrible. I could probably sell it for a fortune.

Another find was a compilation I made myself, but apparently never finished. On the cover there's a picture of the Sleeping Giant in flames and a title written in my seventeen-year-old scrawl: *To Me You Seem Giant.* The track listing from Side A is actually pretty decent. There's a lot of good Canadian stuff: The Hip, Hayden, Thrush Hermit—but it looks like I only finished the one side.

Last but not least were the mystery tapes: no track listing, no hint of their content, save make and model names. Acme C 60: Normal Bias. BASF: Ferro Extra. TDK SA 60: High Bias. Memorex dBS I. On these were our first recordings—some of them were made even before Deacon was in the band. Loud, distorted attempts at covers, snatches of chatter, song ideas, and a lot of false starts. I stayed up all night and listened to all of it.

After lunch, I walk past Vicky on my way to class. She's cut her hair, so it's all short and choppy, and while I'm not usually such a big fan of that style, I have to admit that she's pulling it off. I feel the sad double twinge of lust and regret as I imagine what it would feel like to run my hands through that hair. According to the staff rumour mill, she spent a dirty Easter weekend with Danny Pound in Duluth. I guess she had moved from prebound to rebound, and now, having survived the traditional post-breakup haircut with her good looks in tact, the world was her oyster.

I conjure my most collegial smile and wave. She waves back. Lately, she's been a little more civil. Definitely not flirty, but a lot less awkward than that frightened-deer stuff she was pulling last month.

"Hey," she says and stops me. "I think you left something. In my car." She says the "in my car" part quietly, like being in her car was, in and of itself, a clandestine act. I guess, for us, it usually was.

She produces a Feist CD out of her bag. I forgot I had brought it along one day when I felt like Chad Kroeger's presence was starting to affect my performance.

"Thanks."

"I listened to it a lot. It's good. I really like her voice."

"Well, uh, do you want to keep it?" I hold out the plastic square like an olive branch.

"Actually," she smiles, "I bought my own copy. But thanks. I better run. I'll see you."

"See you," I say to the back of her head. But I knew I wouldn't see her. Not very much, anyway. And that was okay.

In Ancient Civ, Jonathan Heyen-Miller is present, but his seating partner, Alexandra Carter, is not.

"Noticed you weren't in class yesterday," I tell him.

His eyes are locked on a copy of *Franny and Zooey* and he doesn't bother to look up. "Dentist appointment."

"Do you have a note from home?" I ask.

"Tomorrow." He turns a page and laughs quietly to himself about something he's just read.

"Have you seen Alex lately?"

He looks up and eyes me irritably. "I have no idea where Alex is. It's not like she's my *girlfriend* or anything."

As he goes back to Salinger, I scan his face for things he shouldn't know.

For the first week after her arrival, Alex acted like she invented the whole concept of being a student. She took notes, she asked questions in class, she even aced a tricky quiz on Aztec architecture. I guess she was trying to prove something. After a while though, she started skipping classes. A couple Fridays at first, but it's Thursday now, and I still haven't seen her all this week. I guess old habits die hard. For what it's worth, I did due diligence and sent an email to Murdock. I hadn't heard back from him.

At three thirty, Ruth and I belly up to the long cafeteria tables like we're going to play cards and eat sloppy joes. I always hope there'll be coffee at staff meetings, but nine times out of ten, they just have those little plastic juice cups with the peel-off tops we used to get from school lunch programs. It's during these meetings I realize how little time I spent in this place when I was a student. It was always the domain of the Pussies and the loud, skinny girls who competed for their attention. Up at the front of the room, Wayne Trimble taps on a microphone.

"All right, folks, I'd like to get started so we can all get home ..."

Teachers make the worst students. I look around the room and watch seventy or so staff members lean on their hands, check their cell phones, and chat indifferently with their neighbours.

As Trimble's second-in-command, Murdock sits near the front and wills everyone into silence. The head secretary sits beside him and cracks her knuckles. Eventually, when there's a quorum of listeners, Trimble begins to speak. He runs through some basic housekeeping—reminders about what to do if you lose your key, reminders about locker clean-outs, and exam procedures.

"I want to know exactly what part of this meeting couldn't be sent in an email," Ruth says, a little too loudly. She looks at her watch. "Shit. I hope Michael remembers to feed Pepperoni."

Eventually, Murdock steps up to the mic and talks about a new off-campus course the school's running next semester at Old Fort William for at-risk students.

"So, in coordination with Old Fort employees," Murdock explains, "the program gives kids a chance to do all this *brilliant* historical stuff, like work with animals on the farm, fire a cannon, build a canoe. And they get one History and one Tech credit for it."

Jim Lodge puts up his hand. "Do you get to dress up like one of those—what do you call them—*coureurs de bois*?"

"Well, Jim, what you and Mrs. Lodge do in the privacy of your own home is up to you—" he gets a few laughs "—but the at-risk kids don't usually like to play dress-up."

"Ah, forget it then!" A few more laughs.

It would be a pretty sweet gig, and in some ways, I'm the perfect guy for the job. History's my first teachable, and unless things change—which they probably won't—I've got only two contract periods. Conceivably, I could spend my whole day out there. I wouldn't even have to set foot in Mackenzie King all day.

"So, if you're interested in helping out with the program, talk to your department head. Or, better yet, just speak to me directly."

Murdock smiles and sits down. I realize that as long as he's heading up this new initiative, there's no way I'll be teaching anything but Civics and more Civics next semester, especially now that his daughter's about to fail my class.

Just when we've reached the end, Trimble stands up and tells us there's been a late addition to the schedule. There's a unanimous groan, and everyone looks at the cafeteria clock under its wire cage as if they've all suddenly and simultaneously recognized the symbolism.

"We don't usually do this at meetings," Trimble starts, "but it's come to my attention that one of our staff members will be retiring this summer ..."

People start twisting their necks like owls.

"Klukie?"

"Priddle?"

"It's Ellis," Gail says.

"Now, I know Mr. Kohler—" Trimble continues as Gail nods her head sagely "—doesn't like a lot of attention, but I wanted to take a minute to let him know how much he'll be missed."

With about as much panache as he demonstrated in his rousing lecture on textbook return protocol, Trimble biographizes the Führer like he's reading the back of a hockey card. "Ellis Kohler was born in Germany, but lived in Canada most of his life. Before he came to work here at Mackenzie King, he worked as a cab driver and served as a lieutenant in the Canadian Armed Forces."

"Military background. Called it!" I hiss at Ruth.

"He's always been well regarded at this school as a tough but fair-minded teacher with an encyclopedic knowledge of his subject matter and—" Trimble looks up from his notes to deliver his one, practised joke "—a fondness for cardigan sweaters." There are a few chuckles and then a brief silence as Trimble over-anticipates laughter and then struggles to find his place again. "Uh, we have a few parting gifts for you here Ellis, so why don't you come up to the front for a moment ..."

Kohler stands up, red-faced and smiling, and does a slow jog up the aisle. Everyone whistles and hoots as he passes.

"Speech!" demands Doug Klukie. Several other senior teachers shout out a similar request. "Speech! Speech!"

When he gets to the front, Trimble hands him a bottle of wine in a decorative bag and a wrapped gift. The principal gestures at the microphone and seems pleased when Kohler agrees to speak.

"Well, I'm sure as many of you already know—partly," he winks, "because this is a retirement speech—I have taught high school for a very long time. Indeed, during the past thirty-four years, I've developed what some people might call *eccentricities*." He looks over his bifocals, and there are a few knowing chuckles. "People say I have only three sweaters. This is not true! I have six." There is more laughter. He pauses again. "Yes, it is true. I have six—some of them are just the same colour." More laughter. Middle-aged women raise their glasses to wipe happy tears from their eyes. *That Ellis*, they must think, *such a character.*

"So. I have taught History for a long time," he considers, "and in this time I have come to think that education is like a Type 2 commercial Volkswagen. You know this? The 'Magic Bus'? 'Are you going to San Francisco?' Yes? Well, you probably also know that it was Hitler who commissioned the production of a 'people's car' for his 'master race.' Mind you, 'the people' never got these cars ..."

It's been years since I was in Kohler's class, but I'm starting to feel that old, dusty dread I used to feel when he'd ask everyone to take out their textbooks and follow along.

"...and then, after Stalingrad and the Yalta Conference, once everyone was friends again, Volkswagen started exporting these 'microbuses' to North America. The beatniks drove them all over to their Woodstock and their Haight-Ashbury. Lo and behold, a symbol of *das Dritte Reich* becomes a symbol of counter-culture."

I sense the audience getting restless. Everyone, including myself, seems to have lost the thread of his analogy. Klukie is checking his Blackberry and Lodge is reading one of his wife's *Cosmos* behind a briefcase.

"So. It was a good machine. Good for Nazis. Good for hippies. Good for everyone in between. A testament to German engineering!"

There are only a few polite smiles now. It must be clear, even to him, that he's overstayed his welcome.

"But now, I see young people driving the same microbus. Not a modern version, but the very same Type 2s their parents drove in the nineteen-sixties. I don't know. Maybe young people are nostalgic for a time they will never know. But they drive them all the same, and because they are antiques, people criticize them when they break down. People laugh. They say, 'Those hippie buses are no good.' They say, 'Those hippie buses are *shit*.'"

Kohler's speech has been so mannered and reserved that, when he lands hard on the carefully selected expletive, two things happen. First, everybody shuts up and listens to him, and second, we are suddenly privy to a previously unknown reservoir of rage.

"Well, they *are* shit. They are old and they don't work as they once did. Our education system, this Machine for the People, is old, too. Is also broken down. At one time, yes, it was good for everyone, but now, it is *kaput*.

"The politicians, they will vilify you teachers to please the taxpayers—the parents of the children you teach. No matter how good your intentions, you are a two-horned devil, and your horns are called July and August."

I can see Trimble, who's been standing off to the side the entire time, take a step forward. He smiles, and his hands gesture uselessly *Can we wrap this up?* Kohler ignores him and soldiers on.

"But it is you, teachers, who do the greatest damage, because it is you who *perpetuate* the machine. Every day you stand outnumbered in your classrooms, hamstrung by your administration, distracted by the latest teaching trend, and now, confused by this standardized, one-size-fits-all methodology that turns our students into Hitler Youth. Yet, you work and slave and *adapt* and spread yourself so thin until you become the grease between the wheels of this broken machine.

"Young teachers, I beseech you. Abandon the broken machine by the side of the road. Sell it for scrap if you must. Or if you are very brave and don't mind being very unpopular, take it apart and rebuild it. Like the *Six Million Dollar Man*, yes? Better and stronger. I'm sorry I cannot offer you any solutions, but as I said, I am old, and this is a retirement speech. It is not my job anymore. My job now is to sit by a lake and forget all this. Good luck and thank you for such a lovely gift."

"Holy *crap!*," Deacon says. "He just went off like that? *Der Führer*?"

"The very same," Ruth says, unplugging her guitar from the amp.

Pepperoni, who has been hiding upstairs in protest as we practised, materializes and rubs his face against my pant leg.

"Man, I *wish* I had seen that," Deacon continues, putting his bass back in its case. "Did he really call the education system 'shit'?"

"Sort of."

"Wow. Harsh."

After practice, Deacon convinces me to drink a beer and play some *Grand Theft Auto*. I've never been super into video games. I have just enough nerdy tendencies that to embrace one more might push me over the very thin line that separates charmingly available bachelor and hopelessly single man-boy.

"You're a *terrible* driver," Deacon scolds. "You just ran over that old lady for no good reason."

"Is there ever a good reason for running over an old lady?"

Ruth, like most wives and girlfriends I know, has a slow-boil hatred for inane video games. She's wisely removed herself to read upstairs.

"God, if that's how you drive in real life, I hope you never get your licence."

I continue to navigate a battered taxi cab around the streets of Vice City until the engine catches fire. Sirens wail and despite my attempts to evade the cops on foot, they eventually beat me to death in a parking garage.

"Remember that time you let Soda drive the Sabre and he did all those donuts in the student parking lot?"

"Yeah. He missed hitting Jason Sebesta's Suburban by, like, an inch. And then he slammed into the chain-link fence."

"You remember Fat Fuck running down the front steps screaming at us?"

"I couldn't drive my car to school for a month after that. I was sure he'd recognize it. I had to walk to school and it was during that cold snap."

All our laughter gets eaten up by silence after a few seconds.

"It's going to be weird seeing him again," I say finally.

"Yeah."

It's rare for me and Deacon to talk about Soda. There've been so many times when the name *Jesse Maracle* came up in someone else's conversation, or when we heard 'Common Cold Heart' playing on a stereo somewhere, and we have to look at each other and silently acknowledge this weird evidence that proves our friend left us behind. That's usually enough.

"Hey, so," Deacon says, with a tone that deliberately changes the subject, "do you think Kohler's right?"

"About?"

He takes the game controller from me and commandeers a motorcycle.

"Well, Ruth's been on about those standardized exams since the beginning of the school year. And did you read that article in the *Chronicle-Journal* about how much they're costing the province?"

"No. What is it? Few hundred grand?"

"*Shit.* Hold on, I need to steal this garbage truck." Deacon quickly murders a sanitation worker. "Try two million dollars."

"*Two million dollars*? Our department doesn't have enough money for textbooks, and the province is shelling out two million on a bunch of exams we could write for free?"

"Hey, can I show you something?" He drives the truck off a flight of stairs. It spirals in the air like a football, lands on its side, and skids down the pavement. The screen flashes *Double Insane Stunt Bonus.*

"I get it, Deacon. You're really good at driving imaginary trucks."

"No, not that." He hits pause on the controller and pushes up to his feet. "Follow me."

Deacon's office is in the basement, and it's a mess. It's a little drywalled room, just off the unfinished part where we practise. Two desks and two desktop computers dominate the space, but he's also got a printer, and a scanner, and bunch of other black and grey components tied together by a bird's nest of wires. There's a stack of boxes in one corner with names of clients sharpied across the side. He's got a corkboard up with a lot of notes and printouts, some with lines of text highlighted. The only attempts at decoration are a 1974 Steely Dan concert poster for their *Pretzel Logic* tour and a Super Friendz poster that Rita designed about ten years ago. *Super Friendz with special guests Giant Killer!* Aquaman's head is a Telecaster. Ruth had them both framed as an anniversary present.

Deacon sits down at one of his desktops and his hands are suddenly a blur between the keyboard and the mouse. I pull up a chair from the other desk and watch him go. I forget sometimes how good he is with this sort of thing, and it makes me think that maybe I should have paid more attention in grade nine Keyboarding. He leaps through a series of screens and windows and before I know it, we're staring at something that looks oddly familiar.

"Wait—why are we on the school board's website?"

"We're not. We're on the board's diagnostic site. It's kind of a place for the website administrator to test run site design."

"Okay, so why are we on the board's *diagnostic* site?"

"Well, because you work for the public sector, and the public sector is always a little behind the times, especially when it comes to technology."

"Tell me about it."

"I shouldn't be able to access this info, but I *can* because the security is a joke. I mean, come on. It's like they sealed up a bank vault with a beaded curtain."

"So, what? Is this illegal? Are we committing a crime right now?"

"Nah, it's not our fault they left the backdoor open—but *this*—" he cuts a string of numbers and letters from one screen and pastes it into the data field of another "—is totally illegal."

All of a sudden, the screen fills with an enormous list of incomprehensible file names.

"What's all that?"

"These are all the files that the Lakehead School Board doesn't want you to see. Teacher disciplinary notes, H.R. stuff, sub-contracts, all kinds of junk. Even—" he looks at me and scratches his beard "—standardized exam files."

Before I can say anything, he clicks on a file and a PDF of the Lakehead District School Board Grade Twelve Ancient Civilizations Exam appears on the screen. The whole course, reduced to two hundred multiple-choice questions.

"*Jesus*, Deacon. Why are you showing me all this?"

"Because I think you guys are right. You, Ruth, The Führer. Even though I never liked that guy. Did you know he only gave me a sixty-two in grade ten History?"

"Deacon. Focus."

"Well, I thought about showing it to Ruth, but she'd freak because it's illegal. She's kind of like that."

"Most people are 'like that' when it comes to breaking the law."

"Look. Do whatever you want. If you want to warn the board about their lax security and win some brownie points, cool. But if you really want to throw a wrench in the gears, well, here it is." He clicks the mouse a couple times and his printer hums to life.

"What would you do?" I ask.

"I don't know, Pete." He gives me a copy of the test, still warm from the printer. "Just don't complain about things when you can actually change them."

SIDE A

June

"Well, there's nothing we can do about it now."

"We can call the police, is what we can fucking do about it now." Deacon shoves his tuning pedal into his backpack like he's trying to punch through the bottom.

"We're not calling the police. Besides. It was partly his anyway."

"The guy *stole* from us, Pete. Stop trying to defend him."

"I'm not defending him. I'm just saying he *did* own a third of it." Shortly after I found Soda's records in my bedroom, I noticed our four-track was missing from the basement. "Maybe he was trying to pay for it with all the stuff he left."

"What, a bunch of mouldy records, and a cat that needed *three hundred and forty-six dollars'* worth of shots? You know my mom made me pay for them myself? Otherwise, I would've had to take him to the Humane Society."

He slams the lid down on his bass case, picks it up, and slings his backpack over his shoulder. Then he looks around at our rehearsal space. With everything gone, it seems so big now.

Deacon sighs. "Can you grab one end of my amp?"

"Sure."

We lug it outside and into the back of the Sabre. Ruth is waiting behind the wheel.

"Hey," she says. "Sorry to hear about ... everything."

"How come you get driving privileges?" I ask. "When do I get to pilot this beast?"

"Maybe when you get your licence," she says.

"Hey, Pete, you coming tonight?" Evie leans in from the back seat.

"I think so. I got a few things I need to do first."

Martha Dumptruck are opening for Eric's Trip at Whiskey Jack's tonight. It's a pretty big deal, and lots of people are supposed to be coming, so of course Ruth's amp went on the fritz. Luckily, she could borrow Deacon's. It's not like he needs it right now.

"Hey," Evie continues, "I'm still your date for grad, right? Your friend Mike asked me, but I don't want to go with him. He smells weird."

"Yep. Got you covered. And hey, if I don't make it tonight—have a good show."

I watch them drive off until they make a turn and I can't see their car anymore. I should go tonight. Normally, I'd be first in line for Eric's Trip, but I just haven't felt like going to shows lately.

I looked for him. Every day for a week or so, I tried to track him down, just in case Rita was wrong. I went to his house and got barked at by Mauri. I went to the St. James Arcade, Soldier's Hole, Whiskey Jack's. I never saw him. I talked to Emily Gardner, Emily McCormack, Tina Reid, Clarissa Woods. All the girls he messed around with this year. No one had seen him. I even made the ball-shrivelling climb to the top of Mackenzie King just to see if he was hiding out up there. He wasn't. Maybe if I had burned a fifty-dollar bill on the school crest, he would've appeared like a ghost.

But there was one place I thought about checking out and never did.

It takes me about half an hour to get to Banning Street, and another ten minutes or so to find the right house. Honeydew Headquarters. In the fading daylight, it looks more shabby than bohemian. The paint is worn and peeling off the brick, the front porch is slightly askew, and a ratty Canadian flag hangs with half-assed patriotism in the window. Soon some slumlord is going to hose this place out and turn it around to a bunch of second-years. I imagine that eight or nine months of dude and pot stank is about as much as anyone can really handle, so it's a good bet that everyone's already cleared out for the summer. That's why I'm a little surprised when, after I give the front door a half-hearted knock, Sudbury Steve swings open the screen and flashes a purple-gummed smile.

"So. They left you behind too," he says.

I half expect him to slam the door in my face. Instead, he invites me in.

"Here, man, have a seat. You want a beer?"

"Uh, sure." I plop down on a stained couch. On the wall, Jimmy Page pouts at me from behind a double-necked Gibson. Steve disappears around the corner and I hear the clinking of beer bottles and the hiss of meat hitting a hot pan. Steve asks somebody a question I can't quite make out; then I hear that somebody laughing. A minute later he reappears and puts a bottle of Canadian in front of me. He grabs a seat in the adjacent chair, an equally stained La-Z-Boy.

"Sorry," I say, feeling like I need to charge the air with diplomacy, "were you guys in the middle of making dinner?"

"I'm not. Howie's making something or other in there." He takes a sip from his beer and leans forward. "He's an exchange student from Hong Kong. Guy barely speaks any English and just giggles at whatever I say. Check it out ...

"Hey, Howie!" he hollers. "What are you cooking in there? Dogmeat stew? You cooking up a little Jack Russell Terrier for dinner?" Steve lets loose with this high-pitched hyena laugh.

Howie walks out of the kitchen smiling, with the steaming pan in his hand. He's wearing a buttoned-down shirt tucked into crisp, new blue jeans, and I immediately feel sad that fate has dropped him into this house.

"Pork," he says, pointing to the pan. "You ... want?" he offers.

"Uh, no. No, thank you," Steve says, inspecting the pan from the chair. Then he looks in my direction and whispers, as if Howie is only capable of hearing loud noises, "That's totally dog."

Howie says something in Cantonese and returns to the kitchen.

"So, it looks like you and I've got a lot in common these days," Steve says.

"Yeah, I guess so." I take a sip of my beer.

"I heard our friend Kim got caught screwing around with a married man, huh?" He lets out a low whistle. "She always did have a flair for the dramatic."

It's weird talking about Kim with Steve, but sometimes it takes a common enemy to cement a little camaraderie.

"Yeah. And it was my fucking *art teacher*."

"That's right! Howlin' Mad Murdock." Steve pulls a lever on the recliner and I find myself staring at a hole in his sock.

"How'd you know his name?"

"He and his wife came to a couple of our shows. Introduced himself to the band and bought us a pitcher of beer. He kept calling me *Dizzy*, as in Dizzy Gillespie."

"He does that."

"Anyway. He seemed pretty into Kim. He kept talking to her and touching her arm and stuff. I guess his wife must've been in the bathroom or something. Then, a few weeks later, I see him come out of Video Hutch and get into Kim's mom's car."

"The Divorcemobile?"

"Yeah," he rolls his eyes. "The fucking Divorcemobile. At first I thought maybe he was banging Mrs. Kivela—she *is* kind of hot—but when they took off, I could see that Kim was driving."

"Huh."

In the past couple months, the Kim wound had been healing up pretty nicely, but hearing these new details peels the scab back a little too soon. I try to play it cool, but I can tell Steve is getting a kick out of taking me to school.

"So," he continues enthusiastically, "I look up Murdock's number in the phone book and call it one afternoon, all anonymous and shit."

I have a clear and unpleasant vision of putting a quarter into one of the payphones near the main office.

"Mrs. Murdock answers, and I tell her that maybe her husband isn't being completely *honest* with her. I must've put a bug in her ear or something—I don't know, maybe he did something like that before—but I guess she found out. And then I heard she had a total *meltdown* in your high school. Thought he was sleeping with one of his students. Fucking hi-*larious*."

"So you're the guy." I'm not sure if I sound impressed or judgy. Sudbury Steve clearly receives it as the former.

"I do have my moments," he says and takes a swig of his beer.

"You know they have a little kid, right?"

"Hey, what can I say?" he smiles. "All I did was tell the truth. And payback, like our friend Kim, is a bitch."

There's a moment of beer-drinking silence that I use to reroute our conversation.

"So, have you been to see Matty?"

He dismisses the question with a wave of his hand. "Everybody's been to see Matty. Matty's the most popular guy in town, poor bastard. What you want to know," he says, levelling a finger at me, "is if I've seen your friend Sodapop."

"Have you?" The question turns me over and reveals my soft underbelly.

Steve sighs. "Thaler told me Soda gave you guys the ol' French Leave"—he air quotes the expression. "That's pretty cold, man. At least when Thaler kicked me out of the band he did it to my face. Said, 'We don't really *need* a touring trumpet player.' Shit. Like music has anything to do with *need*."

I shake my head and then drain the rest of my beer. How am I supposed to feel now? All I feel is a little sick to my stomach.

"After what happened, Thaler was going to call off the tour. It was Matty who actually suggested getting Soda to sing lead."

Fucking Matty. Even paralyzed and bedridden, the guy seemed determined to ruin my life.

"They all left a couple weeks ago. Thaler's got a rich uncle with this big cottage down in Muskoka. Apparently, they're going to practise there for the rest of June and then hit the road. They've got a booking agent and everything."

"And we're stuck here."

"I thought about going back to Sudbury for the summer—" he jerks a thumb in no particular direction "—but I got hired on at the Old Fort, so no worries. With all the high school girls working there, I'll be up to my eyeballs in teenage pussy."

A little fish of nausea swims around in my stomach. Steve looks at my empty bottle.

"Well, dude, it was good talking to you, but I should let you get going."

He asks me to leave like he's doing me a favour. In a way, I guess he is.

"Oh. Yeah, sorry," I get up and put my beer bottle on the coffee table. "You probably have stuff you want to do."

"What, me? Nah. Me and Howie are going to get stoned and watch *Baraka*. You, though, are going to want to be close to a bathroom pretty soon. You don't have a lot of time."

His statement doesn't register. "Sorry—why's that?" Jimmy Page eyeballs me from behind his mutant guitar.

"Because I put some magnesium citrate in your beer."

"Some ... what?" I feel a confused smile fading on my face. My gut fish flicks a tailfin.

"Magnesium citrate. Kyle left it here. He used to get bunged-up pretty bad. It's kind of like Ex-Lax, but stronger, and works a lot faster."

"*Why* would you do that?" I'm torn between punching him in the mouth and putting my shoes on as quickly as I can. I choose the latter.

"It's like I said, Pete—payback's a bitch."

Steve cackles as I lose my balance tying up my runners. Howie comes out of the kitchen to see what's going on and laughs at me too.

"You are very clumsy," he says.

"You're a dick," I tell Steve.

I push out the front door and start running. Even after my full tilt is reduced to an ass-clenching hobble, I can hear his hyena laughter in my ears. I never do make it to Ruth and Evie's show.

By second period the next day, I still feel like I have to go to the bathroom, but know full well there's nothing left in there. There couldn't be. During my tenure on the toilet, I imagined a variety of violent and detailed revenge scenarios involving Steve, but eventually I realized that I kind of had it coming.

I'm starving by the time the lunch bell rings, so I walk downtown and risk buying a meatball sandwich from Mr. Sub. It's been almost twenty-four hours since I left Banning Street, so I figure I'm in the clear. I squish myself into one of the hard booths, wolf down my sandwich, and chase it with a root beer that's mostly just rattly ice chips. I think about the summer Mark Zaborniak worked here. Soda and I would come down during his graveyard shift to visit him. One time, Mark didn't see us come in because he was crouched down looking for something behind the counter. Soda crept up, turned around, pulled down his jeans, and put his bare ass against the glass display. When Mark looked up, the first thing he saw was Soda's pressed ham. He chased us out of the store, and I'm willing to bet that afterward he made a pretty good show of disinfecting the glass for the security camera.

Fucking Soda. Is this what it's going to be like from now on? I spent the last seven years hanging out with the guy, and now it's like every memory I have of him is tainted. What do you do with seven years of turncoat memories?

When I leave the restaurant, I can see it's becoming one of those real blue sky days. I still haven't heard the latest Eric's Trip album, and I'm pissed about missing the show, so I make an executive decision to skip Murdock's class for the billionth time and walk over to Cumberland Stereo. As of yet, I haven't got a single detention. I guess Murdock hasn't reported my absences to the office, but I'm not sure if he's doing it out of pity or laziness or what.

I make it back to Mackenzie King just in time for Kohler's law class. It turns out to be a work period for the final essay, so everyone's reading books on serial killers or miscarriages of justice when the intercom calls me down to Guidance. As I go, the Führer watches me leave the room like *I'm* the Nazi war criminal.

When I sit down in her office, Mrs. Leedy smiles, but it's not her usual *Hey, how's it going? Want a Jolly Rancher?* kind of smile. It's the kind of sad smile that parents wear just before they tell their kids about a dead pet.

"So, Peter. How are things going in Mr. Murdock's art class?"

I know she's not going to sell me down the river, so I tell her the truth. "Not so good. I haven't really been going a lot."

Leedy breathes a disappointed sigh. "Pete, we talked about how the U of T Admissions Scholarship offer was based on your midterm marks, right?"

I nod. It might be some residual magnesium citrate, but I once again have a bad niggle in the pit of my stomach.

"Well, the Scholarship Board still requires an estimated mark before final report cards—I guess so they can arrange housing and numbers—and Mr. Murdock has estimated your mark at about sixty-five percent. Would you say that's fair?"

I'm not sure if there's anything "fair" about my situation with Murdock, but considering I've missed a few major projects, it's probably accurate.

"I guess."

"Okay." She inflates her lungs sharply, like she's about to jump into a cold lake. "I hate to have to tell you this, but because your overall average is now below 80%, Toronto will be withdrawing its scholarship offer."

"What?" The niggle turns into a nightmarish surge. "*Why*? You just said it's based on midterm marks. My midterm average was, like, eighty-six percent."

"You're *offered* the scholarship based on your midterm mark, *but*, like we discussed, you have to keep your overall average above eighty percent. Your average right now is seventy-six percent."

A horrible bell rings in my head.

"What happened in that class, Pete? You always do well in Art. I thought Mr. Murdock was one of your favourite teachers."

I almost tell her. Right there and then, I almost break down and talk about my *feelings* with a guidance counsellor. I wonder, if I tell her the whole story, whether she'll go to bat for me. But I don't. I'm not entirely sure why. Maybe I'm just tired of acting like I'm some kind of victim.

"So what do I do now?"

"Well," she taps her desk with a pen, "you probably need to have a serious conversation with your parents about whether or not they can still afford to send you to U of T."

"And if they can't?"

"Well, have you taken a tour of Lakehead's campus yet?" She hands me a brochure. "It's actually really lovely this time of year."

I don't go back to Kohler's class. There's twenty minutes or so left, but I'm just not up to it. I realize I left my pencil case and a biography about Ted Bundy called *The Stranger Beside Me* in the room, and while I'm *sure* Kohler will hassle me about it tomorrow, I'm equally sure he won't let it get lost. Teachers are good like that. Most of them, anyhow.

Instead, I go to my locker and grab my backpack. I duck out of the school and walk across the football field. When I get to the big elm, I shimmy the bag off my shoulders and sit down on the hard-packed ground.

The plastic wrapper peels off *Forever Again* easily enough, and when I crack open the case, I can smell the factory off-gas and the printer's ink. When I fish my Walkman out of my bag, I realize there's already something in it—some mixed tape I started ages ago and never finished. There are a bunch of songs by Canadian bands on one side but nothing on the other. I shake it out and throw it in my bag. I slide Eric's Trip into place and put my head back against the tree trunk as the test tone whistles.

The sound of my Walkman reversing gears wakes me up, and before I even open my eyes, I recognize the skunky perfume of weed. For just a second, I think it's Soda.

"Hey. Want some of this?"

Brad McLaren sits against the elm just a foot away from me. He's still wearing his Mackenzie King Lyons jacket, even though he quit the team weeks ago.

I pull my headphones down to my collar. "No, thanks."

"That's cool."

He takes another haul and holds it in his lungs awhile. When he breathes out, the smell reminds me of Matty's basement.

"They gave Dave five years," he says, apparently to me. I guess he's just stoned enough to abandon all attempts at segue. "It's like, you get used to things being a certain way, and then this *one little thing* changes, and it makes everything else change too. You know what I mean?"

I tell him I do.

"It's like that game we used to have in Mr. Rusnak's class—Jenga. 'You take a block from the bottom and you put it on top.' Remember that?"

I tell him I do.

"You take one block out and the whole tower comes crashing down. Man. He had all those old board games. Mousetrap. Connect Four. Battleship. The Game of Life ..."

He's quiet for a few seconds as he smokes. The tip of his joint is a tiny neon sign.

"Life." He repeats the word like it's an old trend embarrassingly out of date, like New Kids On the Block or Zubaz pants. "'Life's what happens when you're making other plans.' That's what life is. Right?"

I nod.

"John Lennon said that ..." He looks out at Mackenzie King the way some people look at a sunset. "Hey, do you like the Beatles?"

"Brad," I say, pushing myself to my feet, "everybody likes the Beatles."

When I get to my house, Kim is sitting on my front steps. Of course she is. Bad luck comes in threes. Or fours, if you factor in today's early-morning diarrhea. She's not teary eyed and repentant looking, like she is in my fantasies, but she is waiting for me. That's something.

"Hey," she says.

"Hey."

She pats the cement beside her, and I sit down, immediately wishing I wasn't so obedient. I haven't seen her since she drove away from me at the Mike's Milk. She looks good. Her blonde hair is pulled up in a loose bun with little wisps hanging down the nape of her neck. She's wearing the blue-and-red beaded necklace I made for her when we were first together. She still smells like Dewberry. It's the smell that gets me the most. I wish that after you broke up with someone they automatically smelled like hot garbage.

"So, I know it wasn't you that called Helen."

"Who?"

"Ken's wife."

"Oh. Yeah."

"Ken's still pretty convinced you had something to do with it."

I'm not sure what to say. I mean, obviously I have a few questions. Does she know about Steve's phone call? Did Murdock and his wife split up? Did she sleep with Murdock while we were still together? I opt not to ask any of them.

"It doesn't matter. I think he was just using me to sabotage his marriage." It's a pretty heavy thing for a teenage girl to say, and she seems to savour the very *grownupness* of being able to say it.

"Shitty."

"Nah, it's cool. We were just cutting ourselves off from the energy of the universe, anyway."

"Sure. Wait, what?"

She sighs, a little impatiently. "Well, when people are in love, they give each other this energy *unconsciously*, right? Like, it just flows back and forth between them. But when you start *expecting* this energy to come from just one person, you cut yourself off from the energy of the universe. I mean, I'm paraphrasing James Redfield, but that's the basic idea."

"Who's James Redfield?"

"James Redfield? You know? He wrote *The Celestine Prophecy*."

I shrug my ignorance.

"You haven't read *The Celestine Prophecy*? You *need* to. Everybody does. Ken gave it to me when we broke up, and it's really helped me."

"Wait. Murdock gave you a self-help manual to help you get over him?"

"It's not a 'self-help manual.' It's a novel. And it's really amazing. It could help you with your whole Soda situation."

Jesus. Does *everybody* know about Soda leaving town?

"If you say so."

"Hey, did you hear about the party tomorrow night?"

I shrug further ignorance.

"They're letting Matty come home for the weekend, so his mom is throwing a party at her house. She's super chill so we can all drink and stuff. *Apparently*, Matty's got tons of this medicinal weed called Quadriplegic because—well, it's for quadriplegics—but it's also supposed to make all your limbs feel totally *numb*."

"Cool."

"You should come."

"Maybe ..."

And for a moment, I really do entertain the thought. I tell myself it would probably mean a lot to Matty, but the truth is—despite everything—the idea of smoking ridiculously strong pot with Kim sounds, at the very least, interesting. Who knows? I mean, here she is, literally on my doorstep. Trying to make amends. Chances are we'll be going to the same school next year. Maybe the universe really is trying to send me a message.

"Tons of people will be there. Janey and Cowboy. Khaled and Tom." She always did that. I don't know any of these people, and she assumes I'm on a first-name basis with all of them. "Brett's going to bring his guitar, and Jay's going to bring his bongos and they're going to jam. And Steve's bringing his cute new roommate from Hong Kong."

"You mean Howie?" That one I did know.

"Yeah. *Howie*. Steve says he's a Buddhist. He seems so ... *spiritual*. Like he hasn't been brainwashed by North American materialism. I'm totally going to fuck him."

"Sure. Awesome."

God. When will I learn? I want to be mad at her, but she's too pretty. That's basically what it comes down to. Beauty is an evolutionary advantage. Pretty people will always be loved. If she was just ten percent uglier, I could recognize her for the terrible person she is and hate her for the rest of our natural lives. Unfortunately, this is not an option.

We sit in silence a moment while Kim reaches into her bag and pulls out a pack of du Mauriers. She offers me one, but I refuse. There's no question I could use one, but my folks still don't know I smoke and I'm about to be in enough shit over this whole scholarship mess.

"Have you figured out where you're going next year?"

"Honestly? I don't think I'm going anywhere." Kim frowns and I hurry to correct myself. "I mean, I think I'm going to have to go to Lakehead. I had a scholarship for U of T, but I kind of messed things up."

And that's when it really hits me. I'm staring down the barrel of at least three more years in Thunder Bay. Three more years of living in my parents' house. Three more years of winters that seem like they're exacting some personal vendetta against me. Three more years of that terrible pulp-and-paper-mill smell that I barely notice anymore, but whenever I do, I feel inexplicably sad.

"Well, Lakehead's okay."

"Really?"

"No." She laughs a little. "Pub Night's fun. But otherwise ..."

"Yeah. Great."

"Pete—the universe has a plan for you. You just have to decide whether or not you want to follow it."

"Thank you, James Hetfield."

"*Redfield*."

"I don't know, Kim. I hope the universe has a backup plan, because so far this one seems pretty shitty."

Kim stands up. "Well, on that note."

I stand up too. She trots down to the sidewalk and looks back at me.

"I hope you come—Matty would love to see you—but it's cool if you don't."

I watch her walk across the street to where the Divorcemobile waits patiently.

"Oh—hey," she says as she opens the car door. "It's at 129 Birchwood

Drive. Up in Cherry Ridge. It's BYOB, and bring a sleeping bag if you're going to crash."

She sits down in the driver's seat and slams the door shut. She starts to drive away, but after about ten feet, her brakes light up and she comes to a sudden stop. Her window lowers, and for a second my heart involuntarily expects her declaration of undying love.

"Could you bring my Mazzy Star album?" she shouts. "I haven't listened to it in, like, forever."

And then she's gone.

I walk up the remaining stairs and put my hand on the doorknob, wondering how I was going to explain losing an eight-thousand-dollar scholarship without really explaining it. I guess the upside of my parents killing me would be that I wouldn't have to go to that shitty party.

SIDE B
Time is a Force

Downtown Port Arthur is a pretty shitty place to party on a Thursday night. I can hear a cover band at Blackjack's faithfully trudging their way through 'Enter Sandman' and I take a pass. From the door of the Phoenix, I hear acoustic guitar and apologetic mumbling. Open mic nights are usually embarrassing for everyone involved, but the performers are also easier to ignore, so I go inside. I figure I can sit through a few songs by some university dude who's been playing guitar about as long as he's been growing his hair. The truth is, I just need a drink. I don't care all that much where I drink it. Deacon called me about an hour ago to tell me that the Wheeler Foundation Fundraiser for Spinal Cord Research had sold over three thousand tickets to the Jesse Maracle concert on Saturday. Three *thousand.* Jesus *Christ.*

I sit down at the bar. The bartender is reaching up on her tiptoes for a bottle of Canadian Club. On the back of her black t-shirt, the words *Phoenix: Live Music* are spelled diagonally across the x-axis of her bra strap line.

As the kid on stage strums his resolving note, I contribute a couple polite claps to the applause. I rubberneck a little when I hear the hollow gong of his acoustic guitar hitting the instrument mic, but when the young hopeful has sufficiently untangled himself, I turn back around to order my drink. Surprisingly, there's already one in front of me.

"I made it a double. I hope that's okay."

Alex turns over an empty pint and hits a button behind the bar. A fountain of water shoots up like a miniature bidet and cleans the inside of the glass.

"You missed a unit test on Tuesday," I tell her. "And some exam review today."

"Oh yeah?" She stacks the glass behind the bar.

"Your dad's going to be pretty pissed if you fail the course."

"That's kind of the point."

"Yeah, but he'll be pissed at *me*."

She shrugs. "It's not my fault your boss is such an asshole."

"You should at least write the exam. You could still get the credit if you do okay."

"Can we not talk about school, *Mister Curtis*?"

I nod and take a healthy swallow of what turns out to be a really stiff rye and ginger. It makes me wince and she smiles a little.

"So, I hear you've got a big show opening for *Jesse Maracle* on Saturday." She says his name with the same fake reverence she used on mine.

"You're not a fan?"

"Oh, he's good. Don't get me wrong. He's just so middle of the road now. I heard him on 94FM the other day. Blah. And what's with him blowing off his hometown for, like, ten years? I know Thunder Bay sucks, but seriously ..."

"Yeah."

"I mean, are we supposed to kiss his ass like the prodigal son because he's *finally* graced us with his presence? Oooh, *Jesse Maracle*. Big fucking deal."

Diplomatically, I continue to drink.

"I guess it's cool you'll get to play in front of so many people," she adds as an afterthought. "Nervous?"

"Terrified." I drain the glass. "Are you coming to the show?"

"Nah. I've got to work. I'm technically part time, but Pat has me here almost full time under the table. You want another?"

"I think I'm good." It's then that my cell phone plays a song I've never heard before. I take it out of my pocket. "That's weird."

"What's weird?"

"That sound. My phone's never made that sound before. That little melody."

"You probably got a text."

"I don't think my phone does that."

"Of course it does. Here." She grabs it out of my hand and navigates easily through a few screens. I feel obsolete when she hands it back to me. "See? You've got a message. '*Up top. Twenty minutes.*' Very cryptic."

Who's sending me a text? My first guess is Deacon, but I don't recognize the number. And then there's that second, impossible possibility. *Up top.* Either way, I can't help but be a little curious.

"I should get going," I say.

She makes an adorable sad face that almost convinces me to stay, but instead, I reach into my jacket and take out my wallet. She waves her hand at me like she's performing a Jedi Mind Trick.

"This one's on me."

The trick works and I put my wallet back into my pocket. As I do, my fingers brush against a folded piece of printer paper.

I had almost forgotten I'd been carrying this thing around with me. It was kind of dumb, I know, to keep something so valuable and so dangerous in my jacket. I was going to take my lighter to it, or throw it out in some anonymous public trash bin, but I guess I never got around to it. I pull it out of my pocket now and unfold it on the bar.

"What's that?"

I hesitate for a moment, just to fully appreciate the stupidity of what I'm about to do, then do it anyway.

"This is the Lakehead District School Board Final Examination for Grade Twelve Ancient Civilizations."

"Hmm. Isn't that supposed to be some kind of big secret?"

I nod.

"My dad said if those exams got out, it would totally fuck up the whole standard practices thing they've been pushing this year."

I nod again.

"So why do *you* have it?"

"Listen," I tell her, "I'm probably not the best person to be giving you advice, but one of the few things I've managed to learn is this: don't screw up your own life just to spite someone else. It never pays off."

Her mouth twists into a question mark.

"What if I told you that you could graduate and piss off your dad at the same time? Would you do it?"

It's her turn to nod.

"Well, then, *this* one—" I push the paper across the bar to her "—is on me."

It's been a long time since I've tried to scale William Lyon Mackenzie King. Almost ten years, in fact. Standing at the base looking up, I remember just how tall the building actually is. Climbing the school never seemed like a particularly good idea, even when I was seventeen and immortal. Now I'm twenty-eight, with a pin in my left knee from a toboggan mishap, and the lung capacity of an overweight tween. Never mind the fact that what I'm about to do is probably a violation of my teaching contract and is definitely not covered under worker's comp.

When I see they've moved the dumpster, I almost give up and go home, but then I notice a new air conditioning unit around the corner by the teachers' parking lot. It takes my weight and gives me just enough height to finger-grip the top of the first-floor addition so I can pull myself up. I climb over onto the air register, which booms with old menace and nearly convinces me that I'm either going to die or get fired or both.

The second-floor lintel is, as it always was, the worst part. It's probably only three inches wide and once I get on top, I have to stretch out my entire body length to the rooftop. That's a hard thing to do and not lose your balance. I'm not sure that a two-storey drop onto asphalt would actually kill me, but it would definitely break parts of me I don't want broken. This is the moment when a very calm and rational voice tells me that I don't have to do this. I don't have to prove anything to anyone. I have a good job and a nice life, and whatever might be at the top isn't worth the risk. It's also the moment when I do it anyway.

Dragging myself onto the roof is a humbling experience. By the time I roll onto my back, panting and safe, I'm sure I've shown half of Thunder Bay my ass. I've also incurred the traditional price-of-admission wounds: three scratches on my abdomen, each adorned with tiny feathers of torn skin.

Soda doesn't turn around when I find him. He's sitting where he always did, legs dangling over the edge, veins racing with his fearless blood. He opens another bottle of beer and puts it beside him when he hears me approach.

For a moment, I want to kick it like a field goal into the student parking lot and scream obscenities in his face. Instead, I sit down a foot away from the edge.

"Sodapop," I say, reaching for the bottle.

"Ponyboy."

I take a drink.

"How come your nickname caught on and mine didn't?" I ask. "That always pissed me off."

He turns around and looks at me. He's got his hood up, and his hair comes out in bunches around his face. "I don't know. I guess you're more of a Pete."

It's weird seeing him in person. I look away before he does.

"Sorry to hear about Mauri."

"Yeah."

We sit and drink our beer for a little while longer. Stoically. I know guys are supposed to be bad at this stuff, but Soda is the worst.

"Well," I finally say. "If you invited me up here for the view, I've seen it." I always hated how he made me go first.

"I heard you work here now. How'd *that* happen?"

"The original plan to become a rock star didn't exactly pan out. How's it going for you?"

He finishes off his beer. "There's no way I'm not the bad guy here, is there?"

"Nope."

Soda lets one of his Mortality Reminders fall to the pavement below. Some poor kid'll probably cut his foot on it tomorrow.

"What do you want me to say, Pete? I'm sorry? Because I'm not. And yeah, things worked out pretty well."

"For *you*."

"For both of us. Come on. Were you really going to stick it out playing shitty clubs for five years? Your parents would have convinced you to pack it in after three."

He's giving me a little too much credit. I quit Filthy Witness after two.

"Still doesn't explain why you dumped us for Thaler and those guys. We were your friends. They were just fucking *burnouts*."

He shrugs and doesn't look at me. There's something a little defensive in his body language.

"You're right. They were burnouts. I mean, yeah, they went to university for a while because their parents had a little bit of money, but they never studied, never went to class. I don't think Thaler even bothered showing up to write his finals. They were all total fucking losers, and that band was the only good thing they had going on. So I knew there was no way they'd leave it."

"What's that supposed to mean?"

"Look—you and Deacon—you've got parents who give a shit, and you always did okay in school. If the whole music thing didn't work out, you had a Plan B. You were going to be a lawyer, and Deacon was going to work for NASA or something, I don't know ...."

For a moment there's just the sound of liquid moving in glass.

"The point is, eventually, you guys would've left me behind. One way or another. So, I guess I just left you first."

I want to tell him he had no right to make major life decisions for me.

I want to tell him how I hate my job, hate my crappy basement apartment, and hate Thunder Bay. I want him to understand how good his life is, and what a steaming pile of bullshit mine has become.

But I don't. What would be the point? There's nothing I could say that would change the last ten years.

"Well, it's a school night," I tell him. It's one of those meaningless excuses that fills the air long enough to get me on my feet. "Thanks for the beer. I'll see you on Saturday."

He looks up at me. A strand of hair divides his face in two. "Hey, wait—hold on a sec."

"Soda, I've got to go. I spent ten years thinking about what I'd say to you when I finally saw you again—and now that you're here, there's nothing really to say. It's like when I run into Kim Kivela at the mall. I'm fine. She's fine. Everybody's fine. That's all anyone needs to know."

"I'm not your ex-fucking-*girlfriend*, Pete."

I laugh a little hollow laugh.

"I don't know *what* you are, Soda. You're not even a person anymore. You're just a *voice* that comes on the radio once in a while to remind me that things don't always work out the way you want them to."

He twists the cap off another bottle.

"Well, I had this whole speech planned out," Soda says, standing up. "It was pretty good, too, but—fuck it. Do you want to come make a record with me this summer?"

"Do I want to *what*?" It comes out irritable, even though I don't really mean it to. All the old feelings cling to my words like cobwebs.

"I'm going to make a record with Daniel Lanois this summer. In L.A. Preproduction starts in a few weeks. I thought maybe you and Deacon would like to be the band."

"*Daniel Lanois*? Wait—don't you have, like, a bunch of session guys on speed dial or something?"

"Yeah. There's other people I could work with, but I want this to be raw—like, *Everybody Knows This Is Nowhere* raw. I want the energy we used to have."

"Have you talked to Deacon?"

"Not yet. I wanted to talk to you first. Plus, you were always better at talking to Deacon than I was."

"What about Bunsen Honeydew? You guys are having the big reunion this weekend. Why not ask them?"

"I think I've gone about as far as I can with those guys. We're pretty much sick of each other. They've all got these side projects now." His brow crumples. "Thaler's really gotten into jazz."

"Oh."

"You could come on tour in the fall if you could get the time off work. Couple weeks in Canada. A month in the States. We might go to Europe in the winter if album sales are good."

All of a sudden, I feel like everything I've had to complain about in the last ten years has been kicked out from under me. I don't have an angry leg to stand on. I should be fucking ecstatic, but all I feel is this tidal wave of tired. I rub the back of my head with my hand and look past Soda at the city.

"It's a lot to think about," is all I can muster.

"Of course, man. Look, I've got a pretty heavy schedule tomorrow—local interviews and some big phone meeting with my label. Why don't you and Deacon come by my hotel room after sound check? I'm at the Prince Arthur. Seven o'clock okay?"

"Yeah. Sounds good." I take a couple steps back and stop. "Hey, are you under Koskinen or Maracle?"

"Neither." A broad grin stretches across his face. "I'm under Barry Hawkes."

"What the hell is Facebook?" Ruth asks, staring irritably at her computer screen. She's been in a bad mood since I told Deacon about seeing Soda.

"This is the *third* one of these emails I've got this week. 'Hi Ruth. I've requested to add you as a friend on Facebook. You can use Facebook to see the profiles of the people around you, share photos, and connect with friends.'"

"How is that any different from MySpace?" I ask. Filthy Witness had a MySpace page.

"I don't know. I can't keep up with all this website-of-the-week bullshit. The last thing we need is another Friendster."

"Who's it from?"

Ruth looks at me sideways. "Molly Pearson."

"You get email from Molly *Pearson*?" I try to disguise the envy in my voice as polite interest. "So what's Molly up to these days?"

"Maybe you'll have to join Facebook and find out ..."

Suddenly the room explodes in shrill noise. Ruth and I look at each other for a second. The phone barely ever rings in here, and when it does, it's usually because someone dialed the wrong extension. Most of our phone conversations entail explaining that this is not, in fact, the Math Office and that Mr. Kaukinen is not, in fact, available.

"Can you get that?" Ruth asks, accepting the terms and conditions of Facebook without reading them. "I'm all tied up over here."

I sigh and pick up the receiver. "Hello?"

"Ringo?"

"Hi, Ken."

"You're a hard man to find, you know. Gail said you might be hiding out in that little storage closet there. Anyhoo—I got a call from Jamie Greene up at the board office. Do you think you could swing by and see him after school?"

"Jamie Greene our superintendent? Why would he want to see me?"

I hear myself ask the question, even though I already know a number of possible answers. Drinking with a student, distributing confidential board documents, and fucking his wife come to mind.

"Couldn't tell you, Mister Starkey, but he's in his office until about five thirty, so if I were you, I'd try to get over there before then."

After Murdock hangs up I look at Ruth. "I think I'm going to need some backup."

She looks at me, one eyebrow raised.

"And a ride," I add.

When Ruth pulls into the visitor parking lot at the Board Office, she takes the keys out of the ignition, leans her seat back, and shuts her eyes.

"You're on your own from here," she says.

"Any words of advice?"

"Yeah." She keeps her eyes shut. "Don't fuck your boss's wife."

When I finally find it, the superintendent's office isn't quite as impressive as I thought it would be. I guess I was expecting to find him surrounded by mahogany and leather, spinning around in a high-backed chair, possibly petting a cat on his lap. Instead, his room was furnished with the kind of laminated chipboard stuff you get at Staples. Stacks of worn-out binders line the bookshelves. A framed poster of the 1986 Montreal Canadiens proclaims them *Stanley Cup Champions!*

"Hi, Peter," he says from behind his desk. "Grab a seat. I just have to fire off this email."

He's younger than I expected and good looking in a cheerful kind of way. I had seen pictures of him in his own house, but he was older now, and middle age had taken away any of the meanness I imagined in his face. For some reason, I don't feel scared. I just feel like a terrible person.

He taps the final keystrokes with a kind of flourish and then clicks his mouse.

"Sorry about that. It never ends around here."

"No problem." I smile as though I have even some basic understanding of what he actually does.

"Thanks for coming to see me. I've been meaning to talk to you for a little while, but I've been completely *swamped*."

"No problem," I repeat mindlessly.

"So," he says, clasping his hands in front of him, "how are things going at Mackenzie King?"

"Good," I say. "Fine."

"Wayne Trimble's been good to you?"

"For sure."

"And how about Murdock? He can be a little, I don't know, let's say, *eccentric*."

"He's cool," I lie. "We go way back."

"Right. So," he pauses and looks me square in the eye, "my ... *wife* has had a lot of great things to say about you."

For a minute, my heart stops, and I lose a little dribble of pee in my underwear. An idiotic smile freezes on my lips and I watch his face carefully for any signs of innuendo. I grip the arms of my chair and prepare myself that he might, at any moment, pounce on me with red-faced, spittley rage.

"She says that you love history, and you've got a knack for working with challenging kids. I think the word she used to describe you was *passionate*."

I stifle a sophomoric snort. I feel relieved and guilty. I'm a terrible, terrible person.

"So, Peter, based on her recommendation, and of course, your great work at Mackenzie King this semester, I'd like to offer you first dibs on leading the Time Travel Program next year."

"Sorry, the what?"

"It's the new off-site program for at-risk students."

"The one at the Old Fort?" It was the job I figured Murdock would never let me have.

"You'd be working in coordination with Old Fort William staff, mostly teaching History, but also helping kids learn a few practical skills. It gets them out of the school for half a day."

"Sounds pretty great."

Pretty great, but no Los Angeles.

"Tell you what," he says. "Take the weekend to think about it and then call me on Monday." He powers down his computer. "Hey, are you going to the Jesse Maracle concert tomorrow?"

When I get out to the car, Ruth is no longer feigning sleep. Instead, she's staring at the speedometer like there's something it can tell her.

"You know we're not actually moving yet," I say as I slam the door. She doesn't say anything. She just turns the key and backs out of the parking spot. We're halfway home before she starts talking.

"You know, when I played music with Evie, we really looked up to you guys. Giant Killer, I mean. You guys were a really good band."

"Thanks," I say, "I always thought—"

"No, shut up and listen."

I realize she's not trying to compliment me. She's working at getting something out of herself, like when you get water in your ear and you have to knock it out of your head.

"I know that, in his own fucked-up way, Soda's trying to make things right. I get that. But you can't just come back after ten years and expect things to be the way they were when you left."

She looks at me. Dares me to speak. I don't.

"Deacon's not going to California. He couldn't tell you last night because we have this agreement not to tell anyone—not even my parents—until we get through the first twelve weeks, because last time we had a miscarriage—"

Now I *have* to interrupt. "You're pregnant?"

"Eight and half weeks."

"Congratulations! Any chance you'll name it after me?"

Ruth rolls her eyes.

On Saturday afternoon, just as we finish packing up the wagon, Evie's minivan pulls up to the curb with Rotten riding shotgun and two little Dora the Explorers in the back.

"Hey, guys. Break a leg tonight," Evie says out the window. "I'm *so* jealous. Totally unfair."

"Come on, Mom! *Vamanos*!" the Doras shout in unison from the back seat.

"That's a pretty sweet ride, Rotten," Deacon says.

"Least it's not my mom's station wagon. Loser."

As Evie starts to pull away, Rotten flips us all the bird. I can hear the Doras scolding him for his rude behaviour, but a moment later they're drowned out by the sound of the Sex Pistols' 'Pretty Vacant.' It makes me glad to see he's still a badass to somebody. Deacon watches them all drive away with a funny expression on his face.

"I never really thought about it before," he says, "but those two kids scare the *shit* out of me."

The show doesn't start for hours, but when we get to the Marina, there's already a crowd forming—people with blankets and beach balls and camping chairs. The bandshell over the stage looks like a massive blue-and-orange kite that's ready to sweep the entire stage into Lake Superior. Part of me wishes it would.

The parking lot is a disaster of pylons and confused teenagers waiving drivers in all directions with fluorescent batons. We have a little bit of trouble trying to get the Sabre anywhere near load-in because the access road is blocked by an irritable security guard, who shakes his shaved head and refuses to make eye contact with us.

Eventually, we find our way to a little fenced-off area behind the stage. We stop and Deacon jumps out to open the back. I reach in to drag my bass drum out, and when I turn around, some guy wearing a bandana and cut-off army pants holds his arms out like a long-lost relative looking for a hug.

"I can take that!" he insists cheerfully.

I smile and lug it over to him.

"Thanks," I say. Then I grab a couple toms in their cases. I haven't walked three feet when a young woman with long hair like a horse's mane reaches down and plucks the handles from my hands.

"Here, let me grab those," she says, before I have a chance to answer or refuse.

I smile at Deacon and shrug. "Looks like we have roadies."

Soon, a small army of hippies is carrying our gear through the grass and up onto the stage like a line of industrious ants.

"Aren't these guys *great*?" Mrs. Wheeler makes her way toward us, trailing a jet stream of frilly scarves behind her. "They come every year to help out with Matty's birthday. Usually there's not so much work to do, but they've really stepped up their game this year."

From the little that I know of Matty's mom, she's one of those people who's so relentlessly positive that you kind of worry about being around when the dam finally breaks. You certainly can't blame her—she's gone through a lot—but tonight her joy seems completely unfabricated.

"Well, I'll let you guys get ready. There's some kegs of beer in the backstage area, and Scooter's mom brought in a bunch of samosas and pakoras, which are just *spectacular*."

There's about thirty or so people milling around the field behind the stage, laughing and drinking beer out of plastic cups. Most of them look like regular attendees of the Bunsen Burner—tie-dye shirts, Grateful Dead skulls and teddy bears. Todd Farkas is sporting some kind of ridiculous jester's hat that he unearthed from 1993. Everything smells just a little like weed.

In the middle of all this, we find Matty sitting in his psychedelically painted motorized wheelchair and talking with a bearded well-wisher. All things considered, he looks pretty good. He's managed to keep his dreadlocks, which, from a maintenance standpoint, are actually kind of practical, and he's wearing a t-shirt with a picture of Ronald Reagan that reads *Shut Up Hippie!*

"Dudes!" he says, winking when we get a little closer. "You ready to tear this town a new one?"

We all smile and nod.

"I just talked to Thaler, and the guys are on their way. You should probably go set up and sound check. I think Keith was looking for you earlier."

Hilariously, the stage manager for the night turns out to be the same living cigarette that did sound for us at the Odeon, ten years ago. It's encouraging, in a way, to know that some people can keep on keeping on fuelled only by booze, tobacco, and the spirit of rock 'n' roll.

"You'll set your gear up in front of Mr. Maracle's band," he hacks at us. "After we check your levels, I want you to play one song all the way through. Just one. Got it?"

We say we've got it, but by then he's bent over and coughing up various parts of his anatomy, and I doubt he's heard us.

After sound check, it takes me and Deacon about twenty minutes to walk over to the Prince Arthur. We invite Ruth, but she decides that in this case, four's a crowd. Or five, I guess, technically.

"Is he really staying under the name Barry Hawkes? That's so lame. If you're going to use an alias, it should be something cool like Keyser Söze or Armand Tanzarian, not boring like your high school principal."

"I think if you're already famous, the point is to try to *avoid* attention."

"Whatever."

When we ask for Barry Hawkes at reception, the concierge trades her professional indifference for starry-eyed enthusiasm.

"Absolutely! And who should I tell Mister, uh, *Hawkes—*" she inserts a little wink "—is here?"

I realize that, because we've got the inside scoop on a Big Deal, she thinks we must be Big Deals too.

"Tell him it's Sundell," Deacon says, butting in. "Jerry Sundell."

It's his turn to wink at me.

To her credit, she lets the phone ring about ten times before she gives up.

"Uh, I'm sorry, Mr. Hawkes isn't answering his phone."

I try his cell, but there's no answer. To quote every *Star Wars* movie ever, I have a bad feeling about this.

"Look," I tell our new friend, "Mr. Hawkes—*Barry*—is a bit of a deep sleeper. We're supposed to wake him up for the big, uh, *meeting* today, if you catch my drift."

She does catch it and nods conspiratorially.

"Do you think you could take us up to his room?"

She looks around, as though someone might be watching us. "Okay," she says quietly, "just give me a minute. Ted," she calls across the lobby. "Can you watch the front desk while I take these two gentlemen up to see Mister *Hawkes*?"

Ted nods knowingly. Everyone's in on it.

We all smile at each other as the concierge knocks politely on Soda's door.

"Let me try," Deacon insists and proceeds to bang on the door until a shirtless and irritated-looking man sticks his head out a couple rooms down.

"Sorry," I say. "Bit of an emergency."

Against what the concierge calls her "better judgement," she eventually opens the door with her master key. Secretly, I think she just wants to catch a glimpse of Jesse Maracle sprawled out on the bed in his underwear—hungover, strung-out, or maybe even worse. Bottles of liquor, lines of coke, a half-naked teenage girl passed out on the floor. But that's not what we see at all.

Instead, the door opens on a perfectly spotless suite. The bedspread is smooth, the closet is empty, there aren't even any towels on the floor. It's a nice room with a pretty decent view. There's just no one in it.

"Are you sure he said seven o'clock?" Deacon asks, taking a quick glance at his watch.

"He said seven."

The concierge watches us, trying not to look too impatient. Just then, my cell phone screams in my pocket.

"That's probably him," I say.

But it's not him. It's Lovely Rita.

"Hey, Pete!" she says.

"Rita? Uh, listen, now's not really a good time—"

"I'll be quick," she interrupts. "Have you seen Soda?"

"Uh." Deacon and the concierge both give me hurry-up eyes. "I saw him on Thursday. We're supposed to meet him right now, actually, but he's not in his hotel room."

I hear the sound of a straw sucking the bottom of a drink. "Well, I'm at this industry thing, and I heard that Divergent Records just got bought out by this big American conglomerate last week. *Apparently*, they've opted not to extend Jesse Maracle's contract."

"What does that mean?" I ask. Deacon and the concierge are watching me now like a television show they can't quite follow.

"It means they're cutting him loose." More background noise. Someone brays at a joke I don't hear.

"How can they do that?" I ask. "He's huge right now."

"Yeah, well, 'huge' is relative. He's huge in Canada. 'Common Cold Heart' was the biggest Canadian single since 'My Heart Will Go On,' but in the States, Britain, Australia, Europe, he's pretty unproven. There're a lot of flashes in the pan these days. The big companies generally tend to be more conservative."

I remember Soda saying something about a meeting with his label. "That's some cold shit."

"Yep. That's show biz," she says. "In any case, break a leg tonight. And when you see Soda, tell him I'm thinking of him."

When I see Soda. *If* I see Soda.

Deacon has the good sense to tip the concierge, and soon we're hurrying back to the Marina.

"So, what are we going to tell everybody?" Deacon asks.

I look across the water to the Sleeping Giant.

"Nothing. For all we know, he just bailed on us. He does tend to do that."

"Yeah, *or* he freaked out and took a taxi to the airport. If he doesn't show up, people are going to be *pissed*."

"Probably," I say. "But let's say we try to shut this thing down now. Best-case scenario? Matty's fundraiser is fucked, and we don't get to play the biggest show of our lives."

"Hmm. What's the worst case scenario?"

"Worst-case scenario? We start a full-scale riot."

"So really, we're just being practical."

"Right. Safety first. Hey, does Ruth know the words to 'Common Cold Heart'?"

Deacon shrugs. "Doesn't everybody?"

When we get back behind the stage, we find Ruth chatting with Matty.

"How's Soda?" she asks.

I try not to look at Deacon. "Good."

"Just good?" Matty asks. "I bet he's fucking *psyched*. That crowd is *insane*! I was just telling Ruth how Soda's bringing me up on stage to sing 'Low Rider.' It's going to be awesome. I can't wait."

"Yeah. That'll be great," Deacon says unconvincingly.

"Super cool," I add with equally forced enthusiasm.

I'm just starting to second-guess our whole strategy when Mrs. Wheeler appears in a whirlwind of fabric.

"Oh, *good*. You're all here," she says. "Listen, I was wondering if you wouldn't mind going on just a little bit early tonight. The crowd's starting to get excited, and the stage manager—quite a wretched little man—suggested that we might start a *titch* sooner."

"What time were you thinking?" Ruth asks.

"Well," she looks at her watch more out of habit than anything else, "*now*, I think would be good."

Lightning bolts of fear shoot through me. Ruth smiles. "No problem, Mrs. Wheeler."

As we walk toward the stage, I hear a voice call my name.

"Hey, Curtis!" it says. "Can I get an autograph?"

I turn and see Molly Pearson standing against the security fence. When I get closer, I can see that her skin is already summer brown and her freckles have multiplied exponentially. She looks happy—happier than I've seen her look before. When I give her an awkward hug over the fence, she still smells like oranges.

"What are you doing here?"

"Didn't Ruth tell you?" Hearing her name, Ruth turns and waves at us. She doesn't seem particularly surprised. "Trimble offered me contract work for September. They basically gave me Ellis's old job. I brought Charlie up for the summer so we can start looking for a house."

"Holy shit!"

"Yeah! Holy shit!" Those words had never sounded prettier. "So, if I don't see you later because you're too busy being a rock star—"

"Pete!" Deacon calls at me from the side of the stage, his bass already strapped to his stomach. "We're on."

I turn back to her and open my mouth to say something more, something probably embarrassing, but she stops me.

"Go," she says. "Do your thing. We'll catch up later."

As I climb the stairs to the stage, I wave at her. She waves back, and just before the crowd swallows her up, I think of that old, unfinished mixed tape I found in the Pizza Pop box. Maybe the reason I never finished it was that I needed someone to finish it for—someone who appreciated a good mixed tape.

In a daze, I sit down at my Uncle John's bright orange 1978 Ludwig Vistalites. Beside me, Deacon plugs in his bass, Ruth checks her guitar, and they both tap their vocal mics. I look at my friends and they smile back at me. Already, the crowd has started to surge against the giant metal barriers. Below us, bouncers pace like caged leopards. In his ridiculous hat, Todd Farkas charges out from the wings and asks the crowd if they're ready. Are they ready to rock? Are they ready for the biggest party of the year? Are they ready for *Ruth Kipling* and her *Gentleman Callers?* I half expect them to say that, no, as a matter of fact, they're not, that they wouldn't mind waiting just a little longer for the main event. For Jesse Maracle. For Sodapop Koskinen. But instead, they say yes. They say yes the way an ocean says yes. The way a newborn baby says yes. *Yes*, we're ready, whether you are or not. The sound is frightening and reassuring.

It stays light out late in Thunder Bay. The sun was still hanging in the sky when we got up on stage, but it'll set behind us as we play and remind everyone that this moment is temporary. That soon, this will be over and time will push us all in one direction or another.

It's a good view from behind the drums. Like Levon Helm said, it's the best seat in the house. From up here, all the faces swirl and blur together in the heat of the evening. Kim's out there somewhere, probably with her brother. Vicky Greene—or Gauthier—is out there too. Evie and Rotten. Andy Thaler. Mark Zaborniak. Jeannie Drew. Toby Watkins. Wayne Trimble and his son. Even Howlin' Mad Murdock will honour us with his presence once again, and I bet if I wade into that sea of people afterward and swim around in their good will, I might just find his daughter ditching work to catch our set. Past the crowd, I spot an enormous black SUV glinting in the sun. It's rental shiny and making its way across the parking lot. I wonder if Soda's inside, but one way or another, he's out there too.

For the first time in a long time, I don't know what's going to happen next. In a month, I could be recording in Los Angeles, or swimming in the summer-freezing water of Lake Superior. I want to figure it all out as soon as possible. I want to see the future stretch out like a straight line into the horizon.

But first, there's something I've got to do.

And that's the great thing about stage fright. When you're terrified, everything else falls away. You're completely cut off from your past lives and potential futures. All you can do is live in the unmitigated present and hope your timing is dead on. Now. Now. Right now. I pick up my sticks and count to four.

This book wouldn't exist without the following awesome humans:

Sarah Wyche, Cara MacMillan, Amanda St. Jean, Wilma Aalbers, Meaghan Mazurek, Dave Harvey, Douglas Davey, Mark Rhyno, Kate Lee, Justin Armstrong, Robert Green, Cheryl Misener, Alex Richman, Vish Khanna, Mike Nelson, Sloan, Kathy Olenski, Bill Hanna, Leslie Vermeer, Claire Kelly, Matt Bowes, Mom & Dad, the Wyches, and last but not least, the Lockharts, without whom there would be no Thunder Bay.

GREG RHYNO was born in Toronto, Ontario, but grew up in Thunder Bay. His work has appeared in *PRISM international,* Vocamus Press, and he is a recipient of the J. Alex Munro Prize for Poetry. In addition, Rhyno has toured and recorded with such rock n' roll outfits as Phasers On Stun, the Parkas, and Wild Hearses. Currently, he works as a high school teacher and lives with his family in Guelph, Ontario. This is his first novel. Find him online at gregrhyno.com.